Merely Magic

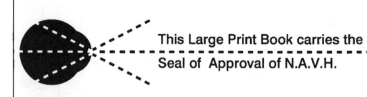

This Large Print Book carries the
Seal of Approval of N.A.V.H.

Merely Magic

Patricia Rice 1949-

Thorndike Press • Thorndike, Maine

Copyright © Patricia Rice, 2000

Published in 2000 by arrangement with NAL Signet, a division of Penguin Putnam Inc.

Thorndike Press Large Print Romance Series.

The tree indicium is a trademark of Thorndike Press.

The text of this Large Print edition is unabridged.
Other aspects of the book may vary from the original edition.

Set in 16 pt. Plantin by Anne Bradeen.

Printed in the United States on permanent paper.

Library of Congress Cataloging-in-Publication Data

Rice, Patricia, 1949–
    Merely magic / Patricia Rice.
        p.   cm.
    ISBN 0-7862-3024-X (lg. print : hc : alk. paper)
    1. Northumberland (England) — Fiction. 2. Witchcraft
— Fiction.   I. Title.
PS3568.I2925 M47 2000
  813'.54—dc21   00-047923

For Robin,
who had the faith and courage that I lacked,
and the supreme self-confidence to act on both.

Prologue

"Mama died."

"Because she did not listen to me, love." Smelling of rich evergreen and roses, the old woman pulled her ten-year-old granddaughter into her plump arms.

"Papa doesn't want me." Ninian tried not to snivel as she curled into the first welcoming embrace she could remember receiving.

"Because you are a Malcolm, and men fear what they do not understand. You'll see when you are older."

"Papa says I am a witch, Grandmama. I'm not a witch, am I?"

"You're a Malcolm, dear, and that's nearly the same. Witches can accomplish great good if they listen to their elders and do as they're told." The old woman set her away and straightened Ninian's shoulders. "Sit up here beside me, and I'll read you a

7

story." She patted an ancient leather-bound book in her lap.

"My mama didn't want me to be a witch," Ninian whispered, suddenly frightened as she climbed onto the chair and sensed her grandmother's determination.

"Your mama denied what she was, love, and she died of it. Never deny who you are, and you'll live a long and happy life."

"Who I am?" she inquired, snuggling into her grandmother's powdery embrace, momentarily reassured by her promises.

"A Malcolm, my dear," the old lady repeated. "Be proud and grateful for your heritage. We can have anything we want, if we want it hard enough. We just must never deny who we are, as the story tells us. An Ives once tried to force his Malcolm lady to deny her heritage, and it nearly destroyed the village."

Ninian loved stories. Happily, she settled down to listen.

One

Northumberland, 1750

Alone on the edge of the clearing, Ninian Malcolm Siddons sat on an overturned stone from the circle that had once dominated this hill and contemplated the bonfire and laughing couples below. It was a very lonely business being a Malcolm. Tonight, she'd much rather dance and sing and shout for joy in the firelight like everyone else.

She wanted to scream and yell, "I'm here! Here! It's just me!"

But there was danger in achieving that kind of attention. She could not indulge her volatile nature and throw tantrums at the unfairness of life; it would only enhance the village's fear of her. As her grandmother had taught her, she must remember who she was, what she was, and be proud of it. She had a gift and a talent no other had been granted, and she must use them wisely. Making the villagers fear her was not wise.

She sighed and rolled her eyes in exasperation. "Gifts" and "talents" weren't quite as valuable or exciting as the magic in fairy tales. If only she possessed *real* magic, she could summon a lover to dance with her. She smiled as the fantasy formed in her mind. What kind of lover would she summon? Dark and passionate? Fair and loving? One who would give her fat, jolly babies?

One who would dance with her.

She'd never even considered sharing her life with anyone until Granny died last winter. Given her circumstances, it didn't pay to consider it now. She must dedicate her life to the people of the village of Wystan just as Granny had done — or deny her heritage and forfeit everything as her mother had.

The bonfire leapt higher into the starry May night as someone added new brush to the flames. With the aid of the moon above, the glade sparkled with the silvery glow of a thousand candles, filling the night with enchantment.

Beltane was a night to celebrate the earth's richness, to throw off the dark of winter's cold. She should exult in the promise of spring, not fret over what she could never have. It was time to shrug off her grief over her grandmother's death and go on with the business of living.

If only she knew precisely what that was. Tending her herbs, healing the sick, and delivering babes did not hold the promise she'd hoped now that she faced those tasks alone.

Eagerly, she straightened as an excess of hilarity and high spirits buffeted her with the approach of the dancers.

"Have you heard? Lord Ives is repairing the castle!" Tom, the wheelmaker's son, crowed as he and several others gathered to catch their breaths.

"We'll all be rich!" Alice, a farmer's daughter, expressed her excitement with glee.

"This time next year, we'll have fat pigs in our pens and geese on our tables." Son of a sheep farmer, Nate passed his cup of ale to the next person.

The return of an Ives to Wystan after all these years worried Ninian. She'd thought the legend in her grandmother's storybook was little more than a fairy tale and had never feared it, until now, with the recent return of the mysterious nobleman.

According to the story, long, long ago,

Ives and Malcolms had been the nobility of this land, building castles and protecting their people. But according to the legend, disaster destroyed that happy land upon the marriage of an Ives lord and a Malcolm lady. Prosperity had fled, the Ives lords moved away, and only Malcolms remained to care for the people as best they could. As others left to seek riches elsewhere, the village shrank, and there was no need for more than one Malcolm here. So even the Malcolms left. Ninian's aunts had followed their aristocratic husbands and moved on to better things. Ninian's particular gift fared better in the isolation of the village, so she had been chosen to remain behind.

Why had a legend walked out of her storybook as soon as her grandmother died? And if this Lord Ives could make the village wealthy, would they need Ninian at all? Or would he bring the tragedy the storybook predicted?

Clamping down a frisson of fear and blocking out such silly superstition, Ninian watched the unaccompanied bachelors expectantly as the musicians struck up a new song.

Nate grabbed his companion's hand, and Gertrude giggled and ran off with him to join the dancers. As the other young men chose partners and the laughing couples dashed toward the revelry, leaving Ninian behind — again — her dimples disappeared and her shoulders sagged with the weight of loneliness.

It shouldn't matter that they didn't ask her to dance. They were simple, uneducated village boys, and she was a Malcolm. Malcolms were not only witches, but nobility, educated far beyond the simple means of a farmer. She understood. She really did. But the music was so lively and the moon so beautiful . . .

An old lady laughed as Gertrude slapped Nate's face and flounced off. "That one has aught but one thing on his mind," the old one said to her companion.

All the village girls knew about Nate's hot hands and sweet words. Still, even well plied with ale, he danced a fair step, and Ninian wouldn't have minded one whirl about the fire. Just one.

It wasn't as if she expected love.

A pagan fertility rite, how appropriate.

Standing in the deepest shadows of the forest's edge, Drogo Ives, Earl of Ives and Wystan, crossed his arms and watched as the bonfire in the clearing blazed skyward. The hypnotic notes of flute and fiddle carried on the wind along with the sounds of laughter.

He'd come to this deserted outpost of northern England in hopes of studying the stars, not human behavior. Heaven only knew, he had sufficient specimens for study in London should he wish to take up the science of people, but he preferred the distance and mathematical precision of stars. At least stars were predictable.

The bonfire had aroused his curiosity when he'd seen it from his windows. He'd spent a long and grueling day over the estate accounts, correspondence, and decisions regarding his brothers' latest escapades, and inexplicably, he'd been drawn to the sight of the leaping flames.

A lone figure lurking in the half shadow between him and the convivial couples in the clearing captured his curiosity. He might not be from these parts, but he had sufficient knowledge of folklore to recognize the village's celebration of Beltane. As spring fertility rites went, this one was fairly tame. He even recognized the primitive urge within himself to procreate. The warmth of a new May eve, the hum of nature's nocturnal creatures seeking mates, the gravid fowls and burgeoning plant life of spring stirred even the most stoic of mankind into desiring to create replicas of themselves within a woman's womb.

Drogo clanged a steel door shut on that thought as he watched the solitary figure in the clearing.

Her pale hair glimmered with moonlight, curling in wild ringlets over her shoulders and halfway down her back, uncovered by cap or cloth. He had caught a glimpse of her face earlier as she exchanged words with some of the couples. She had a round face of ivory purity with mysterious light-colored eyes he could barely discern in the silver swath of moonlight.

And she had a figure men would kill for. He surveyed her ample bosom and trim waist with jaundiced gaze. Country beautiful, built for breeding. Why then was she not part of one of the amorous couples cavorting around the fire? She should have men dancing attendance at her fingertips.

He had no intention of becoming so involved in village affairs that he might ask. He craved a solitude he couldn't achieve in London, and he didn't need another woman mucking up his life or his mind. He'd do better to return to his studies in the tower or to the tedious stacks of frantic messages from London.

The silver goddess turned just enough for

him to perceive the yearning in her expression, a yearning that so matched his own, the loneliness of it nearly crippled him.

He *wouldn't* feel this way. He had no right. He had far more on his table than he could possibly consume as it was. Asking for the delicacy that wasn't his was obnoxious selfishness.

As if sensing his tumult, the moon maiden gazed into the forest where he stood. His sudden fierce arousal at the sight of her starlit features decided the matter. He would not become his father, dancing heedlessly to temptation's call, following his cock like a tail.

Let her find another partner for this night of amour. He had nothing to offer.

Thinking she saw a shadow slip into the darkness, Ninian shivered. Perhaps Satan walked on a night like this, as her grandmother had warned, for only a soulless devil could escape her notice. Her gift for sensing human emotion might not include understanding what she felt, but it gave her the ability to discern someone's presence.

Granny had taught her how to deal with external devils, like dangerous men. Ninian wished she'd taught her how to deal with internal devils, like doubt and loneliness.

Granny had thought everything easily cured by herbs and amulets, but as far as Ninian was concerned, amulets couldn't cure anything. Still, she would respect her grandmother's memory and keep an open mind. Granny had known a great deal more than Ninian could ever hope to learn.

The music changed and laughing couples drifted from the fire. Instead of leaving as she ought, she lingered, hoping against foolish hope that at least one of the men would dare ask her to dance, now that they had more ale in them. She tried her best to smile naively as the other maids did.

"They say the earl has three wives." Nate laughed as he approached, his arm once more wrapped firmly around Gertrude's shoulders.

"They say all Ives are devils who only walk the night." Tom grinned as Alice shrieked in horror and cuddled closer under his arm.

Perhaps Ninian wasn't the only one who'd noticed a presence at the forest's edge. She glanced over her shoulder again, but the shadow had disappeared.

"You know what they say happened the last time an Ives walked this land," Nate whispered in the ominous tone of a man relating a ghost story. "He mated with a witch and the entire valley flooded."

All heads turned in Ninian's direction.

Ninian's stomach soured at the attention. No matter how hard she tried to be one of them, the curse of her heritage always erected barriers. She didn't know why she had joined them tonight, except that sometimes her empty cottage echoed with loneliness.

Harry, the shoemaker, shifted attention back to himself. "Since this Ives already has three wives, he's not likely to need more, is he?"

The lads guffawed. The women tittered.

Grateful for Harry's diversion, Ninian clung to her dimpled smile and watched the dancing as the conversation swirled on without her.

Even Harry, who'd defended her verbally since she'd set his broken finger, would never do more than nod in her direction. It would take a brave man, indeed, to court a Malcolm witch. She should be used to rejection by now.

The villagers' superstitions about her origins didn't cause her undue concern. England hadn't burned a witch in — oh, a hundred years or more. They hadn't hanged one in twenty or thirty. They had more civilized methods of destroying witches these days. A wrong word or look, and she'd see nothing but their cold backs. And with the poor harvest of these last years and after the bad winter — she couldn't blame them. Unlike Granny, she couldn't convince people to do what was good for them with amulets and promises. She could only heal the sick with her knowledge of herbs. Her gift for empathy was singularly useless, and more nuisance than help.

She wished things could be different. Just once, she would like someone to accept her as she was, to hold her close and dance with her in the firelight, like normal people.

And she *was* normal, she told herself fiercely. She just knew a little more about herbs than most, had an unpredictable ability to sense what others felt, and the intelligence to apply both. She wasn't a witch. She was a Malcolm.

Yet, in the minds of many, there was no difference.

With a wistful sigh, Ninian drifted from the glade into the forest, away from the celebrations, away from the sight of the others slipping pair by pair into the shadows of the grass and trees, there to create the bumper crop of babies she would deliver come winter. Babies she would never have. The ache at that thought was best excised with work.

Strolling among the trees, putting the bonfire and the amorous crowd far behind her, Ninian sought the babbling burn where the herb she required dwelled. In the full light of the moon, the agrimony should contain all the power she needed for the morrow's work. She wished the stream ran through her grandmother's property so she needn't stray so far to obtain it, but no one had ever complained of her trespass on Ives's land. Of course, until recently, there had been none to do the complaining.

Lord Ives had certainly stirred a controversy by returning after generations of neglect, but Ninian didn't indulge in gossip. Surely, no man could legally have three wives. She knew enough of human temperament to doubt even his ability to have three mistresses under one roof, although contemplating the nature of such a man aroused dangerous fantasies in her mind.

Deliberately turning her thoughts to the herb and the best means of persuading Mary's little boy to drink an infusion of it to soothe his aching throat, Ninian didn't catch the presence following her until it was too late to hide.

She knew at once who it was and why. Nate. Even as she caught the strength of his arrogance, coupled with his muddled anger and a whiff of fear, he staggered into view from around a bend in the road.

Caught in the open with nowhere to run, she donned her best defense, the one she used to make children giggle. Blinking innocently, she wrapped a curl around her finger. Her dimpled features, blond ringlets, and blue eyes could deceive any man into doubting legends. Weren't all witches dark and dangerous? "Why, Nate, whatever are you doing here? Gertrude will be most disappointed without your company."

"Gertrude went off with that oaf, Harry. You're much prettier than she is. You shouldn't have left so soon." He sidled closer, eyeing her bosom.

She could smell the ale on him and sensed his reckless determination. Despite her short stature, Ninian knew she was strong, but Nate not only stood taller, he outweighed her by several stone.

"Why, Nate, how thoughtful of you to see me home," she replied airily, "but you needn't, really. Go back to the fun."

"Ives land is the long way around to your cottage," Nate said with suspicion.

"Oh, but I so wanted the watercress in the burn!" Ninian slipped away as he reached for her. If she wasn't good enough to dance with in front of one and all, she certainly didn't intend to dally with him in private. Lonely she might be, but crazy she was not. "I'll be fine. Do go."

"You know there's no other man in the village for you but me." He tried a cajoling tone as he stepped toward her. "My father has the most sheep and the most land. I'm strong. I can do the work of three men."

Ninian knew the kind of "work" he had in mind and suppressed a wry grimace at his vanity. "Why, Nate! You flatter me." She couldn't run fast enough to elude him, but she had five times the wit he possessed, especially when he was muddled with drink.

"I'll show you how good I can be." Apparently encouraged by her lack of coyness and a good dose of grog, Nate threw aside his fears and grabbed for her.

Prepared, Ninian sidestepped, thrust out her ill-shod foot, and let him trip over it. In his alcohol-induced haze, he slipped in the mud, threw his arms up to steady himself, and splatted nicely in the icy stream. That should drown his overheated ardor.

With behavior like this, Ninian supposed she deserved the epithets he spewed as he sat up, gasping.

"I'll get you for this, witch!" he howled, shaking his fist at her while water rivulets trickled down his forehead.

Well, so much for warding off ill will. She might as well throw sticks and stones while she was at it. "If I were truly a witch, I'd rot your balls, you silly fool!" she shouted back. Granny would not have been happy with her. After all these years of taking the safe and narrow path, she was throwing it all away in a fit of spite. She knew better.

Cursing, Nate righted himself on the slippery rocks, splashed to his feet, and lunged for the bank and Ninian. Well, perhaps she hadn't completely forfeited her innocuous facade. He didn't fear her enough to run.

As he grabbed for her, a cool voice intruded from the darkness of the trees.

"Is there some problem?"

Startled by that voice from nowhere, Nate slid back down the bank and hit the water again. In the act of retreat, Ninian froze.

She hadn't *felt* any presence. How could that be? No one *ever* walked up on her like that without her extra sense picking up some warning. Wide-eyed, she swerved to stare in the direction from which the voice emerged.

Swiping water from his eyes, Nate shakily climbed to his feet again. "Who's out there?" he demanded.

Ninian suspected he was shivering with more than cold. Despite his boasts, Nate possessed the same ignorant superstitions as most of the villagers. Right now, at the sound of that eerie disembodied voice, Ninian understood his fear of the unknown.

"We are having a disagreement over my ability to see myself home," she replied boldly, willing the stranger to show himself. The absence of any human emotion from the direction of the voice scared her as much as the absence of a physical presence.

To her relief, a solid shadow separated from the trees. Male, taller than Nate, with wide shoulders and a disturbingly graceful physique, the mysterious intruder hid his features by remaining out of the moon's light. "You're trespassing," he stated with the same lack of inflection as when he'd first spoken.

"Lord Ives!" Nate hastily backed out of the burn, scrambling up the bank on the far side. He cast Ninian a terrified glance. "He *is* the devil, and you're in league with him!"

Sighing at this inevitable conclusion, Ninian raised her arms, waved the ruffles of her long sleeves, and threw an eerie "Boo!" in Nate's direction. She laughed as Nate fled, screaming, into the forest.

"I'm glad that amused you," Lord Ives said from behind her, with what might have been a hint of dryness. "Would you care to explain what it meant?"

Of course, his lordship was new to the area. He didn't know the local folklore about Malcolm witches and Ives devils. Turning to judge his reaction, she had to look up much farther than she liked. Through slivers of moonlight, his silhouette was breathtakingly impressive and much too close.

Her grandmother had taught her about the temptations of dark forces to which witches were drawn. She should be wary.

"Welcome to Wystan, my lord." She curtsied as she'd been taught long ago. Straightening, she added wickedly, "I'm Ninian Malcolm Siddons, resident witch." Her grandmother had also sworn an imp lived inside her instead of sorcery.

Instead of laughing or stepping away in fear as would any normal man, Lord Ives cocked his head with interest. "Ninian? A saint's name?"

Not only fearless, but with a knowledge of ancient history. Interesting. Grandmother had said men didn't take well to learning. "My mother had a strange sense of humor," she admitted. How odd that he queried her name, but not her reputation.

"I see." The hint of dryness disappeared into cool tones again. "I don't think it safe for a young woman in these woods at night. I'll escort you home."

"Please pardon my trespass, my lord," she said belatedly, "but there are herbs I need along this stream. Do you mind?"

"Would it matter if I said 'yes'?"

Observant, also. She shook her head. "I might be very sorry to go against your wishes, but I would not leave young Matthew with a sore throat."

"Quite." He seemed to withdraw within himself, or perhaps the moon shifted behind a cloud. "Then let us be on with it. I take it you are an herbalist and not a witch?"

"I see you are a natural philosopher," she commented evasively as she scanned the burnside where the agrimony grew. She didn't care what he believed, and she refused to succumb to the temptation of too much Beltane fantasy.

Many men were tall and physically graceful, with voices that could command attention with just a whisper. Granny had told her the devil possessed such charms, while promising much and producing evil. If she pretended the earl was Satan, she could safely ignore the unusual pattering of her heart at his proximity. Just because she had wished for a lover didn't mean she would fall for the charms of any man who came along — and *certainly* not an Ives.

Frowning, she crouched down to better study the streambed. Perhaps the darkness concealed what she knew to be there.

He must have heard her muttered curse of frustration. He stepped closer, his long boot-clad legs halting near her hand. "What is it?"

"It's gone. It used to grow thick . . ." She pushed past the undergrowth, searching closer to the water. "The watercress is gone, too, but that could be . . ." She prodded the moist soil at the edge with a stick. "Nothing kills violets," she muttered in puzzlement. "The sweet rushes are dead!" she exclaimed a moment later. "That's not possible!"

He crouched beside her and prodded his walking stick along the embankment. "I don't see much of anything but rocks. Are you sure you have the right place?"

The fine hairs on the back of her neck rose as his hand brushed near hers, but faced with a disaster of this proportion, she had no patience with her odd reaction. The burn provided a goodly portion of her remedies. If she couldn't heal, she had no place here at all. A cold chill iced her blood. Surely the legend of Malcolm and Ives bringing disaster couldn't already be coming true. Maybe it was Ives men alone who caused it.

Refusing to panic, she pushed farther upstream. "I *know* this is right," she muttered, mostly to herself. She wasn't accustomed to anyone accompanying her, and the black void that was her companion registered very strangely, enabling her to ignore him on a comfortable level. "Here's the path I made. This is where I added ashes and manure to sweeten the soil. I *know* . . ." She stopped and broke a branch of willow hanging over the embankment. "Dead," she whispered as the branch snapped.

"Trees die," he said from behind her. "In this cold damp, it's a wonder they live."

"No. No, it's not right . . ." Stepping carefully through the darkness, she broke a branch here, crouched to examine a tree root there. "I'll have to come back in daylight, follow the stream . . ." But fear licked along her veins. Without her remedies, she was less than nothing. She must discover —

"You'll do no such thing," he informed her. "In fact, it's time I saw you home."

Muttering to herself, she tucked the dried leaves and branches she'd gathered into her apron pocket and strode back to the path. According to her grandmother, in the scheme of things, men had only one purpose — the same services as the devil offered Eve. But the earl owned this property, and she had to at least pretend to listen to him.

Striding down the path, analyzing all the reasons the plants might have died, refusing to believe all was lost, Ninian jumped as strong fingers caught her elbow.

"You will break a leg walking so heedlessly."

Prickles crept along her skin where his fingers pressed through her shift sleeve. The sensation unnerved her. Had her idle wishes for a lover summoned this man? She should have paid heed when Granny warned her about wishing for what she could not have, especially on a night of power, like Beltane.

"Witches see in the dark," she said blithely, giving his grasp a not-too-subtle tug.

The long fingers only clenched her tighter. "Unlike that lout, I'm not inclined to superstition and I mean you no harm. I will see you safely home."

Wisely, Ninian surrendered the fight, lest he grasp her tighter still. His touch unsettled her as much as his lack of emotional presence. Never had her awareness been centered only on the physical. And never had the physical been so deeply felt as with this man. She could not sense whether he lied or laughed at her, but perversely, she trusted what he said. A wealthy aristocrat would have no interest in a village wench, or if he did, he would have offered her coin by now.

"Have you studied natural philosophy, my lord?" She would make the best of this enforced detour by picking his brain. Perhaps he would have a suggestion to chase away her fear about the absence of growth along the burn.

He hesitated before answering. "Somewhat," he reluctantly agreed.

"Do you know aught of the ways of water?"

"It's wet."

This time, she was certain she heard the dryness of his tone. He thought her a lackwit. So be it. She spoke aloud to hold back the uneasy awareness encompassing them.

"I know more of plants than water," she admitted. "I wonder if it's possible for water to become bad for plants as soil does when it goes sour."

Silence. Ninian fumed at this lack of response. She really needed someone who could discuss these things with her. Without Granny, she had no one with her level of knowledge.

"I have never noticed a stream without

plant life at this time of year," he said reflectively.

She sighed in relief. "Not even after an unusually harsh winter?"

Again, the long thoughtful silence before his deep voice broke the night. "I am not overly familiar with these climes, but even in the Highlands, I have seen plant life along streams in May."

"That's what I thought." Satisfied at having a part of her theory confirmed, she mulled over the next hypothesis.

"Is your home very far from here?" he asked, breaking the lengthening silence.

Startled anew at thus being awakened from her reverie, Ninian blinked and glanced around. While she'd fretted, they had left the forest and now traversed the road toward the village. "Not far."

She listened to the night around her, the soft hoot of an owl in a nearby field, the cheerful cries carried by the wind from those around the bonfire, and shivered at an all-too-familiar drunken anger she sensed nearby.

"Nate's hiding in the bushes outside my gate," she said calmly, nodding toward a picket fence covered in a thicket of overgrown roses. "By morning, he'll be convinced he saw you with horns and tail, riding the sky on my broomstick. You might wish to have a talk with him."

He shot her a sharp look and glanced at the bushes rustling outside the fence. "Talk seldom penetrates thick skulls," he replied.

Releasing her elbow, he strode determinedly toward the gate and jerked Nate from his hiding place.

In fascination, Ninian watched Lord Ives stride off, effortlessly hauling a struggling, protesting Nate without a single by-your-leave.

She thought she had every right to be afraid of a man like that.

Two

"What the devil are you doing here?" Drogo demanded, returning from a dull day with his steward and irritated to discover that one of his brothers had tracked him there. Second in line for Drogo's title but handsome enough to already have proved his Ives ability to procreate, Ewen crouched on the over-grown castle drive and attached a gear to what appeared to be a junk heap of scrap metal.

Drogo scraped at the mud on his boots as his brother reached for a wrench. His steward had insisted that he survey the bleak hills belonging to this barren estate, but unless they had coal under them, Drogo really wasn't interested. He needed to be back in London. Let the local sheepherders have the mud.

And let them keep the moonstruck little witch, too. She had haunted his sleep last night. How the devil had she known that rogue hid outside her gate? And why did he see her laughing eyes in every dark corner of this damned dungeon? She'd have him believing in witches at that rate. Could witches relieve him of disastrous siblings?

It would profit him to concentrate on the here and now rather than on the unattainable. He studied the tangle of wire and metal his brother was assembling.

"I could ask the same of you," Ewen replied as he threaded a pipe through a wheel, adjusted the gear, and sent the whole assembly wobbling down the drive. "I had to threaten to send Joseph up in my next balloon before he'd reveal your whereabouts. I didn't take you for the rural sort. I thought that was Dunstan's role."

A pity Ewen didn't possess their brother Dunstan's penchant for farming; Drogo could assign the neglected Wystan estate to this youngest of his legitimate brothers. But Ewen would sell the castle for wires and tin.

Eyeing the alarming contraption that couldn't possibly have been created in the few hours of his absence, Drogo assumed his most dour expression. "*I'm* establishing a coal mine and canal for transport, and increasing our profits in the process. The question is, what are *you* doing besides building children's toys? Looking for handouts?" From London to Wystan was a damned long uncomfortable distance for Ewen to have traveled for a friendly visit.

From beneath an uncut hank of raven hair, Ewen didn't lose his cheerful grin. "I'm developing a better method of making iron more malleable that would require the heat generated by the coal in your new mine. Don't you think that would be useful?"

It would, if Ewen had any chance of actually accomplishing one of his far-flung fancies. Drogo didn't see any hope of that since Ewen inevitably lost interest in practical applications once he solved a theoretical problem. "And I suppose your creditors are threatening Newgate?"

"Actually, I just sold my capacitor and plans for an electrical circuit to a colonist." Ewen shrugged. "I can't see how he'll trigger the electricity or what he'll do with it if he does, but that's his problem. But malleable iron . . . That's something we can use."

"For less expensive swords." Drogo could see the value. He just knew Ewen's capricious mind would move on before he profited from it. Giving up on his muddy boots, Drogo climbed the castle's crumbling stone steps. "So, what is it you want? My coins or my coal?"

"Both. I want to start a foundry." Leaving his contraption in the courtyard, Ewen eagerly followed. "No one would let me inside. What are you hiding in there?"

"Sarah's lost souls," Drogo said curtly, not expounding. "Come along then. I have a thousand things I need to do today, and you weren't among them."

"You need a woman, big brother," Ewen said cheerfully. "Do you never take time to look at a pretty girl or embrace the wind?"

"Keeping up with the lot of you is about as futile as embracing the wind," Drogo replied dryly. He didn't bother telling his rattlepated brother that he wasted his nights gazing at stars and admiring moon maidens. Someone in the family had to keep a sound head on their shoulders and their feet on the ground as an example of how normal, sane people lived. Their father, God rest his troubled soul, had never done so. As eldest, Drogo had been designated as the person in charge of responsibility.

Stargazing didn't fit the image he wished his brothers to emulate.

Ewen whistled as they crossed the enormous great room. "This place looks a hell of a lot better than your London place. Is that our stepsister's touch?"

"Probably." Drogo shrugged, indifferent to the polish the servants had been applying since their arrival.

At the sound of voices, Sarah appeared at the top of the stairs, her powdered hair immaculately curled, her brocade gown rustling as she glided downward. "Ewen! You have found us. I despaired of ever seeing civilization again."

Grinning, Ewen executed an exaggerated bow on her behalf. "Has Drogo kidnapped you and buried you alive out here?"

Sarah pouted prettily. "Mother threatened to dispossess me if I poisoned one more suitor, so I ran away. Only Drogo doesn't trust me to run by myself."

Impatiently, Drogo started up the stairs his stepsister had just descended. "You invited yourself, as I remember. Something about the stars being in the wrong house. I offered to send you to Brighton to find a husband instead."

"I don't want a husband," she called after him. "And we're all getting entirely too old for you to tell us what to do, Drogo Ives. What will you do when you don't have us to coddle any longer?"

"Watch after all the Ives bastards my brothers beget, I imagine." Ignoring Sarah's not-so-subtle jibe, Drogo led Ewen up the stairs into his tower study. He reached for the pen on his desk and glared at his brother. "How much?"

Along with an assortment of strings, coins, gears, and other mysterious objects, Ewen produced a scribbled list from his coat pocket and handed it over as he stubbornly pursued the more personal subject. "Even my bastards have mothers to coddle them. We're not all as irresponsible as our father. We can take care of any brats we produce."

"Fine then. The next time you produce one I won't increase your allowance." Sitting at his desk, Drogo scanned the list of supplies, sighed, and dipped his pen into the inkwell. It was a damned good thing he knew how to manage money better than his father had, or their continually growing family would all be starving in the street by now. Despite Ewen's fine protests, Drogo already supported two of his handsome brother's by-blows.

A shame none of his half-dozen younger brothers had learned the trick of high finance, or keeping their breeches buttoned.

Frowning, Ninian shut her grandmother's storybook and left it on the front parlor table. She shouldn't have opened it. She should forget last night's encounter with Lord Ives and not be looking at a childhood tale embroidered by generations of Malcolm women. Malcolms had odd talents, but even her grandmother couldn't cause natural disasters. Of course, there was that time Aunt Hermione had soured all the milk . . .

Ridiculous. That was coincidence. Much of her grandmother's power had been common manipulating, like telling Gertrude the lavender love charm would win Harry's heart, when all it did was instill confidence in a girl hampered by shyness.

Just because somewhere in the mists of time a Malcolm and an Ives had made an unhappy match did not mean she had to believe all Ives caused disasters. She still didn't have a right to think about a man with three wives.

This was an age of naturalism. Lord Ives wouldn't believe in legends, or witches.

Sighing, Ninian slipped from the cottage into the profusion of plants spilling over her garden. By starting seeds inside early, she had bay leaves big enough to harvest, mint thick around her ankles, columbine and foxglove blooming in glorious abundance in every nook and cranny. Plants, she knew how to handle. Men — it was best not to think about them.

Ninian poured a spoonful of honeyed willow bark water down young Matthew's throat. It wasn't as effective as the agrimony, but she wasn't yet prepared to admit that the source of half her herbs had mysteriously gone bad. As soon as she left here, she needed to examine the stream in daylight.

"The earl grabbed Nate's jerkin and carried him off. I don't have any idea what he said to him." Ninian related the prior night's events to Matthew's mother, Mary, as she persuaded more medicine down the boy's throat.

"Good gracious," Mary exclaimed. "The earl must be a very strong man to drag Nate anywhere."

"Taller, but no heavier, I think. Nate was drunk." Making faces back at Matthew until he giggled, Ninian wiped his mouth and tucked his covers more securely around him, basking in the gratitude and love he radiated.

It seemed cruel that she could never have a family of her own when she had so much to offer. Her heart ached, but she told herself that God must have His reasons.

"You are not interested in the man, are

you?" Mary asked with suspicion. "You know what the legend says about Malcolm and Ives destroying the land."

Ninian shrugged and tucked away her jar of medicine. "If he has three wives, he certainly has no interest in me. He'll be gone back to his city life soon enough."

"They say the castle once belonged to Malcolms," Mary said slyly.

"So? The cottage I have is much too big for me as it is. What would I do with an entire castle?"

"Have balls and servants," Mary dreamed aloud, apparently giving up her suspicion for the moment. "Dance all night and drink chocolate all day."

"And if I did that, who would make the willow bark for Matthew's throat?" Ninian asked pragmatically and finished packing her basket with jars of salve and medicine.

"Well, there is that," Mary agreed. "Still, your mother must have had grand gowns and pretty lace and danced all night. You could have the same."

"Yes, and my mother died young." Covering the basket, Ninian stood and brushed down her old wool skirt, unadorned with so much as an inch of lace or a bit of embroidery. She preferred it that way.

She'd been only ten when her mother had

died after the last of a series of miscarriages. Granny had warned that Malcolms could only bear their babes in Wystan, and Ninian's aunts had all dutifully done so. Not Ninian's mother. She'd birthed Ninian here, then gaily immersed herself in London's frivolities, denying her heritage and never returning to the place of her birth.

It was a tale Ninian had heard often, though she believed the tradition of returning to Wystan to give birth was her wily grandmother's way of controlling rich and powerful daughters who had strayed too far into the heathen life of London society.

Her grandmother's admonitions hadn't been necessary for Ninian. As curious as she might be of the roles of wives and mothers, as much as she loved children and wished for one of her own, she'd known for years that her place was in Wystan, where she was needed, where she was comfortable. As interesting as she found Lord Ives, he was still an Ives, and no temptation at all. Almost no temptation at all.

"Yes, but that doesn't mean you can't dress as pretty as Lord Ives's ladies," Mary said as she walked Ninian to the door. "Two of them visited Hattie's last week, and I've never seen anything so elegant."

"If they're reduced to buying Hattie's

caps, they won't be elegant for long," Ninian observed. "She's nearly too blind to see the stitches these days. And it rained all last week. Surely they did not drag their best silks and laces through the mud?" Ninian retained fond memories of her mother's silk and laces, but it had been over a decade since she'd outgrown the last of hers. They were useless in this cold, damp climate, and she'd never considered buying more, although she could have all the silk she wanted, if she'd wanted it. Which she didn't.

"I suppose you're right, but did you never dream of other places, Ninian?"

As a child, she'd seen other places, and chosen Wystan, but Ninian didn't try to explain that to Mary. Granny had called Ninian an emotional weather vane, buffeted by whatever winds of passion brewed nearby. The explosive emotions of London's immense populace had often disoriented her and spun her like a whirligig. She preferred the isolation of Wystan, a quiet world that she knew and understood.

Saying her farewells, Ninian swept out of the cottage with every intention of exploring the mystery of the barren burn. If Lord Ives only walked the night, he wouldn't know if she trespassed during the day.

Two women with their silk-covered panniers flapping in the breeze stood in the village square, hanging on to their preposterously wide straw hats and arguing with Harry, the shoemaker. Ninian blinked in astonishment at the bewigged apparitions. They couldn't have been more out of place in this simple village had they rode in on elephants.

Glancing around, she wasn't certain whether to be relieved or disappointed that she saw no sign of Lord Ives. Perhaps he really did only appear at night.

Imagining the ladies' difficulty in explaining what they wanted to unimaginative Harry, Ninian smiled wider. She could not understand why the taciturn Lord Ives would want two magpies for wives, much less three, and she certainly wouldn't carry that thought as far as the others had. His sleeping arrangements weren't her concern. Remembering the odd warmth she'd felt in his lordship's proximity, she didn't pursue that avenue either.

As she hurried down the path into the woods, she didn't worry about dirtying her practical leather shoes. Rural fashion appealed to her. The big pocket of her apron held all the herbs and plants she liked without need of tying pockets inside her homespun skirt, and her petticoat wouldn't carry her off in the wind like a giant kite as surely panniers and all that trailing silk would.

Musing on wires and silks and kites, she reached the burn much sooner than expected — and stopped short at the sight of Lord Ives standing a few feet away, poking his walking stick in the dead debris.

Amid the gray shadows of new leaves and clouds, he appeared nearly as formidable as he had last night. Tall, garbed in unfashionable black, and unsmiling, he frowned at Ninian's approach.

"The soil is coated with a malodorous slime," he said to her.

Shaken but undeterred by his presence, Ninian dipped down to examine the soil more closely. She rubbed her fingers in it, then sniffed them. "Sulfur?"

"Quite possibly."

She didn't sense his surprise at her knowledge so much as see it in the slight uplifting of his dark brows. Lord Ives had the most disconcertingly dark and piercing eyes, with thick eyebrows that curled upward at the ends. She couldn't call him a handsome man, so much as a compelling one. Her stomach lurched uncertainly at the intelligence staring back at her, intelligence she craved in a companion.

She hastily tested the soil again. "Sulfur, and something else." Thoughtfully, she wiped her fingers on her apron and gazed in dismay at the brown leaves and crumbling foliage that had once been a fairy garden of emerald hues. "It's as if it has been blasted by the devil," she murmured.

"More likely a type of acid, unless you prefer to search me for horn and tails."

His tone was as dry as the brittle leaves they walked upon, and Ninian warmed in appreciation of his humor. She glanced up, and her smile faltered beneath the impact of his intense stare. She didn't want to look away.

Taking a deep breath, she broke his spell. "I have already explained to the villagers that horns and tails do not fit well under silks and wigs." Daringly, she lifted an eyebrow at his unadorned black hair. "Although surely they can see for themselves that you are hiding nothing in that department."

He shrugged and returned to poking at the rocks along the bank. "I shouldn't think sulfur a naturally occurring chemical in water."

Reminded of her place, Ninian pulled her cloak more tightly around her. "Then I must explore and see where the blight begins."

"So you can cast a spell upon it?"

"Or wave my magic wand," she replied airily, striking out upstream.

"I think not." He caught her elbow and drew her back.

The spring air warmed around her, and heat sang through her veins. She didn't know whether to respond with interest or panic, but heeding her grandmother's more practical warnings regarding men, she pulled away.

Unable to read the earl's thoughts or emotions, she studied his harsh features for answers. He had a sharp blade of a nose, a stiff, stern jaw, vestiges of laugh lines around his eyes, and a sensuous curve to his upper lip that particularly captivated her. Masculine interest flared in his eyes at her scrutiny.

Shaken, she returned to their argument. "You cannot stand guard over the entire stream, day and night."

"I will send someone better prepared to walk these woods alone." He glanced pointedly at her diminutive figure. "It's my property. When the source of the blight is found, I'll deal with it as I deem appropriate."

Anger simmering, she hid it behind disarming dimples. "Not with witch's incantations? How unspirited of you."

His dark brows drew down into a V. "There is no such thing as magic."

"Of course, there isn't," she soothed. "I'm sure there's a purely natural reason for the stream to die and a thoroughly natural solution. I'll just consult a few trees, shall I?"

Her skirts swung tauntingly as she walked off. An unexpected beam of sunlight shot through the screen of clouds and leaves to catch on her golden ringlets, reminding the earl with a shock of her ability to recognize an intruder concealed by shrubbery.

Perhaps she just had uncanny eyesight.

Her challenge awoke an unholy curiosity in him that wasn't entirely intellectual but heated his blood far more than was good for either of them.

Three

Staring at the night sky, Drogo adjusted the telescope on his desk, tried to jot down a note, and cursing the dry quill, dipped it in an inkwell. He should hire a secretary.

He didn't want a secretary. These few moments he hoarded for himself were the only pure pleasure he possessed in a life of constant demands. People always asked too much of him, and secretaries were people. Besides, it was too late to hire anyone. His business with the coal mine was almost done, and he doubted he would linger in the area another week.

Adjusting the telescope one final time, he grunted in satisfaction, and bending nearer the flickering candle, noted the location and date of the celestial object he'd observed. He was almost certain he'd found a hitherto unknown planet. He needed better equipment. And more time for his studies.

He could buy the equipment. Time was more difficult to obtain.

After carefully sanding his notes and placing them in his leather folio, he looked up and caught a glimpse of another project he'd started out of curiosity stirred by a forest nymph. He didn't generally waste time listening to women, nymphs or not, but she'd engaged his intellect in the puzzle of the blighted stream.

Drogo wandered to the tower windows he'd had installed upon his arrival. This far north of London's smoke and fog the vista of starlit firmament spread out before him as far as heaven itself — as distant as the peace he craved.

Briefly, he wondered what it would be like without the responsibilities of his title, to come and go as he pleased, to act on impulse without thought to consequences. He might as well picture life without his half-dozen younger brothers. He didn't have the imagination for it. He did what was necessary and savored these rare moments of quiet when they appeared.

The moon was waning, but its silver light poured over the ancient forest below, returning his thoughts to the moon maiden. More than enchanting, she fascinated him — he supposed because of the night and the moon and his own curiosity.

Mostly, women were a mysterious other world to him, one of soft fragrances and whispery silks and incomprehensible giggles. He enjoyed the sensual pleasures when he visited their world, but he wasn't likely to linger among them. They weren't logical and didn't provide sufficient intellectual stimulus. The baffling moon maiden hadn't provided silks and giggles, but she'd stirred his interest. Odd.

He glanced down at the experiment the encounter had inspired. He'd set out pots of grass he'd dug from the yard. He'd watered half the pots with liquid from the dying burn and half with water from the castle well. All the grass looked seriously unhappy.

The witch would no doubt tell him his own malaise blighted the plants.

Grimacing at that illogical thought, Drogo watered the plants again. *Witches.* In this day and age. Silly, superstitious twits.

A corner of his mouth turned up as he remembered her flapping her sleeves and terrifying the bumpkin, Nate, into flight. He'd often wished he had that ability. Maybe he could hire her to stand on the tower stairs and terrify the castle inhabitants into leaving him alone.

Too late for tonight though. He heard the

patter of feminine feet on the stone even as he thought it. He swore they knew the instant he rose from his desk. Maybe all women were witches. His limited experience would certainly indicate something decidedly hellish about them upon occasion.

"Drogo!" The door burst open on Sarah's usual breathless note. "Come quickly! I swear, the ghost is walking. Hurry!"

He did no such thing. He tilted his head, heard the sound of the wind picking up, and looked at his stepsister with disfavor. "The branches are rubbing the windows again. Don't be such a goose, Sarah."

"Don't be such a stubborn ass, Drogo!" Several years younger than he, but a widow now and far more worldly-wise than she ought to be, Sarah tossed her powdered head of curls. "There's moaning, and footsteps, and, I swear, something crashed. Claudia is in hysterics, and Lydie could go into labor any minute out of sheer fright."

The thought of Lady Lydie in labor frightened Drogo more than any threat of haunts. Why the devil had he let them follow him here?

Because Sarah's mother had thought her daughter safer away from society's wagging tongues after she'd nearly poisoned her last suitor with one of her witch's brews. At the time, he hadn't anticipated his stepsister bringing along an unwed mother and an unhappy companion. The potential for trouble was enormous, which was one of the reasons why he'd sent Ewen away. Of course, his brother's invention of a "ghost-catcher" that had crashed through the ceiling in the middle of the night had speeded his departure.

Drogo was used to dealing with his brothers. He wasn't used to dealing with women and babies. Definitely not babies. He'd expected to be long gone before Lydie delivered.

Gritting his teeth, Drogo surrendered any idea of a peaceful evening reading the pamphlets on astronomy he'd received in the day's post. "There are no such things as ghosts," he reminded Sarah as he followed her down the stairs. "There may be squirrels in the attic or mice in the walls, but there are no ghosts."

"Well, you just come down out of your almighty tower and tell Lydie there are mice in the walls," Sarah answered tartly, lifting her wide skirts by the armful to negotiate the narrow stairs. "But I suggest you do it after you've called the midwife."

A midwife. By all the saints in heaven, he hadn't thought about midwives. Did the village even have one?

"Isn't it a little early for that?" he asked cautiously. His experience with Sarah as a child told him she was capricious, irresponsible, and capable of causing him grief just for amusement. She was supposed to be an adult now, but he still took anything she told him with an entire cellar of salt.

"It most certainly is, so I fervently hope you can trap your wretched mice. Or ghosts."

The dual screams echoing up the stairs from the rooms below warned that the night's theatrics had only just begun.

Sarah flattened herself against the wall as Drogo pushed past and raced downward. In the candlelit darkness, he didn't see her smile of satisfaction.

"It's all in the diary," Sarah said defensively, clutching a peeling leather volume to her chest in the face of her friends' dubious expressions. "It says so right here." She opened the frail, cracking pages and pointed out a paragraph. "All Malcolm women are witches, so it must have been a Malcolm witch who cursed the Ives."

"You don't really believe Drogo is cursed, do you?" Lydie asked, wrinkling up her nose in confusion.

"*All* Ives are cursed!" Sarah declared grandly, slamming the book closed and gesturing dramatically. "Just look at them. They all have miserably unhappy marriages and bear nothing but bastards. Boy bastards," she added in emphasis, as if that were curse enough. "I have three of them for half brothers, so I ought to know."

"There wouldn't be any earls left if that were true," Claudia, Lady Twane, pointed out. "And if I remember correctly, Drogo has two younger brothers and neither of them are bastards."

Undaunted by this hole in her theory, Sarah smiled. "That's a matter of opinion. My point is, what are we going to do about it?"

"Do about it?" Lydie squeaked, her eyes growing wide as she realized Sarah was off on another of her schemes.

"If a Malcolm cursed an Ives, then a Malcolm could uncurse one, couldn't she?"

"But, Sarah . . ." two voices protested at once.

"It doesn't matter. The stars say the time is propitious for Drogo to marry and have a son, and we will do what we can to see that accomplished."

As Sarah triumphantly returned the tattered leather volume to the library shelf, her companions exchanged knowing looks.

"If Drogo has a wife and heir, he'll have his hands so full, he won't have time to see what Sarah is up to," Lady Twane translated.

Lydie rolled her eyes.

Drogo located the moon maiden dreamily gathering rosebuds from the rampant brambles along her picket fence. The bushes at the castle weren't blooming. Wasn't it a little early for roses?

Obviously not, if she was picking them. Sarah was the one who believed in ghosts and witches and impossible feats of magic. Rampant roses in early May were not magic.

He felt a fool for seeking out the little herbalist on such a pretext, but Sarah had insisted, and he'd seen no real alternative — not if he wanted any peace at all.

Ninian looked up at him as if he'd materialized from another world but said nothing as Drogo explained Lydie's condition and the foolishness of the women's complaints.

"I will pay whatever it takes," he stated dispassionately when, seeming struck dumb by his appearance, she didn't reply to the ladies' absurd request that she come to rid the castle of ghosts. Captured by the enchantment of her cornflower-blue eyes, he wondered how anyone in his rational mind could consider this golden-haired innocent a witch, providing anyone rational could believe in witches.

His gaze dropped to the swell of a generous bosom disguised beneath the folds of her muslin kerchief. Men might call her sorceress, but for her physical charms, not her magical ones.

Drogo lifted his gaze again to discover a mischievous dimple peeking from its hiding place. Pouty pink lips parted in a teasing smile as if she knew precisely what he was thinking.

Which, of course, she did, because all men must look at her that way. "The women are hysterical," he repeated calmly, despite his sudden surge of lust. He wondered why she did not let him past the gate, invite him into the house. In his experience, women fell all over their feet to entertain the Earl of Ives, one of the many reasons he'd fled to Wystan's isolation. This female smiled enticingly, but twiddled with a rose like a simpleton. Perhaps he'd mistaken her intelligence. Anyone who called herself a witch probably had a cog or two missing in her brainworks.

Patiently, he tried again. "Lady Twane has a nervous condition and Lady Lydie is expecting her first child shortly. I understand you're a midwife. You must know the delicacy —"

She shook her head. "Call for me when she goes into labor. That, I can help with. Ghosts are not within my realm of knowledge."

So, she could speak when she wanted, fluently and with the educated accents of London. Unusual. The golden ringlets hid a brain, even if it was slightly cracked.

Bewildered by her benign smile, and wondering what could possibly be racketing through that strange noggin of hers, Drogo refused to accept defeat. He merely changed tactics. He nodded complacently. "Of course, I perfectly understand. Ghosts are a figment of the imagination and you cannot promise what is not possible. I respect your honesty. However —"

Again, she interrupted with a shake of her pretty curls. "Ghosts are real enough. But I believe they should be left alone. You're the intruders. Those ghosts could have been there for hundreds of years. Why should they leave their home because trespassers are annoyed with their presence?"

Exasperated by her lack of logic, Drogo gripped the pickets of the gate that separated him from her. He did not have a temper, he told himself. Given his excitable but generally scientific family, calm logic had always served him best. Silly females who believed in ghosts weren't rational. Fine, then he would be irrational.

"Then don't disturb the ghosts. I'm concerned about Lady Lydie. Examine her, if you will. However, I'd be much easier if you could convince these infernal women that you've tried all within your power so they'll leave me in peace. If they believe in ghosts, they'll believe in the power of witches, too. Merely sprinkle smelly things about the place, mutter a few magical words, yell 'boo' for all I care. I'll have the men on the roof searching for loose slates on the morrow."

She slipped the tip of a soft white finger between her rosy lips and stared at him from her crystal blue eyes as if they were the insurmountable dividing wall between his world and hers. She blinked once, frowned quizzically as she tilted her head and studied him, then her befuddled mind apparently reached some decision, and she nodded.

As if that were a signal for her to return from a trance, she straightened her shoulders and her apron, and smiled beatifically. "I'll come tomorrow, shall I?"

Slightly mystified but satisfied with the result of his task, Drogo relaxed enough to notice the lush profusion of purple, pink, and white flower heads bouncing on thick stalks just over her shoulder. The castle kitchen garden had barely revealed a poor shoot or two the last time he'd looked. Perhaps he needed a new gardener.

Dismissing the flowers as irrelevant, he nodded at her acceptance, and walked away. On a whim, he made the mistake of glancing back. The nymph waved at him from her bower of rose canes as if she really were the fairy queen of a flower realm. Ridiculous thought. He straightened his shoulders and returned to the reality of the road ahead.

As he strode away, Ninian admired the aristocratic line of the earl's fitted coat, the determined pace of his gait, and the way the sun glinted off his ebony hair. She knew the dull brown of his long-tailed coat was less elegant than those of the gentlemen in London, but it was far above the crude jerkins of the townspeople, and it not only exactly matched his cockaded hat, but revealed the silver hilt of a sword — a weapon not often seen in these parts. The rich leather of his riding boots and the ornate head of his walking stick spoke of the wealth his coat did not.

She could not fathom why a lord of the realm, a man with riches beyond imagination, would require her poor services, as witch or midwife or anything else. And because she did not understand him, she felt compelled to try, despite the legends. Seldom did she meet someone she could not read, particularly a man. Women often confused their emotions so badly that she couldn't sort one from the other, but men — men were usually simple.

Her grandmother would have been proud of her restraint. The legend had it that the last Ives man to cross a Malcolm threshold had carried off the lady against her will.

Well, she hadn't let him cross the threshold.

Four

Refusing to believe she could be entranced by an aristocrat wearing a fashionable coat and expensive high-topped boots, Ninian firmly closed her portmanteau as she prepared to leave for the castle the next morning. The image of Lord Ives standing at her garden gate, hat in hand, raven hair gleaming in the sun, had haunted her all night, but it was his eyes that held her spellbound. Deeply set, shadowed by heavy black lashes, framed by those thick curling eyebrows, his eyes opened fascinating new worlds.

Still, she thought it mainly curiosity that drove her to agree to this visit. She wanted to know more about the blighted stream and the castle ghosts and . . . Lord Ives.

She supposed she really ought to search Granny's library for some source of the story about Malcolms and Ives before *she* crossed *his* threshold, but recklessly, she

62

chose to find out the truth on her own. It was time she explored a wider world.

She wouldn't admit to the restlessness Beltane had stirred in her. She just needed something new and exciting in her life.

Could she chase away ghosts? It didn't seem likely, especially since she didn't like to try. But her grandmother had assured her that Malcolms could do most anything they applied their minds to. Ninian had no proof of that. She couldn't make amulets work. She had packed her grandmother's ancient book of incantations, but it might as well be a chemist's manual for all the good it was. Maybe one of her aunts or cousins could work the spells, but she'd only found success in healing remedies. She'd discovered and tested any number of effective herbs on her own, but she'd never laid a ghost to rest, made a love potion, or bewitched a cow. Or a man.

Laughing at that thought, she set out for Wystan Castle.

Portmanteau in hand, her hooded cloak pulled firmly around her against the dew, she stepped through the garden gate and nearly walked straight into a two-wheeled cart.

"Mornin', miss." The driver touched his battered felt hat. "His lordship sent me to wait on you."

"How thoughtful." Surprised and pleased, she threw her bag into the back of the cart and, with the help of the driver, clambered up. No one had ever been thoughtful enough to offer her transportation. Perhaps the road was longer than she'd realized. She had never traversed the woods as far as Wystan Castle because no villagers lived in that direction, and the forest was too dense there for her to waste time exploring it without reason. Castles didn't hold as much interest for her as plants did. "Is it very far?"

"Not so far as a bird flies, but people can't fly."

Ninian digested the truth behind this platitude sometime later as the cart finally ambled off the pitted, rutted main road onto the narrow drive leading to the castle. After years of disuse, the lane had nearly reverted to its natural state. The forest and underbrush beyond the drive looked impenetrable.

"Will his lordship be clearing the grounds?" she asked casually, eyeing a marvelous clump of birch almost lost in brambles.

"His lordship has interest in naught but books," the driver grumbled. "Ain't natural." He peered at her from beneath the crumpled brim of his hat. "There's them that says —"

"Oh, look at the woodbine!" Ninian exclaimed at the cascade of greening vine ahead, cutting off any descent into gossip. She didn't want to know what people said about Lord Ives any more than she wanted to hear what they said about her.

The driver lapsed into silence and Ninian savored the trill of birdsong and the fresh scents of evergreen. Too much of England's forest land had been stripped bare or landscaped into unnatural quadrangles of neatly trimmed hedges, straight paths, and tidy flower beds. She preferred Lord Ives's method of leaving the land alone.

Of course, she would prefer cultivating the more beneficial trees and plants to allowing this kind of impenetrable wilderness, but perhaps, given time . . .

The horse slowed and Ninian glanced ahead. The formidable stone walls of Wystan Castle towered across the road. Fortified at a time when border wars ravaged the countryside, it had never been fully modernized. The main block of the house loomed through the trees, with high stone walls and narrow windows that would allow little light inside. The rocky ground on which it had been built would once have been cleared of brush and trees, but years of neglect had brought the forest nearly to its doors.

The clouds parted overhead, and a shaft of light illuminated glass in the upper reaches of the tower. How odd, Ninian thought as she scrambled from the cart. Lord Ives had installed windows in the unheated watchtower.

A housekeeper let her in, and Ninian followed her stout, black-clad figure through the great hall and up the steps to the private floor.

Little had been done to improve the ancient decor. Moldering tapestries had apparently been cleaned and patched, but nothing could restore them to their medieval grandeur. The covers on the furniture had been removed and the wood beneath dusted and polished. The towering carved walnuts and oaks of an earlier age looked foreign and uncomfortable.

An old-style upholstered bed draped heavily in crewel-embroidered linen with faded blue silk linings filled the center of the room to which the housekeeper led her. At first, Ninian assumed she'd been brought to the bedchamber of Lady Ives, but the servant opened Ninian's bag and began laying her drab homespun into a chest of drawers inlaid with carvings more elaborate than the embroidery.

"I'll do that," she said hurriedly, taking her best apron from the woman's hands. She didn't want anyone touching the herbs and book at the bottom of the bag.

The woman nodded. "The lady will call for you," she said, before ambling off.

With a sigh, Ninian scanned the enormous room. Since the age of ten she'd lived simply, with plain country furniture and lathe and mud daub walls. She hadn't seen wainscoting and ornate ceilings since London, and she'd never seen tapestries like these. The room would burst with color had age not grayed the threads.

She started to examine a cloth swarming with trees and white figures, but the carved step beside the downy thickness of the bed distracted her. A bed so tall that one needed a stair to climb into it warned of bitter drafts about the floor. The room had no fireplace. The purpose of the heavy hangings and the thick carpet was evident.

The image of Lord Ives appeared, imprinted over the reality of the ornate bed. She could see him like some medieval lord in shirtsleeves waiting for his woman to disrobe and join him. She'd never had such thoughts until she'd looked into the earl's haunting eyes.

Her gaze dropped to the soft bed, and the air warmed around her. The perfume of roses tickled her senses, returning the image of the earl's dark gaze. Her breasts tingled as if he'd touched them.

She'd never possessed a sensual awareness of a man's masculinity until she'd met Lord Ives. Intellectually, she knew how men viewed women and what they did to them when they could. Emotionally and physically, she'd never quite understood why a woman would invite what seemed to her as rather awkward indignities. Now, understanding rippled just beneath her skin.

She hadn't come here out of curiosity about ghosts or blighted streams. She'd come to test her powers as a woman and a witch.

Uncomfortable with that self-discovery, since Lord Ives was beyond her limits and she really didn't think she could chase ghosts, Ninian escaped the scent of roses by slipping into the hall. Arrow slits illuminated the far ends of the corridor, revealing only a row of doors and a worn carpet adorned with miscellaneous tables along the wall. She wondered if the other doors belonged to the women of the household. Perhaps the earl really did keep a seraglio.

She took the stairs down to the public

rooms. The original great hall had evidently been added onto in a helter-skelter pattern she couldn't discern. She peeked in on a library and a gentleman's study with billiards table and a ladies' parlor and a small breakfast room. But the earthier scents of plants and soil drew her onward.

She halted at the sound of voices coming from behind a partially open door. Perhaps the hope of female companionship had drawn her here as much as anything else. The earl, she must remember, wanted her abilities as a witch, not a woman. Spirits dropping, she would have hurried past, but one cheerfully ribald feminine voice rang out clearly.

"Well, it's a pity I'm in an 'interesting condition' or I'd volunteer. Drogo is surely a more thoughtful lover than my Charles, although admittedly, he's not very sympathetic to you, Sarah."

Another woman twittered. "When he looks at me from beneath those dark brows of his, I'm fair to fainting. But I fear I am barren," she finished sadly.

"And a good thing, too. You're a married woman and could only bear him bastards," the younger first voice declared firmly.

"Now, girls, this discussion has grown quite old. We all owe Drogo more than we can repay in the usual way."

"If we disappeared tomorrow, Sarah, he wouldn't notice," the sad voice replied.

"Well, we know why that is, don't we?" Sarah continued. "But the stars say we have a chance to correct that. I've brought the herbs from London, and if we're in agreement that it's up to us to correct the . . ."

Ninian hurried away as the voice came closer and the parlor door closed firmly. Heart pounding, she nearly fell through the door at the far end of the hall.

It didn't sound as if any of the women were married to Lord Ives, but it certainly sounded as if they knew him as a lover.

She couldn't imagine the enormity of such a thing. She'd read tales of Oriental harems, but Lord Ives was *English*. And the one lady was *married*. Was the other bearing his child? Three mistresses rather than wives. She couldn't comprehend it at all.

Uneasiness skittered across her skin, but she ignored it as she discovered the door to which she'd been drawn.

On the other side of the threshold, the frames for enormous windows ran along the entire length of the back wing of the castle. Tile floors still held the remnants of broken glass. Small oak saplings struggled to survive amid the debris of many autumns, protected by the warm stone of the outer wall.

A conservatory. The castle once had a conservatory. How very, very odd.

With her foot, Ninian brushed aside years of dead leaves, exploring the unfurling frond of a fern, the probing stems of valerian. Valerian! Ninian stooped to clear away pot shards and leaves to examine the root. No one willingly grew a plant that smelled so bad unless they meant to use it for sleep disorders or magic rituals.

Exploring farther, she uncovered evidence of old clay pots and disintegrating wooden planters. A few straggling herbs, ones hardy to the region, still survived exposure to the elements. Whatever else had grown here had long since died.

Mary had said the castle once belonged to a Malcolm. The Malcolm women were all purported to be witches.

Ninian cleared aside glass to uncover designs in the tile. She recognized the symbols for sun and moon and stars. This had been the heart of the Malcolm castle then — a wonderful conservatory of healing plants and a tribute to the earth that produced them.

It saddened her to see the soul of the house broken and neglected like this. Maybe this — and not Lord Ives — was why she'd been drawn here.

Even as she dared to think it, the object of her thoughts intruded upon her reverie.

"I should have known I'd find you here."

Ninian dropped a sprig of mint and whirled to meet the master of the household.

He wore a black traveling cloak and looked as if he'd just come in from a ride. As usual, he wore no wig, and his somber hair was drawn back in a ribboned club. The beginnings of a beard darkened his jaw and his craggy brows shadowed his eyes as he gazed upon her. Ninian shivered. She had remembered him as an imposing presence, but on her own territory, she had not feared him. She was in his territory now, with nowhere to run should she need to. And he was everything masculine she'd ever dreamed about. The earthy scents of soil and plants surrounding them seemed somehow fitting, and intoxicating.

"It is a pity this room was lost." She gestured at the rotted frames, seeking solid ground as her senses reeled from the impact of his proximity. Was that the scent of male musk mixing with her own oil of roses?

The earl gave the structure a look of disinterest and shrugged. "I had the fallen tree removed, but there's little worth saving here. No furniture, only a few broken tables."

In his knee-high boots and billowing cloak, with those piercing eyes beneath curled eyebrows, he could have been Satan declaring the earth beyond redemption. Bravely, Ninian stooped to retrieve the mint, crushing it to fill the air with freshness. "This was the heart of your house," she said quietly.

Dark eyebrows raised. "Not to me. It's the tower that I prefer."

Male and female, earth and sun, the distance between both was so great it was a wonder plants grew or children were born. Looking up from her crouched position at the length of the earl's booted calves and the shiny silver buttons on his breeches-clad thighs, she blinked and looked away again when her gaze traveled a smidgen too far.

His cloak had fallen back from his hips to reveal the tight cut of his breeches. Lord Ives was a very big man. Even the fresh smell of mint couldn't distract her from a vivid awareness of his masculinity.

"May I see the tower sometime?" Visiting his lair seemed suddenly important to her understanding of this man.

He quirked one eyebrow as he gazed down on her uncovered curls. She'd forgotten her cap. Hastily, brushing off her hands, she stood up. His gaze didn't rise with her, but now rested on her bodice.

"Only if you have need of me," he replied enigmatically.

With a swirl of his cloak, he stalked out, leaving Ninian feeling as if she'd just been stripped naked, examined, and found wanting.

Five

"What on earth are you doing?" the lovely woman in the doorway asked, peering from the conservatory threshold but not setting a silk-shod foot beyond.

Ninian halted her sweeping. She'd found enough dried grass on the grounds to fashion a decent broom and had uncovered a large portion of the tiles in the decimated conservatory. "I'm not accustomed to sitting still," she replied mildly.

"Obviously." The woman glanced at the little garden of plants Ninian had repotted in an old bucket. "I'm Drogo's stepsister, Sarah. Let me provide you with more . . ." She didn't complete the sentence but turned to leave, gesturing for Ninian to follow.

Stepsister! Not wife. Curious, Ninian wondered if a stepsister could be a mistress.

"I will need to wash." Having never been a

servant, she didn't follow orders well. Setting aside her broom, she stepped over the threshold into the house. She felt inadequate enough in the lady's stylish presence; she didn't need to feel dirty, too.

Sarah schooled her obvious impatience and nodded toward another doorway. "The kitchen is through there. They'll have . . ." She waved her hand vaguely.

Well, Ninian was accustomed to washing in kitchens. She and her grandmother had practically lived in the service room during the winter to keep from lighting more than one fire. Not that they couldn't have afforded more fires, but Grandmother had always been tightfisted, and Ninian had had more important things to tend than fires.

She brushed herself off, washed as best as possible, and returned to the hall to find Sarah still waiting.

The elegantly slim lady looked her up and down, sighed faintly, then straightening her shoulders, marched toward the hall and the stairs.

Well, she'd always known she wasn't cut out to be a graceful swan of society, Ninian thought ruefully as she followed Sarah up the stairs. She had a sturdy peasant's build she couldn't change with any amount of magic. And no need to change, she reminded herself. She did not look out of place in her own home.

Sarah led her to a bedchamber in a different wing than where Ninian was situated. This wing looked slightly newer and more recently refurbished. She had time to glimpse gleaming mahogany and a brilliantly patterned carpet before her escort pushed open a door and introduced her into a room full of sunlight and exotically garbed women.

Including Sarah, three exotically garbed women, to be precise. Ninian quickly reduced the sensory bombardment to count her escort in blue silk and powdered coiffeur; a hugely pregnant young girl in layers of flowing emerald and a frilled cap of dainty lawn; and a thin, timid woman hiding in the shadows.

"Ladies, meet Ninian Siddons. Miss Siddons, Lady Twane, and Lady Lydie, good friends of mine. And of Drogo's, of course."

The pregnant girl giggled. Ninian noted the flash of vivacious dark eyes and surmised that Lady Lydie had hair as dark as the earl's beneath her cap. She was younger than the others, scarcely old enough to be carrying a child. Under Ninian's study, she smiled. "I thought midwives were old, gnarled creatures," she stated disingenuously.

"You are referring to my grandmother." Ninian smiled to relieve the effect of her bluntness. "Her hands were arthritic, so I acted as her hands. I learned all she knew, which is more than most London physicians know." The sarcasm was instinctive. It was in the hands of London physicians that her mother had lost five infants.

"We've inquired, and you come highly recommended," Sarah replied soothingly. "We have no doubt that you're the best person for Lydie's lying-in. But it's the . . ." She fluttered her hands helplessly and looked to the others. "I feel so foolish saying this . . ."

"The ghost," Lady Twane stated firmly, still staring at Ninian. "We want you to send the ghost away. It is most distressing to be woken in the middle of the night by invisible temper tantrums."

Ninian didn't think there was a thing she could do about the spirits haunting Wystan Castle, but these women would never believe her until they saw for themselves. They were born of wealth and privilege and thought all their wishes could be carried out on command. They wouldn't understand that some things were not of this earth and could not be commanded.

"As I told Lord Ives, I am an herbalist, not a ghost-chaser. For that, you will need a priest. But if you wish, I will try talking to the spirits. I make no promises."

"Priests wear fancy robes and silk scarves and carry incense and candles," Lady Lydie said thoughtfully, gazing with interest at Ninian's simple garb. "Perhaps ghosts would be more impressed with your power should you wear something more . . ."

"Fashionable," Lady Twane finished caustically.

"Rich and powerful!" Sarah exclaimed. "That is exactly it! We shall give you the power of the church by ornamenting you with . . ." She waved her hand in a manner Ninian was coming to recognize. "Lydie, you are much the same height as Miss Siddons. You are certain to have something . . ."

Although Lady Sarah failed to finish sentences, she scarcely seemed the type to fear ghosts. These women hid themselves well behind layers of powder and silk and feathers, but this particular scheme spoke of subterfuge. Ninian sensed it in the air. "I do not think this is at all necessary —"

"But it is!" Lydie intruded. "We are all so bored sitting out here in Drogo's hideaway

79

with naught else to amuse ourselves. Dressing you like a fashion doll would be oh so amusing, and it's certain to impress any ghosts lingering in the walls. Say you will, please? Then we can go ghost-hunting after dinner."

Ninian thought she should tell them she wasn't poor and could afford her own silks if she had any desire to wear silk. But the trust fund Granny had left in her care wasn't anyone's business but her family's.

Sarah was already riffling through Lydie's trunks, searching for the perfect gown. Lady Twane picked at the discards with a disdainful finger, but even she seemed to be interested in the scheme. She radiated pain, Ninian thought. All that submerged anger and grief and pain would be sufficient to wake any ghost from hiding. She suspected removing Lady Twane from the premises would quiet the haunts faster than she could.

"The blue!" Lydie ordered from her reclining position on the upholstered daybed. "It never suited me, but it will be perfect for her fair hair and eyes."

Ninian thought she ought to remind them that she was several inches shorter than anyone in here, but then she remembered the wealth of undergarments holding up their fashionable material and, panicking, shook her head. "No, please, I cannot . . ."

"Never say you can't," Sarah called from the depths of the trunk. "Look, won't this cap look sweet if we dress her hair . . ."

Ninian's hand flew to her hair. "No! I won't have flour or pomade."

"Of course not." Lydie waved away the protest. "Your hair is much too fascinating as it is, and surely ghosts come from a time when hair wasn't dressed. The cap with the blue ribbons, Sarah. It's just a wisp of lace."

Sarah shook out layers of rich brocade. "Perfect. No panniers. We need a heavy underskirt, Lydie. I saw a white one with gold thread . . ."

Dazed and bewildered by this sudden barrage of beautiful silks and colors, Ninian allowed them to replace her coarse linen with a frail lawn chemise adorned with layers of lace at sleeve and neckline. She gasped as they tightened the whalebone bodice until she could scarcely breathe, but her protests went unheard until she declared the ghost would never hear her should she faint from lack of air.

The beautiful sky-blue brocade slid over her shoulders and underskirt like a waterfall, and she surreptitiously smoothed the sensuous material as they nipped and

81

tucked it into place. As expected, it fell past the tips of her toes, but they fashioned a sash of darker blue silk and hauled the excess material around her waist and tied it in place. She felt like a stuffed pig, but the ladies oohed and ahhed and praised their own work so highly, she couldn't be so rude as to say so. Besides, the silk felt wonderful, and decadent.

"I don't suppose you have knowledge of astrology?" Lady Lydie asked as the others arranged Ninian's attire. "The stars tell us such wonderful things. Sarah has found this astrologer —"

Sarah hastily cut her off. "Miss Siddons knows about herbs, Lydie, not stars. We need her to teach us how to rid this place of ghosts."

Covering her mouth with a giggle, Lydie said not another word. Ninian could sense the confusion of emotion surrounding her, but it was impossible to tell what came from whom and why. She just knew they were hiding some conspiratorial secret, and it didn't take much thought to figure it had to do with her.

They attacked Ninian's hair next, cutting a fringe of curls around her face and brushing out thick ringlets until they billowed over her shoulders and down her back. They pinned it all in place with the scrap of lace, then stepped back to admire their handiwork.

"The modesty bit isn't very modest," Lady Twane noted, just as a gong tolled from deep within the bowels of the castle.

Ninian leapt at the booms. The ladies looked unconcerned by the constant ringing.

"Well, she is a little more well endowed than Lydie," Sarah agreed. "But we haven't time. Drogo will disappear into the wood-work if we —"

"Wait! I can't go." Ninian glanced down at the scrap of transparent cloth scarcely covering the valley between the swells of flesh pushed up by her bodice, but Sarah caught her arm and dragged her toward the door. Ninian had seen her mother wear less, but she'd never seen herself as her mother.

"Of course, you can, dear. It's just us, and you look marvelous. Lydie, dear, do you want your meal sent up or are you able to manage the stairs . . . ?"

That instantly diverted Ninian's thoughts from herself. "No, she should not be walking those stairs at this stage! I will fetch a tray and bring it up for her."

Sarah laughed. "We have servants, Miss Siddons." She glanced over her shoulder at

Lady Lydie, who didn't seem interested in stirring from her reclining position. "We'll tell you all about it later, Lydie."

"I want to be there for the ghost hunt!"

"No one comes with me . . ." Ninian started to protest, but no one was listening.

Laughing and giggling, Sarah and Lady Twane drew her relentlessly toward the stairs to the public rooms where the earl awaited his dinner. Feeling as if she wore more clothes than she owned but still shivering from exposure, Ninian surrendered the useless fight. She would put on her show of ridding the place of ghosts and leave in the morning. If they wished to make a toy of her in the meantime, what harm could it do?

The instant she saw Lord Ives's dark gaze fasten on her, Ninian knew the harm it could do. Her breasts swelled beneath his stare, and her nipples puckered. Had she seen that look on Beltane beneath the moonlight, she would be a lost woman by now, like all the other foolish girls that surrendered their virtue in a moment of moon magic.

After what seemed a thousand eternities, the earl finally lifted his gaze to Sarah and her companion. "I see you found something to amuse you this day," he said mildly, before offering his arm to Ninian. "Witches should always wear blue." With that ambiguous statement, he led her into the dining room, leaving the other women to follow.

So nervous she didn't think she could eat, Ninian clasped and unclasped her hands in her lap as Lord Ives seated the other ladies, then returned to the seat at the head of the table, beside hers. She was uncomfortable with this new awareness of her body. It had served her fine as a place to hang clothes. Her arms were meant for sweeping floors, not looking bare and enticing beneath a fall of expensive lace. She had never thought to have babies so considered her breasts a nuisance, until Lord Ives glanced at the way they pushed above her bodice, and his look burned all the way down to the place between her thighs.

"And this is your idea of ghost-hunting clothes?" he inquired of the table in general as a footman passed around the tureen of soup.

"Of course, Drogo, the very latest . . ." Sarah gestured and laughed.

"Nay, my lord," Ninian said at the same time. "But the ladies insisted."

"The ladies are bored and amuse themselves at our expense. Do not let them make you do anything you do not wish to do." Lord Ives returned his attention to his soup.

"He never notices us when he's studying the stars," Lady Twane whispered in her ear. "It does him good to know other people exist."

"No whispering, Claudia," Sarah warned from across the table. "He will ignore us no matter what we say. He's already calculating arcs and angles in his mind, or pounds and pence, and doesn't hear a word. He thinks we're so far from trouble out here, he can forget our existence."

His lordship did seem particularly taken with his soup, which he ladled up without noticing if the spoon was full or not. Ninian watched as he finally discovered the bowl was empty, looked surprised, and blinked back to his surroundings.

The look in his eyes was irresistible. He had such warm, dark, vulnerable eyes, eyes that could stir — an imp of mischief.

"That was a delightful chowder, my lord," she said demurely.

"Yes, yes, it was." He looked a bit perplexed, then signaled for the next remove and lost himself in the fish as it appeared.

Oh, dear. A flawless, powerful earl might leave her cold, but this one . . . This one was lost somehow inside his head. The soup had been a broth, not a chowder. Ninian raised a questioning eyebrow to Sarah.

"It is quite deliberate, I'm convinced," she replied with a shrug. "He shuts us all out by counting stars or whatever on earth it is he does in his head while we chatter on. He has not even noticed that Lydie is not here."

Ninian didn't think the earl was quite as oblivious as the ladies liked to think, but she didn't express her opinion aloud. A lifetime of keeping her thoughts to herself served her well now. She didn't think she had imagined his reaction to her. The earl wasn't just shutting out chatter. For whatever reason, he was denying the existence of feminine company. She didn't like being denied the masculine attention she had craved for so long. Experimentally, she brushed her hand over the sleeve of his coat.

The earl jerked to instant awareness, his eyes blazing with something dark and powerful as he turned to her. She felt the heat of that look deep within her, in a place never stirred before.

A shriek pierced the air, echoing off the towering stone walls.

Into the silence that followed, Lydie could be heard shouting, "That wasn't me! It must be the ghost!"

Six

Drogo leapt to his feet. "Stay here!" he ordered, stalking toward the staircase. He'd had quite enough of these practical jokes and he would end them now. Sarah's latest preoccupation with astrology and witches and the supernatural had gone beyond the realm of scientific inquiry into the ridiculous. She'd practically poisoned her last suitor with some concoction she'd claimed would make him more amorous. It was evident she had made up the ghost nonsense just to lure the pretty herbalist into the castle for amusement. Well, he was not amused.

To his annoyance but not to his surprise, Miss Siddons ignored his command and ran after him. Knowing the wicked humor of Sarah and her friends, he assumed she was as much a butt of this joke as he was, and not one of its perpetrators. That didn't relieve his irritation. He preferred people to obey his commands.

"You'll tumble down the stairs and break your silly neck in that gown," he said harshly as she caught up with him.

"No thanks to your ladies." Showing no umbrage at his insult, she lifted the skirt until he could see her stocking-clad ankles and ran lightly ahead of him.

She'd probably wrapped those ankles around half the sheepherders in the village, he grumbled to himself as he increased his pace to catch up with her. He hadn't missed the grunts and groans in the shrubbery during the bonfire the other night. Pagan rituals celebrating the earth's fertility inevitably resulted in a crop of wailing infants in nine months' time. Maybe he should have indulged that night. Even if the fertility gods didn't oblige, he wouldn't be looking lasciviously at the heels of the local witch now.

The eerie screams had halted the minute they'd leapt from the table, but his guest aimed unerringly for the room from which earlier disruptions had emanated. Maybe she was part of Sarah's plot, after all.

The door she halted at led into the sitting chamber of a suite of rooms. From the size and location, Drogo figured it had once been the master suite, but he preferred the privacy of his tower to this central location.

No one currently occupied the suite, but the women had rooms nearby.

"Stay here," the little witch ordered, twisting the latch and peering into the darkness beyond.

Seriously annoyed at being the recipient of his own command, Drogo produced a candle and flint from the niche beside the door and lit the wick. Once he had a flame, he shoved against the solid panel, ignoring the female slipping in beside him.

The room was icy as hell and filled with shadows from the flickering candle, but nothing leapt out and screamed at them.

"I can't sense anything with you in here," his buxom companion complained. "Stand outside and let me listen."

Ignoring that foolishness, Drogo lifted the candle and began a careful search of the cobwebbed draperies and ancient furniture. Lydie had probably produced the inhuman screech. She would do anything Sarah told her.

Miss Siddons stood in the center of the carpet, apparently communing with the spirits. Remembering the massive bed through the next door, Drogo wondered if she might be seduced into staying the night, waiting for another emanation. All that soft blond voluptuousness could easily entice him to spare a few hours from his watch of the stars.

He tested the latch to the bedroom. Locked. He'd have to do something about that.

Without his realizing it, Miss Siddons had abandoned her listening post. Her small hand took the latch he'd just released and — opened it.

Raising his eyebrows, Drogo followed her into the bedchamber. She didn't seem at all aware of his presence or the proximity of the enormous bed. The females he knew would be giggling self-consciously at being caught alone in a bedroom with him. Or, more likely, they would be throwing themselves into his arms in mock fright or open seduction. He'd swear the little witch knew he was here, and just didn't think him worth noticing.

He'd used his Northumberland mining venture as an escape from a barrage of family demands as well as the ploys of marriage-minded females. He had no reason to be irritated because this female didn't require his attention like everyone else, but he was.

Annoyed that he was annoyed, Drogo continued his search while the lovely lackwit drifted to the fireplace and listened to the wind in the chimney. In his opinion, the wind occasionally caught some loose stone or tree branch to produce the earsplitting shrieks. He'd hire a chimney cleaner and a tree pruner in the morning.

"There's no one here but us," she informed him, dropping her long skirt and sweeping toward the exit. "I'll come back sometime when you haven't disturbed the spirits. Is this the only room where they dwell?"

"There's nothing here but moldering furniture, rats, and drafts cold enough to freeze our ars . . . toes," he amended. Despite appearances to the contrary, he'd assume she was a lady and protect her ears accordingly.

"And your cat." She bent to lift a bundle of fur into her arms.

In the flickering light, the gray cat seemed to shoot him a malevolent look from the haven of the lady's bosom. "I don't have a cat," he said coldly.

In response, her dimples appeared in a bewilderingly unreadable smile as she stroked the cat until it purred. "If you say so, my lord. This must be a ghost cat."

Flummoxed by the enchanting smile and irritated by the illogic of her answer, Drogo struggled for a rational reply. Resorting to the superiority of his position, he nodded condescendingly and steered her from the suite into the hall. "A stray accidentally locked in here while chasing mice. It must have been his yowls we heard."

"Of course, my lord," she answered meekly, but there was nothing meek about her dancing dimples.

He'd like to kiss the mischief off her rosy lips. He shouldn't be looking at her lips. Stiffly, Drogo slammed the door.

Let the ladies have their fun. He had better things to do. From experience, he knew she'd end up in his bed sooner or later. They always did. He didn't believe it was because women found him so overwhelmingly attractive, but his wealth and title overcame any objection to his character or looks. And since Sarah had started that rumor about his wanting a child . . . He should have wrung her neck long ago.

Nodding curtly, Drogo released her elbow. "Give my excuses, but I've work to do. I'll see you later."

He strode off to the isolated recesses of his tower.

Ninian shook her head as she watched him go. The room they'd just left reeked of anguish and anger, but she didn't expect a believer in naturalism to notice.

Wondering what Lord Ives did in his lonely tower, Ninian descended the stairs patting the lovely cat. Her grandmother had never allowed her to have pets — no sense in arousing the village's superstitions more than necessary — but she loved animals.

The cat's rumbling purr almost made up for his lordship's rudeness.

With bold ink strokes, Drogo completed his calculation, jotted down his observations, and reached for his smaller telescope.

Before he could lift the sight to his eye, he heard the unmistakable patter of feminine footsteps. At last, the little witch had decided to explore his chambers. That one certainly didn't possess a shy bone in her body. Intrigued despite himself, he actually laid down his telescope in anticipation. Would she have some sorry story of a dying relative or a long-lost love? Or would she just boldly present herself for his approval? By now, Sarah had probably told half the British Empire of his admission that he would marry any woman who carried his child. He should have thrown Sarah from the parapets long ago. The possibility of bedding and wedding an earl had provided an irresistible temptation for every unattached female in the damned kingdom, when all he'd meant was that he refused to support a herd of bastards as his family traditionally did.

It was a good thing he didn't mind occasionally trading feminine machinations for the erotic delights of seductive sighs and satin skin. His normally all masculine household was sorely deprived of feminine delights, but he saw no need to suffer permanent leg shackles when women came to him readily, without his having to lift a finger. And he could be rid of them just as easily.

He hid his disappointment as Sarah peered around the corner of his door. "Are the demons haunting your sleep already this evening?" he taunted, turning back to his telescope and lifting it to the north-facing window.

"I'm lonely." She pouted.

"I warned you," he replied without compunction.

"I had no choice. Mother threatened to disown me. Besides, Lydie needed a hideaway."

Flouncing her skirts, she arranged herself in the window seat below his telescope. She leaned forward to expose the tempting mounds of her breasts. "We're not blood kin, Drogo," she whispered. "I could be the wife you need."

Drogo closed his eyes and cursed under

his breath. Sarah had done her best to be circumspect since her arrival. It looked as if the act had finally fallen flat.

"I'm perfectly aware of our relationship," he said without rancor. He'd been down this path too many times to take anything personally. "You were born well before my father brought your mother into his household. But you still grew up as my younger sister. I can remember pulling your hair and calling you names when you kicked me. Don't make me regret offering you shelter."

She leaned back against the pillows with a frown, once more the busybody sister and not the temptress. "It might work, Drogo. Why not try? It's better than both of us living out our lives in loneliness."

"I'm not lonely and you shouldn't be. You could have any man of your choosing."

"I don't want another man who holds the purse strings." Resting her head against the wall, she stared at the night sky beyond the window. "But I want children. They wouldn't be a nuisance, Drogo. You could . . ."

"No," he said firmly. "I don't need children when I have the lot of you to contend with. Haven't you learned anything from our parents' marriages?"

She shrugged her nearly bare shoulders.

"What choices have we? We lead expensive lives and cannot support ourselves without land or money. Your mother is fortunate that the courts forced your father to pay for her house and expenses. And you are fortunate that your father dropped dead and left you his wealth before you came of age. Life is a gamble. We can only choose which game of chance to place our money on."

"Very philosophical, my dear, but this game of chance is closed. Find another."

Grimacing would have creased her powder so she settled for a reflective gesture of finger to lips. Drogo appreciated the performance, but his patience was wearing thin. He had hoped for a more natural bundle of blond curls and pink lips tonight.

Drogo hoped the little witch wasn't quite as mercenary as Sarah. Miss Siddons seemed as if she might have a trainable mind. That could prove just as interesting as her abundant charms.

"The family won't leave you alone," Sarah warned, rising from her seat with a rustle of petticoats. "You can hide out here as much as you like, but like it or not, you are the official head."

"And arms and hands," Drogo muttered, returning to his telescope.

"Beastly man." She kissed his cheek and

floated from the room.

Her scent filled the tower long after her departure. Cursing at the distraction, Drogo stared at the night sky, wondering for the millionth time if he'd made the right decision when he'd decided he didn't need to marry.

It seemed the only rational decision he could make. He remembered only too well the shock and anguish of the day his father had thrown his weeping, hysterical mother from their home. His younger brothers had screamed day and night after her departure. His father had drunk himself into a stupor. He wouldn't wish that emotional devastation on his worst enemy.

In the years since then, observing other people, other marriages, he'd reached the conclusion that the only way a man and a woman could live together in any kind of harmony was if they shared common interests and intellect, avoided emotional scenes, and abided by clearly defined rules. In the world he inhabited, that was nigh on impossible.

For the sake of an heir, he'd been inclined to attempt the impossible, until two things had gradually dawned on him. As his brothers grew older and more mature, he realized they could accept their share of responsibility, and he'd begun to understand that he really didn't need a child for an heir. His brothers would suit that purpose nicely.

And since he had yet to produce any of the bastards for which his family was infamous, it had become apparent he could never sire a child. The only good reason for marriage was to produce a legitimate heir.

Ergo, he didn't need to marry.

He couldn't help it if logic didn't erase a yearning for the child he could not have, the child he'd never been, the child he would never hold.

In all the years of providing for his siblings, he could not remember ever once holding one in his arms.

"What are you doing?" Drogo demanded as he entered his tower chamber and daylight revealed an easily identifiable feminine silhouette near his windows. He'd wanted her last night, not today.

The little witch spun around. Back in her customary drab homespun and apron this morning, she appeared to be stroking a kitten. A kitten. A second glance located last night's gray cat perched on his chair, watching him with a calculating gaze.

"Your nonexistent cat has apparently had nonexistent kittens. I'm petting one." She explained this with kind sincerity, as if he were an idiot who couldn't see what was right beneath his prominent nose.

He didn't know whether he was more annoyed with her for treating him like an idiot instead of an earl, or with himself for being disappointed that she hadn't sought him out last night. "Did you have some purpose here?" Briskly, he strode to his desk to fetch the papers for his steward.

"Sarah sent me to look for a wrap she said she'd left here last night." Ninian thought she kept the accusation out of her voice quite nicely, but the earl's knowing look discounted that theory. She turned her back on him and examined the plants in the window. They definitely didn't look healthy. "What are these?"

"Grass." His curt answer came from just behind her shoulder.

She tried not to jump at his proximity, but she grimaced at his typically terse response. "Were you experimenting in drowning it?"

"No."

She thought he would end it there, but to her surprise, he lifted a watering pot. "I took this water from the burn and I'm using it on these pots here." He pointed out the dying grass on one side of the window. "The other pots I'm watering from the well."

Excitement lit little fires along Ninian's skin as she recognized the import of his experiment. "So you can see if it's actually the burn water causing the blight?" She had only her grandmother's teachings to guide her, but this man had learning and knowledge well beyond hers, and she thirsted to acquire it.

"Yes, but they seem equally blighted." Indifference returned to his voice.

"No, just overwatered. They have no air or sun here, so cannot absorb much liquid. They would fare better in a conservatory, with more sunshine and windows that open." She poked at the grass with the blighted water. "The soil in these pots is smellier."

"Perhaps I should carry the pots outside."

She thought she heard awakening interest in his voice this time. It was difficult interpreting the signs people gave off in word and gesture when she was accustomed to just feeling what they felt, but she was learning with this man.

"That, or water them less," she agreed.

"Would you like to see what I've done with your brook?" he asked abruptly, holding out his hand to her.

She looked at his hand as if it were the devil's cloven hoof, but gingerly accepted it.

"You have found the source of the problem?"

Her pulse pounded beneath his fingers, and Drogo refused to let go as she tried to pull away. Women seldom aroused his curiosity. This one did. He would hold her captive until he'd dissected the reason for that.

"No, but I thought if I filtered the water, we might stop whatever damage the acid is causing." Her cold fingers warmed inside his. Idly, as he led the way downstairs, Drogo wondered how much interference he would receive if he installed the little witch in the castle and took her for mistress while he was here. She hadn't offered herself to him yet, but perhaps she was distrustful of his rank.

"We'll have a storm tonight."

The irrelevant comment jerked Drogo's attention back to the present. They had traversed the hall and stood in the doorway overlooking his sadly bedraggled grounds. His companion studied the heavy clouds above as if they were the only thing of consequence in her surroundings. Perhaps she needed to be reassured of his interest. He had yet to meet an available woman who was not tempted by the promise of title and wealth.

"Are you afraid of storms?" he asked with

what he hoped was sympathy, or under-standing. "I've seen some magnificent ones from my tower." He tucked her hand into the crook of his elbow and led her down the path he'd had cleared to the brook. With the trees in leaf, no one could watch their prog-ress.

"Storms have their purpose," she said enigmatically, kicking at last year's leaves. "The sky's passionate attraction to the earth can be a trifle unsettling though."

Drogo grinned to himself. Her mind might take a warped approach, but she knew what he was about.

Once inside the cover of the trees, he slid his arm around her back, and drew her to him. She was soft and malleable in all the right places as he brushed his lips lightly along hers, testing his welcome. Sparks ig-nited everywhere they touched.

She sighed with pleasure and melted against him, brushing exploratory fingers along his jaw, but before he could engage her more fully, she pressed a hand to his chest and shoved him away. "The earth and the moon fight their attraction with vio-lence, my lord. I would rather we not do the same."

She stepped away and disappeared so swiftly into the woods, it was as if she'd merged with the trees.

Drogo cursed under his breath and struggled to regain control. He wouldn't let lust rule his head. He simply needed to find the right pattern of behavior that would entice the wretched sprite into his bed.

It was a simple matter of problem-solving, like a mathematical equation.

Seven

As she fled down the path, Ninian covered her mouth to hold on to the texture of the earl's lips imprinted on hers. They'd been slightly rough, narrow but with a sensuous fullness as they'd softened, tasting vaguely of coffee and sugar. The heat of his breath and brush of his whisker stubble still burned on her cheeks.

No one had ever touched her so intimately.

If she tried very hard, she might recollect her father lifting her into his arms and pecking her cheek when she was quite small. Her mother had never offered such caresses, as if she feared the child she had borne. Granny had welcomed her with hugs when she was young, but nothing could have taught her to expect what she had just experienced in the arms of Lord Ives.

She couldn't believe how magical something so simple as a human kiss could be.

She heard him crunching through the leaves behind her. Why had he kissed her? He had three elegant ladies at his beck and call. Was he like Nate, needing to conquer every female who crossed his path?

She didn't like to think so. She wanted to believe he felt the pull of the moon and earth as she did.

She must leave this place. The legends were right — Ives men were dangerous.

His long strides caught up with her without haste. She was intensely aware of his physical presence. He didn't even touch her and yet a shiver raised bumps on her skin as he fell in beside her and adjusted his stride to hers.

"How does a filter work?" she inquired when he said nothing.

"I hope to catch the damaging particles so only clear water flows downstream."

He was very adept at hiding his feelings. His voice reflected nothing more than his intellectual interest in the experiment. One would think the moment back there had never happened, that for one point in time their hearts hadn't beat as one. Excitement prickled along her skin and her pulse accelerated at just his nearness, though he appeared to be completely indifferent.

"What could catch something so tiny as a particle?" She could play the same game. She had a strong will and an inquiring mind. She didn't have to wonder what his kiss would have become if she'd allowed him to continue.

Was it only her own desire vibrating between them now? Or was that truly interest in his dark glance? It was very frustrating not knowing these things.

"I am experimenting with a number of materials. Rocks and sand are easiest." He spoke as if from a lectern. "Plants have been known to work occasionally, but I have found none that survive in the substances in the brook."

"You have studied filters?"

"Not thoroughly, no. It's not a problem with which I've been presented before. My library is inadequate. But there are certain basic conclusions one can reach given the available evidence."

Ninian halted as she sensed a horse and rider nearby. The burn babbled just beyond the next copse.

Lord Ives looked down at her with curiosity. "Is there a problem?"

"Someone is studying your filter." Unhurriedly, she continued walking. She sensed no danger in the newcomer.

"Payton!" Lord Ives shouted as they passed through the copse and the rider became visible. "What news have you?"

Ninian idled on the edge of the forest as Lord Ives walked ahead to converse with the rider. The stranger was a slightly built man of no more years than the earl. His coat was of sturdy quality, but not expensively elegant. His placid mare nosed the grass farther up the bank from the stream, and Ninian noticed the rider didn't allow her to drink the water. A commonsensical sort of man, she concluded, one who did as told and did it well, but without ideas of his own.

He nodded to her as she approached, and Lord Ives introduced his steward.

Payton touched his cap politely. "Miss Siddons. I have heard the village folk speak of you."

She dimpled and curtsied. "And you do not fear being cast under my spell?" She really shouldn't say these things. It tempted fate. But she'd been so very, very good at resisting temptation, she had to do something naughty for balance.

Payton looked vaguely startled but smiled. "I'm certain all men must be caught by your charms, mistress."

Lord Ives snorted. "You speak of the witchery of all women. Miss Siddons specializes in healing, not seduction. Tell me what you have found upstream."

She had not thought the earl had noticed or cared about her preferences. Noblemen tended to have more important things on their minds than local superstitions. Perhaps she should be flattered, but she was more interested in what Mr. Payton had to say. She crouched to examine the odd dam of rocks crossing the stream as the newcomer spoke.

"Plant life is failing for miles upstream but recovers slowly the farther downstream I go. Your filter is too new to have evidence of its success yet."

"You still haven't found the source?" the earl asked sharply.

"No, not yet."

Ninian sensed an aura of uneasiness about the steward as his mare sidestepped nervously. She started to speak, but Lord Ives beat her to it.

"The stream divides?"

"And has numerous tributaries. This stretch seems to be slower moving than others, which could be part of the problem."

"There is evidence of damage along one of the tributaries?" Ninian prompted.

Both men stared at her as she rose from the stream bank. Perhaps they weren't used to women speaking. She rather liked the light of interest in the earl's eyes.

Payton formulated his reply carefully. "The tributaries are smaller, faster flowing. I have noticed . . . a lack of lushness . . . in one, many miles from here. I haven't had time to explore its length."

"But you have some idea what it flows through?" Ninian prodded. The man wasn't telling the whole story.

Payton shrugged. "It flows from the hills beyond this property. I can't say more."

She frowned, considered questioning him further, and decided against it. Men tended to become stubborn when pressed. She wished she had a horse of her own so she could explore farther, but she wasn't much good at riding. She returned to studying the intricacies of the filter the earl had constructed. He'd used lumps of coal among the rocks, and layers of gravel. Mostly, he'd caught dead leaves and branches. He'd have a large pond when the rain broke.

She sensed the steward's departure and tried to distinguish the earl's emotional presence from his physical one as he approached. She couldn't. He vibrated with a masculinity she responded to as if he were her life's blood pounding through her veins.

"He doesn't tell the whole truth, my

lord." Brushing off her hands, she stood up again. She was tired of him looming over her.

Dark eyes studied her from behind his emotionless mask. "How so?"

"He must suspect the origins of the tributary carrying the poison, but is reluctant to verify it."

"And you can tell all this because . . . ?"

She turned around and started back up the path. "A little bird tells me." She didn't waste her breath explaining. She had told him what she knew. He could either act on it or not. That was his choice.

He didn't comment on her evasion. Instead, he returned to their original intent. "What do you think of the filter?"

"Very ingenious, my lord. It should be interesting to discover if rocks can stop poison. It should be even more interesting to see how tonight's storm affects it."

"I've thought of that, but without further experimentation, I cannot say. If it's a poison, as you call it, some are diluted and rendered useless by heavy quantities of fluid. Perhaps a good downpour will clear the poison out."

She nodded in admiration at this assessment. "An excellent thought, my lord. I hope you are right. The stream provides valuable resources I cannot replace." She didn't think it healthy for her life in the village if she could no longer make remedies either, but he wouldn't understand the precariousness of life on the thin edge of superstition.

"At least the damage is limited to my land. We can hope for the best."

Ninian accepted the earl's hand in assistance as she climbed over a fallen log. His hand was warm and hard and much stronger than hers as it clasped her fingers and held them. She could almost summon reassurance from that grip, and she was reluctant to withdraw from it once she reached the other side of the log. He didn't release her of his own accord either.

It was as if they communicated through contact. Struggling to shake the sensation, she concentrated on her reply.

"I must warn the villagers not to use your stream," she replied slowly, trying to adapt to the current of sensation flooding through her hand and up her arm. Was this how Ives men bewitched their women? Did the earl possess some power stronger than her own?

"I'd best take a look at the kitchen water," Lord Ives said thoughtfully, staring ahead as if he had only the burn's problem in mind.

She couldn't take the eerie physical bond anymore. Tugging her hand free, lifting her skirt, she fled down the path to safety.

They returned to a house in an uproar.

Lady Twane stood in the great hall, clasping and unclasping her hands, moaning in terror as she gazed up the stone stairway.

Screams and a crashing clatter emanated from the haunted suite above.

Lady Lydie leaned on the upper banister, staring down the hall toward the suite, her hand protectively covering her prominent belly as she hesitated over descending the stairs. She screamed an obscenity at Sarah, who stood beside Claudia, alternately urging Lydie to hurry down and Claudia to shut up.

"Where are the damned servants?" Sarah shouted as glass smashed overhead.

The gray cat sat on the newel post, tail twitching, watching their antics.

Lord Ives muttered a profanity worse than Lydie's and rushed toward the stairs.

As he caught Lydie and helped her down, Ninian had to assume the lady's child was his, since he played the part of solicitous protector so well. She recognized a tug of jealousy but the wails of the unhappy inhabitant of the upper suite demanded her more immediate attention.

Ignoring the earl's command, Ninian raced past him up the stairway. She had hung birch and rowan branches in there earlier, and scattered the hearth with dill. Perhaps she should have chanted Granny's protective charm as well. She wished she had a flint to light her divination incense.

She shouldn't need divination incense if the ghost's presence was strong enough to demolish a room.

She burst into the darkened suite, expecting an onrush of icy drafts or a chair flying at her head.

All within was calm.

She halted to catch her breath and slow her pounding heart. The drawn draperies shrouded the room in darkness and the growing gloom of the coming storm prevented even a crack of light. She wished for Lord Ives and his candle, but she inched cautiously inside, seeking the source of the violent anguish vibrating the air.

A sigh whispered in her ear, and startled, Ninian froze. Her gift did not lend to reading minds or hearing ghosts.

"Are you there, Ghost?" Ninian whispered hesitantly.

She was aware of Lord Ives entering behind her, listening. She thought he had a candle and a weapon in his hand, but he did no more than stand guard behind her.

She could sense consternation and frustration as the window draperies blew outward and the chairs rattled. But she received no reply.

Able to make neither head nor tail of this, Ninian wished she possessed her grandmother's wisdom. She crept farther into the room, seeking with her senses. Pain, heartbroken torment . . . These she could feel, but not the thought rendering them.

"What must I do?" she asked of the air around her.

Lord Ives edged to the fireplace, inspecting it with a poker, hitting on nothing but solid stone.

"How can I help? What will make you rest in peace?" *Do you intend evil or good?* she wanted to ask, but feared the reply. Given her attraction to an Ives, the arrival of a ghost in conjunction seemed ominous, at best.

The frantic emotions grew faint, and Ninian sought harder for the source. Lord Ives poked at the drapery, apparently oblivious to the sensations.

"Don't go," she called, but she already sensed the presence had departed.

She received no reply.

Lost, she waited, hoping the spirit would return, that she would be struck by a blinding insight into the quandary she'd been handed. All she sensed was Lord Ives losing interest in the draperies and coming to place a hand on her shoulder.

"Are you all right?"

The heat of his hand reassured her in a way she could not explain. Perhaps communicating with a world beyond the mortal one had consequences requiring a human touch. Whatever, she jerked as if he'd awakened her.

"I'm fine. I've never communed with a ghost before."

"Did the ghost talk back?" he asked with a trace of irony, steering her gently toward the doorway.

"Do you know aught of your family's history?" Perhaps the answer lay there. The ghost certainly wished to tell her something.

"Very little." He opened the door to discover all three women waiting anxiously outside. "Have the servants bring up lamps and clean up the glass," he ordered. "I think the walls must be shifting. I'll have a stone mason check them."

He not only didn't believe, he wasn't listening. Angry now, shaken by the unearthly experience, Ninian halted where she stood, refusing to be guided by his comforting hand. "She's in pain!" she cried. "She's trying to warn us. We must listen and try to understand."

Lord Ives quirked an eyebrow.

She glared back. "Was this place once owned by Malcolms?"

Lord Ives shrugged. She could see the frown of concern creasing his brow, but he had no interest in ancient history.

"The original land deeds call it Malcolm Castle," Sarah replied. She lifted her hands helplessly as everyone turned to stare at her. "I have nothing better to do with my time than poke through old papers."

"Then I would research the means by which the Malcolms were dispossessed and the Ives acquired their land," Ninian said coldly. "The ghost is very angry and unhappy. I cannot take responsibility if you will not listen."

Ninian thought to stalk back to her room, gather her things, and march out of their aristocratic lives, but a thunderclap overhead and a cacophonous downpour on the roof slates halted her.

Into the silence following the thunder, Lord Ives spoke. "If you think to take back what your ancestors lost, you are dealing with the wrong man."

The wind howled, or maybe it was the ghost moaning.

Eight

"No, you cannot leave tonight. We won't hear of it." Lady Sarah swept Ninian's bag from the bed, caught her arm, and steered her down the hall to the ladies' wing of the house. "We are all scared senseless. You must tell us what to do."

Ninian was just a little bit tired of being steered and guided wherever these people wanted, but she no more desired to go out in the storm than the ladies wanted her to leave. She wished she could look on them as the friends she craved, but she feared they thought of her more as a toy to be played with.

"There is naught I can tell you," she protested feebly.

"Tell us what the ghost said!" all the ladies commanded as they closed the door on Lydie's room and turned to Ninian.

"Ghosts don't speak," Ninian said with a

sigh as Claudia held a shimmering blue-green gown up to her shoulders. She really needed a nap more than another session as a fashion doll. Dealing with ghosts was draining.

Sarah began unfastening Ninian's gown and said, "It's obvious there is some tragic history in this castle that we must right."

Amazed that flighty Sarah had laid her finger on the problem, and suspecting she did so only out of a fondness for sentimental fiction, Ninian didn't argue as they stripped off her gown and draped her in pannier hoops. "Perhaps if you have papers in your possession, my lady, you might research the castle's history." She pushed the women in the right direction, though she didn't expect much as a result.

As they dropped the gown over her head, Ninian stroked the fragile damask and ignored the excited chatter. She had her mother's love of fine fabrics, it seemed. The panniers held the layers of silk off the floor. She still felt like a fashion doll, but the cold draft blowing up her legs beneath the wiring told her she was made of flesh and blood. She didn't like the way the tickle of the wind reminded her that she was young and restless, and a man stood ready to please her anytime she beckoned.

Where had that thought come from? She couldn't read the earl's emotions. She couldn't know his intent. Perhaps noblemen bestowed kisses thoughtlessly. He certainly hadn't seemed as disturbed by their kiss as she had been.

But somehow she knew Lord Ives was as aware of her as she was of him.

"There are journals and ledgers and stacks of dusty books and papers in the library." Sarah hooked the fastenings of the gown's bodice with precision while Claudia adjusted the back lacing to fit Ninian's slimmer waist and fuller bosom.

"Perhaps, after you've discovered the story . . ." Ninian suggested tentatively, gasping as the lacing pulled tight and the whalebone structure dug in, "you might call me back again. Perhaps then I can understand —"

"Nonsense." Sarah stepped back and dusted off her hands as she gazed at her handiwork with approval. "You must stay and give us advice as to where to look . . ." She waved her hand. "Drogo is likely to leave at any time, so we must solve this mystery. . . ." Abruptly, she turned to Lydie with a small frown. "Shall we leave the ringlets loose again, or try something more sophisticated?"

Ninian didn't know where to begin protesting. She held her hand protectively to her hair and backed away. "I cannot —"

"She needs jewelry," Lydie decided. "Her obvious charms draw attention without it, but a little extra adornment never hurts."

Ninian's gaze dropped to the exaggerated plumpness of her bare breasts above the very narrow square cut of the bodice. "A modesty piece will suffice —"

Lydie's laughter cut her off. "Not with that gown. It's French. Isn't it wicked? Turn, and let me see how the train falls."

Ninian was buried in enough silk to clothe a village, yet she was half-naked. "Wicked" wasn't the half of it. "Obscene" might come close. She shook her head and tried to find the dozen tiny fastenings molding her into this monstrosity.

Sarah grabbed her hands. "Don't be silly. It's perfect, as if it was designed for you. Lydie, you have some paste . . . ?"

"That's all I have," the young woman replied with bitterness. "In the top drawer, Claudia." She indicated her massive trunk. "I thought I'd at least have jewels to sell."

"Well, yours wouldn't be the first family to sell off the family gems," Sarah drawled. "Perhaps if they'd told you of their precarious financial situation, you wouldn't have been quite so foolish as to get yourself with child on a man with no wealth."

"Would it have been better if she'd married a man with wealth and had her virginity taken by a beast?" Claudia asked caustically. "At least she's had some pleasure of it."

Ninian's head spun so with the barrage of information, she forgot her protests as Sarah fastened a gaudy tangle of glittering glass around her neck. She didn't know the difference between diamond and crystal, but the necklace picked up the colors of the gown and reflected it in a breathtakingly iridescent sparkle.

More importantly, she tried to unscramble the clues of their conversation. Lydie's child was by a poor man? Not the earl?

"I should have come to you for the herbs you told me —" Lydie popped her hand over her mouth with an "oops" before Sarah had time to cut her off.

These women were up to something. Maybe she ought to leave.

The dinner bell gonged, echoing through the high stone corridors. This time, Ninian didn't jerk with surprise. Numb from an overabundance of information, her thoughts spinning, she escaped the room under the guidance of both Sarah and Claudia.

Lord Ives awaited them at the bottom of the stairs. He'd made no attempt to play the London fop. The discreet embroidery of his black coat and gold waistcoat and the expensive quality of his lace cuffs spoke of generations of wealth and aristocracy. Coal-black hair caught in a ribbon gleamed in the lamplight, and even though he was freshly shaved, the shadow of his beard accentuated the stark masculine planes of his jaw. Dark eyes glittered as he studied the bejeweled rainbow descending the stairs.

"You play their games well, Miss Siddons." He bowed mockingly and took her hand on his arm as Sarah delicately pushed her in his direction.

"No, I don't," she muttered under her breath.

He cocked an eyebrow but didn't inquire further as they reached the linen-bedecked table. Candlelight glimmered against silver, casting light on the storm's gloom.

"We have decided to research your castle, Drogo," Sarah declared cheerfully. "Miss Siddons will interpret for us."

"I have no . . ." Ninian shut up as a footman materialized to pour the wine. Why argue? She'd simply leave before the ladies called for their chocolate in the morning. The rain pounding against the windows warned of the foolishness of leaving tonight.

"An interesting project, I'm sure." Lord Ives lifted his wine, nodded his approval to the servant, and sipped. "And if you find nothing of interest, are you prepared to argue with a ghost?"

He was mocking them, Ninian knew. A man of science, with a toplofty intellectual bent, wouldn't heed things of the spirit, things that must be taken on belief without material evidence of their existence. It didn't matter. She could see no answer to the conundrum the ghost presented. Likely, the lady had existed here for centuries. She could exist a few more, until someone wiser interpreted her unspoken plea.

As Ninian sipped the rich wine, she noticed the earl's gaze drawn to the immodest exposure of her bosom. A warm flush crept along her skin, and she swallowed a large gulp of the wine. She coughed as fire burned down her throat.

"Gently, Miss Siddons," he admonished. "Wine must be sipped, not guzzled. Have you come to any further conclusions about our ghost?"

She practiced sipping, just to show she knew how. The wine really did affect her body temperature, she noted. She no longer felt the room's chill. Or perhaps it was the heat of his gaze on her neckline while his finger traced the edge of his glass.

"Since you do not believe in the ghost's existence," she answered tartly, "I cannot think you have any interest in my opinion."

"Now, now, Miss Siddons, do not judge dear Drogo so harshly." Sarah leaned over and patted her hand where it rested on the tablecloth. "He must see to believe, admittedly, but I cannot think him beyond hope. He just needs someone who can make him see through different eyes."

Ninian withdrew her hand and clasped it around the crystal stem of her goblet. "I wish you well of that task, my lady."

Drogo chuckled. "She has you there, Sarah. I think you underestimate Miss Siddons's perspicacity."

The footman refilled his glass as a maid removed the soup course and a third servant presented the vegetable course. Ninian noticed that tonight his lordship was more interested in the quality of his wine than in the food on his plate. The creamed potatoes were rather overspiced, admittedly, but she ate rather than swim in wine.

It seemed odd that he didn't shut them out as he had the previous night. Why was he staring at her like that? And was that perspiration forming on his forehead in this damp air? His grasp on the goblet seemed oddly tense.

"The jewels look like something Lydie would wear," Lord Ives observed as Claudia and Sarah chattered. "They are tantalizing, but they do not really suit you."

The husky rasp of his voice and the odd intensity of his gaze seeped through her flesh into her racing blood. Her own skin felt tight and feverish.

Since she did not believe jewels or this gown or this company suited her, Ninian refrained from replying. She couldn't reply. Her head spun too uncertainly. She was increasingly aware of his attention, of the flickering candlelight, of the steady pour of rain against the roof and windows. Lightning crackled, illuminating the candelabra-adorned table with ghostly illusions, and she had to blink not to see other people and earlier times in this hall.

She had always been attuned to the world and its essence around her, more so than most people. Usually, she was on the outside, wistfully watching as if she were the audience and all others, actors on a stage.

Tonight, she felt as if she were actually a part of the performance, at one with the drafts and the flickering candles and the ghosts laughing and drinking at the far expanse of the table beyond the candlelight.

She tried not to include the imposing man at her side in the world she sensed, but he filled it with his every breath, every movement, as if, in some time or place, they had belonged together. An odd urgency to test that theory swelled within her, but she didn't know how to act on it.

Without looking, she knew the moment when the shock of awareness hit him — the moment when he recognized the flow of energy between them. Somehow, she knew he felt the same heated demands pounding through his blood when he set his empty wineglass down, and cursed beneath his breath. She didn't have to turn to see the reason for his curses because it raced through her own veins, desire dancing in its wake. She didn't know if she sent out these vibrations or if he did, but they were as real as if he'd touched her and spoken the words aloud.

"Sarah, I will make you pay for this," he intoned ominously as he shoved his chair away from the table.

Ninian stared at the way his long fingers clenched the linen, at the silky dark hairs nearly hidden by the starched white lace falling over his hand. He had strong, sensuous fingers that would appreciate the texture of a woman's skin, fingers that would instinctively seek the erotic places . . .

She blinked in surprise at the path of her thoughts. Never in her entire life had —

"Come, Miss Siddons. Let us escape before they poison us further." The strong brown fingers locked over her helpless white ones.

Oblivious to the company, she stared at their joined hands. Once again, his heat soaked through her skin, and she watched in fascination, hoping to observe the miracle, as if their flesh might become transparent.

Amusement laced his voice. "Obviously, you're not a very good witch, Miss Siddons. Don't you know any protective spells against other witches?"

Other witches? Knowing she looked an idiot for blinking again, Ninian followed the tug of his hand and rose from her seat, focusing on his face for enlightenment, ignoring the smug smiles of their companions. The sardonic curl of the earl's lip should have told her something, but she could never read this man as she did others.

"Sarah has a friend who deals in magic potions. Isn't that what witches do?"

She shook her head in denial but didn't have the words to explain. He didn't seem to require a response. His heated look said everything as he held her hand trapped in his.

"I think I like you like this, Miss Siddons," he observed as she followed him compliantly across the towering hall. "You are usually much too wrapped up in your herbs and ghosts and healing. Being an object of your intense study is a pleasant change."

She should be embarrassed that he'd noticed her fascination, but she wasn't. She didn't even flinch as his strong arm circled her waist to steady her ascent of the stairs. She had the strangest notion that he craved the closeness as much as she did.

"Am I drunk?" she inquired soberly.

He chuckled again, a deep, perversely pleasurable chuckle that rumbled up from his insides and into hers.

"Victim of your own sorcery, I suspect. Or do you not dispense aphrodisiacs?"

"Aphrodisiacs work only on the deluded . . ." she started to say scornfully, then blinked again. He would think she had eye spasms, but she kept seeing things from strange angles. "I'm not deluded," she said firmly, to reassure herself, though she'd been suffering delusions from the moment she'd met this man.

"Probably not," he agreed, steering her down the darkened hallway to her room. "Just feeling the old pull of the moon and the tides like the rest of us mortals."

Thunder rolled overhead but Ninian gave it no notice as she pondered his words. "Are you saying Sarah put something . . . ?" She stumbled over the question as he pushed open her bedroom door, brushing unnecessarily close as he did so. She looked down to see the white of her breasts pressed dangerously near the dark cloth of the earl's coat, close enough for the lace of his jabot to tickle.

"That, or alcohol and excess stimulation have released our inhibitions, freeing us to act on our rather fundamental attraction to each other."

Attraction. He was attracted to her. The knowledge shivered down her spine, but her mind was too muddled to define its true meaning. She didn't think it was alcohol or aphrodisiacs burning through them, but she didn't know enough to explain the uncanny bond, the seemingly natural need to be with him.

To just once feel close to a man. This man.

The hand at her waist slid higher, pressing her closer. She was aware of dark eyes piercing the privacy of her heart, pinning it as it thumped, but she couldn't look beyond the lace at his throat to verify her awareness.

"I see," she murmured foolishly.

"Come, Miss Siddons, it is no more than the throbbing excitement of a night beneath the full moon in a lover's arms. We may choose to indulge or not, as we please. It's rather pleasant having one's inhibitions removed, is it not?"

Somehow, he had her beside the high bed, with the door closed behind them. Ninian refrained from blinking again as she realized someone had lit candles all around the room, and drawn the window draperies open on the electrifying flashes of lightning outside. The bed hangings were drawn open, too, revealing a bed turned down in open invitation. She wasn't too drugged or stunned to understand the precipice she was walking now. She could feel the edge crumbling as clearly as she could feel the carpet beneath her feet.

She had been lured to this castle for a purpose.

The brief revelation dissipated the instant Ninian lifted her eyes to Lord Ives. The dark reflective pools she looked into revealed her future more clearly than a crystal ball, if she could believe what she saw staring back at her — raw hunger, heady passion, and the uncertainty of loneliness.

She required the breezes of human emotion to function. He had nothing but lust to offer.

"We do not have to do this, you know," he reminded her, even as his dark head bent and his lips whispered over her cheek. "We can thwart the ladies' joke, say good night, and you can be on your way in the morning."

She could, but she already knew she would not. Logic had fled her wits, but instinct poured through her fingertips. She caressed the rich satin of his waistcoat, felt the tense hardness of the muscles beneath as he held himself still. She'd yearned for this sort of closeness all her life. Yearned for it, imagined it, questioned its existence. She could not deny her need to know — to take one step beyond the narrow world she knew.

"I am not beautiful," she murmured senselessly.

"That is like saying the moon has no charm," he scoffed, threading his fingers through her hair.

Shivering, Ninian wrapped her arms around the earl's broad shoulders, and basked in the warmth and power of his hunger as he caught her against him. She'd never known a man's dominance, never walked in a man's world. What could it hurt to try just once?

Her grandmother's warnings fled with her wits. As Lord Ives drew her into his embrace, his wool coat wrapped her cold flesh in heat.

The flick of his tongue against her innocent lips tumbled all remaining barriers, plunging her into the depths of paradise.

Nine

Brain fogged with Sarah's damned liquor and the perfume of the moon maiden's roses, Drogo descended swiftly from the logic of his mind into the passions of his body. Love-making had become too clinical for him these last years. The joy and exuberance of youth had faded with the cynicism of experience. Ninian's innocent kiss welcomed him to the excitement of his first time again.

Ninian. A saint, not a witch. Smiling at the odd path of his muddled thoughts, he drove his fingers deep into her hair and drank joy and wonder from the melting of her lips. He experienced her excitement as well as his own, arousing his senses doubly, heightening his desire with unprecedented speed.

Urgently, he demanded more, until her mouth opened beneath his, taking his tongue as if it were a holy wafer and not the possessive claim it was. Perhaps she considered lovemaking to be a religious experience. In this case, she could be right. The sweetness of her breath breathed life into his soul. He wanted to inhale her. His grip tightened, pressing her breasts into his coat, until his breathing matched hers, their hearts pounded together, and the clothing between them was unnatural.

For a brief moment, Drogo wished the harpies hadn't imprisoned the nymph in this tent of whalebone and wire. In her simple attire, he could have thrown up her skirts and joined her without the delay of hooks and laces and acres of silk. Instead, he lowered his hands to the hooks of her bodice.

Ninian's awe-filled gasp as he released her bodice and his knuckle brushed the underside of her breast repelled any urge to hurry. Despite the burning urgency of his body, his mind functioned clearly enough to want this to happen slowly, seductively, and for the rest of the night. He needed to fill his hands with her flesh, taste of her skin, revel in her softness.

In the flutter of light and scent of a dozen candles, with the nurturing pour of rain from the skies, he could almost convince himself that this was the woman who could swell with his child.

His mind danced past that thought as shadows danced past the curtained bed. He wanted her, and she wanted him. For the first time in a long time, that was enough.

"I give you this last chance to say no," he warned, releasing her mouth to draw his finger inquisitively over a pouting pink nipple. It drew up tighter, and he smiled. Her body answered more clearly than her words, he noted in relief, since he didn't think he *could* stop. For the first time in memory, he acted on instinct alone — the instinct for survival. If he did not have her, he surely would not survive. He cupped the fullness of her breast and stroked again, feeling the tug in his groin that she must feel in her womb.

"It's not right . . ." she protested weakly. Her breasts flushed with color at his attention, and her fingers dug more firmly into his shoulders, giving the lie to her denial.

He located the tapes of her skirt and loosened them, knowing there were things he should be saying, yet unable to form the sentences logically. The wire baskets at her hips collapsed on the floor, taking the lengths of silk with them.

She froze as he removed the soft lawn of her chemise, and she stood naked before him. Light played against skin finer than cream, unmarred except by a beauty mark where thigh met hip. No hollows or planes or hard angles here, he observed with a connoisseur's satisfaction, only rounded curves and a pillowed softness a man could lose himself in. He slid his thumb along the curve of her breast and waist, down to her hip until it rested just above her mound. *His,* his muddled mind declared, focusing on the welcoming entrance between her legs.

She tried to cover herself with her hands, but he caught them and spread them wide to better observe her.

"Exquisite," he murmured. "You were meant for better than sheepherders."

"My grandmother would kill me," Ninian whispered in one final protest, though she felt the power of him drawing her in already, and knew the futility of words. Thousands of protests jumbled through her mind, but she could voice none of them. A creature of instinct, she could only act.

He released her wrists to throw off his coat. "As Sarah has no doubt told you, I have vowed to marry any woman who bears my child. Otherwise, who's to know what we do here? Or care?"

His waistcoat fell to join his coat, and

Ninian stared at Lord Ives in wonder as he loosened his jabot. In shirtsleeves, the earl stood tall and wide-shouldered, muscles rippling beneath his fine linen. Every arrogant inch of him screamed nobility and privilege. Only a man accustomed to riding the swiftest horses, gracing the most elegant drawing rooms, indulging in the idle games of archery and fisticuffs, could develop the easy grace and power he possessed. Here was no studious scientist, but a stallion in the prime of life, willing and able to service any mare he cornered.

Then his mocking comments regarding children and marriage sobered her. If their joining produced a child, he would marry her, and a Malcolm would once again occupy Malcolm Castle. The ghost's appearance seemed strangely prophetic. Was the ghost warning her against mating with an Ives? Her grandmother had said to be true to herself and avoid all Ives. But right now, being true to herself meant forgetting everything and everyone but this Ives.

"Ready to try your luck at becoming a countess?" he taunted, dropping his shirt on the floor.

Ninian gaped at his chest in awe. "No, that's not what I want," she whispered. Unable to resist, she ran her fingers through soft dark curls, and pleasure surged through her at his sharp intake of air.

"Good, because it's not likely." Without warning, he grabbed her by the waist and dropped her onto the downturned bed linens. She sank into the feathers and did not have time to struggle up before he fell beside her, pinning her with a leg still clad in breeches.

"Does your skin taste as rich as it looks?" he asked, tickling her earlobe with his tongue. His hard, dark body leaned over her, trapping her until her breasts tightened and her flesh tingled with his nearness. But instead of touching what she wanted, nay, *needed* touched, he continued his exploratory kisses along her throat, to her nape.

Just when she thought to scream a protest at his teasing, the earl claimed her mouth again, and his tongue took another intoxicating foray that left her breathless.

"If not for the storm I would continue this in my tower, under the stars," he murmured as he released her lips to press another trail of kisses down her throat. His tongue lapped gently at a nipple so achingly hard with need that Ninian practically launched off the bed in pleasured surprise. "But then, perhaps a storm is appropriate for this night."

His mouth fastened more fully over her

breast, and Ninian uttered a primal cry of joy and deep, powerful desire. Moisture pooled in her womb, and her body readied itself for this act she'd never expected to know.

As if understanding the strength of the tug between breast and womb, Drogo slid his hand between her thighs and spread her until she cried and shuddered beneath him. "You are as eager for this as I am," he said with satisfaction, rubbing lightly with the heel of his hand. "It's good to know it's not just the promise of wealth and title you crave." The feverish gleam in his eyes belied his words, as if he struggled to separate mind and body — and his body was winning.

"I . . . never . . . wanted that." She gasped as pinwheels of light spun behind her eyelids and she realized she had no control over her own limbs. They spread wider at his urging, recognizing only the demands of the earl's questing fingers.

"Ahhh, but you can have that, all for the price of a babe in your belly. Imagine that, will you? A simple thing, one any woman can do."

Somewhere in the recesses of her mind, Ninian knew the fallacy behind his seemingly casual comments, but she had no interest in his worldly temptations. She wanted only the joining that would seal her fate and put her forevermore under his mastery. She knew the fallacy of that, too, but no longer cared.

As his thumb deepened the pressure and stroked higher, her back arched and her hips rose and twisted and sought what only he could provide, until she screamed a protest at his delay and drove into his hand. Only then did he lower his head to suckle at her breast and apply the strokes that released the tension throbbing in her loins, in her womb, in every thread and nerve of her body.

She cried as her world exploded, and through her sobs, Ninian heard his chuckle of satisfaction. She couldn't react. She floated somewhere outside herself, unable to sort right from wrong, reality from illusion. She only knew — it wasn't enough.

She muttered an objection as he took his hand away, and he brushed a kiss against her cheek in response. "A moment, greedy moonchild."

The bed shifted, but lethargy held her too firmly in its grasp for her to turn and see where he went. She felt empty, deprived in some manner, but too content to question. This wasn't the form in which her grandmother had warned her that devils staked their claim.

"My turn," he announced from somewhere above her.

With difficulty, Ninian opened her eyes and stared straight up — into the dark features of a completely naked Lord Ives. Through the open bed hangings, lightning still flashed in the windows, framing him. Thunder roared and rain poured. Candle flame glowed and billowed in the cold drafts from the walls. Shadows played across flesh darker than hers, flesh covered in a soft down of black hair, muscled flesh that rippled with tension as he kneeled between her spread legs. He loomed enormous, his curled eyebrows drawn down in concentration as he studied her while she studied him.

Gulping, fighting a shiver of panic at the irrevocable claim he would make next, she lowered her gaze to the arrow of hair on his chest as he leaned over, trapping her between corded arms. In the dim light, she could see the gleaming jut of his man's part, and even as terror spread, she opened her legs wider and lifted her hips to accept him, understanding the reason for the ache of emptiness there.

"Ah, you know your place well, moonchild." Kissing her lips, teasing her breast into readiness, he positioned himself. "Do you wish to chant a spell for good luck?"

He didn't give her time to answer. In one powerful stroke, he penetrated her moistened passage, ruptured the barrier, and planted himself deep beneath her belly.

A cry of mixed rapture and pain tore from Ninian's throat.

Drogo hesitated.

Then, with a curse, he withdrew and pumped again, driven by the consuming hunger between them.

She was too narrow and he was too big. Only a devil would split her asunder like so. Ninian dug her fingers into the strong arms trapping her, but she couldn't pull away any more than he could stop. Instead, she opened wider still and met his thrust.

Driven by the urgency of the madness they'd plunged into, he stroked deeper, filling her more completely, claiming her in the eyes of God and man.

She wanted to scream, but couldn't. She wanted to cry, but only a whimper emerged as he plundered her body with a sureness she no longer thought to escape.

The wind picked up outside, dousing the candles one by one. The strain and determination on her lover's taut features didn't falter as he drove her harder, forcing her back to the glorious heights through sheer strength of will.

Her hips lifted, and he growled approval deep in his throat, thrusting so high he carried her with him. Once started, she couldn't stop. She matched him stroke for stroke, taking him deeper, accepting his domination, giving up some piece of her soul in trade for the changes he promised.

"Yes!" he sighed through his teeth. "Now!" he commanded, caressing her urgently with his thumb, using the trick he'd already taught her.

And well taught, Ninian exploded all over again, inside, outside, through every racing particle of blood as he penetrated the hollow beneath her belly and poured his life force deep inside her. He shuddered and groaned with the power of his own release, and Ninian's muscles contracted to hold him tighter.

For one brief moment, his soul touched hers, and joy poured through her at that brief whisper of knowledge. She saw inside of him, felt him, like a flicker of warmth . . . and then, it was gone, leaving her alone again.

Moisture trickled down her thigh as she slipped from full consciousness. She was aware of the man leaning over and suckling at her breast. His teeth grazed her nipple, and the connection returned, the tug between breast and womb, the pointed reminder of what a woman's body was designed to do. She had no doubt he'd done it, she realized sleepily as his mouth released her but his spell did not. The moon was in its proper phase. Her body had been primed and ready, and Malcolm women were always fertile. Too fertile, her grandmother had said. And they always bore witches.

What had she done?

Lord Ives — Drogo — rolled over beside her, letting his hand play sensuous games with her breasts.

She didn't know what to say. She couldn't seem to care what she'd done, what she would do again, given a chance. Perhaps he was right and Sarah had actually found an herb that would act as aphrodisiac. She didn't think so though. This connection was more than just of the body. It burned through her soul, as if she were truly possessed.

"I apologize."

Startled, Ninian found the strength to turn her head. He didn't look remorseful. He looked remarkably pleased with himself as he rode his hand over her belly and examined the birthmark on her hip.

"For what?" she asked, for lack of a better response.

"For not believing you a virgin." He collapsed back against the bed, forming a pillow with his hands as he stared up at the canopy. "I was a dolt."

"A drugged one," she suggested, wondering if he still believed that.

He shrugged, and she admired the play of muscle in his broad shoulder.

"Not unless I've been drugged for days. I generally avoid virgins, so I suppose I convinced myself you weren't one."

She smiled. The studious professor was returning. "I'm well past the usual age of bedding," she admitted. "And I'm not inclined toward virginal simpering."

"That's it. You obviously deluded me into making an ass of myself."

He leaned on his elbow over her. He didn't look angry or menacing, so she decided he was teasing. It was hard to tell with a man who wore his face like a mask.

But the play of his hands on her flesh conveyed a message she could not mistake, nor deny. She arched beckoningly beneath his touch.

"I've always wondered what it was like." She caressed his bristled cheek, sampling this male texture she'd never encountered in her all-female world. His jaw twitched, but he did not pull away. She smoothed the ribbon hanging loosely from his long dark hair as it fell over his shoulder. "It was difficult counseling young girls when I knew nothing."

He nodded. "Glad to be of service. Anytime you like, I'm at your command."

He had to be teasing. She stroked the moisture of his lower lip. "Now?"

He tensed, obviously struggling again in the battle between mind and body. This time, however, his strength of will won. "You're sore, and still feeling the affects of Sarah's mischief-making. I'll not take advantage of you again." Reluctantly, he pulled the covers up around her. "I'll put out the candles."

When he swung his legs over the side of the bed, she could see he was fully aroused again. Yawning, she admired the pride of Lord Ives until the candles smoked out. He was a very big man, in more ways than one.

With the rain still pounding on the roof, she snuggled into her pillows, and slept.

Drogo carried the last candle to the bed, and looked dispassionately down on her golden curls. He'd given up thought of wife and child many years ago. Cynicism had arrived with the events of the past year. Women would do anything for a title. This one did not strike him as so conniving, or desperate, but then, neither had the last one.

It was simpler and more productive to immerse himself in the mathematics and astronomy he loved than to indulge in painful human relationships.

But just for one night, he'd known real passion again. He would thank her for that.

And in the course of things, when he left here, as he knew he must, he would see her taken care of, as he took care of all the people in his life.

Ten

Ninian woke to a cold bed. The heavy draperies had been pulled to prevent drafts, so she could see naught, but she knew it was still night, and she was alone. She frowned at the constant pounding of rain and the rising howl of the wind. She fretted over the safety of her home and the village in a storm as vicious as this one. In all the years she'd lived here, she'd never known the like. Still, there was little she could do to stop the wind and rain, and she could not travel at night. She would have to wait for morning.

She lay still, contemplating her new status of fallen woman. She'd been bedded by an earl. She'd never dreamed of such a thing, but it didn't feel wrong. If he was truly the devil as the legend called all Ives, shouldn't she feel raped and violated now? Shouldn't his promises be turning to ashes in her mouth?

She'd not been brought up to consider human mating more than a natural extension of the earth's fecundity. One plowed and planted in spring to bring forth fruit in fall. Society placed impediments on this natural cycle for good reason, she supposed. Human children needed years of care and protection before they could go out on their own, so society required a man to protect the woman and the fruit they produced.

But Malcolm women didn't need a man's protection. Malcolm women had the means to take care of their own. That had become a family tradition dating back to the first Malcolm woman who had lost everything to an Ives.

Uneasiness stole over her. She didn't mourn the loss of her virginity. She'd never expected to marry, and she had enjoyed the lesson he'd taught her. But the thought of bearing the child of an Ives . . .

She really didn't need to be arguing with an earl about heirs and titles and all those worldly concerns she'd rejected when she'd chosen to stay here with her grandmother and accept her responsibility as the Malcolm healer.

Shivering at the enormity of the problem, deciding she couldn't worry over things that couldn't be undone, she sat up and pulled a blanket with her as she sought her chemise.

She had to depart in the morning. She didn't like wasting what remained of her time with the earl. Perhaps now was the time to test her power as a woman.

Drogo didn't hear her enter. He looked up from his desk to see her standing in the candlelight, her golden curls tangled around her face, only her thin chemise protecting her bare shoulders above the blanket she'd wrapped around herself. She looked the part of enchantress she claimed to be.

She appeared vaguely startled at his smile. So innocent. He wished he could believe that innocence would last, but it really wasn't necessary. She'd given him what no other woman had, and he was properly grateful.

"You'll freeze," he admonished, rising to throw a few more coals on the brazier. Blood surged to his groin at the mere sight of her, and he knew damned well any silly potion Sarah could have used would have worn off hours ago.

"I did not mean to disturb your studies," she said primly, not flinching as he halted in front of her. He knew his size and possibly his station intimidated her, but she seemed to have no sense of vulnerability, even after the pain he'd inflicted on her. She drew a deep breath and daringly met his eye. "Why did you leave my bed?"

The demands began already, but he supposed he owed her an explanation. "Because I no longer had the excuse of too much drink should I ravish you again." She had such a bright and open expression that it blinded him. He couldn't tell what went on in the diverting byways of her mind.

She met his gaze steadily. "You wanted to ravish me again?"

"Repeatedly," he agreed grimly.

He could no longer believe Sarah's potion was responsible for the remarkable experience they'd shared. He'd just spent hours in a cold tower with nothing but mathematical equations dancing through his head, and the instant Ninian had walked in the room, he wanted her again. As he had since Beltane.

He'd never needed a woman as he hungered for this one, and he didn't like the knowledge.

He paced to his desk and played with his pen, protecting her from his lust while wrestling with the illogic of the situation. Perhaps he should have tried virgins sooner. He hadn't thought himself so crass as to be aroused by the power of total possession.

Even as he thought that, he turned to watch the vivid expressions fleeting across her face and wanted her more.

She didn't have the grace to look mollified at his admission but continued challenging him with wariness. "Do you fear bewitchment?"

Startled, Drogo choked on a laugh. Turning more fully to admire her, he dipped his gaze to the place where her blanket slipped and a flash of lightning illuminated the pearl of her breasts. "I'm not a superstitious man," he reminded her. "I only feared harming you."

"I am not harmed."

To his astonishment and deep, abiding pleasure, she dropped the blanket and stepped from its folds, blessing him with the sight of firm curves draped only in gossamer.

"I will warn you, though, that you will get no heirs from me. Malcolm women only bear girls."

"Once, there must have been a Malcolm man to lend you his name." The spurious debate over his nonexistent children had no importance to him. He'd come to terms with that long ago. He had not had time to come to terms with the witch's charms. Drogo reached for her, dragging her from the cold floor so they saw eye to eye, glorying in her responsiveness. "Do not cry rape come morning," he warned.

She wrapped her rounded arms around his neck and pressed his lips with a kiss he'd taught her, then added a mischievous lick of her own. "So long as you do not," she agreed.

Laughing for the first time in months, Drogo carried her downstairs to his chamber, where he could plant himself between her soft thighs, heedless of the consequences.

An ardent student, she responded with alacrity to his lessons. He taught her so well, he actually forgot the stars and slept.

Ninian woke to the sun blazing in the west window of a strange chamber. Groggy with more than the prior evening's heavy wine, she winced and covered her eyes. Other aches replaced the one in her head. Her cheeks and breasts burned with a fiery rash. Her nipples ached. She never noticed her nipples. She peeked from beneath her arm to stare down at them in amazement where they purled tight in the cool air, ready for plucking.

The soreness deep between her thighs jerked her more fully to consciousness. She had done it. She had mated with Lord Ives. It hadn't been a vivid dream after all.

Remembering the bright fire of passion in the earl's eyes, the shadows of a harsh jaw, the way raven hair fell forward as he pumped into her, she couldn't regret what she'd done. If she'd been possessed by a demon, he was kindlier than most. He'd covered her thoroughly in his rich blankets and set a fire burning in the grate.

Of course, demons were experts on fire. She giggled as she gave into the ridiculousness of her superstition. She was as bad as the villagers. Lord Ives had blighted nothing but her virginity, and that was no loss.

Listening, she heard no sound of rain. She must go back to the village and see what damage the storm had done. They might need her there.

Her head spun as she sat up, and she steadied herself against the mattress. The result of too much wine and whatever foolish herbs Sarah had introduced into both wine and food, she surmised. What on earth had possessed the silly woman to push her into bed with his lordship?

Well, it didn't matter now. It wasn't the end of the earth if she carried his child. The Malcolm trust fund ensured that no Malcolm female ever need go hungry. She could easily raise a daughter in the same way she had been raised.

A daughter. She smiled at the thought. She'd never considered an infant of her own before. She'd best start thinking about it now. In the meantime, she needed to return to the people for whom her gift was intended, to the village, where she belonged.

Wishing for a good birch bark tea to ease her aches, Ninian traipsed down the tower stairs to gather her things. She wished she could dally, but she feared the joining of Ives and Malcolm would bear a high price.

She debated bidding the earl farewell but decided it was best not to disturb his studies again. The women would tell him soon enough.

She descended the stairs carrying her bag, fully expecting an argument should anyone see her in the hall. But the day was fine and she had strong legs. She could walk the distance home. She didn't need anyone's help.

She hadn't expected all three women to be sitting around the fire, waiting for her. Perhaps it was well past noon, but she didn't consider herself of such importance that anyone would expect her company. They all looked up and watched her with interest as she crossed the flagstones.

"You're not thinking of leaving, are you?"

157

Lydie inquired brightly as Ninian approached. "We've only just begun to search the library."

"You should not be climbing stairs," Ninian reminded her sternly.

She laughed and held a hand to her bulging belly. "I expect to be delivered of him any day, and if climbing stairs brings him sooner, I'll not complain."

"He may not be in a proper position if you deliver him sooner. For the child's sake as well as your own, stay upstairs." Ninian nodded to Sarah and Lady Twane. "You must see she obeys. I am not always available when a child decides to arrive."

"Oh, but of course you will be," Claudia said with dismay. "You'll be right here. You can't go anywhere yet."

Patiently, Ninian tried to dispel that foolishness. "I have a mother about to deliver in the village. When Lydie's time comes, if you send the cart, I'll be here in time."

"Oh, don't worry about that," Sarah replied airily. "We've sent word to the village so they know where to find you."

A small shiver of fear shook Ninian's spine. Were all of London nobility this selfish? If so, how had her mother tolerated them? Remembering her grandmother's curses of her father and his friends, she wondered if she should have listened more closely. "It is not so simple as that," she explained cautiously. "I have my garden to tend, herbs to dry, things I cannot do here."

Claudia brightened. "We'll ask Drogo to rebuild that old conservatory you were working on. You could grow all sorts of marvelous plants there. It will be lovely having our own apothecary in residence."

The thought of the conservatory was tempting. She could grow tender plants she had only heard about, plants that could be very useful . . . Ninian shook her head as she recognized temptation when she saw it. "No, thank you very much, but I must go."

Sarah stood and hugged her. "I am sorry to hear that, dear, but you really cannot leave, you know. After that last foolish chit got herself pregnant by another man and declared the child Drogo's, we simply cannot put him through that again. If you are carrying his child, as the stars say, we must prove that it is his, beyond any possibility of doubt. We cannot do that if you go into the village."

Stunned, Ninian thought she had not heard her rightly. She sifted her brain for the proper response for something she couldn't have heard.

"He's gone into the village to check on the

storm damage," Claudia offered. "I'm sure he'll bring back any news."

Ninian didn't know what his lordship's relation was with these three women, but she had no intention of being added to their circle. Smiling falsely, she nodded. "I'll wait for him then."

Accepting a scone and tea, she ate unhurriedly, then returned upstairs with her bag, leaving the ladies chattering of researching the library. Instead of dropping her bundle in her room, she slipped down the hall, found the servants' stairs, and descended to the kitchen, easily retracing her path to the conservatory. Within minutes, she was in the woods and on her way home.

Evidence of the storm's havoc surrounded her as she picked her way over fallen trees and trudged through mud and pond-sized puddles. Perhaps the heavy rain would have cleared the stream, and vegetation could return again. She didn't want to believe in superstition and think what she had done last night had unleashed some inevitable fate. Her gift was not magic. She had no power over weather.

Hurrying to investigate the damage to the village, Ninian stepped off the beaten path into the overgrown jungle of the woods. She knew her directions well, and she didn't fear the fairies as the villagers did. If fairies were actually spirits waiting to be reborn, as her grandmother's tales said, they could scarcely harm a living person.

She'd welcome their guidance right now. She'd just given herself to a man she could never marry, a man whose odd company of women thought to hold her prisoner for his sake, or for the sake of his purely imaginary heir. Really! Sarah had been reading entirely too many medieval romances in that library. Ninian wasn't certain which of them had run mad — the ladies for dreaming up this scheme or herself for falling into it.

She wondered what stories Sarah had found about Malcolm women and if they might be why she'd sought Ninian out. Surely any legend would relate the disaster of Ives joined with Malcolm. Sarah couldn't be so mean-spirited as to . . .

Ninian halted beneath a rowan tree on the edge of a glade she'd never crossed before. Sunlight danced on a fairy ring in the dew-laden grass, and sensing a presence she could not see, she hesitated, her fingers digging into the rowan's bark.

The instant her hand touched the bark, something moved inside her, just as Lord Ives had last night.

Gasping, she released the bark and her

hand flew to cover the space between her hips. Recalling how Lord Ives had kneeled above her last night, claiming her as his own, she murmured a hurried protective incantation against evil. Surely they couldn't have created a child in one night. But if they had . . . Her grandmother had been right about the fairies. A spirit had just been reborn within her.

She looked down at the place her hand protected. A child? Mother of all that was holy . . .

A Malcolm, the wind whispered. As long as there were Malcolms in Wystan, there would be Malcolm witches.

Lord Ives would call it superstitious folly. He was probably right. These were modern times. Fairies didn't exist. But she felt what she felt, and alive with the knowledge, she skirted around the glade, pretending the quickening of her womb was no more than an aftereffect of the night's passion.

She had truly eaten of the fruit of folly.

Granny had said denying her instincts denied her power. But the difference between instinct and desire was so hard to differentiate . . .

Perhaps she just wanted a child so badly, she imagined the fairy touch. But instinct was also telling her disaster loomed ahead.

What did that portend?

Worried, Ninian hastened down the path. Detours around the debris scattered by the storm took more time than she'd antici- pated, even with the shortcut. It was late af- ternoon before she arrived at the beloved picket fence of her garden. She frowned at the broken rose canes and the place where the old oak had lost a limb and smashed a fence post. Safe within solid stone walls, she hadn't fully realized the storm's severity. A broken oak was a bad omen.

No longer denying instinct, suddenly fearful, Ninian raced toward town.

Eleven

What had she done?

As she ran toward the village, Ninian quaked at the extent of the storm's damage. The late-evening sun breaking through the overcast clouds didn't warm the chill running down her spine. Broken tree limbs grabbed her clothing as she ran. The washed-out road threw obstacles in her path so she tripped and fell in her haste. She shivered as she saw a dead cow in the field and heard the rush of fast waters in the usually bubbling burn. Never had a storm wreaked such destruction.

Malcolm and Ives once may have created havoc with their domestic battles, but surely one night of lovemaking couldn't produce a storm. She hadn't denied what she was or who she was, as the Malcolm in the legend had. Lord Ives hadn't asked her to. It was all silly superstition.

But what if her grandmother had been right? Was this the devil's reward for giving in to temptation? What had seemed so beautiful by moonlight, revealing its ugly face at dawn? This time instinct told her to be afraid, and Grandmother had said she shouldn't deny her instincts. Fear rode high in her throat as she approached the battered village.

Stumbling into town, mud-splattered and numb, Ninian didn't feel any surprise when Gertrude grabbed her sisters and shoved them inside at the sight of her.

She told herself she must look a fright with her hair every which way and her clothes ruined, but then Nate's father made the sign against the evil eye and slammed his door in her face. She'd known it would only take a simple slip, a rash mistake to turn them against her. A hollow opened inside her heart. She'd tried so hard, for so long . . .

A Malcolm had joined with an Ives, and disaster had struck. What further evidence did they need? At the sound of rushing water, Ninian turned from the village square. As if in answer to her question, a once quiet tributary of the burn roared through the lot where the milliner's shop used to be.

Where had all the water come from?

As fearful now for the villagers as for herself, Ninian glanced toward the little shop that housed the shoemaker and his family. Harry had always been her bulwark of security against wagging tongues. The churning stream filled his yard, seeping over doorsills. Had his family come through safely?

The door opened, and Harry stepped through the water, helping his limping mother to dry ground. Seeing Ninian, he looked at her unhappily and turned his back. He didn't call to her or ask for aid in dealing with his mother's injury. They didn't want her help.

How could they know where she'd been, what she'd done? How could they believe in a foolish legend instead of in her, who had never hurt a soul?

It didn't matter. The entire village had been brought up on tales of the wealth that had died in the disastrous joining of Malcolm and Ives. They were always wary of Malcolms. They had been even more so since the return of an Ives. Now they had visible confirmation of their worst fears. They held her responsible. They had trusted her, and in their eyes, she had betrayed them.

Mary. Mary wouldn't turn her back on her. She'd taught Mary and her children their letters. Ninian had delivered her babies, nursed them in sickness, played with them in health. Surely, Mary couldn't believe that she would deliberately do anything to hurt her.

Cautiously, Ninian slipped around to the back. Mary's cow nibbled at a muddy patch of grass amid the debris left by the swollen stream. A tall hedge hid her from prying eyes. Surely, if no one saw them . . .

At Ninian's knock Mary peered cautiously around the door. She almost slammed it before Ninian had the sense to shove her heavy shoe in the crack.

"Mary, for the love of God! Tell me what's wrong," she pleaded.

Hesitantly, Mary stood in the crack, blocking all access to her children. "You've been with Lord Ives, haven't you?" she demanded. "You've brought this disaster on us!"

"How can you believe that? I've been tending to a woman about to give birth!" But deep in her heart, she already knew. She'd always been one step away from their superstition, and that step was too easy for mere mortals to avoid.

For years, she'd played the part of simple healer, shying from any behavior that would label her "witch," but the people in the village weren't fools. While all was well and she helped the needy, they tolerated her. She could see with her own eyes that all was no longer well, and the dreaded word had risen with last night's wind.

"The stream turned into a river and washed out our livestock and tore down all that we've built," Mary whispered harshly. "Don't tell me the legends aren't true!"

"Mary, I'm sorry, I'm so sorry." Ninian rubbed her eyes, fighting terrified tears. "But I didn't do it! Can't you see that?" No amount of words could drive away the stabbing pain of this rejection. Somehow, she must make them see differently, but how? She couldn't believe what she'd done was wrong or that the earl and his household had any knowledge of witchery. It just wasn't possible.

"I don't know what to do," she whispered, panicking, pleading for Mary's help. Where would she go, what would she do, if the villagers no longer trusted her? Who would she heal? What would be her purpose in existing? Tears poured unchecked down her cheeks. "The earl has nothing to do with any of this," she cried. "You must believe that. It has to be the stream. I've warned you . . ."

Mary looked wary but didn't turn away. "We've used that water for generations. It's never turned on us before."

"I don't know why. I need time . . . Please, Mary, what can I do?"

"Go back to your own kind," Mary said, her earlier harshness softened. Then, as a gray cat stepped out of the shrubbery and wrapped around Ninian's ankles, she slammed the door in horror.

The loneliness of the ten-year-old she once had been blew through Ninian now, only this time, she had no grandmother to run to. Tears stinging, she picked up the cat that had apparently followed her from the castle. She'd always known she was an outsider. She hadn't arrived in Wystan until she was ten, but she'd thought the villagers had accepted her over the years because Malcolms had lived here since the dawn of time. The tenuous nature of their acceptance was now apparent. She didn't belong anywhere.

Biting back a sob, hugging the cat for comfort, Ninian trudged back to the road. Doors and shutters slammed as she passed. No one wanted her near. It would take weeks to send for her aunts in the far south of England. The roads would be impassable after the storm. And her aunts really didn't want her either. They had troublesome daughters of their own.

She could go to the castle and see if the ladies would persuade some of the male servants to aid the village, but it would be tomorrow before she could walk there and back. And it had to be those same servants who had reported the castle events to the villagers. Everyone knew what she had done.

Guilt and shame flooded her as it hadn't before. It had all seemed so right with Lord Ives holding her. Somehow, he had blinded her to reality. She had fallen to the devil's temptation, and he'd destroyed all she knew and loved.

Even as she thought of him, she walked straight into his arms.

The earl caught and steadied her in the dying shadows of daylight. Even now, with her life crumbling in pieces, his arms provided a haven of security.

"You shouldn't be here."

"I live here," she whispered as the cat fled her arms and her head spun with uncertainty. She used to live here. The whole world had turned upside down, and she didn't know if she was falling off or climbing on. The earl's strong grip offered safety, just for this minute, just until she found the ground beneath her feet.

"I'll take you home."

She didn't even know which home he meant, his or hers. Ninian shook her head in denial. She had to get away from the earl, from the village, and return to the only real home she'd known — her grandmother's cottage. She didn't know what she would do once she got there. Tears spilled down her cheeks again. "The village," she choked, "I'm responsible . . . I have to *help*." The word cracked on a sob.

He didn't hug her, probably didn't know how to offer hugs of sympathy. He merely glanced down at her tearstained face and drew her deeper into the shadows, toward the cottage.

"I'm taking care of it," he said in utter certainty, as if she should have known that.

And to her amazement, Ninian finally saw through her haze of grief to see he was doing just that. Men appeared out of the shadows carrying shovels, hoes, and pitchforks. On the village green, the earl's steward directed workers toward dead animals and swollen drain ditches. Others, carrying ladders and thatch, tugged their forelocks as the earl passed, exchanging brief words as to which houses needed repairing next.

They didn't need her. Maybe they'd never needed her. Her mind spun blankly at the blow. The earl could give what she could not.

Drogo stopped to correct the manner in which a ditch was being diverted, gazed thoughtfully to where the water poured from the forest and toward the village from a new streambed, then caught Ninian's arm and steered her onward. Too stunned to entirely accept what was happening, she didn't fight his guidance. He was an Ives. And the villagers were following him, not the Malcolm who had lived among them. She couldn't think beyond that incredible obstacle.

To Ninian's weary surprise, Sarah awaited them in the kitchen. "I've gathered her things," she told him. "As quaint and charming as I'm sure this place is, I have no wish to remain here. The ghost was weeping when I left. Claudia is frantic. And Lydie vows the baby will arrive at any minute."

"You'll come home with us," the earl commanded Ninian, leaving it evident he expected no argument by steering her toward the door.

Ninian knew she should resist. Granny would want her to stay here, to tend the garden, to find some means of helping the village. That was her place in things.

But Granny had left her here all alone, and the village didn't want her.

For the moment, she could not summon

172

the spirit to fight. She'd always thought friendship worked both ways, but it seemed no one wanted her except when she was useful. She wasn't useful now. Not to the village. Not to anyone. Maybe she never had been. Maybe her gifts were just products of Granny's imagination and her own pride.

Silently, Ninian followed the earl and Sarah from the cottage. She was needed at the castle. Maybe in a few weeks, things would return to normal, and she could come home to her garden again. Perhaps she would see things more clearly then.

Not looking at the broken rose canes of her garden, she closed the cottage door and walked out the picket gate to the carriage waiting to take her to the castle of her ancestors and the future fate had in store for her.

Drogo rubbed his weary eyes as the candle guttered in a puddle of wax. He'd thought Ninian would have come to him by now. He'd left her in Sarah's care, but he didn't expect Sarah to offer much in the way of commiseration. He'd seen that blank gaze of grief before and knew the little witch needed more than sympathy.

In his experience, the first thing a woman did when confronted with disaster was turn to a man. The second thing she did was look around to see if he was the best man to feather her nest. Since he was the only man on the horizon, he assumed Ninian would be up here sooner or later, looking for the promise of a title. He really couldn't blame her. A woman had to have strong survival instincts in this world.

He would gladly offer the comfort of his bed. Unfortunately, he wasn't prepared to offer more unless his price was met.

The sound of feminine feet on the stairs outside his observatory stirred his tired brain, and he smiled. Women were so predictable.

His smile faded as Sarah entered, wearing only a thin night robe.

"I thought you would be entertaining our guest." She set her candle on the corner of his desk.

"Your meddling has done this to her," Drogo said coldly.

Sarah picked up one of his papers and fanned it. "My meddling caused the flood?" she asked. "My, I am much more powerful than I thought."

"You know what I mean. Had she been at home where she belonged, those superstitious idiots wouldn't be turning their backs on her now. Putting that damned concoction in our drinks last night had to have been your idea. If you don't leave those damned potions of yours alone . . ."

"Don't be ridiculous, Drogo." Sarah swung her makeshift fan back and forth, watching him over the top, smiling faintly. "You are the last person in the world to need any help in *that* direction. You merely acted on your own fantasy."

He usually knew when Sarah lied, and he saw no evidence of it now. Yet, if he believed the damned woman, then he had no one to blame but himself for what had happened last night. He'd taken the innocence of a simple maiden, robbed her of her home, ruined her in the eyes of her neighbors . . . out of pure lust.

If it wasn't Sarah and her potions, then the moonwitch had bewitched him as no other woman had the power to do. He was always careful. He never lost control to the extent that he acted blindly.

So blindly that even now he refused to explore the matter further. He didn't want to know what had driven him. He knew he wouldn't like the answer.

He couldn't let Sarah know how completely he had fallen. She would ride him endlessly if he did. Shuffling through a drawer, Drogo produced a fresh candle, and lit it with the dying flame of the first. "I have work to finish. I have to return to London in the morning. Did you want something?"

Her mouth turned down, but she watched him with more curiosity than disappointment. "Your guest is still awake. I heard her crying as I passed by."

"She knows where to find me if she needs me," he answered curtly, returning his attention to the page of numbers on his desk.

"What if she doesn't need you?" Sarah asked softly. "She didn't strike me as the weak sort, like the rest of us."

She walked out, but her words nagged in her absence. Drogo glared at the numbers on the page but couldn't make sense of them any longer. Everyone needed him for one thing or another. The little witch wasn't any exception, just more stubborn than most.

And more tempting.

He shoved back his chair, and picking up his candle, wandered down from the tower to the wing where Sarah had conveniently placed Ninian. Women always came to him, not the other way around. He'd never pursued a woman in his life. He wasn't pursuing this one. But he owed her for his drunken actions. It had to have been the wine.

He just wanted to see if she was all right. He really didn't have time for a mistress, but he couldn't seem to prevent himself from stopping outside her door.

He could hear her sobs as he stood there. He had no experience in dealing with female hysterics, but he couldn't bear hearing her cry. She'd been so full of light and mischief yesterday, he hated to hear her pain now.

Last night, she'd invited him in. He could see no reason why he should stand on propriety. He tested the latch and opened the door.

She gasped, as she almost always did when he appeared. He wondered if he really was so terrifying to look upon, and only Ninian in her innocence was open enough to show it. She didn't seem terrified though. She grabbed her sheet and covered herself as she sat up, and she looked furious enough to spit nails. In the flickering light of his candle, he could see streaks of moisture on her cheeks, but he was more interested in the tangle of golden curls falling over her rounded breasts.

"What do you want, my lord?"

"I heard you crying," he said simply, having no other words to offer. He wasn't a particularly gentle or compassionate man.

He vaguely understood her disillusion but knew no real solution other than time. Physical comfort, however, he knew how to give and would willingly offer, if it was acceptable.

"I cry when I'm unhappy. Don't you?"

He thought she was being sarcastic, but he considered her question anyway. Logic usually worked best in emotional situations. "No," he finally answered. Not since childhood, anyway, but he didn't need to explain that. "I waited for you to come to me."

In this light, he couldn't tell if her eyes widened with surprise or anger. At least he'd given her something to think about that stopped her crying.

"I refuse to be one of your coven," she announced stoutly. "You may strike me dead, if you like."

Not a moonchild, but a typical woman, using irrationality instead of logic. Staring down into her vehement expression, Drogo sighed in bewilderment and lowered the candle to the table. It was a good thing he was leaving in the morning. "I won't pretend to understand what that means. I'll leave you with this. Good night."

"You won't pretend to understand that you've brought death and destruction to Wystan?" she demanded.

He glanced at her over his shoulder, so beautiful with her luminescent face lit by the candlelight, and her defiant chin tilted proudly. He'd never understand what went on behind that lovely facade. "The *storm* brought destruction," he answered carefully.

"The burn never flooded like that before. It never died before. Ask your steward what he's hiding from you. My grandmother was always right. An Ives has ruined us again."

If he lived to be a hundred, he would never forget the wonder and beauty of a golden-haired witch bathed in candlelight, even an irrational one.

As utterly befuddled by his reaction as hers, Drogo nodded politely and escaped.

Twelve

Ninian was awakened by daylight pouring through the windows. Briefly, she entertained the idea that she'd dreamed the last few days, or perhaps just last evening's strange encounter with Lord Ives. As she dragged herself from bed in search of food and knew she no longer slept in her own bed, she reluctantly accepted that it had all been very real, and now she must decide what to do about the rest of her life.

She could return to the cottage, raise cats, and plant herbs no one would ever use, and grow into the witchy old lady the villagers expected of her. Alone.

Unable to accept that forlorn future quite yet, she sought the ladies in the same place as the day before — or at least two of them waited there. Sarah had an immense dusty tome on the table before her, while Claudia embroidered the hem of an infant's nightshirt.

Sarah glanced up from her reading and gestured at the empty chair. "You've just missed Drogo. He's off to rescue my brother Joseph from Newgate. Have a scone. The jam is heavenly."

Not certain whether to be relieved or not at news of the earl's departure, Ninian took the chair indicated and accepted a cup of tea. "Joseph? He's an Ives?" The legends had said to beware of Ives. How many of them were there?

"An Ives from the wrong side of the blanket, but we all grew up together."

Ninian wasn't certain she was prepared for so much information about the immoral society she had turned her back on. She buttered a scone to keep from thinking too deeply about anything. Pain lay only a thought away.

"Might I ask how many of you there are?" Perhaps she could grasp enough facts to keep her grounded. Really, if she knew more about these people, maybe she wouldn't be so afraid of them. Remembering her tirade at the earl last night, she thought again. Maybe she should be afraid. She wasn't certain they brought out the best in her.

Sarah wrinkled her brow in thought. "Well, Drogo is the eldest of the legitimate Ives, of course, since he inherited his father's titles. Dunstan is the second eldest. He manages the Ives estate. Ewen is third. I believe it must have been at that point poor Lady Ives decided she could not bear a fourth boy and denied the late earl her bed. I'm not at all certain of cause and effect, you understand, since Drogo's father is not mine, and I was scarce more than a child when the late earl and my mother met."

She pushed the plate of scones toward Ninian. "Have another, dear. You must keep your strength up if you are to be a Countess of Ives."

Sarah didn't even take a breath after that strange announcement, but continued following the path of her own thoughts. "Ives men are infamous for their prolificacy. There is scarce two years between Drogo and each of his brothers, and my mother bore the earl three more boys once they set up housekeeping. All bastards, my brothers are, of course, but Drogo supports them. He could scarcely do less, since they grew up in the same household."

Battered by both the barrage of Sarah's words and the tension of repressing her hysterical thoughts, Ninian sipped her tea and eyed her manic hostess with caution. "I see. Of course, you do realize I am a Malcolm?"

"Oh, yes, Drogo did mention that. I'm

sure the Malcolm ghost will be gratified to know a Malcolm will once again reside in Malcolm Castle. Although . . ." She puckered her brow slightly. "Drogo will never be able to stay here for any length of time. I'm certain he will wish to introduce you to the family, and he takes his place in Parliament quite seriously."

Ninian smiled and nibbled her scone, wondering if Claudia would join in the idiocy. "You don't seem to understand," Ninian replied demurely, wishing them both to the devil. "Malcolms only bear witches. Female witches," she clarified, not wanting there to be any doubt that she would never bear an Ives heir, wishful thinking or not.

Lady Twane chirped quietly at this announcement. Sarah only shrugged.

"Well, that should make for some enlightening entertainment nine months hence, but it's of no matter. Drogo will marry you once he ascertains you're with child. You see, he thinks he can't have children."

And Sarah had thought to provide him with one? How considerate of her.

A servant chose that moment to arrive and announce that Lady Lydie appeared to be in labor.

As Ninian rose from the table to follow

183

the servant, she accepted that now that the earl had departed, she didn't have to leave just yet. Her gift was needed here, even if the castle's inhabitants were all quite mad.

Drogo set down his telescope with disgust. The fog off the Thames and the smoke from a thousand chimneys blotted any vision of the night sky, no matter how high he climbed in this doddering edifice he called home.

He almost missed the crumbling castle in the north. At least there he'd been able to complete his calculations and verify his results on clear nights. In London, there was no such thing as a clear night.

In London, there was no such thing as moonstruck witches.

Cursing his inability to put Ninian out of his mind, Drogo started down the attic stairs. The aging town house echoed empty these days with Dunstan married and living in the country, Ewen off melting iron in the north, and his half brothers all at school.

Theoretically. He frowned as he noted Joseph lingering in the shadows of the lower hall. "I thought I sent you back to Oxford."

Twenty, lanky, and more inclined toward living inside his head than the rest of his brothers, Joseph never quite fit in anywhere.

He still looked like a gangly youth with hands and feet too big for the rest of him, but Drogo knew better than to underestimate Joseph's clever mind.

"I don't want to be a vicar," he declared sullenly. "I don't care if you've left the living at Ives open for me. I don't like people."

Drogo groaned inwardly as he entered his private parlor and threw another coal on the dying fire. For May, it was still damp at this time of night. "Fine. Don't enter the ministry. You're welcome to starve, if you choose. Or find a wealthy wife."

"I fail to see why I can't make a living as an architect. It's not as if I'm in line for the title," Joseph said resentfully, dropping into a wing chair.

Drogo rolled his eyes at this eldest of his bastard brothers. At the moment, Joseph had chosen to ape him by refusing hair powder and wigs and going about in unadorned plain frock coats. Convenient for the family budget, at least, although Drogo suspected the informal attire was more a result of his brother pawning his more expensive clothing to fund his experiment in card-counting which had landed him in Newgate.

"You can't draw," Drogo answered succinctly, taking a seat at his desk where the estate books had collected dust in his absence. "You will have grave difficulty supporting yourself on ideas you can't present."

"I can learn," Joseph muttered. "I just haven't had the right teacher."

To school his patience, Drogo drew a mental image of his castle tower, complete with velvet skies and twinkling stars and Ninian shining golden naked beneath them. Even if he couldn't visit paradise in truth, his thoughts served him better than reality, for in his head, Ninian could be as brilliant in mind as in form.

The thought relaxed him sufficiently not to follow his first impulse to throttle his half brother. "Then go to school while you look for the right teacher."

Giving up on the calculations on the desk in front of him, he propped his boots on the battered fireplace fender, opened a desk drawer to produce a handful of sweetmeats, and didn't reward Joseph with any. Drogo popped a candy and dallied with the image of Ninian a little longer. Was she really superstitious enough to think him the devil? If he returned to Wystan, would she still be furious with him and refuse his bed? Or would her unpredictable humor have changed to prefer a try at becoming a countess?

Joseph slumped deeper into his chair. "Our father should have stopped while he was ahead. There's too damned many of us and not enough blunt to go around. I don't know why you let Dunstan have the estate."

"Because he loves farming, and he's my heir. Someday he will have children who will inherit the lot. Makes sense to me."

"How do you know I wouldn't be good at farming?" Joseph muttered rebelliously.

"Because you were raised in town and don't know one end of a sheep from the other. How do you know you wouldn't enjoy the ministry?"

"Why did Dunstan and Ewen stay with your mother in the country and you didn't?" he countered.

Drogo sighed. Joseph had been but a lad of five when their father died. Not overly inquisitive, he'd always accepted their erratic family ties. Drogo supposed it was time his brother began to ask questions. He threw Joseph a walnut kernel from the mix. He missed.

"That was the separation agreement the courts allowed. My father kept his heir and my mother was allowed to raise Dunstan and Ewen. My mother was allowed one of the smaller farms as her residence if she did not come to London and interfere with my father and your mother. It happens all the time. Remember it when the time comes for you to consider marriage." He recited the facts easily, without calling up the wrenching pain of the memory.

"Never!" Joseph replied vehemently. "I'll not let any hellcat sink her claws in me. I might not be book fodder like you, but I'm not addlepated enough to saddle myself with whining women and clinging brats and courts demanding every last penny I earn."

"You've not earned any," Drogo observed wryly. "Have you decided on the military or the priesthood?"

Joseph scowled. "Are those my only alternatives?"

"Well, we could apprentice you to a solicitor. Just think of all the blunt you could earn from us writing marriage settlements for a living."

"And separation agreements." Gloomily, Joseph sought the missed kernel in the folds of his coat. He sighed as he located the treat and popped it in his mouth. "Might as well try law, then. I'd rather grow rich in boredom than be shot at on the battlefield."

"Smart choice. I'll make the arrangements." Relieved that this latest crisis hadn't resulted in the usual sort of temper tantrum, Drogo turned back to his books.

"Damned good thing you never married, Ives," Joseph drawled, standing up. "A wife would either pitch us all out on our ears, or run home to her mother."

"Heaven forbid," Drogo agreed fervently. "I have enough on my hands. Can you imagine what it would be like in the next generation if I had a brood of boys of my own plus whatever bastards the rest of you breed?"

At thus being acknowledged as adult enough to breed bastards, Joseph brightened. "Can you imagine what would happen if an Ives produced a girl child?"

"There's Sarah," Drogo pointed out, though Sarah couldn't really be counted as a blood relation. Still, she had grown up amid Ives, and they had managed well enough. Drogo winced at the memory of her latest mischief, and retracted that thought.

Maybe God hadn't given him children because he already had a family of them.

Morosely, Ninian dug her fingers into the dead sludge of the burnside. No amount of manure or ashes had returned plant life to the part of the stream running near Wystan Castle. The banks were as barren and muddy as they'd been after the flood.

The storm had wiped out the earl's filter.

It had been nearly two months, and he hadn't returned to rebuild it. What had she expected? That the devil would repair his cruelty?

Or that he'd be longing to see her again as much as she craved his return?

Knowing better than to think such thoughts, she picked her way upstream, searching for the lichen she'd discovered along a faster flowing part of the water.

"The castle almost certainly was the dowry of a Malcolm lady," Sarah argued as she stepped gingerly alongside Ninian. "I cannot read ancient legal language well, but that's the way the account books read to me."

"That does not mean the ghost is a Malcolm or that she protests some imaginary wrong done." Unsympathetically, Ninian bent to dig up a root she needed for her demolished garden. She hadn't told Sarah about her grandmother's storybook. Despite the havoc the storm had wreaked, she refused to believe she'd personally aroused the legend about Ives and Malcolms destroying a place they had obviously loved, and apparently lost. The true story was no doubt lost to the mists of time.

"The villagers believe it," Sarah said triumphantly. "They believe you're a witch and that you've gone the way of the Malcolm who drove the Ives from Wystan."

"Would that you were an Ives so I could do the same," Ninian muttered.

"You don't mean that. I'm the one who will return peace and happiness to both families," Sarah declared brightly. "I knew the stars had some purpose in directing me here, and I have found it. You will provide Drogo the child he desires and the two of you shall return prosperity to Wystan."

"And Drogo will give you financial freedom in return?" Ninian asked cynically, having already learned Sarah's most frequent complaint.

"Or you will," she answered confidently. "What does this place hold for you? Nothing. But as Countess of Ives . . ." She gave a characteristic shrug.

"A Malcolm cannot marry an Ives," Ninian said adamantly. "And I belong here. I'm a healer, not a countess." She sensed the despair behind Sarah's bright words, but her gifts did not lend to healing emotional wounds.

Her gift might not heal emotional injuries, but it had saved Lydie's baby, both from childbirth and from Sarah's plans to put the infant out for adoption. In return for the reprieve that the castle inhabitants provided from loneliness, Ninian let Sarah spin her idle fantasies about Malcolms and Ives. Using the excuse of Lydie's infant to stay where she felt needed, she didn't have to face the scorn of the villagers just yet.

She turned down the path to the castle garden she'd been cultivating. The parts watered by rainwater were flourishing. The plants watered from the burn had all died.

"You're doing Lydie no favor," Sarah scolded as Ninian stopped to admire a fern.

"And you are a more meddling and manipulative witch than my grandmother ever was." Ninian gently eased the root from the ground and into her basket.

"I'm just trying to help," Sarah protested. "Lydie's unwed and only sixteen. Her family cannot introduce her to society with a child in her arms. They're telling everybody she's visiting friends in Scotland. In a few weeks, she can go home and find a good husband."

"A wealthy one, you mean." Ninian lifted a kitten from the hole she'd just dug and rubbed its furry face against her own. The cats followed her as much as Sarah did. She loved their easy acceptance. Selfish creatures, they only required feeding. "That should be Lydie's decision, not yours."

"Lydie is young and too foolish to know

what's good for her. No man will take her with a bastard. She can keep the child and starve on the streets, or she can give the child a home and start a new life for herself, a safe one, with a man who might come to love her."

Ninian sat back on her heels and wiped the dirt from her hands. "Men are not the solution to everything. Does Lord Ives threaten to throw her from the castle?"

Sarah shrugged. "Drogo never threatens. But her parents can cause a scandal if they discover he's protecting her."

Ninian tilted her head to look up at her. "And you'll do anything to protect Drogo?"

Sarah looked annoyed. "You see entirely too much. Hurry up, now. Claudia may have found that volume of family history by now."

Ninian didn't point out that if she possessed any gift for seeing, it hadn't helped with the village. Lord Ives had sent the money and the tools to rebuild, but the people still turned their backs on her, the burn still failed, and she was no closer to a solution to any of her problems. She was certainly a failure as a witch.

It had been two months since her night with Lord Ives, and she suspected she was far more successful at one part of her Malcolm legacy than others.

Granny had always said Malcolm women were fertile.

Thirteen

August 1750

Ninian clung dizzily to the potting bench and blocked out Lydie's chatter as she concentrated on remaining upright. Her knees wobbled. Her legs wouldn't move.

Lydie shoved a stool beneath her. "It hit me that way, too. I was afraid to stand up for a week."

Heart pounding, Ninian sank onto the stool, not registering anything Lydie said. Three months, and the earl hadn't returned. She couldn't wait any longer. She'd have to solve her problems on her own. She'd have to ignore Sarah's hysterics over leaving the castle. The women had comforted her when she needed friends, but she knew her duty. It was time to return to the village, whether they wanted her there or not.

"I'll call Sarah," Lydie said breathlessly.

"She wanted to know the instant you quickened. So many women lose their babes in the first months."

As Lydie departed, Ninian rested her head on her knees, just as Granny had taught her. The dizziness faded, replaced by what she had tried to deny.

Lord Ives had possessed her and stolen everything she possessed in return, leaving her with something far more dangerous — his child.

She carried the child of an Ives, of an earl, of a man she barely knew. In begetting this child, she'd lost the respect of the village and the only life she'd ever wanted. Had the begetting of the innocent soul in her womb been the cause of the ruination of Wystan?

How would she raise a child who would be scorned by every person in the vicinity?

"Ninian, are you well?"

Sarah's question seemed to come from a distance, but Ninian managed to nod her head. Maybe she would create her own village of unwed mothers, take Lydie and her babe home with her so she wouldn't be alone.

Not a chance. Sarah had plans for everyone. She would have to escape before the web tightened. She wouldn't give up her child. Never, no matter what nonsense these

London lunatics dreamed up.

Taking Lydie's arm, Ninian stood up. Her head still spun, but not badly. The morning sickness had taken much of her strength, but it shouldn't last much longer. She'd be fine enough to return to her cottage any day now. To her empty cottage.

Before she left, she would be sure of Lydie's safety. "You have heard nothing from your baby's father?"

"The father is a footman," Sarah said scornfully. "The child belongs here among the peasants, despite Lydie's sentimental silliness."

"I want to keep her," Lydie protested. "She's all I have that's truly mine."

Sarah shrugged. "Then good luck finding employment to support her." Her eyes narrowed as she turned to Ninian. "You're pale. Come inside where it's cool. I'll not have you losing Drogo's son."

Foolishly, Ninian had hoped Sarah really didn't believe her wishful thinking about stars and ghosts and other supernatural portents. Equally foolishly, she'd hoped she'd hidden the truth of her pregnancy. Mostly, she feared what Sarah intended to do about it.

"I've written Drogo," Sarah said placidly.

Ninian swayed beneath this confirmation

of her fears. She'd told the earl? Catching the kitchen table as they returned inside, she lowered herself into a chair.

As if she wasn't exploding still another cannonball, Sarah continued, "He should be here to fetch you in a day or two."

Fetch her? The earl? May The Lady preserve her!

Ninian's gasp finally caught Sarah's self-absorbed attention.

"Did you think he wouldn't want to know?" she asked incredulously. "The stars said you would carry his son." Contentedly, she handed Ninian a teacup. "I can help you gain a little town polish, and Drogo won't be able to call me a silly female any longer. He will have to give me an allowance if I'm your companion, and I won't have to live with Mother or marry anyone I don't wish to marry."

The rest of Sarah's chatter became a distant buzz in Ninian's ears. The earl knew.

What would he do?

Was he reading this right? Could it possibly be true?

Drogo struggled through Sarah's illegible, cross-hatched letter again, threw it on his desk, and stalked to the window to stare out at London's nightly fog. He jammed his hands in his coat pockets and clenched them into fists. He gritted his teeth and wrestled with the wildness pounding at the scarred walls of his heart.

He had to have misread. Sarah would do anything to move out of her mother's house. Or she had thought of a new scheme to get even with him for unleashing her mother's rage. He and Sarah had a long history of seeking revenge on each other.

But he knew that beneath the bombast, Sarah only sought his approval.

Terror slithered in through a hitherto unknown crack in his guard. He must have misread Sarah's chicken scratching. He needed to reread it, prevent another dashing of his hopes. He'd barely survived that episode last year when the lying slut he'd bedded once claimed to carry his child.

Joseph wandered in, trailed by his younger brother, David — the eldest two of his trio of half brothers. Drogo wished his stepmother would keep a tighter rein on her sons, but she hadn't even insisted that David complete his schooling after he'd been heaved out for digging up a Roman bathhouse — under the provost's cottage. Drogo had to buy the man a new one after the old one collapsed into the cellar.

"There's a new orchestra at Vauxhall,"

David suggested hopefully.

Drogo couldn't pull himself out of his fog to reply. Sarah's letter seemed to grow larger and more demanding the longer he let it lay there.

"Could I have the cavalry colors Joseph doesn't want?"

David had never been as insouciant as Joseph. He'd always fought for attention in the tumultuous upheaval of the Ives household, and he'd learned to do it well. At eighteen, he was taller and broader than Joseph, and faster to come to blows.

He'd have to leave his brothers on their own if he returned to Wystan.

The dread rising in Drogo's soul had naught to do with his brothers. He turned and picked up Sarah's letter.

"You can join the cavalry after you've completed your education," he answered absently, staring at the paper in his hand. Was that an "m" or an ink blot in front of "other"? "Ninian, mother"? Was she telling him Ninian had adopted Lydie's child?

"Ain't that Sarah's letter? Is she coming home yet?" Joseph wandered over and tried to look over Drogo's shoulder. "She never did learn how to spell."

Maybe that was it. Maybe she had misspelled something and it had come out "child." What could she be saying here? Chilled?

"There's no sense in going to Oxford if I take colors," David protested, pacing the study. "I just need to know how to sit a horse and point a musket."

"And look good in a uniform," Joseph added sarcastically, giving up on the letter and helping himself to the sweetmeats in Drogo's desk.

"You'll gain promotions faster if you can at least write a letter better than your sister," Drogo muttered, collapsing in his chair and muddling through another sentence. They'd done what? Held Ninian captive? He shuddered to think of it. What sounded like "captive"? Or looked like? Cap? Tiv? Tin. Captain. They held Ninian captain?

"Girls don't need to write," David declared disdainfully. "She ain't had any teaching. I could write better than that when I was in leading strings."

"You never were in leading strings." Joseph sprawled in a chair in the same fashion as Drogo. "You ran wild all the time."

"No more so than Paul," David objected. "He needed caning —"

"Shut up, both of you." Drogo slammed the letter down and stood up. "I'm bringing Sarah back from Wystan. We may have guests. Tell Jarvis to prepare rooms. Tell your damned mother I'll fund her visit to Scotland if she leaves by day after to-morrow." He strode toward the door.

Beneath nearly identical dark curls, David and Joseph exchanged surprised looks. As far as they were aware, Drogo had never offered to send their interfering mother out of town before. Sarah always stayed with their mother.

A major Ives upheaval was afoot.

Cursing his foolishness, cursing Sarah, cursing the lazy horses he'd hired at the last posting house and urging them faster, Drogo raced his carriage through the night.

His terrified coachman had long since retired to the interior with a flask of gin. The lurching and swaying of the lumbering coach had nearly unseated the man more than once.

Drogo didn't miss his company. His own jumbled thoughts provided entertainment enough.

He'd given up on Sarah's letter. The only way he could determine the truth was to confront the women personally. He knew Sarah could look him in the eye and blithely tell him entire books of lies. He hoped the moon maiden was less sophisticated.

He was hoping a damned lot more than that.

As the night wore on and weariness crept in, he couldn't believe he not only had the ability to still hope, but that he could be interested at all.

He'd meant what he'd told Joseph. Marriage wasn't for him. He'd given it considerable thought before Dunstan decided to marry. By that time, it had become morbidly apparent he hadn't sired a single bastard on any woman who'd crossed his bed. Marrying for any reason but heirs was of no purpose. The family he had was sufficient proof that Ives weren't meant for monogamy, love was nonexistent, and children were far overrated, or so he'd told himself, repeatedly.

He didn't need a wife. He didn't need an heir.

But what if he'd finally, after all these years, begot one?

"Impossible!" he exploded as the three harpies all talked excitedly at once.

"Impossible!" he declared later as he cornered Ninian in the privacy of her chamber and stared at her still trim waist. A proliferation of fern fronds in the window behind her blurred the lines of her silhouette. Fern fronds?

Instead of exploding with anger as she had every right to do — Sarah had actually locked her in to prevent her from leaving — the golden-haired witch tapped her finger against her lips and eyed Drogo as if he were a particularly recalcitrant schoolboy. "Well," she said, "as a naturalist, you must know it's not *impossible*. What we did results in babies."

He threw up his arms in exasperation and stormed through the room's shadows. She'd pulled back the draperies to allow the meager sun through mullioned windows, but there wasn't enough light in the world to enlighten this mess. "What we did is nothing I haven't done ten thousand times before, and *I've not made babies!*"

She remained curiously unperturbed by his belligerency.

"If you're saying it's impossible after just one night . . . ten thousand?" she inquired, diverted by his declaration. "Well, you might be right that it's unusual after just one night, if the moon wasn't in its proper phase, but unfortunately, it was. Not that I expect you to believe that," she added blandly.

Drogo swung around. "How very convenient." He could swear the fern wrapped a frond around her shoulders to shelter her.

She ignored his acidity and continued

ticking off her list. "I suppose I could have gone into the village and seduced every man there after you left, which might make the child unlikely to be yours, but still, I wouldn't call the child *impossible*."

"I can't have children," he said adamantly.

She showed no sympathy. "Well, since I haven't been with any man but you, and I'm definitely experiencing every symptom of pregnancy known to womankind, you've either been misinformed, misled, or haven't tried hard enough. *Ten thousand* times?" she repeated in wonder. Then shaking her head, continued, "Or would you prefer to believe I'm the victim of a second Immaculate Conception?"

He wanted to throttle her. He'd been through this before, let his hopes soar, swung high with reckless abandon on joyous rainbows, only to have the clouds pulled from under him. This time, he couldn't see how she might have become pregnant by another. She'd been an innocent when he'd taken her, of that he had no doubt. And from what he knew of her, she wouldn't have lain with any other man. There must be another trick.

"I've known women to claim they're with child and then mysteriously lose it directly after they've gained what they wanted."

Offended, she drew herself rigid and glared. "I don't *want* anything. I'm not the one who wrote you. But if it's my word you doubt, I'll be happy to retch up the contents of my stomach on you for as many mornings as it takes to convince you."

Buffeted by their conflicting logics, Drogo stood bewildered in the face of her certainty. He'd thought her a simpleton, a pleasantly innocent miss with unpredictable moods. She didn't seem quite so simple now, although her mood was definitely odd.

With some trepidation, he eyed her stomach. She hadn't dressed for the occasion, he noted wryly. She wore her usual apron stuffed with God-knew-what plants and dead leaves, and a bulky homespun gown that revealed nothing. Perhaps her waist was a little thicker? Had her breasts always strained the seams of her bodice?

"I'll have a physician examine you when we reach London," he decided coldly. He could see no alternative. He would have to go along with Sarah's little farce until it played out. He couldn't foresee any real danger to anything but his already jaded cynicism.

Delicate, rounded eyebrows rose. "London? I think not, my lord. My child will be born here, as all Malcolms are."

"That's a lot of superstitious claptrap," he said scornfully, finally standing on firmer ground. "If you carry my child, as you claim, we'll be married in a church, in London, with friends and family as witnesses. The child will be an Ives, not a Malcolm."

"The father's name has no bearing on the matter." Now that she'd won her point, she clasped and unclasped her hands, then turned to the plant-bedecked window. "I promised my grandmother I would not leave Wystan, and I certainly won't marry an Ives."

Again, he wondered about her sanity. He'd just offered marriage, and he was quite certain she had turned him down. Perhaps it was her way of driving a bargain.

He hadn't run herd on a pack of unruly siblings by losing his patience. Logic and reasoning always prevailed. He took a deep breath and counted stars in his head.

In calming his temper, he noticed delicate purple blooms on the plants she stroked. How did she make plants bloom in this light?

Shaking his head, he returned to the focus of his concentration. If there was any chance at all that Ninian carried his heir, he must have it verified immediately by a reputable physician. He'd do whatever it took to accomplish this.

"You cannot bear a child alone," he said, seeking an opening in her defenses. "Do you have other relations you can call on?" He supposed, if a marriage came of this, he ought to know who to invite. But he'd vowed not to do as his father had done. Any child of his would have a name, regardless of the mother's foolish protests.

"My aunts," she replied carelessly. "But I don't need them. I'll be fine here. I have a family trust fund."

"If we marry, you'll have more than a trust fund," he wheedled mercilessly. "You can have all of Wystan Castle, and more. But you must come to London first."

"No," she replied quietly. "I cannot."

He'd driven himself without sleep for days, worn the ragged ends of hope and despair until they'd frayed through, and his patience slipped a notch at her stubbornness. "I cannot marry you here. There is no church."

"I don't need a husband," she said indifferently. "I suppose you needed to know you've sired a child." She hesitated, and with great reluctance added, "And I suppose I cannot argue if you insist on giving her a name, since it would be for her good.

But it could not be a real marriage. If you must insist on this absurdity, it can be done across the border in Scotland. It's only a few miles away, and a church isn't needed."

"I'll not let the lawyers eat away the estates after I die while my brothers dispute the legitimacy of my son because of a heathen wedding," he shouted in frustration. "It's London and a church in front of all the witnesses of family, as befits an earl."

Her shoulders sagged. "It won't be a son. You're doomed to disappointment if that's your desire, my lord."

"I've been doomed to disappointment all my life." Growling, he returned to pacing, fighting a gnawing panic. "If we leave now, we can reach London by week's end."

She turned, and the desolation in her eyes nearly cracked Drogo's hard heart wide open. Suddenly, she seemed no longer a helpless child, but a woman who knew far too much of life's dark secrets.

"I am a witch, my lord, and from all appearances, not a very good one. Why would you take me for wife?"

Drogo thought it might be a test of some sort. He stopped in his tracks and sought some logical reason for so illogical a question. He really couldn't believe the brain behind the beauty was cracked. "You're a beautiful woman and you carry my child," he offered.

"I'm far less beautiful than Sarah's ladies, and any woman can carry a child. Send your women to me and I'll advise them of the proper phases of the moon. Or sleep with them every night without fail, and you'll be a father as often as you like."

Wondering if this pint-sized asp knew things he didn't, if possibly his hectic life with its constant interruptions that prevented his taking a regular mistress might possibly be the reason he'd never sired a child, Drogo struggled between her warped logic and his own determination. Determination won.

"I crave neither wife nor child," he assured her, although he lied about the child. He wanted this one desperately or he'd never have broken his neck to get here. The wife part bloody well worried him, but he would do whatever it took to make it work. "But a child needs a father and I would give my support. For the child's sake, come with me to London and let the physicians verify your assumption. You can always return here later."

Promising support without the threat of marriage seemed to mollify her resistance. She searched his face. "I would like to see

London and my family again, but I cannot stay, and I will not marry you," she warned. "If you want what is best for this child, you will return me here before the snow flies."

It was already August. Much later than September, and she risked herself and the child with the exigencies of travel.

It didn't matter. If she carried his child, he had no intention of returning her here unless he could come with her, which wouldn't happen until he could spare the time from his duties. That happened seldom, if at all.

But he'd won this round. In return, he offered the flattery all women liked. "That's time enough to become better acquainted with all your moods. I think I like the seductress best." Drogo brushed his fingers over her fair cheek, loving the feel of her peach-warm skin. He could have her back in his bed again.

At his impudence, Ninian slapped his hand. "Then marry an actress, my lord," she said sweetly, "not a witch."

Fourteen

"We really must clear out your musty nursery, Drogo," Sarah chattered as the coach swayed through another rut.

Fighting the churning in her stomach, Ninian glanced at the man who had fathered the child within her. Lord Ives sprawled with apparent unconcern on the leather seat across from her, his arm behind his head as he leaned against the window, one booted foot on the spare cushion beside him. Sarah accompanied them, but Lydie and Claudia had opted to stay in Wystan.

The earl didn't appear to be a man worried about his virility or considering marriage to a witch. He didn't even seem much interested in his stepsister's chatter. But Ninian sensed his tension at the word "nursery," and she thought she was possibly missing an undercurrent. Lord Ives's ability to conceal his emotions from her was a se-

vere impediment to their ever understanding each other. Absently, she stroked
the gray kitten that had hidden in their food
basket and considered the problem.

If he had no children, why would he have
a nursery? Without the perception of her
gifts, she had to reason out the undercur-
rents. Had he furnished a nursery in expectation and been disappointed?

From their conversation earlier, she
would assume so. A man did not set up a
nursery for no reason. She would feel sympathy for him, if she could. Right now, all
she could summon was stomach-churning
terror.

She had to do this, had to venture into the
outer world to seek the help and advice of
her family, to learn more of who and what
she was so that she could return with the
knowledge that would let her live among the
people of Wystan again. That her daughter
would gain the support of the Earl of Ives in
return was an added benefit. But despite all
her reasoning, the knowledge of what she
had done, and was doing, terrified her.

The earl easily controlled every aspect of
their journey. He knew every road, village,
and inn, and when and where they would arrive, barring any accident. With solicitude,
he told the coachman to halt whenever

Ninian felt queasy, stopped early at the best inns so she could rest, placed no demands on her at all — not even that she share his bed. He'd scarcely looked at her in that way, although more than once she'd caught him watching her. She didn't think her condition showed yet, but he seemed determined to detect the signs — or lack thereof.

His occasional sidelong looks stirred wistful yearnings best left buried. She would dearly love a friend, someone with whom she could share her despair and her hopes. Sarah's scheming left Ninian too wary of friendship there. She couldn't hope a busy man like Lord Ives would understand, or even care, about anything but the child she carried.

"Are we almost there?" Ninian murmured into a gap in the conversation. The sun had lowered in the western sky, casting long shadows over the road.

With indolent grace, Ives sat up and peered through the curtains. "It will be dark before we reach the house, but I think we're safe enough at this hour. Or are you growing weary? I know an inn . . ."

She shook her head. "I would be there, if you don't mind. The sooner we arrive, the sooner I can leave."

Sarah's sharp intake of breath warned she

hadn't been informed of this part of their agreement, and Ninian lifted a quizzical eyebrow.

He shook his head slightly at her in warning. "London is not so bad as that," he answered blithely. "Society will be returning from their country houses, and there will be a round of balls. Don't rush us until you've seen what we have to offer."

The conspiratorial intimacy of his look quaked her insides, but she bestowed a scowl on him and returned to watching the window. She didn't know why he protected Sarah from their arrangement, but surely it would be safe enough to visit London for a few weeks. She supposed she really ought to see her family — and her father.

Wrinkling her nose at the vision of that confrontation, she subsided into silence.

Drogo paced up and down the hallway outside the bedchamber he'd assigned to Ninian — the one adjacent to his own. With Sarah to babble, he didn't have any secrets. He'd been chided and glared at and been the recipient of more jests than he'd care to acknowledge from the array of brothers who'd straggled through the house already this morning. Joseph and David had been at school through his earlier fiascoes. They'd never let him live this one down.

Drogo could hear the physician's low murmur through the door if he tried, but he was too nervous to try. Ninian had turned stony with rage at being told she would have to submit to the indignity of a man examining her. He'd thought he would have to hold her to the bed, but he'd promised her a tour of the pleasure gardens and a visit to the seamstress to order baby linens and Sarah had whispered assurances until she'd finally capitulated. It was a damned good thing she didn't prefer gold and jewels or he'd be bankrupt within weeks. He hated being at the mercy of unpredictable females.

He detected what was almost certainly Ninian's giggle from behind the door. He'd never heard her giggle. Hell, he'd never heard her laugh at all, but he already knew she had more moods than all his brothers combined. Just what he didn't need for a wife — an emotional arsenal.

For a wife. If all went well. Not wanting to face that hurdle yet, he returned to wearing out the carpet. Was it a good sign that she was giggling and not heaving things at the physician's head? He supposed it didn't really matter. He could handle any female tantrums, much as he controlled his brothers' machinations. People were people, he reassured himself. He'd find what made her happy, she'd settle down to her own pursuits, and he could return to his. It would just be a minor upheaval considering others he'd endured in his lifetime.

If she was breeding.

Damning himself for hoping, not understanding why he hoped, Drogo stationed himself across from the door as he heard the sounds of impending departure. Leaning with one shoulder against the wall, his arms crossed, he sought an insouciant pose as the doctor stepped out, pulling the door closed after him.

The physician beamed. "Congratulations, my lord, you're about to be a father."

All the air left Drogo's lungs. His heart halted. His knees crumpled. The wall was all that held him up. He stared at the doctor's outstretched hand a moment too long before recovering and shaking it fervently, accepting the older man's too-familiar slap on the arm.

Glancing anxiously at the closed door, Drogo let the doctor find his own way out. Heart pounding so hard he thought it would break loose of his chest, he straightened his neckcloth, tugged his cuffs clear of his coat sleeves, and cautiously opened the door.

At sight of him, Ninian broke into a gale of laughter.

Obviously part of the conspiracy, Sarah joined in.

Disgruntled, Drogo glared at them both. Ninian wore only a flimsy nightshift borrowed from Sarah for the occasion. Her golden curls flowed in a cascade over the linen, but there was nothing childish about the woman sitting up against the pillows. She represented every female seductress portrayed in art or literature. She had a knowing gaze that saw straight into a man's soul, and a seductive full-lipped smile that told him she could provide all his secret desires. At the same time, she had eyes so blue and innocent he could swear she'd never taken him into her bed or spread her legs for him.

He had a momentary vision of those shapely legs spread across his bed and almost passed out from the rush of blood to his groin.

"It seems you've accomplished what others could not," he said dryly, approaching the bed with wariness.

That produced another gale of laughter.

He stood at the bedside, gazing down at the mysterious woman who would become his wife despite her protestations, and wondered what the hell he'd done. "Am I allowed to hear the jest?"

Still giggling, Ninian bit her lip and shook her head as a signal that she couldn't speak just yet. Schooling his patience, Drogo sat on the edge of the immense bed. He'd have to wallow across the covers to strangle her, he surmised. It was easier to wait.

Sarah offered her a sip of water, and gratefully, Ninian took it. She hiccuped once, then regained her composure. Drogo thought almost any other woman in the world would be looking at him skeptically about now, weighing the advantages of his wealth and title over his dubious appearance. He knew his wasn't a pretty visage, one the ladies swooned over, unless it was in fear. His thick eyebrows and dark coloring were sufficient to classify him as closer to Gypsy than earl. The sharp blade of his nose and the square angles of his jaw, not to mention his blasted height, presented a fearsome appearance. He'd used it quite successfully in terrifying his siblings into behaving.

His intended bride — not a frightened bone in her body — grinned hugely. "That was quite edifying, my lord."

Drogo shot a glare at Sarah, who hastily stood and brushed out her gown. "I'll be leaving the two of you alone now to . . . ahh, discuss the wedding." She hurried out, closing the door firmly behind her.

Drogo returned his glare to Ninian, intending his look to ask what he would not.

She sighed. "Do you never smile, my lord?"

"You have not yet met my brothers," he replied grimly. "Smiling is not the general reaction to events in this household." He waited.

She grimaced. "You really don't want to hear the reason for our laughter," she warned. "It will not make you in the least happy."

"Why does that not surprise me?" Relaxing, he leaned back against one hand. "I prefer knowledge to ignorance, however. Let me hear it."

She almost looked embarrassed. She rearranged the lacy coverlet near her breasts and looked down. "Ummm, your London physician just asked questions."

Drogo played with that for a moment, but couldn't see the humor. "And?"

"That's it, my lord. You brought me all the way to London so your physician could ask questions about what you already know for yourself." At his impatient glare, she shrugged. "He asked if we'd had 'sexual congress' and how long ago. He asked for the last date of my" — she struggled for a polite word — "woman's time. And so on. He then merrily declared me *enceinte*, and offered his congratulations."

Temper shooting from nil to explosive in a matter of seconds, Drogo forced his tone into politeness. He didn't want to terrify her. "He did not examine you?"

"Didn't touch me," she replied. "It seems that's not 'done' in polite circles."

"Sarah knew," Drogo replied through clenched teeth. "He's her physician."

Ninian grinned again. "That's why I agreed to your preposterous suggestion." Her smile slipped away. "I'm sorry, my lord. Sarah should never have written you. The only way you'll have any proof that I carry any child at all is to wait a month, until you can see for yourself. And that still won't prove the child is yours. What would you prefer I do?"

Her only concern seemed to be for him. That struck Drogo as odd to the extreme, but the puzzle she presented demanded his attention more. He couldn't believe her wanton enough to have slept with any other man. He accepted that he was the only devil in her bed. But he definitely wanted to ascertain her pregnancy before he committed both of them to an institution in which his family had never fared well. Maybe she wasn't trying to trick him, but she could be mistaken. She might have some passing malady.

"Then we must wait a month," he decided reasonably.

Any other woman would be indignant. This one took his delay with indifference. "My only interest is in doing what is best for the child. I think it will be good for her to have a father who acknowledges her and will support her should anything happen to me. Beyond that, I merely ask that I be returned to Wystan as soon as possible."

She had as odd a notion of parenthood as his parents. Drogo didn't intend to inform her that he kept what was his, and that included her as well as the child. It didn't matter if he'd impregnated a maid or a witch. He'd accept the responsibility and the burden.

Maybe in a month's time she would come to enjoy what the city had to offer and not have any interest in returning to the cold dreariness of the north. It would behoove him to work toward that goal.

He cast an interested gaze to the swelling curves above her bodice. "Would you care to take more chances at conception, as a precaution against disappointment?"

He watched as her nipples tightened and

thrust against the thin cloth, until she hastily pulled the covers up to her chin. "Not a chance, my lord. If you can't trust my word, I'd spend the rest of my life locked up in this room."

Adjusting the suddenly too-tight press of his breeches, Drogo admitted the truth of that. He'd not only seen too many cases of marital infidelity, but he'd been victim of female treachery one too many times. He preferred the certainty of the stars in the heavens over the vagaries of human nature.

He nodded curtly and rose from the bed. "I'll have Sarah take you 'round to the dressmakers. You'll be entertaining for a few months, at least. Spend what you wish."

He strode out, leaving Ninian staring after his broad back long after he'd departed. Months? Had he said "months"? Surely, she was mistaken. Or had it been a slip of the tongue? The earl had much on his mind and hadn't paid attention to what he said.

She smoothed the soft fabric taut across her slightly rounded belly. It was impossible to tell what was her and what was the infant. She just didn't doubt its existence in the least — unlike the poor babe's confused father.

If she'd been impregnated by the devil, he

was a fascinating one, at least.

She had to quit thinking like a supersti-tious, ignorant villager. She was in London now. She must learn from her betters and enlarge her education.

She sighed and collapsed against the mountain of lacy pillows. Maybe she shouldn't have refused his offer of another tumble in bed.

But the blasted man thought she *lied*. She'd have to teach him better than that.

Fifteen

Gut churning in frustration after leaving Ninian's chamber, Drogo eluded his brothers and bolted the door to his study.

To have the damned doctor grant all his hopes in one minute, and have them dashed by Ninian the next, was too much for his shattered nerves. Ten in the morning, and he needed a brandy.

He didn't pour one. He couldn't teach his brothers not to imbibe like drunkards if he did so himself. The mantle of responsibility was a damned nuisance. Just once, he'd like to get drunk, throw a tantrum, or in some way behave as monstrously as the rest of the family.

But then, who would rescue him when he got thrown in Old Bailey? Despite their generous allowances, not a one of them would have a farthing saved to bail him out.

Ignoring the mountain of ledgers from his

various estates and enterprises — ledgers on which he'd cut his first mathematical teeth — Drogo picked up the sheet of calculations he'd begun in Wystan. If he was right, he could very well have discovered a new planet. That accomplishment was surely greater than producing a child. Anyone could produce a child.

Sighing in exasperation as his thoughts instantly returned to the woman upstairs, Drogo whittled at his pen nib. No matter how he denied it, something very human in him would like to have a son, even if he didn't need one.

So, there was his weakness. Everyone was entitled to at least one. He wanted Ninian to be breeding. He wanted to watch his child grow, dandle a babe on his knee, teach his son to ride and search the night skies for stars. He wanted to show all of London that he could produce an heir and a spare, just as his father had.

Pride goeth before a fall, he muttered, applying his attention to his calculations.

A discreet knock at the door interrupted his concentration.

Drogo considered ignoring it, except he knew none of his brothers would rap discreetly. They'd pound and yell. It had to be Jarvis, who would never disturb him for anything less than a crisis involving spurting jugulars.

Perhaps one of the dolts had experimented with flying and broke his fall on a vegetable cart. It would be easier if they'd just get drunk and gamble like normal people. Ives males had never been known for normality.

Dropping his pen in the stand, Drogo unbolted the door. A florid, dapper gentleman shoved past Jarvis, shouting something incomprehensible about "daughters" and "responsibility." Jarvis, straight-faced, merely bowed and shut the door, leaving Drogo trapped with a raving lunatic. Lunatics seemed to be popular these days. He wondered if it was an epidemic.

Since he had no daughters and couldn't remember dallying irresponsibly lately, Drogo merely took his chair and waited for the old fellow to rant it out. Of a decade-old fashion, his caller's clothes had seen better days, now that Drogo observed more closely. Although impeccably pressed and cleaned, the frock coat's gold buttons had gone missing at the top, and his neckcloth linen was thin enough to read through. His old-fashioned bagwig had lost a curl on one side, causing a decidedly lopsided look. A gentleman, but one fallen on hard times.

"If you do not do right by her, I'll call you out, sir!" the gentleman shouted. "She's my only daughter, and I'll not see her ruined by an unprincipled rake!"

Unprincipled rake? Drogo considered that unexpected and rather dashing image of himself. Perhaps the man was referring to one of his brothers. Admittedly, he wasn't a monk, but these days he limited his attentions to courtesans and widows and other would-be countesses. He wasn't much inclined toward virgin . . . Ninian.

With a nasty taste in his mouth to add to the churning in his gut, Drogo asked him, "Might I have the pleasure of your name, sir?" he asked icily, hoping for a madman, but preparing for the worst.

The stout gentleman drew himself to his full height — a good head shorter than Drogo's. "Viscount Siddons, sir, father of the child you've molested and hidden away in your house of horrors. I demand satisfaction, sir. I *demand* it, I say!"

Dumbfounded at both the accusation and the knowledge that the little midwife had a father among the *ton,* Drogo sought a conciliatory reply. After all, he had done just as the viscount said, although calling this old tomb a house of horrors was pushing it a little far.

Before a sufficient reply came to mind, the study door silently slid open. In astonishment, Drogo watched as Ninian wafted in, just as if he'd called for her — or as if her father's rage had drawn her like a magnet.

"Hello, Father." Self-consciously, she pulled at the billowing skirt Sarah had apparently dressed her in.

The pale yellow didn't suit her, Drogo decided, but the expanse of the panniers was very effective in distancing her from the room's occupants. As Drogo rose at her entrance, she scarcely looked at him. She didn't seem inclined to embrace her father either.

The viscount looked stupefied at the vision of loveliness addressing him. Embarrassed, he stuttered a bit before remembering his purpose. He swung to face Drogo. "This is an outrage! You will marry her at once, I say."

Drogo detected a hint of amusement in Ninian's tone as she interrupted the tirade.

"How are you, Father? You look well. In case you're wondering, I am quite fine."

"I can see that," the old man said testily, returning his gaze to her. "Decked out in all the finery he's bought you. Well, no daughter of mine —"

"Grandmother died last winter," Ninian

interrupted again, obviously pursuing her own goals. "I wrote and told you and you didn't reply."

"The old witch left you plenty enough to live on, and you've got wealthier than me to call on, if she didn't." The viscount huffed and glared. "It's not as if you ever expressed any interest in living with your poor old father."

Drogo saw the sadness behind Ninian's smile even if her father didn't. Perhaps he didn't know much of the mysterious little witch, but he'd just learned a little more. She had a heart, and it broke as easily as anyone else's. He understood the need for a parent's approval, and the despair at a parent's rejection. The viscount had left Ninian alone and at the tender mercies of the world in favor of the comforts of London. Drogo's defensive instincts rose without hesitation.

She was to be his wife. She deserved his protection, whether she wanted it or not. Gently, he rested his hands on her shoulders and looking over her head, forced her father to face her completely.

"I had no interest in living in London," she corrected. "And no interest in asking Grandmother to support me without giving her anything in return. You, on the other hand, only wished to be free to spend my mother's money without acknowledging where it came from. It comes from Malcolms, Father. Don't you think it might be tainted?"

"That's all faradiddle the old biddy's filled your head with! You're my daughter, and there's the end of it."

"I'm my mother's daughter, and deny it as she might have, my mother was a Malcolm witch, just like me."

The viscount harrumphed and reddened slightly, then swung his gaze up to Drogo. "No matter, any of this. You've ruined her, and you'll pay the price."

Like a candle flame, Ninian brightened the darkness her father cast. Amusement again laced her voice. Never hasty to speak, Drogo let her have her moment.

"No, he won't, Father. Grandmother's trust is mine, to do with as I wish. Even should we marry, Lord Ives cannot give it to you."

That was the first Drogo had heard of this. He wasn't certain he approved of a woman possessing her own funds — especially one with as befuddled a mind as hers. He didn't need her pennies, though, and he rather enjoyed the way she flaunted them in her father's face. He just didn't wish the scene to descend to the hysterical. "I think,

231

perhaps, my dear," he interrupted cautiously, "your father merely wishes to ascertain that marriage is what I had in mind when I brought you here."

Over her shoulder, she threw him a look of annoyance with nothing befuddled about it. "My father is always short of funds, although I suppose I can give him credit for not actually trying to sell me."

"Ninian!" the viscount shouted, outraged all over again.

"Marriage among the aristocracy is a form of monetary exchange," Drogo clarified for her, pacifying the old man's temper. Ninian looked more amused than irritated at his generous interpretation. "Perhaps, if you'll excuse us, I can assure your father that I am an honorable man."

"It should be interesting to know how much I'm worth, my lord. Just remember while you're haggling that I can only bear daughters, that I'm a witch, although he'll deny it, and I have no intention of marrying." She said the last quite emphatically, before slipping from his hands and out the door, taking the sunshine with her.

Drogo sank into his chair again. The viscount wiped his brow with a wide handkerchief. The faint scent of roses and pine lingered between them, along with the image of golden curls and female mockery. Drogo thought he had a better definition of "witch" now. The blasted woman could read minds.

"I wish you well of her, my lord," the viscount said heavily, sinking into a leather chair without invitation. "Her mother was a delight, a pure delight. The most beautiful woman, with the sweetest nature, you've ever met. But those harridans she calls family . . ." He shivered in remembrance.

"Ninian is an exceptional young woman." Drogo thought it wise to defend the potential mother of his child. He also thought it wise to find out more. "She mentioned aunts . . . ?" Discovering a viscount on the family tree was shock enough. He had been dilatory in researching his potential bride. He would correct that immediately.

Muttering, the viscount shoved his handkerchief back in his pocket and cursed as the pocket corner tore. "Persephone — my wife — was the youngest, so they didn't mind if she married a mere viscount," he explained disparagingly. "But Stella and Hermione . . ." He rolled his eyes. "Stella is the Duchess of Mainwaring. Hermione is the Marchioness of Hampton. And in case you're wondering, they both thoughtfully married widowers who already had heirs.

They've got half a dozen girls or more between them, last I counted. All the babes my wife lost were girls, too." He looked chagrined. "Couldn't be less than honest about that."

A marchioness and a duchess! Drogo collapsed against his chair back and groaned mentally. He'd bedded a simpleton in peasant's clothes and acquired a family more powerful than his own. The little matters of an all-female family or lunacy or even witchcraft scarcely compared in importance to a duchess and a marchioness. He could take care of himself, but his family's reputation was precarious, at its best. He would not destroy any chances his brothers had to make places of their own in the world by creating powerful enemies.

"What the hell was she doing living like a peasant in Wystan?" he demanded, for lack of anything more rational to say as he struggled with a world turned upside down.

The viscount shrugged. "She's a Malcolm and the old virago's heir. Ask them."

Drogo groaned mentally and surrendered the struggle. He'd lost any choice in whether or not he would marry Ninian in a month's time. He'd ruined a flower of the aristocracy, and he knew the penalty, even if his intended bride did not. He would worry about how to tell her later, when his head quit screaming. He bit down hard on a candy from the dish in his desk.

"I'll apply for the license in the morning." Drogo forced himself to speak calmly. "We'll be married in four weeks' time, so Ninian may prepare her bride clothes. I'll be happy to discuss the settlements."

Viscount Siddons brightened.

He might as well make peace with his prospective father-in-law. The viscount might be the only ally he'd find in a marriage with an unwilling bride from a matriarchy containing both a duchess and a marchioness.

No wonder Siddons never had any money, Drogo concluded as he wandered the dark halls to his bedchamber later that night. The man didn't know a valuable when he saw one, and he couldn't drive a bargain to save his life. The viscount's only interest had been obtaining whatever amount he'd felt his mother-in-law had deprived him of by keeping it in trust rather than giving it to him upon his wife's death.

Since Drogo had no idea what funds Ninian possessed, he'd told the old man they'd have to wait until they'd located her solicitor. He'd seen how Ninian lived. She couldn't have much. Good thing the viscount didn't seem to realize Drogo would willingly pay half his fortune for a wife who carried his child. His brothers would strangle him if they knew the depths of his obsession. Fortunately, it looked as if he'd acquired her cheaply.

As things stood, though, he had no choice but to take Ninian for wife, even if she carried no child. He could feel his last chance of progeny seeping away, his only hope hanging by the bare thread of Ninian's honesty. Perhaps he could seek solace in the knowledge that with Ninian as wife, he'd never have an empty bed. He could easily adapt to a lifetime of nights like the one they'd shared. If the actuality was even half so good as his memory of that night, it would be more than enough to keep him satiated and happy.

He didn't think he'd tell Ninian of their impending marriage just yet. No point in starting out on the wrong foot. Let her formidable aunts be the bearer of bad tidings.

On impulse, he stopped at Ninian's chamber door. Sarah had taken her shopping, he knew. They'd probably run up his accounts in every establishment in the city, most of it for Sarah. It was a game she liked to play, helping out with their brothers and helping herself at the same time. She knew he knew it. She knew he'd make her pay in other ways. He hadn't figured out how to make her pay for a disaster of this proportion.

Drogo knocked, and received a vague acknowledgment he assumed meant welcome. He'd never kept a woman in this house, not with his brothers appearing unexpectedly at inopportune times. He was trying to adjust to the idea of having a woman at his beck and call. He opened the door without further hesitation.

Bareheaded, hair curling in wild lengths over her linen chemise, Ninian stood on the cushions of the window seat, staring over the London rooftops. She didn't even turn to see who entered.

"The fog is like an unhealthy wraith stealing down the chimneys," she observed. "It's a wonder anyone survives the air. Are you ready to send me home yet, my lord?"

She had sounded brave enough when she'd confronted her father, but he heard her sadness now. Drogo doubted he had the ability to assuage it since he had no intention of playing the role of father. Still, he could offer what little comfort he possessed. He reached for an unlit candle. "If you'll climb down from there and pull the draperies, I'll light this, and you'll find no fog in here."

She crossed her arms and didn't move. "I don't need light to know what's here. Has my father convinced you that I am a ruined woman and you must marry me and turn over all my funds to him?"

"Your father couldn't convince a cat to drink milk," he observed wryly, as the kitten leapt from a chair to wrap around his ankles. "We've sent for your grandmother's solicitor to determine the legality of the trust. You needn't worry. The money will remain yours, no matter what they decide. I don't have need of it."

Gazing upon voluptuous curves silhouetted in the window, Drogo wanted her with an urgency so potent he almost crossed the room and dragged her from her perch. If he had to marry her anyway, what difference did it make if she carried a child or not?

Because she knew as well as he that he'd never trust her out of his sight until he knew she was safely bearing his seed, and that could mean keeping her prisoner here forever if he bedded her now. He'd already harmed her enough.

Ninian climbed down from the seat of her own volition. He could barely discern her silhouette against the fading light of the moon, but she was round in all the places he craved, curved in all the places he wanted to hold. Like some pagan fertility goddess, she exuded sexuality, and he was drawn to her like a condemned man to freedom.

"I'm to trust your word as you trust mine?" she asked sweetly.

She had him there. He didn't light the candle but admired the shimmer of a golden curl. Grateful she didn't condemn him, he kept his voice even. "We'll learn. I'm a patient man."

She laughed lightly, a fairy breeze more than a human sound. "You're a stubborn man, my lord. I may not be able to read you as I read others, but I know that much."

She would be his wife. He didn't know what to expect of one. He certainly didn't know what to expect of one as fey as this. One moment, she glittered with moonlit seduction, the next, she teased like a child. He'd seen her tears and heard her laughter. Wary, he remained where he was. "I have found that I accomplish my goals better when I give up no ground," he admitted.

"It seems that you stubbornly kept trying until you found the woman who could give you a child," she acknowledged. She stood within reach, tempting him. "You *will* be a father come the new year, I promise. But that doesn't change anything. I'm still a witch, and my place is still in Wystan. I must return there."

"One thing at a time, moonchild," he answered gravely, keeping his distance and promising nothing.

Sixteen

Given the freedom of Drogo's absence while he conferred with his men of business, Ninian spent the next morning exploring his world. Apparently the Ives family didn't believe in selling property just because it was no longer in a fashionable neighborhood.

The deteriorating old house near Charing Cross overlooked a street crowded with fish and vegetable carts as well as court carriages carrying the aristocracy from the center of town to the newer suburbs of St. James and Hanover Square. The once sedate area teemed with so many lives and emotions that it formed a kind of dull roar to her extra sense. Ninian missed the quietness of Wystan, but the cacophony of sensation didn't affect her as much as it had as a child. Perhaps she had learned to live with her gift a little better since her last sojourn in London.

241

The old house rambled through dark rooms with narrow windows much as the old castle did, but apparently Sarah hadn't been allowed to interfere here. Without a woman's touch, it harbored drafty fireplaces, soot-coated carpets, and tottering furniture. The library contained not only books, but also bridles, saddles, and a sadly worn pair of boots.

Ninian had sought the library hoping to find a book on water or blights, but after an hour of fruitless searching, she had found nothing.

Setting a book back on the shelf, she noticed a light glimmering through the shabby draperies in a connecting room, illuminating entire villages of small wooden buildings scattered across the fading carpet. Drawn to investigate, she discovered each represented an architectural work of art. Some were of churches she recognized, some of buildings she assumed were the Houses of Parliament. The ones she liked best were of lovely homes with gracefully arched windows and pediments and delicate porticoes.

"That's the house I want to build."

Startled, Ninian nearly dropped the model in her hand as she swung to face a man who was considerably younger than

Drogo, and not nearly as formidable. Still, the shock of midnight hair, planed jaw, and wide shoulders marked him as an Ives.

He shrugged diffidently as he sauntered into the room, but Ninian recognized his curiosity as his gaze swept her from head to foot. She guessed him to be younger than herself, but still very much a forceful male animal.

She held out the model of a Palladian mansion. "It is quite lovely."

He took the model and held it up to the spare light from the dirty window. "They're easily done. Most of them are copies. I want to design buildings of my own." As if realizing his rudeness, he lowered the hand holding the model. "I'm Joseph, the eldest of the bastard brothers."

Ninian blinked in surprise at this blunt introduction. She was beginning to believe the danger of Ives men was their power to turn Malcolm women into stunned puppets. She nodded tentatively in greeting. "I'm Ninian Siddons." She didn't dare introduce herself as a witch, although the shock value seemed relevant.

"I know. Sarah told us." He set the model on a table. "Women don't last long in this family. My mother refuses to live here. Drogo's mother left long ago."

Ninian's expressive gesture took in the dismal room and a dying potted plant. "I can't imagine why. I thought the harp with harpsichord keys very inventive, and I'm certain that contraption in the dining parlor has an excellent purpose."

Joseph fought the beginning of a grin as he glanced around at the chaos of toy models that rendered the sofas and chairs useless. "Ewen wanted more sound out of the harp, and William thought he could speed delivery of meals with the other contraption. I prefer building things to tearing them apart."

She nodded as if she understood completely. "An excellent philosophy, I'm sure, given the state of things around here." She didn't remember Sarah mentioning a William, but if all the brothers were this imaginative, perhaps one of them could shed light on the dilemma of the fouled burn while she was here. "William?" she inquired.

Embarrassed, Joseph shrugged. "Ummm, our half brother by the dairy maid."

Ninian thought that was more than she needed to know, and changed the subject. "Are there servants, or is someone building them also?"

"Drogo threatened to disown the next one of us who tried to make a better servant.

Mostly, they stay out of our way. Do you play cards?"

"Ninian! Ninian, where are you, dear?"

Looking up from her attempt to learn piquet from Joseph — who had an extraordinary method of counting cards she didn't think quite fair — Ninian tilted her head and listened to the emotional weather storm racing her aunt down the hall. She might learn to live with the roar of London's populace outside the door, but tempestuous individuals like her aunt could still shatter her serenity.

"So, does she always sound like a battle-ax dripping honey or does she reserve that voice for straying nieces?" Joseph asked, raking in his winnings. They were playing for Drogo's sweetmeats since neither of them had any coins.

"How do you know who she is?" Ninian demanded. The perceptiveness of Drogo's half brother left her wondering if he wasn't half witch, or warlock, himself.

"I spy." He winked, and a thick black curl fell over his forehead.

She kicked his ankle under the table as the Duchess of Mainwaring sailed through the open doors. In the last few days Ninian had met three of Drogo's half brothers, and she understood well his need to remain in London to keep the lot of them under lock and key.

"There you are, Ninian, darling!"

Rising from the table, Ninian let herself be engulfed in her aunt's sweet-powdered, rustling silk as the duchess hugged her and kissed both cheeks.

"It's good to see you, Aunt Stella." She coughed as several pounds of powder wafted through the air between them. Apparently her aunt had decided to storm the bastions in full battle gear: powdered wig, powdered cheeks, and powdered silk, all reeking of expensive Malcolm perfumes. "How did you know to find me here?"

"A little birdie told me, of course." Her aunt trilled with false laughter, glared at Joseph, who sat taking in the scene with a huge grin, then tugged Ninian's elbow. "Come, let us have a little girl talk. Where is your sitting room?"

As if Ninian had always had sitting rooms. Sighing, she shrugged at Joseph and led the way down the hall to her chamber. Sarah was visiting, and Drogo was at the solicitor's with her father — again. She supposed Aunt Stella had used her "gifts" to time this visit for a moment when her niece had no defenders. Stella didn't precisely read minds;

she just knew what everyone was doing and when. It was a distinction that eluded Ninian.

With the thoroughness of a general on a battlefield, Stella swept through the bedchamber Ninian had been assigned. She nodded approvingly at the small fire burning on the grate, raised an eyebrow at the gold satin hangings of the enormous bed, and checked the adjoining door to Ninian's dressing room, and the one leading into the next chamber.

"Why isn't there a fire in there?" she demanded, sweeping back from the luxuriously furnished sitting room. "And is that *his* room on the other side?"

"I don't need two fires," Ninian answered, unperturbed, "and I assume it's his lordship's dressing room on the other side, just as mine connects here."

"You *assume?* You mean you don't know? You're living here in the chambers assigned for mistress of the household, and you've never been inside his rooms? Have you or have you not married the Ives devil?"

Ninian opened her mouth, but nothing pertinent emerged. How did she explain her current situation to her formidable aunt? She had done the unforgivable, mated with an Ives, and it did look highly suspicious that she now resided in his home, even with Sarah as companion. She'd assumed this was the only empty bedroom, given the comings and goings of Drogo's brothers, but it must look even worse if this was the chamber intended for the lady of the house.

Still, she would willingly share Drogo's bed again once he believed her about the babe, so her aunt would just have to get used to it. Gradually, perhaps.

"His lordship's sister invited me to London," she said. "I thought you would be in the country at this time of year."

"You won't come to the city when we invite you, but you'll come for the likes of that flibbertigibbet? Fustian!" She paced, examining every ornament on the shelves.

"Aunt Stella, are you here for a reason? I know how busy you are, so I'm sure you'll want to return to the demands of your family as soon as possible. How may I help?"

"You sound just like my mother, may the goddess preserve her." Huffing, Stella flounced her silk and panniers into one of the fireside chairs. Her elegantly curled wig tilted slightly, and she shoved it indecorously back in place and glared at Ninian as if it were her fault. "Sit, child. Tell me why on earth you're here."

"Because I thought it would be nice to see my family again?" she asked disingenuously, using her best dimpled smile. "Because I was lonely all by myself?"

"Nonsense." Stella sat back so hard, she raised another cloud of powder. "You're breeding. Even I can tell that. I haven't seen a notice in the paper. Where the devil is your father? Ives may think he's above the rest of us, but by my faith, he'll —"

"And a good day to you, too, Your Grace."

Gasping, Ninian swung around to find Drogo lounging in the doorway, his broad shoulder propped against the doorjamb, his curled eyebrows raised in devilment. She wanted to slap him for sneaking up on her like that. No one could ever sneak up on her as easily, not even his brothers. But he looked so imposing in his flared black coat and lace-frilled jabot, she couldn't help but admire the picture. He winked.

She definitely wanted to slap him.

"There you are, you young scapegrace! What do you intend to do about my niece?"

"Make her my wife, of course." He strolled into the room and propped a proprietary hand on the chair behind Ninian. The lace of his cuff brushed her shoulders, and a shiver quaked deliciously across her skin. "What else does one do with the most beautiful, most talented woman in the world?"

Perhaps she would kill him. Slapping didn't seem quite sufficient. A good sound curse to start with, then pins through his limbs . . .

"She'll not breed you sons, Ives," Stella said bluntly. "And your family has a poor reputation in the marriage mart. Ninian is special, as you've obviously discovered if it's your child she's breeding."

Ninian interrupted their mutual posturing. "I have no interest in marriage. Malcolms cannot marry Ives, and I cannot live in London, so the matter is quite decided."

Hidden beneath her hair, Drogo's fingers scratched gently at her nape. She hated the way his touch sent gooseflesh up and down her arms. It had been well over three months since he'd taught her the pleasures of her body, and the mere touch of his hand reminded her of all that they'd done, of what they could do again, if her aunt would just end this nonsensical argument.

"Nonsense," Drogo said quietly.

"Fustian!" Stella shouted. Then realizing what Drogo had said, she glared at him. "I take it the matter isn't quite decided?"

"I have found the most beautiful, talented

woman in the world, but she's also the most unpredictable and thoroughly incomprehensible creature alive. You'll have to give me time to bring her around to our way of thinking." Drogo sounded almost apologetic.

Ninian would wager he didn't look in the least apologetic. She started to utter a scathing reply, but his fingers squeezed her neck warningly.

"Well." Stella threw her hands in her lap, and her panniers sailed upward. Oblivious, she focused on Ninian. "My mother has filled your head with foolishness, no doubt, but I'm head of the family now, and it's best you listen to me, young lady. It's a pity you won't be able to give Ives his heir, but he has brothers aplenty who will do their duty in time. Your duty is to that daughter you carry. Should anything happen to you, she will need the support of all the family she can get. She'd be lost with the rest of us, just as you were, but as an Ives, she will be treated like a queen. They don't get girls often."

The duchess looked to Drogo. "You've spoken to that worthless father of hers?"

"We've reached an agreement," he said solemnly. "I have the license. You are all welcome to the ceremony and breakfast, once I persuade your niece to the proprieties."

Stella glared at Ninian. "There's little enough we can do now that you've done the thing, except hope for the best. He'll wed you, and you may come live with us afterward, if you wish. You needn't stay with the devils; they'll run you mad."

Ninian knit her fingers together. "I'm a healer, Aunt. My duty is to Wystan," she murmured, not expecting anyone to understand or even listen. Drogo and her aunt both seemed to consider her wishes far less important than this legendary meeting of Malcolm and Ives.

"Of course you are, dear." Stella leaned forward and patted her hand. "But you have a husband and child who need you more. Family comes first."

Stella truly believed what she said. Since the villagers had turned their backs on Ninian, her aunt might be right, but then, of what use were her gifts? The people of London would only laugh at her, as her father did. "But I have no purpose here," she protested.

"All sciences require study," Drogo said reflectively from behind her, as if reading her mind. "Perhaps you could spend your time here learning more about herbs and medicines. I could introduce you to a few botanists."

"Ninian doesn't need idiot men." Stella bustled to her feet and focused her mighty forces on Drogo. "Her talent is natural. You'll marry her, give the child a name, and let her do as she wishes. That will teach you to keep your breeches buttoned. You might teach those rogue brothers of yours the same."

Ignoring the argument, Ninian considered Drogo's proposal. If she stayed here, she could learn more of why the plants at the burn had died and perhaps prevent it from happening again. She'd already studied her grandmother's limited library and found nothing. Perhaps it was time she ventured further. But marriage?

She tilted her head so she could see Drogo's sharp features. She knew he wasn't a particularly harsh man; his responsibilities just made him look stern. She liked him well enough, for what little she knew of him. She knew two things, though — he desperately wanted the child she carried, and she had no fear of their marriage bed. Was that enough on which to base a marriage? Both Drogo and her aunt seemed to think so.

"I'm a healer, not a countess," she said over top of their running argument, stopping both Drogo and her aunt in mid-speech.

Drogo looked down on her with the patronizing expression she knew she'd have to wipe off his face sooner or later. "The title is just a word," he reassured her. "What's more important is that you will be my wife and mother of my child."

Ninian turned to her aunt. "If I marry him, he will be my husband, as well as an Ives. You will have to accept him and his family as they are, despite the legend. Do you think the family can do that?"

Stella's lips tightened. "It will not last. No Ives marriage ever does. And no Malcolm could tolerate an Ives for long. It is a measure of your talent that the two of you came together without killing each other. But the child must have a name."

Drogo's hand tightened on her shoulder. Ninian couldn't read his emotion as she read others, but she could tell just from the way he touched her that he was troubled by her aunt's words. She supposed he had a right to be. She searched his impassive expression. "Are you certain this is what you want to do, my lord?"

She thought his gaze softened slightly as he looked down on her.

"I think we will rub along nicely. We're

two intelligent people capable of discussing problems rather than emoting them."

Those weren't the most reassuring words she'd ever heard. She'd spent the better part of a lifetime containing her volatile nature so as not to frighten the villagers. She supposed she could continue doing so, for the sake of the child. She just wasn't certain she wanted to do it for Drogo's sake.

She eyed him skeptically. "I tend to solve problems rather than discuss them, but I could learn, I suppose."

"There, that's settled," Stella announced, as if that admission sealed the matter. "I recommend St. John's. They've had experience with Malcolm ceremonies. I'll take care of that. If you're planning on having the breakfast here, you'd best find more servants. Your entry hall is a scandal, and the parlor not much better. Ninian has been raised for more important concerns than dealing with servants."

Ninian was beginning to recognize the dry humor of Drogo's brittle voice as he accepted Stella's orders. "I'll see that it's done, Your Grace."

Ninian didn't bother seeing her aunt out. With fingers still clenched tightly, she stared into the fire, waiting for Drogo to leave. He didn't.

After closing the door behind her aunt, he settled into the chair Stella had forsaken. His long legs sprawled across the space between them, shoving aside her full skirts as he leaned forward and tried to force her to look at him. She wouldn't.

"The child deserves a name." He took her hands and pried them open.

"You believe there is one, then?" She darted a look to his face, saw the thoughtful frown, and knew he didn't.

"It doesn't matter much, does it? If there is one, it will be provided for. I'd not meant to marry, so there is no harm done."

Scowling, Ninian jerked her hands from his. "And what if I'd meant to marry? Does my opinion not matter?"

Now that he had her attention, he sat back and draped an arm over the chair back. "Who would you marry? Nasty Nate? I sent him to the coal mines to work. He needed something better to do with his time than tickle the lasses. Is marriage to me so appalling?"

"I can't know that, can I?"

Drogo sat perfectly still until his eyes compelled her to stare into them, and she couldn't look away.

"You have the means to walk out on me should I ever lift a hand to you. I know you don't fear me. What else can I do to persuade you this is best for the child?"

Her hand rested over the place where their child slept. Her own father had rejected her because of who she was. She couldn't bear her daughter to suffer the same. Drogo had the power of great pain in his hands, and the legend claimed Ives men wielded it well. He was a natural philosopher who would never believe in witches.

He was a man who desperately craved a child. A man who had loved her well and would do so again, should she let him.

"Your daughter will be a witch, just as I am," she said softly. "Can you accept us?"

"I will accept that's what you believe," he said carefully, "if you will accept that I can't believe in the supernatural. I believe you are beautiful and will make a wonderful mother and that we can be happy together, if we try. Is that not enough?"

She felt his words deep down inside her, in the empty places he'd explored and made his. Some part of her already belonged to him. She couldn't tear her gaze away as she studied his words. Could she trust him? She was accustomed to knowing enough of people to trust them implicitly or be wary. With Drogo, she was at a loss.

His eyes promised sincerity, but even if

she dismissed superstition and instinct, she had no experience with men to know whether to believe the promises of eyes.

Shaken, confused, she didn't know what to do. She dug her fingers into her palms and stared into the fire. All she had to do was go against all she knew — as she had already done — with such disastrous results.

Perhaps this was for the best. The people of Wystan no longer wanted or needed her. She had a responsibility to the child she carried, and she couldn't punish the man before her for what had happened in the past. Maybe the worst was over, and it was time to look forward, to explore the world beyond the one her grandmother had known.

Not looking at him, she bowed her head in surrender. "I don't seem to have much choice, my lord. I will try to be as you say."

He caught her hand and kissed it, and Ninian knew the thrill of physical excitement. They would be married, and she could share his bed again.

Somehow, she would have to learn to be true to herself in a world that didn't recognize her talents.

Seventeen

"I'm not sure this is for the best, my dear."

Ninian's aunt, the Marchioness of Hampton, anxiously tugged one of her silk scarves through her fingers as she drifted about Ninian's sitting room. Without her usual wig or pomade, her short frazzled yellow curls bounced and sprung about her face as she whirled around. "I know Stella believes it's best, but he's an *Ives*, dear. They are barely civilized. And you know what the tale tells us. I cannot believe they've changed all that much over the years. They don't *believe* in us, Ninian. We simply can't survive like that."

Aunt Hermione was the younger and gentler of her aunts. She had a gift for creating perfumes that brought out the best in everyone, and her subtle lily-of-the-valley scent wafted through the room as she paced. She literally exuded gentleness and reassurance so that Ninian had to smile, even as she disagreed.

"The tale tells us that we cannot survive if *we* deny what we are," Ninian said, "not if others deny us. I have no intention of pretending I'm anything else but a witch, and Drogo accepts that. He doesn't understand, admittedly, but he's willing to accept me as I am." Yet, even as she said it, doubt niggled.

Could she live with mere tolerance? That was second cousin to rejection, and she'd experienced enough of that for a lifetime.

How could she do what she must and be an Ives countess, too? Drogo would demand that she behave as a wife, and her tendency was to please him. If he did not understand, she wouldn't be able to help the village. Already, she felt torn in two.

Was this the danger of an Ives, then? Did they have their own power of bewitchment in the strength and confidence with which they convinced a woman that she craved their shelter?

It had been much too easy to retreat behind Drogo when the villagers turned their backs on her. She had turned coward and forgotten her responsibility. Drogo might repair the damage wrought by the storm with hammers and hoes, but people weren't so easily cured. They needed her, whether they knew it or not.

Perhaps the legend's warning that disaster would follow the joining of Ives and Malcolm had more than one meaning. A Malcolm witch diverted from her true purpose might perish from neglect, as surely as the burn was dying from her ignorance.

She had to return to Wystan. If he wished, Drogo could come to her when he had the time and inclination. Surely, Drogo in small doses would be less overwhelming than Drogo haunting her every move. She simply must be firm, as she had not been in the past.

Hermione glanced out the window, and her pale, delicate brow wrinkled at the sight below. "That must be an Ives arriving now. He doesn't look happy, my dear. You simply have no idea what kind of family you are entering into . . ."

Ninian could feel the thundercloud of anger drifting in as the butler answered the knock at the front door. She hadn't met this Ives, whichever one it was. Aunt Hermie was right. He was definitely not a happy man. "I don't sense any danger, Aunt Hermione. I know Drogo's brothers are a bit rough around the edges, but they're quite interesting young men. Could it really hurt for us to know them better?"

Hermione looked at her with curiosity. "Stella holds the reins because she is eldest, but Mother chose you to follow in her footsteps. You are the one with her abilities. Is this what she would have chosen for you? What of Wystan? Are you not needed there?"

Ninian hid her discomfort by peering out the window. Apparently, the visitor had entered but had not asked for her. She needn't go down and greet him.

"I think, for a while, I must learn of other people and places, Aunt Hermie," she said slowly, unskillfully working her way through a maze of logic. "The people of Wystan have turned to Drogo, not me. There must be a reason. And perhaps if I am gone for a while, they will forget their prejudice when I return."

Hermione sighed, wrapped a pink silk scarf around her throat, and patted Ninian's shoulder. "Well, I always thought you much too intelligent to be buried alive in Wystan. Perhaps you're right, dear. I just wanted you to know that you and the babe always have a home with us, whatever you decide. If we learned nothing else from that old tale, it's that Malcolms must look out for themselves."

"I must make a new perfume for you,"

Hermione said in a firmer voice. "You've outgrown the old one."

She swept out, leaving Ninian watching the street below for Drogo's arrival.

After a particularly argumentative session of Parliament, Drogo stormed into the house, threw his hat toward the hall table, and watched blankly as it hit the floor. He was quite certain there had been a table there just that morning.

Shrugging, he left the hat where it had fallen and strode to his study where he kept a decanter of brandy. A man was allowed a glass of brandy in the evening. It was practically a social requirement. He just didn't feel sociable right now.

Entering the study, he halted in amazement at the sight of Dunstan gazing into a potted plant that had miraculously begun shooting out new leaves these past weeks. Drogo wasn't even certain why the plant was in front of his window or who had first moved it there. It had served as the repository of cigar ashes and leftover brandy in a dark corner of the room for as long as he could remember.

"It's growing," Dunstan said in greeting, without turning to see who had entered. Evidence that this brother didn't idle his time behind a desk rippled in the thick muscles of his broad back and shoulders straining at the seams of a coat three seasons out of fashion.

Drogo dragged the decanter from its hiding place, noted it was two inches lower than it should be, and shrugged. "Get used to it," he answered curtly. "Things change when women arrive. You're married. Give me some pointers."

Dunstan snorted impolitely as he turned and helped himself to another glass. Unfashionably shaggy, his inky straight locks proved his connection to the legitimate side of the family. Their younger half brothers all possessed their mother Ann's curls. "I lived with our mother all my life. I'm a lot more used to it than you ever will be. But even Mother couldn't make plants grow in a dungeon like this."

Drogo dropped into his desk chair and sipped appreciatively of the liquor, eyeing his brother as he did so. Dunstan never came to London if he could avoid it. His brother had grown up with country manners and detested the false politeness of society. He lived for the estate and its sheep and cows and other annoying animal nuisances. "So, have you come to see if you're being disinherited?"

264

Dunstan's wide brow wrinkled in thought. "I could fight it in the courts, I suppose. You have only Sarah's word that the child is yours, and everyone knows Sarah is non compos mentis."

"Well, at least one of us got something out of his education." Drogo took a deeper sip and regarded the thriving plant with suspicion. "Sarah isn't a total lunatic. She got out from under her mother's heavy hands by shepherding Ninian."

"If you want to take her word for it." Dunstan dropped into a heavy leather chair and tossed back a swallow of brandy. "I'll still fight it."

Unperturbed, Drogo picked up a letter opener and tapped the desk with it. "I'll cut you off if you do." He'd learned at an early age how to control his unruly brothers. His financial acumen had served them well in more ways than one. "If there is a child — and that's a matter of some dispute still — it could very well be a daughter. Don't make a fool of yourself until it's necessary."

"There will be a child. Sooner or later, there's always a child. Women arrange these things." Dunstan threw back the rest of his brandy and reached for the decanter.

Drogo slid it away from him. "Problem at home?"

Dunstan glowered. "None of your business. You've suffered female conniving before and emerged unscathed. This one must be more devious."

Drogo thought about it, bouncing the letter opener against the wood as he did so. "No. You'll have to meet her. Admittedly, she's not the simpleton she looks, but she's not devious. If anyone's the mastermind here, it's Sarah. Ninian . . ." He glanced over his shoulder at the plant. "Well, Ninian makes things grow."

Dunstan chuckled with a half-drunken hiccup. "In her belly, right?"

Calmly, Drogo threw the sharp steel blade of the letter opener into the shelf behind Dunstan's head. The handle thrummed with the force of the impact.

Dunstan instantly sobered and held up a hand in surrender. "I apologize. You're not making my life easier, though."

Tapping his fingers against the desk, Drogo sipped the brandy again. "The title doesn't mean anything to you, does it?"

Dunstan shrugged his rugged shoulders. "Maybe not to me, but to my wife, and to any children we have."

"Celia's expecting?"

Dunstan looked uncomfortable. "No." He glared at Drogo's lifted eyebrows. "It's

Celia, not me. You know that."

He did. Drogo leaned back in his chair and propped his feet on the desk. Dunstan had been overly fond of one of the maids in his youth. He'd been supporting the results for years. Ives men had no problems creating sons. Most of their problems resulted from creating legitimate ones.

"I can arrange for you to have the country estate for your lifetime," Drogo conceded. "You can use your share of the profits to invest in land for your children."

"Celia would rather invest in a London town house," Dunstan replied gloomily. "You don't have any idea how wives can wreak hell with your peace. Yours will probably want the country estate plus a new town house and a wardrobe fit for a queen. There won't be anything left for the rest of us."

Drogo's lips curled reluctantly at that observation. "Ninian will want me to rebuild Wystan, reroute a river, and clothe half the countryside, but she'll not ask me for anything for herself." He hadn't given this much thought until now, but he recognized the truth as he spoke it. Unlike the rest of his demanding family, Ninian asked for nothing frivolous. He wasn't entirely certain how to deal with that.

"You're fooling yourself if you think it will stay that way," Dunstan warned. "They're all sweetness and light before they get their hooks in you. Once you're trapped, they turn into demanding harridans."

Considering what he knew of the forceful powers of Ninian's aunts, Drogo could see that happening, but he couldn't quite believe it. He itched to go upstairs to Ninian's chamber now, listen to her naive description of the day's activities, and relax in the pleasure of her soothing voice. She could heal with that voice. She didn't need herbs and magic potions. He rather liked the quaintness that saw nothing wrong with his entering her chamber anytime he liked. And her observations on city life were not only astute, but from an entirely new perspective to him. "I don't think 'harridan' precisely suits her."

"Then she's probably as crackbrained as Sarah. Between the two of them, they'll have you jumping out windows."

Without surprise, Drogo noticed the door opening and knew who it was before she entered. Ninian had an odd habit of appearing whenever he thought of her. But then, he spent a lot of time thinking about her these days.

She wore a pretty lavender wool dress unlike anything he'd seen on ladies elsewhere, but considerably more alluring than the peasant costume she'd adopted in Wystan. He might question his sanity and hers in developing this relationship, but he didn't question his attraction to her at all. She looked like an angel straight down from heaven, but an angel with a lusty streak that had him salivating for their wedding night.

"Hello, my dear. Come meet my heir, Dunstan. He thinks we're both crackbrained."

"All Ives men are crackbrained," she agreed solemnly, drifting into the room.

Drogo bit back a smile at her riposte. A delicious heat shot through him as she touched his shoulder, melting the smile out of him. How the hell did she do that?

Apparently oblivious of her effect, she held out her hand to Dunstan. Drogo raised his eyebrows as his brother actually stood up and bowed over it. Dunstan could be rude, crude, and uncouth when he chose to be, but apparently, he wasn't drunk enough to insult the next Countess of Ives.

"You're not like Drogo," she said in wonderment. "You radiate pain and rage and . . ." She twisted up her nose and pondered. "Spurned love? Is that possible? This city vibrates with so many emotions, it's difficult to sort them all out."

Dunstan raised a questioning eyebrow at Drogo.

Drogo shrugged. "She's trying to convince me she's deranged so I'll send her home."

"A witch, not a lunatic," Ninian said gently, patting his shoulder but still watching Dunstan. "Drogo won't believe anything I tell him, so you needn't think I'll reveal your secrets. I'd like to meet your wife sometime. I have a feeling the few women in this family ought to know each other better."

Dunstan remained standing since Ninian didn't take a seat. "She loves any excuse to come to town. I'll bring her for the wedding."

"Good." Apparently satisfied, she focused her regard on Drogo. "Offer your brother a room for the night. I'll have them send up a warm bath and food."

Drogo leaned back and held her gaze. He loved the way he could command her complete attention. "What happened to the table in the hall?" he asked.

"Aunt Stella said we must make the place presentable, so Sarah has ordered the old pieces hauled away. I thought it might be easier to clean before the new ones are brought in. Joseph has a keen eye for design, so he's picked out a few things."

"There was nothing wrong with the old table," he said mildly, more curious than perturbed by this rearrangement of his living quarters. "And Joseph is quite likely to choose something with more arches and pediments and statues than Westminster."

"Actually, he recommended a house-keeper." Patting Drogo's shoulder again, Ninian curtseyed to Dunstan and glided out.

Collapsing back in his chair, Dunstan looked as if he'd been hit by a brick. "A *witch?*" he muttered. "My God, she looks like Venus. Too bad she's got maggots in her attic." He stopped and thought about that a minute. "I suppose that's the only way a woman could survive this family."

Drogo tented his fingers and regarded his brother coolly. "I think you'd best find that room she offered. I would have thrown you in the street."

Dunstan let that run right off his back. "No, you wouldn't. You'd leave me here to drink myself under the desk. The food sounds more appealing now that I've met your lovely intended." He flashed his white grin of old. "This marriage will be a plea-sure to watch. I have a feeling the immovable object has just met an irresistible force."

Drogo slowly emptied his glass after his brother departed. He'd never doubted the intelligence of any of his brothers. Dunstan could very well be right. He'd not ever considered himself an immovable object before, but Ninian was definitely an irresistible force. He wanted her desperately. And she didn't need him at all.

Pain? Rage? *Spurned love?* What the hell had she been talking about?

Realizing Ninian's arrival had distracted him from questioning Dunstan about his marriage, he glared at the healthy, uplifted leaves of the plant. Already, he could feel the reins slipping from his hands.

Eighteen

September

Idly, Drogo stroked his useless telescope and gazed out his bedchamber window. The moon was out there. Even the thick London smoke and fog couldn't conceal it. But the stars were out of his reach tonight. He thought of how clearly they sparkled in Wystan and yearned for the peace of his tower. With Ninian there, it had been the perfect escape.

One thought leading to another, he turned his gaze to the closed door between his chamber and the room connected to Ninian's. Tomorrow was their wedding day. He wondered if his reluctant countess had decided to flee yet. After these past weeks of enduring the constant quarreling of his fractious family, she may have preferred the coldness of her neighbors in Wystan. He really couldn't blame her.

She might be alone and frightened. A young woman should be with her family on her wedding eve. He'd thought he would have to argue with them to keep her where he and his family could watch over her. Ninian must have said something to her aunts because he'd never heard a word of objection. Odd family. They seemed to think Ninian needed no support from anyone. He supposed she was far more independent than the females he knew, but that didn't mean she didn't experience loneliness like everyone else.

He wasn't entirely certain when he decided to visit her, or if he decided at all. Carrying his wedding gift, he rapped lightly on the door to her chamber, not bothering to wait for her reply. She had never denied him, nor had she ever invited him. She just seemed to exist in here, a possession provided for the sole purpose of his use. He would have to learn to deal with that. He'd not only never imagined having a wife, he'd never imagined having one who didn't want him for husband. It made things deucedly awkward.

Entering, he saw no candle or fire to light his way, but a silver light illuminated the chamber, revealing an untouched bed.

Drogo squelched an instant's panic. Laying down the gift on a bedside table, he passed the curtained bed, and checked the tall window.

She stood with arms outstretched, silhouetted in a square of moonlight on the carpet, her golden hair streaming in a cascade to her waist as she reached for the stars, swaying to a music only she could hear. Oblivious to his presence, she spun and danced and reflected the moon's light as her gossamer gown drifted and clung and revealed far more than it concealed.

With avid hunger, Drogo sought the high curves of her breasts, the hard points pushing at the frail lawn of her gown, then drew his gaze downward, to the definite outward curve of her abdomen. With the fecundity of the statues of Druidic earth goddesses he'd seen in museums, she burgeoned with new life — positive proof substantiating theory.

In five months time, he would hold a child of his own in his arms.

He couldn't separate the thrill and terror of that knowledge from the thrill of pure lust for the woman dancing in the moonlight. Primitive instinct warred with civilized protectiveness. A woman in her condition should be cosseted, not ravished.

A golden-haired witch demanded ravishing.

He stepped into the circle of silver light, and she danced into his arms as if she were the part of him that was missing, returning home.

"You carry my child," he said gruffly, not knowing whether he asked or commanded as her lips parted beneath his. Finally given the freedom of access he'd been denied, he accepted hungrily, devouring the sweetness of her breath, the quickly heating desire between them.

Drogo possessively stroked the protruding curve of Ninian's belly and something very like joy pried its way into the shriveled remains of his heart. He had planted his seed and she had nourished it. Both humbled and terrified, he didn't know how to behave.

Her tongue stroked his, distracting his decidedly muddled thoughts. Her soft fingers parted his robe and flattened against his chest, nipping at sensitive points until he groaned against her mouth and forgot the child.

"Yours and mine and God's," she agreed, rubbing against him like a cat.

He could swear he heard her purr as he filled his palms with her breasts and pressed his kiss deeper. The damned cat must be in here. It didn't matter. He needed her too much to hesitate now that she'd given him direction. He untied her ribbons and pulled the bodice down until her bare flesh rubbed his own. He crushed her aroused nipples against his chest and bit at her lips until she parted them again. He had been starving for this for four long months.

Right now, possessing this elusive nymph seemed more important than anything else on earth.

He inhaled her breath and sampled her tongue and lifted her from the floor. "You'll not deny me now." He stated it as a matter of fact, a line read from the book of knowledge. She was wild and free and not wholly of this earth, but he knew in every pore of his body that she was completely his.

She carried his child. Elation swelled within him, as if he'd conquered the stars.

"I cannot deny you," she answered simply. "The bonds are too strong."

She confirmed what instinct told him, although he understood neither the words nor the feeling. Right now, he only knew his arms were full of delectable woman, sweet-smelling, soft, and desirable, and he had gone four months wanting her. He tugged her gown down and lifted her as it pooled on the floor, then carried her to the bed.

"Tonight, and every night," he vowed, to her, to himself, to the powers that be. He wouldn't lose this woman as his father had lost his.

"Every night until I return to Wystan," she promised carefully.

He ignored her amendment. Despite his earlier wishes, he had no reason to return to Wystan anytime soon, and he wouldn't let her go without him. He laid her half across the high bed and spread her legs so he could stand between them.

She looked up at him as if he were all the gods in the world. Aroused to the point of bursting by the power she granted him, Drogo offered her pleasure before he sought his, suckling her breasts until she writhed with need, stroking her when she arched into his hand, easing her past the first peak with his fingers until she convulsed with the pressure.

Only then did he open his robe and claim the exquisite pleasure of entering her.

Ninian cried out with the sudden strain. Her muscles constricted against his invasion, then melted beneath the liquid fire of penetration. Her body was no longer her own, but his, contracting upon his command, parting with his thrust, lifting spasmodically with his rhythm until she no longer was herself, but part of him. For a moment, this loss of self frightened her. But then, as she realized she felt not only the male part that possessed her, but all of him, her soul sang with happiness. Without a qualm, she followed him to the highest peak and over.

The free-fall sensation as she floated back was frightening, but Drogo held her close, wrapping her legs around his hips and straining to stay with her until she landed, as if he understood she needed this grounding. Only with their return to earth, she lost the connection that had momentarily bound them. She missed the warmth he kept hidden.

Physically, he remained lodged within her, stirring again even as he leaned over to brush her cheek with kisses and tease her breasts with wanting. "I think I'll keep you close, moonchild," he whispered so softly she almost didn't hear. "I will want you every hour of the day."

To know him that well sounded exceed-ingly pleasant, and she slid her arms around his neck. "Good thing we can make only one child at a time," she murmured as his magic hands created ripples of sensation from her breasts to her womb.

"Then I suppose we must make love instead."

And he did, with a thoroughness that left her gasping.

Later, she lay within his arms and wondered anew at what she had done. Once upon a time, she had been a free woman, innocent of anyone's dominion. Then she had experimented with temptation and fallen into this man's bonds, silken though they might be. Now she carried his child and agreed to carry his name, and in some manner she could not define, he claimed her. That was the natural way of things, she supposed, but she didn't understand his hold on her. Why was it that he need only touch her and she surrendered to his wishes? It seemed more magic than natural. She had not been jesting earlier; she could not deny him. It did not bode well for her escape should he forbid her to do as she thought best.

How could she be true to herself if she were a part of him? She did not want to be controlled as Drogo controlled the rest of his unruly family.

"I brought you a wedding gift," he murmured against her ear, breaking her reverie as his hand tenderly stroked the place where their child grew.

"So I see," she replied lightly, moving

against his growing arousal.

He chuckled, a strange sound she heard seldom. She liked the way it rumbled in his chest and throat.

"That's not what I meant, although you're welcome to it." He lifted himself on one elbow and reached for the night table. "It's not the same as jewels, but I thought you might like it more."

In surprise, she accepted a heavy, musty-smelling leather tome. She sneezed and wondered if her husband was as odd as the rest of his family as she rippled the page edges in the darkness.

"It's the diary of a Malcolm lady," he explained. "I found it in the library the other day. It's in Latin and the writing is difficult, so I doubt if it's ever been read."

Reverently, she stroked the binding now that she knew what it was. The gift was all the sweeter for his recognizing how much it would mean to her. "Malcolms do not surrender their books lightly. However did this one come to be here? I've read the few we have. They're always in Latin."

He was silent for a moment, then caught her by surprise again. "You are much more intelligent than you allow people to know. Why do you insist on believing in superstitious nonsense?"

"Who can tell what is superstition or truth?" She hugged the book to her breast and struggled to find the words to make him understand. It was suddenly important that this man she would take for husband understand who and what she was. "We made a child in one night. Is that not a kind of magic?"

Sitting up against the pillows, he cuddled her against his shoulder, stroking her hair. He never answered without careful thought, but she wished she could follow the path of his mind now.

"As you've said, what we did makes babies," he said slowly, "but I suppose, if you wish to call the success of Sarah's manipulations magic, then it was magic that we discovered each other."

She should be satisfied with that, but she was not. She knew he did not fully accept what it meant for her to be a Malcolm. "Is it such a jump to believe that I have powers others do not?"

He kissed her brow and stroked the place where their child lay. "You will be my wife, Countess of Ives, mother of my child. Isn't that enough?"

"No. That's the same as saying I'm your table and chair. Being possessed is meaningless. I must be who I am, and I am the

Malcolm healer, if naught else. If you cannot accept this, you had best reconsider our marriage before it is too late."

"It's already too late." He removed the book and set it aside. "Call yourself what you wish, but others will call you countess. It's not an easy position to fill." His hand stroked higher, filling with her tender flesh. "I'll do what I can to help, but as I've said, I wasn't prepared for a wife. We'll learn together."

As he kissed her into surrender one more time, Ninian remembered why she had fallen into this man's bondage. He not only possessed the temptations of the devil, but he possessed an open mind that did not exclude her as so many others did. She could accept that, for now, just as her body accepted his.

In the carriage seat across from Ninian, her husband-to-be scowled at the crowd forming at the foot of the church steps. Drogo was not a handsome man, nor even what one might call dashing. She thought those words too close to "pretty" to describe the Earl of Ives. Drogo was much more striking and definitely more aristocratic than pretty, and his scowl was fierce enough to frighten the ravens from the Tower, though it no longer had the power to cast her into terror.

"They're *all* here," he complained. "I never thought to see the entire lot of them under one roof."

"They're not exactly under a roof yet." Ninian leaned over to look out the window. The street seemed to be lined with carriages. Weddings weren't precisely fashionable. They were just legal procedures necessary to bind the complicated entanglements of families and fortunes. They'd sent announcements, but they hadn't anticipated this kind of audience. Several of the carriages had crests painted on the doors. Her aunts. "Would you care to postpone this to another day?" she asked nervously.

He shot her his infamous scowl. "Not under penalty of death. Let's get this over, and then they'll leave us in peace."

Ninian had serious doubts about that as the footman opened the carriage door and Drogo climbed down to help her out. The morning fog had scarcely lifted beneath the September sun, and a cool breeze tugged at her cloak. Her aunts and cousins had no doubt taken refuge inside the church.

"Perhaps I should warn you," she started to say, before a barrage of emotions slammed into her so forcefully, she almost staggered. She was learning to handle the effects of her "gift" in the city, but the tumult she suffered now was more potent than the scattered feelings of passersby. This was directed at her as much as anyone.

Clinging to Drogo's arm, she glanced up to meet the dark eyes of a man taller and older than Drogo. She'd not met him before. He nodded curtly at her. At the back of the crowd, he merely stepped inside the church and disappeared once he'd seen her. With his brothers all shouting for his attention at once, Drogo didn't seem to have noticed.

She scanned the crowd of anxious dark-eyed, dark-haired Ives men, wondering how she could ever fit into this tumultuous brood. Dunstan leaned his plowman's shoulders against the cathedral's stone wall as he drew one last smoke from his cheroot and eyed her warily. Joseph shoved his hands in his pockets and offered a shy shrug. Various other cousins and offspring clamored for Drogo's attention or simply milled about restlessly.

"To the devil with you!" Drogo shouted, swiping hands off his crushed coat sleeve. "Are you afraid to face the women and so stay out here? Go inside where you belong."

"Have you seen those women?" one of them called. "They're all fair as your bride, with their noses stuck halfway to the ceiling."

Ninian giggled. She thought the one speaking was Drogo's youngest half brother, Paul. He couldn't be much more than sixteen and newly down from school. His head swiveled at the sight of any female. Her cousins would have him spinning in circles.

"Have you seen what they've done to the church?" David shouted above the rest, his eyes dancing with curiosity. "They have trees!"

Ninian winced as all those dark eyes turned questioningly to her. She cleared her throat. "Malcolms usually marry in forests. My aunts have adapted for changing times."

"Is there aught else I should know before we go in there?" Drogo asked with that dispassionate tone she knew too well.

She probably should have warned him sooner, but they seldom spent much time talking. Still, she felt a little guilty at not explaining her family more thoroughly.

"Is there anything that would change your mind about going through with the ceremony?" she asked with more cynicism than anxiety.

He didn't think about it for long. Keeping an eye on his family as they shoved their way into the church, he glanced back to where her simple white gown still disguised her growing belly. "No, I cannot think there is."

"Then there is little point in delaying the proceedings." Determinedly, she took another step.

"Why are you the only one here who isn't nervous?" he muttered, gripping her arm tighter as they proceeded upward.

"Your brothers aren't nervous," she replied as she watched her new family race inside for the best seats. "They're angry and uncertain, a bit jealous, and all of them are suspicious, probably of my cousins. I assume they've heard the legend, too. Who was that tall man who stood in back?"

She met Drogo's completely blank gaze. For once, she thought he wasn't hiding from her. He really didn't know. "He was an Ives," she insisted. "He looks more like you than any of the others."

"Poor sod," Drogo muttered. "Hope he has lots of blunt to balance things out."

"He's not happy about something," she insisted.

Drogo looked at her curiously. "And you can tell this how?"

She patted his arm. Now wasn't the time for that explanation. "Because I'm a Malcolm. Would it help you believe if I waved a magic wand or rode a broom?"

He glared and caught her arm more firmly as he led her up the stairs. "We're not a family of storytellers. If your foolish legend is causing suspicion, it's your family spreading the tale."

"This is all your idea," she reminded him as they reached the door. "I warned you. My grandmother said Ives and Malcolm should never mix. We have no idea what kind of disaster we could be creating."

"I have a very good idea what kind of disaster is created if a child doesn't have the proper support," he countered. "We will make this work."

Overwhelmed by the riot of emotion boiling through the church as they entered, Ninian didn't attempt to argue. On her side of the church, a flower garden of colorful silks and blond heads and powdered coifs abounded. On Drogo's side, a sea of dark faces, somber coats, and knowing dark eyes turned to stare. She had the dreadful sensation that they were about to venture where angels feared to tread.

"Well," she said as she examined the crowd, "at least my uncles and their sons aren't here. They apparently consider this a purely Malcolm event, not worthy of their exalted attention." She wrinkled her nose. "But I do believe that is my father talking with the lady on the near end of the pew."

"My mother." Drogo clutched her hand tighter as a cluster of women wearing white cloaks bore down on them. "Your father and my mother. I don't want to even think of it. Let's get this done before all hell breaks loose."

Considering the rampant emotions bombarding her as they waited for her attendants, Ninian could see his point. She tried to concentrate on the happy ones, as her grandmother had taught her, but her Malcolm family regarded the crowd of Ives men as a dangerous threat, and Drogo's family —

Putting it politely, surrounded by a sea of blond femininity, all those dark Ives men were drowning in lust.

Ninian made a mental note never to invite both families for Beltane.

Nineteen

Drogo watched impassively as Ninian's cousins — he assumed they were cousins by the fairness of their hair — cloaked her in a white satin cape and settled a circlet of what appeared to be twigs on her unpowdered hair. The twigs were wound with purple and white flowers, although he couldn't have named them had he tried, which he didn't. He had little patience with ceremony of any sort. He just wanted this over before his brothers figured out how to swing from the enormous medieval chandelier overhead.

He scowled as one of the older women approached him with a dark cape to match Ninian's in all but color. Glancing up from watching the girls fasten a golden chain to the cloth, Ninian caught his look.

"They're symbols," she whispered. "They're all just symbols. Don't worry about it." Despite her words, she frowned at the gold band closing around her neck.

Over her shoulder, Drogo saw a wave of dark heads turn to watch and whisper. He'd never live this nonsense down. He tried to find the stranger Ninian had mentioned, but the chandelier wasn't lit and the foggy morning light didn't penetrate the church's gloom.

Whispers echoed loudly in the Gothic acoustics of the cathedral, but actual words weren't discernible. He was better off not hearing the opinions of his family. Stoically, Drogo accepted the cloak, ignoring the woman fastening the gold band. All Ninian's relatives seemed to be blond and fair. No wonder his brothers were all atwitter.

"Be thankful they won't make us jump the broom," she whispered as two young girls emerged from the shadows carrying baskets of flower petals.

Broom? What the hell kind of pagan ceremonies did these women attend? Since the flower girls seemed to indicate the proceedings had begun, Drogo didn't inquire. He frowned in puzzlement as they led the way down the right side of the church instead of the center aisle, but Ninian held his arm and followed them as if it were perfectly natural to approach the altar in a circle instead of a straight line.

Ninian. Drogo permitted himself the luxury of a feeling of well-being as he remembered the open welcome he'd found in her bed last night. Glancing down at her golden head with its circlet of flowers, he relaxed even more. She had taken him with as much pleasure as he'd received from her.

She had taken his seed and nourished it as she nourished the plants around her. She would make a good mother, and an exciting bed partner. What more could a man ask?

As they approached the altar from the side, Ninian's graceful cousins in their flowing white capes formed a half circle at the center aisle, and Drogo could see the trees his brothers had mentioned. They'd imported a potted oak and what appeared to be a rowan. The clergyman didn't seem to mind. Garbed in the traditional robes of a good Church of England bishop, he waited calmly for the procession's end.

If that was all the ceremony involved, Drogo could handle it. The gold band at his throat was a nuisance, the cloak a ridiculous affectation, but so was all this churchly ceremony. Marriage could be reduced to a few lines on a sheet of paper and he'd be content. But women, for whatever reason, needed appropriate pomp.

Counting heads, wondering if he'd provided enough champagne for the breakfast, and hoping he could spirit Ninian back to his chambers immediately after the toasts, Drogo didn't pay much attention to the prayers. He kneeled when Ninian did, stood when called upon, and admired the innocent translucence of his bride's complexion as the pale light from the rose window fell upon her.

She wasn't a classical beauty, he admitted, but there was a purity and innocence — and goodness — to her rounded cheeks and chin and sparkling eyes that appealed to him. Perhaps he should have sought a wife from among the less sophisticated sooner. This one wouldn't connive behind his back, deceive him with pretty words, or flutter her lashes at other men. He had complete confidence in that, even if he didn't have complete confidence in the odd workings of her mind.

Patting himself on the back for being logical enough to accept that a woman's mind didn't work like his, Drogo didn't catch the bishop's intonations until he heard the whispers rise behind them. Ninian's hand squeezed his, and he returned to the moment.

Now that he had Drogo's attention, the bishop repeated his question. "Do you vow to love, honor, and take this woman in equality, for so long as you both shall live?"

Equality? "Love and honor" were familiar meaningless phrases he'd heard all his life but *equality?* The word seemed to whisper ever louder through the church, echoing back and forth and rising to the soaring rafters.

What the devil was this *equality* business?

A hushed expectancy fell on Ninian's side of the church. A growing rumble of protest rose on his side.

An explosion of gunpowder shattered both. Pelted with an odd hail but feeling no pain, Drogo instinctively caught Ninian and, rolling to the floor, sheltered her with his body as all hell broke loose.

"You idiots, now look what you've done!" Dunstan shouted in the annoyed tone he reserved for castigating their younger brothers.

"Duck!" Joseph yelled through a chorus of male whoops.

A frenzy of feathers flapped overhead, creating a crescendo of disconcerted female screams.

Feathers? As one drifted down to tickle Drogo's nose, he ventured to look up, while keeping Ninian safely tucked beneath him, although her shaking felt suspiciously like giggles.

"Devil take it, where did the damned pigeons come from?"

That had to be William. Cautiously, Drogo peered over his shoulder — and dodged a flapping wing.

"My aunts must not have been able to find doves," Ninian whispered.

Understanding dawned, and with a roar of fury, Drogo rolled to his feet and strode down the aisle after the culprits who were breaking for the door.

Amid the resulting confusion as Drogo's brothers pounded after one another, shouting and hollering, Ninian sat up and gazed in wonder at the magnificent chaos erupting all through the once-peaceful cathedral. The bishop had dropped to kneel and pray behind the protection of the pulpit. Scattered bits of grain still flew through the dusty air and covered the aisle and half the pews. She recognized the inventiveness of Drogo's fleeing brothers in the cannon shot of grain pellets. They'd evidently intended to shower the wedding procession with grain in a less than traditional fashion, but the birds that were always part of Malcolm ceremonies had been too tempting. The pigeons, ignorant of the chaos they'd caused, settled down to peck through the chaff on the marble floor.

The humans were doing nothing so peaceful.

Ninian's aunts had ordered their broods into a protective ring at the first sound of gunfire. Now, they shot dagger glares at the remaining men and boys whooping with laughter and disrupting the sacred ceremonies. The moment certainly didn't bode well for this first joining of Malcolm and Ives in untold centuries, but if this was all the disaster their marriage wrought, she could live with it.

Ninian's giggle died as soon as she realized her groom had disappeared out the church doors in hot pursuit of his younger brothers. Once it sank in, that vow of equality might drive him to keep going and not look back. Trying not to acknowledge the pain and fear of that possibility, she rose and poked amid the pews until she found the blunderbuss the boys had used to shoot grain.

"I don't think a pretty thing like you needs to be playing with a man's weapons," a deep voice admonished as he caught her by the waist and confiscated the shotgun.

She'd felt the muted animosity of his approach, but she'd ignored it as a part of the chaos around her. Sometimes her gift was not at all helpful. Allowing irritation to override her fear, she defiantly met the grim expression of the intruder Drogo couldn't identify, the man who most certainly had to be an Ives.

"The damned earl really doesn't know what he has here, does he?" the stranger asked, with almost a thoughtful tone, not releasing her from his grasp.

The hostility behind his calm words frightened her. Her newly developing powers of observation warned his grip was not playful, and she suppressed a scream of panic. She wouldn't scream. Malcolm women didn't scream. Generally, they didn't fight either. But Ninian had always been a malcontent, as her grandmother had told her often enough, and this man exuded danger.

She might not possess magic, but she possessed a strong instinct for protecting herself and her child. Grabbing the man's jabot, she jerked his head down, and fastened her teeth into his extremely prominent nose. She would make him think twice before manhandling her, and thrice before he hurt her daughter.

He yowled in both pain and surprise. He caught her hair and tried to rip her away.

Ninian bit harder and kicked his shins to force him to release her. Her pointed kid slippers weren't as useful as her heavy country clogs, but they did their job. Her attacker began leaping about to avoid the blows.

"Drop her, and she'll let go," a voice spoke steadily from behind her.

Drogo. Ninian sighed in relief not only at the heavy hand falling away from her waist, but at Drogo's return. She hadn't realized how afraid she'd been that he would leave her standing at the altar. Generously, she released her grip on the man's nose as Drogo caught her and pulled her back against him.

Holding his injured nose, the stranger focused his attention above her head. "You would do well to look further into the origins of the family you marry into," the man said flatly. "Equality!" he snorted. "I suppose you're getting what you deserve."

Without further ado, he stalked down the altar steps and past the men reluctantly returning to their seats. He skirted around the women — several of whom stopped whispering to admire his masculine form — and removed another musket from an Ives brother, who was loading it with grain from his pockets. With scarcely a hitch to his progress, he marched out the front door.

"Who *was* that?" Ninian murmured from the comfort and safety of Drogo's arms. She didn't think her knees would lock under her if he let go. Again, she'd sought the security of the shelter he so swiftly offered.

"Devil if I know," Drogo answered, although his voice held a thoughtful note. "I daresay he won't stick his nose in our business again."

Ninian almost certainly heard him chuckle — whether at his witticism or her handiwork, she couldn't tell. With the congregation coming to order, and the pigeons under control, Aunt Stella sailed toward the altar as the bishop emerged from hiding, all but shaking his ruffled feathers.

While Ninian's aunt and the clergyman fell into a heated conversation, Dunstan hauled the last of their brothers to a pew, then turned a wary glance to Ninian. "Remind me never to put my nose in your vicinity."

Too caught up in the whirlwind of emotions swirling around her, Ninian didn't even have the grace to blush as she leaned into her bridegroom's embrace. "Just don't stick it in my business." She repeated Drogo's words pertly, although uncertainty held her in its grip. Would Drogo call off their wedding now? Or would the bishop?

"Who the hell was that your bride nearly maimed?" Dunstan demanded, turning to

299

Drogo, apparently satisfied Ninian's penchant for cannibalism didn't involve him.

"Damned if I know, but I mean to find out." Drogo lifted Ninian's chin and forced her attention back to the conversation. "What did he say to you?"

Beneath his dark gaze, she blinked. He was forever doing that to her. She'd never known that much heated attention, and she needed time to become used to it. "Nothing we don't both already know," she answered without thinking.

Drogo raised his eyebrows and waited.

Ninian grimaced and pulled from his grasp, reaching to set her coronet straight. "If I may quote him directly, he said, 'The damned earl really doesn't know what he has here, does he?' But what that has to do with anything is beyond my understanding. I've not met an Ives yet who made any sense to me."

"Ives?" both Dunstan and Drogo said at once.

She glared at them impatiently. "Of course. Did you not look at him? He's every bit an Ives." She glanced at Dunstan. "And he's even angrier than you are."

Aunt Stella chose that moment to descend upon them. "We're to take the rest of the ceremony to the church steps. The fool won't risk his precious church on the lot of you any longer. Ives, if you don't keep better control of those young nuisances . . ."

While Stella scolded, Ninian met Drogo's gaze. Did he intend to go through with the ceremony, or had he had time to realize they were wedding chaos to calamity?

She held her breath and watched as his gaze dropped to the place where their child rested, then rose to study her face. Shaking his head with that bewildered expression she saw so often when he looked at her, he reached to clasp her hand firmly over his elbow. The brawl with his brothers had half torn his black cloak from his shoulder, but the gold band remained fastened around his neck. She thought he looked more dangerous than a medieval knight returning from the Crusades.

"Marrying on the church steps is much more to my liking," he declared, hauling her with him down the aisle. "Equality?" he whispered in her ear as they hurried forward. "What the hell does that mean?"

Twenty

With the doves — pigeons — dispersed and the grain already thrown, the rest of the wedding was anticlimactic. As Drogo grimly repeated his vows — including the one of equality — and Ninian accepted the ring that bound her to him, he almost sighed in relief.

Leaning over to seal his vows by kissing his bride, Drogo tried to ignore the murmurs wafting from their feminine audience, and the ribald laughter and shouts erupting among the males. Feeling like one of the beleaguered characters in the political cartoons posted in news shop windows, Drogo limited the kiss to a highly unsatisfactory nibble. Last night hadn't been enough to assuage his urgent need to take his bride to bed and stay there for a week — without interruption.

"Scotland would have been better," he muttered against her lips.

"Or not at all," she answered sweetly.

She might very well have the right of that. Warily watching the crowd for any sign of the mysterious man who was bloody lucky to still have a nose — Drogo eased Ninian through the cheering mob of well-wishers.

"You don't suppose they'll all follow us home?" he asked glumly as he assisted her into their waiting coach. He'd left a footman and a driver standing guard while they were inside, but he ordered a final hasty inspection while Ninian took her seat. His brothers were capable of unfastening wheels or placing Chinese firecrackers under seats.

"I suppose they'll not only follow us," Ninian replied as he climbed in beside her, "but I also suppose my uncles and their sons will be waiting at the house to welcome you into their ranks. They do like a free meal."

"They're not Malcolms, are they?" It didn't look as if he would be bedding his new bride anytime soon, Drogo concluded with disgruntlement.

"Of course not, but I'm sure they'll be happy to console you with all the trials and tribulations we bring. Were it not for the lack of available men, Malcolm women should never have left the forest."

He'd had enough warnings. He really needed to start paying closer attention to the annoying details now that he had what he wanted. As the coach halted in the convoluted traffic of a narrow intersection, Drogo studied the bland, innocent features of his country wife. "Are you trying to tell me *all* Malcolm women believe they are . . . witches?" He had difficulty even saying the preposterous word.

Ninian tugged at the gold band fastening her cape. "To some degree. Of course." The band snapped open and she sighed in relief before looking up at him quizzically. "Did you have some doubt?" She continued without waiting for an answer. "Actually, from studying what books we have at the cottage, I'm theorizing we're descendants of Druids. The white robes and other of our traditions are an inherent part of that cult."

Drogo was used to facing the world and its caprices with impassivity, but even he was having difficulty swallowing a lump this large. "Druids? Tree-worshipers?"

She shrugged. "Trees have their powers, just as herbs do." She touched the halo of twigs in her hair. "Aunt Stella will have laid an enchantment on this rowan, offering me protection. Actually, though, rowan seeds are poisonous and can be used to disable enemies. You should approve of the logic."

"We should force rowan berries down my

brothers' throats?" It was easy to slip past her superstitious silliness while watching Ninian's luscious lips press together in an inviting bow. If only they had time, he could slide his tongue between that sweetness and have her skirts up shortly thereafter.

He checked the jam of horses and carts outside the window. If they delayed much longer . . . The coach lurched into motion. Damn.

"Your brothers are worried they'll lose your attention now that you've married."

Her words jarred him back to the moment. She'd pulled the trick of describing people's feelings once too many times and a little too recently for comfort. Drogo warily eyed her innocent-miss composure. "I suppose you know that the same way you know Dunstan suffers from spurned love and that the man with the sore nose is angry? Not that any man wouldn't be angry after being bitten." Mentally, he rubbed his own prominent beak.

"Of course." Complacently, she glanced out the window at the row of older town houses they passed.

Other women never stopped talking. He'd married one who didn't know when to start. Curbing his impatience, Drogo tried again. "I thought witches cast spells, not read minds."

She shrugged, but he noticed she clasped her hands a little tighter. "I don't read minds. I have a gift for empathy. People call us witches for lack of any better word. We don't cast spells on people. We just have . . . special talents."

She looked so perfectly sane and beautiful when she said things like that. Her golden curls were a picture of angelic purity, her blue eyes reflected the openness of the sky — and then she hit him with lightning bolts of lunacy from out of nowhere.

Sighing, Drogo leaned back in his seat and tried to quench a hot surge of ardor. If there was any witchcraft at work here, it was in the way she bewitched him with lust. She already carried his child. He should be satisfied with that.

"Talents," he repeated flatly, desperately looking for a thread of rationality. "Not the painting, musical sort?"

"Well, Lucinda has a talent for painting wonderful portraits." She didn't seem to think the topic irrelevant. "Unfortunately, her paintings tend to reflect the subject's character a little too clearly. If you have any deep, dark perversions, don't sit for her."

Drogo rubbed his temple and wondered if he should have Ninian sit for her artistic cousin, but decided he didn't want to know the secrets of her soul — or her cousin's talent — that well. "And your *talent* is healing?"

She nodded diffidently, clasping and unclasping her fingers. "I just seem to have made a bit of a mess of it."

Healing made sense. Living in the rural countryside without proper medical care, many women learned healing arts. He couldn't imagine that any of them were very good at it, lacking scientific methods, but even trained physicians often relied on the efficacy of herbal medicine.

"Sarah said you delivered Lydie's baby safely, and helped it to thrive."

"Any decent midwife can do that," she scoffed. "I should have understood how Lydie's unhappiness affected the child and treated her accordingly, but I didn't. I was too worried about myself."

That veered a little too far from the rational path. Taking a deep breath, Drogo built a safe bridge over his new wife's lack of logic. "Sarah says you were better than any London physician. Don't minimize your talents."

The look she gave him should have scalded. "London physicians are quacks."

He'd intended a compliment. Momentarily floundering, he grasped for a more stable topic, one that would satisfy the taunting questions his family would ask.

"Exactly what is the meaning of that vow of equality we took?" he asked bluntly. "What happened to the usual thing, the 'love, honor, and obey'?"

Obviously still disgruntled at being compared to a physician, she bunched the white satin of her cape into a ball. "The Malcolm ceremony used to make the groom promise obedience, but the duke balked at that. Grandmother said he and Aunt Stella fought for six months before they reached a compromise. It's not a difficult concept to embrace, is it?"

"Women aren't equal to men." Already battered by the idea of Druids and unnatural talents, Drogo refused to let the lunacy continue. The coach drew up to the house, but he ignored the orderly line of servants waiting on the steps. He wanted to set this straight before his countess developed any more delusions. "Women can't sail ships, build buildings, learn law, or govern countries. I'd be surprised to find one who could explain how their funds generated income."

Sky-blue eyes narrowed into hostile slits above apple-round cheeks. "Did my father succeed in gaining access to my trust fund?"

"Of course not. It's tied up tighter than the Crown jewels."

"A Malcolm woman established that trust," she said warningly. "Malcolm women control it and Malcolm women fund it for the use of Malcolm women. And I know precisely how it earns interest and where to invest it. Aunt Stella may be head of our family, but Grandmother made me the treasurer." She flung the wad of satin to the opposite seat, composed her features, and offered him one of her dimpled, deceptive smiles. "Shall we go in?"

Not only bewildered, but stunned, Drogo closed his eyes and shook his head in denial. She knew *precisely* what she was worth.

The solicitor had refused to disclose the extent of her trust fund, but he had made it apparent that there were sufficient funds to support an entire army of Malcolms.

Ninian was not only wealthier than he was, but she *knew* it, and she had still married him. She didn't need him in any manner that made sense to him. No wonder she hadn't wanted to marry. With her wealth, she was doing *him* a favor.

He had no control over her at all.

"The earl does not look like a happy bridegroom," Stella commented as she nibbled on a petit four from the lavish buffet table and watched Drogo sipping morosely at champagne while the cluster of men around him laughed and pounded each other's backs. None of them pounded Drogo's.

"My husband is a serious man," Ninian replied demurely, passing up the delicacies in favor of a dry biscuit to settle her queasy stomach.

"Do not play the witless fool for me, young lady," Stella snapped. "Did he blame that disaster of a ceremony on you?"

"Of course not." Ninian sipped her tea. "Drogo is a very rational, very patient man. He is an upright pillar of society, a man of genius, a man who dedicates his life to family, and friends, and friends of family and . . ."

"Your sarcasm is no better." Her aunt sighed, as if she were bearing the burdens of the world. "Surely you're old enough not to have romantic notions. Lucinda weeps daily because her father insists she marry a man of stature instead of the wastrel beau who recites poetry. In my day, we knew our duty to family."

Ninian pointed her biscuit in the direction of her young cousin. "If it's a man of stature the duke wants, he'd better steer her clear of young Joseph. He cheats at cards and won all my sweetmeats."

"Then play him for hazelnuts." Stella frowned at the laughing pair. "It's time we take our leave. Drogo might be a fine catch, but that illegitimate lot of rapscallions he calls brothers are nothing but trouble." She patted Ninian's cheek. "You'll be fine once you learn not to expect romantic fantasies. He may be a little stiff and unbending, but he's a good man. He'll take care of you and the babe. Call on me if you need anything."

"You're returning to the country?" Ninian really didn't need to ask. Malcolms needed woods as roses needed rain. She just wanted the reassuring presence of the familiar for a little longer while she tried to settle into her new role.

"You know how to reach me." Stella patted her again, then hurried to rescue her daughter from the charms of a roguish Ives.

"We'll be going, too, dear." Hermione appeared from out of nowhere. Quiet and unassuming where Stella was bold and loud, Ninian's younger aunt was still a force to treat cautiously. "These Ives men are much too . . . how do I put this delicately . . . *virile* to tolerate easily." She smiled prettily from a face unlined by her middle years. "I'm sure you'll fare well, dear. I don't mean to insult

311

your young man. But" — she sighed, glancing toward Drogo, who now stood alone — "he is a bit of a thundercloud, isn't he? Perhaps if I —"

"No, Aunt Hermie," Ninian hastily interrupted. "He's having a little difficulty accepting us, is all. He'll be fine."

Hermione looked doubtful. "If you say so, dear. I do hope you're reading him rightly. He does look a bit like Old Nick, doesn't he? But you're the expert. I'll bow before your greater knowledge." She blew Ninian a kiss, and trailing bits of lace and ribbons, mother-henned her chicks toward the door.

Of course, that was the problem, Ninian acknowledged. She understood nothing about Drogo. He could be plotting her demise right now, and she wouldn't even know he was angry.

Still, she couldn't subject Drogo to Hermione and her erratic spells. Hermione might have a genius with perfumes, but she simply couldn't accept that she didn't possess any mystical, occult, or psychic powers. The last time she'd attempted one of the lesser spells in her chap book, heat had curdled all the milk in the dairy for a week.

Ninian smiled at the memory of her two aunts arguing over that incident. Hermione was as gentle as Stella was arrogant, yet they'd quarreled without once hurting each other. Perhaps Malcolms were strange to others, but she thought they could teach the rest of the population a thing or two.

Noting the strain on Drogo's jaw as her aunts and cousins fluttered around him to say their farewells, Ninian swallowed her doubts and crossed the room to relieve him of his onerous task. If Drogo was anything like his brothers, the feminine bombardment of scents, voices, and touches would drive him to the brink, much as all those *virile* Ives men were distracting her cousins. She thought the families together might resemble multiple Adams and Eves after their apple-tasting orgy, but Drogo's house was no Garden of Eden.

He turned and reached for her before she could speak her presence. Although he often appeared totally self-absorbed, he always seemed to know when she was there. Odd, since she could never sense him.

"Now, if you could only chase away my brothers," he whispered in her ear as he shook the duke's hand and watched the last of the Malcolm females flutter out the door.

"Abracadabra," she murmured in return, feeling her own female flutter at the warmth of his breath.

He didn't laugh at her jest but regarded

her with suspicion. Ninian sighed. She liked him much better as a natural philosopher who thought her a silly twit and not the arrogant male who protected all under his roof. She could already see the disadvantage of being a wife.

Fear prickled across her skin at that thought. She was married. Her child had a name. Would her husband ever allow her to return to Wystan, or would she be a prisoner of her decision?

Drogo's hand rose from her shoulder to tease at a sensitive spot just below her ear. "If I leave them with the champagne, do you think we could disappear upstairs?"

She wanted to turn and head for the stairs right now. Just the husky suggestiveness of his voice aroused a tingle that danced along her skin. The memory and anticipation of his lovemaking had haunted the back of her mind throughout the day's chaos. The bond between them was deeper than the physical now, blessed by church and family. There was no reason at all to deny what they both wanted.

Except a Malcolm instinct for self-preservation. "I would like to leave for Wystan soon," she said innocently, testing the boundaries.

"Parliament is not over, moonchild. I

cannot leave." He murmured the endearment seductively, as if no other word but that one mattered.

"I can travel alone," she suggested, but the queasiness in her stomach lurched in expectation of an answer she didn't want.

"When we travel, we travel together," he said firmly.

"Then pray we travel soon, before the heat consumes us." Donning her best dimpled smile, Ninian bobbed a curtsy, and sailed off for a long chat with Dunstan's wife.

She no longer saw her husband as the fantasy devil of legend, but as a man. Devils wreaked havoc and ruin, then had the courtesy to disappear. Men lingered to cause trouble a lot longer.

Twenty-one

"Drogo! What are you doing in here on your wedding night?" Sarah swept into the library just as Drogo turned the brandy glass to his lips.

All the guests had departed, and Ninian seemed to have disappeared with them. He hadn't thought their little discussion earlier of any significance. Mayhap, she had thought differently, because he couldn't find her.

Of course she thought differently. That was half their problem. Their minds didn't work the same.

Sipping his brandy, Drogo tried to pretend Sarah had left with the other guests, but he didn't succeed. "The question is, what are you still doing here? Ninian no longer needs a chaperone. You may go back to your mother's house, where you belong."

"And leave you to botch things as your father did? Not likely. Now that you have a bride, you'd best find time for her, or she'll flee back to Wystan."

Drogo tried not to wince. What had gone wrong between his parents was a long time ago, but the repercussions resounded to this day. He would do well to take Sarah's warning to heart. It might be fashionable for spouses to take lovers after providing the required heir and spare, but it wasn't sane. And above all else, Drogo intended to approach marriage sanely.

"I'll do my best." He hesitated. It had been a long day, and where he'd hoped to be closer to his new wife by the end of it, it seemed they were more distant than ever. He had little in the way of female guidance to explain what he'd done wrong. Sarah was as close as he would get. "But I have little practice at it," he admitted.

"Think of her as one of those stars you prize," she said dryly, gathering up her skirts. "Study her as you do the night skies."

He was afraid of what he would discover if he did. She already fascinated him far more than he had time to act on, and he couldn't keep her as distant as the stars. With a grimace, he finished his brandy as Sarah swept out the door.

The September sun had disappeared into

the fog banks over the river by the time he set out to find Ninian. He'd see no evening star twinkling through this murk. His brothers had already departed to their own separate activities, expecting him to celebrate his wedding night with his bride.

He didn't know where the hell his bride was.

Drogo climbed the stairs to see if he could locate her in her chamber. She didn't seem to think it necessary to tell him where she was going or what she was doing, even on their wedding day. She'd lived like a creature of the forest most of her life and was more independent than most females of his acquaintance. He supposed he could adapt to that. He just couldn't help worrying about her.

No candle lit Ninian's room. No fire warmed her grate. No graceful silhouette danced in the misty light from the windows. More disappointed than he was willing to admit, Drogo turned to his own room, but he had little hope of finding her there. Only once had she come to him, and that had been back in Wystan, on her own home ground.

Finding his chamber empty, as expected, he ordered fires in both grates and set out in search of his straying wife. This was their wedding night. He'd had high expectations of this day, but as he'd told her before, he was used to disappointment. Still, he didn't give up. There was all the night ahead of them. He'd not understood how little joy he had in his life until he realized how much he was looking forward to nights in Ninian's bed.

All his life he'd been the responsible one, the one who had led his drunken father home, the one who returned his mischievous brothers to their tutors, the one who managed the account books and the solicitors and the matters of estate. His stolen moments he'd devoted to stargazing and the astronomical calculations that so fascinated him. He didn't have an imaginative mind, but he liked to think there might be life on other planets, or perhaps the Greek gods resided there, and that someday he would find proof. It was the only fantasy he allowed himself, outside the bone-deep desire for a child of his own.

He didn't even know why he wanted the child. He'd never held his brothers as babies or dandled them on his knee. He'd always considered them a constant source of interruption and little more. Perhaps it was his one arrogance to have what he thought he could not have. He had little experience with women, seldom took them seriously, avoided them at all costs except in bed, but they possessed the one ability he could not duplicate — the ability to procreate. For that, he was willing to allow Ninian into his life.

After checking all the public rooms and inquiring of the servants, Drogo still hadn't found her. The house wasn't as extravagantly large as the castle. It had been his father's and his grandfather's, but Sarah's mother, Ann, had detested it. His father had built a more modern one for her in the suburbs of Hyde Park Corner. Once he'd come of age, Drogo had insisted on moving in here to attain some privacy from his motley lot of brothers. That had lasted just long enough for the first one to be kicked out of school. His house had gradually become a home for his brothers, but it wasn't large enough to get lost in.

Unless Ninian had run away — and he thought she had more courage than that — there was only one place left to find her.

Taking the back door above the kitchens, Drogo lifted his lamp and searched the darkened garden. His heart caught in his throat as he saw her lonely figure sitting on the damp ground, with the fog swirling around her cascade of hair. She never wore her curls up as other women did, and he was glad of it. He loved their wild abandon.

He stepped softly, not wanting to frighten her, but she must have seen the lamplight. She turned and looked up at him through the wet fog. She looked almost haunted, so pale were her cheeks, and his heart did another panicky leap. "Are you well?"

She regarded him soundlessly, then returned her gaze to the blighted garden. "The soul is gone out of this land."

She'd drifted off on another of her mental journeys. Some days, she gave him reason to fear he'd taken a madwoman to wife, but whatever she was, she was a gentle soul, and she tugged at his hitherto unknown heartstrings. "You'll catch a chill."

"I don't, generally." Sitting cross-legged on the bare ground, wearing one of her old gowns, she sifted dirt between her fingers. "There are carriage wheels on your roses, and a burned-out kettle in the thyme. I believe even savage Indians take better care of their land than that."

Drogo took a seat on the garden bench above her. She might not mind the damp ground, but he did. "Savage Indians must eat off the land. We do not. My brothers have used this yard as a play lot for years. I did not see the importance of keeping it up."

She twisted her head to look up at him. "That is where we differ, my lord. I am of this earth. I must take care of it. I sometimes wonder if you are not of the sky, and if we will ever meet. I believe in things of the spirit, but you see only with your mind."

Perhaps she was not so much out of her mind as in another place besides the one he inhabited. "I don't claim to fully understand you," he admitted. "But we've made a child together and must now learn to live with what we've done. What would you suggest?"

He thought she smiled. In the gloom, it was difficult to tell. He wanted to pull her into his arms and warm her, but he suspected she would slip through his fingers like the fog should he try.

"I like the way your mind works." She leaned over, plucked a clover from the beaten grass, and handed it to him. "It has four leaves," she informed him. "You are a very lucky man. There is an entire patch of them here."

Drogo bit back a sigh of exasperation. He wanted logical advice. She handed him superstitious good-luck charms. "We should go in."

"You may, if you like. I need to think, and I think better outside."

He shrugged off his coat and leaned over to place it around her shoulders. "All right, can I help you think so you will come in sooner?"

She shifted the coat more snugly around her. "Thank you. I cannot read you as I do others, but I think you are a very nice man, just a little too intellectually elevated above the rest of us, perhaps. I exist, you know."

He stared down at her golden head and wished he knew what went on inside of it. He liked mathematics because it was clear-cut and simple to understand. His wife was no such thing. "Of course you exist. I never thought otherwise."

"No, you think I'm a convenience, like the bench you sit upon. That's not the same thing. There is a Me inside of me. A person. You've never met me, and you don't seem much interested in knowing me, so I've tried not to get in your way. But that isn't going to work if we live together, is it?"

A hollow opened inside him, a gaping, echoing hollow he recognized from long-ago nights as a young child in a strange bed, in a strange house, without the familiarity of his mother or brothers around him. He tried not to let that emptiness speak through him. Carefully, logically, he applied his mind to whatever she might be trying to say. "I'm not used to having a woman in the house, if that is what you mean."

"No, that isn't what I mean. You had Sarah and Claudia and Lydie in your castle, but you didn't know they existed either. You shut them out. Sarah is here now, and you seldom speak with her except in passing, as you would speak to your valet when you want your boots shined. I'm different, and that bothers you, but you're still trying to reduce me to the position of bootblack or whatever." She stroked the grass at her fingertips. "I think . . ." She hesitated as she formulated the phrases. "I think you've consigned me to the role of Wife. A wife sleeps with you when you want it. She buys things and her bills end up on your desk. She occasionally speaks, and you try hard to listen, but you don't really hear. Your mind is elsewhere."

He waited for her to go on, and when she didn't, he figured he was supposed to say something. He had no idea what to say. He could stand in front of the Lords and speak for hours, but he couldn't talk to his bride. Men talked about subjects he could understand. Women talked of things beyond his comprehension.

"I'm sorry. I really don't understand. You're my wife now. Wives and husbands

324

share a bed. That's the purpose of marriage. What would you have me say?"

"That you will allow me to do as I see fit because you know I am as capable and intelligent as you are."

The panicky feeling returned, and Drogo hastened to quiet it. She wanted to return to Wystan and leave him. No woman ever stayed with an Ives for long. But he couldn't let her leave him. He had to explain. He hated explaining himself, but Sarah had said he must work at this, and so he would.

"Come here," he ordered. If he was going to do this, he would do it on his terms.

She looked up at him again, and then unquestioningly, she stood up and settled beside him, curling her warm, soft fingers into his. Her rose scent had developed a decidedly more sensuous undertone than the evergreen mixture she'd worn earlier. Just the scent of her aroused him, but he had to be logical right now. He laid his hand over her gently sloped belly and stroked. She was round and firm and he could almost feel the life blooming there. He took a deep breath. "You know my parents lived separately?"

She nodded. "Sarah explained."

"My mother is from a modest family. Her brother is a vicar. Her father owns a small estate close to the Ives holdings. My father was an arrogant man, raised to be an earl, the eldest and most spoiled of several sons. He always did as he pleased."

She wriggled slightly beside him and Drogo realized the bench was hard. This was no time for these unveilings, but he would have it done. He took his hand from hers and pulled her on his lap, where she settled gladly. Her breath whispered against his cheek, and he breathed easier as he wrapped his arms around her plump waist. He could do this.

"It pleased him to seduce my mother. It did not please him when her father went to his and demanded that he do the honorable thing, nor did it please him when my grandfather agreed. But threatened with disinheritance, he did what was right, and they had the three of us in the first few years of their marriage."

"You and Dunstan and Ewen," she recited, apparently confirming her memory.

"Yes. But my grandfather was still alive at the time, and he refused to give up the reins to his holdings. My father was bored and sought entertainment elsewhere, challenges which drew him to London, leaving my mother behind with us. He stayed away for a year or more. My mother retaliated by finding a man who would love her as my father did not. My father sought revenge by bedding every woman who consented. This tale becomes worse with the telling. Would you rather go inside?"

She snuggled closer and leaned against his shoulder. Taut with the pain of his recitation, Drogo breathed the fresh scent of her, rested his chin upon the silken warmth of her hair, and tightened his arms around her and his child.

"I know of at least one bastard he created in his dalliance across the countryside. I have a half brother, William, by a dairy maid in the village. My father set her up with a small competence. At the same time, he filed a petition for separation with the courts and demanded my mother be removed from his home."

"How old were you?" Her breath warmed the chill in Drogo's chest.

"Six." He gritted his teeth and continued. "You must know the rest. With the proof of my mother's adultery, the court granted his petition, with the provision that Dunstan and Ewen be left with my mother. My father met Sarah's widowed mother, Ann, and set her up as mistress. After she birthed Joseph, he moved her into his home in my mother's place since the separation agreement does not allow for remarriage. I do not know what hold Ann had on him, but after that, my father was content to settle down. Perhaps the death of my grandfather gave him the challenge he needed, but I saw little of that. I was fourteen when he died, and the responsibility of the earldom fell on me."

"And why do you tell me this?" she asked softly.

Drogo curbed his impatience. "To explain why I will never leave my wife as my father did. A wife and husband must live together, work together, play together, become one as my father and Ann did. He never strayed after he took her into his home, and I like to think they were happy together. That's what I want."

He held his tongue even though she made no immediate reply. Neither of them were talkers by nature, it seemed. He could live with that. He could not live without her beside him. He needed her in his bed at night, to remind him of why they were together. He needed his child where he could see him, watch him grow, be part of his life — something his father had denied Dunstan and Ewen.

"Your father and Ann must have loved each other to have managed a life together, even under such terrible circumstances.

They had some common bond, whereas your father and mother did not."

"My parents had three children together," he said grimly.

"Ives men are very . . ." she chuckled and added, "*virile*. And with her upbringing, your mother would have tried to please him. Children are easy to make."

He growled and Ninian turned her head up and patted his cheek. Drogo imagined his bristles burned her soft palm, but he reveled in the touch. He'd reached deep down to a place he didn't like to relate this story. He didn't want to ever go through it again. He wanted her in his bed right now, and if they didn't go soon, he would take her here on the grass. He needed to be deep inside her, outside of himself.

"Children really are easy to make, if the circumstances are right," she assured him, "else there would not be so many in the world. Raising them is another matter. And making a relationship between two grown people is even more difficult, I expect. We really have gone about things in reverse."

"That's Sarah's fault."

"No, it's ours. We played with fire and got burned. I do not regret it. I want this child, but if you mean what you are saying, if you mean to keep me at your side and see this child grow, then we have a very difficult road ahead."

"I don't see how," he said grumpily. If she would just come to his bed, the road would smooth considerably. "I'm wealthy enough to support you comfortably. I will not beat you. I am trying very hard to listen to you because I know I'm not good at that sort of thing. I've even told you what no other but my mother knows so we might understand each other better. What more can I do?"

"Believe I'm a Malcolm healer and that my place is in Wystan," she answered firmly, wiggling out of his grasp and standing. "Until you understand who I am, and recognize Wystan is as important to me as Parliament is to you, we can never be happy. I will try very hard to show you who I am, but we have left this too late. The child will be born in five months, and according to tradition, she must be born in Wystan."

"There is nothing in Wystan," he argued. "The session won't end for months, and then the holidays are upon us and my brothers are here. I assure you, my steward is looking after the village. There is no reason to return there until spring."

"And until you understand and believe me, we are at cross-purposes. Good night, my lord. I'll see you in the morning."

She walked away. Drogo stared after her in disbelief. He'd unbared the secrets of his soul, and she'd walked away. On their wedding night.

He jumped up to follow but stumbled over a rusting water can. In a fit of unusual temper, he flung it as hard as he could. It crashed into the assortment of carriage wheels leaning against the fence, and the clatter and bang did nothing more than cause his neighbors to open their windows and yell, and dogs to howl all across the city.

Twenty-two

Devil take it! He'd not let her get away with this. This was their *wedding* night. A husband had rights.

With dogs still howling in the distance, Drogo stomped up the stairs, delayed by a stop to reassure the servants they wouldn't be murdered in their beds by a gang of tin-can-throwing thieves. He'd learned to be firm with his brothers. He saw no reason why a wife should be any different.

Prepared to batter down her locked door, he nearly fell in as it swung open. Righting himself, he glared at the candlelit bed.

Ninian had removed her gown and sat in a simple shift against her pillows, reading the book he'd given her. At his entrance, she glanced up with curiosity but no fear.

He felt like an ogre. Sighing, he took a deep breath and plunged his hand through his hair. Unlike his half brothers', his hair was thick and straight instead of curly, and the ribbon fell out easily. He must look like a wild man.

"This is our wedding night," he reminded her.

"We've already had our wedding night," she corrected. "That's the problem. We did this backward."

Ninian watched her husband standing there in all his masculine confusion and almost backed down. Firelight flickered over the taut planes of his dark features, and she remembered the night they'd met when she'd thought him the devil. She still thought it sometimes, but for better or worse, he was her devil. She admired the way he controlled his temper before speaking. She also liked the way one thick strand of hair pulled loose to hang beside his ear, an obvious sign that she'd disturbed his usually ordered life.

She craved his attention and affection, and the heat in his eyes nearly burned through her resolution. She wanted to throw down the book and open her arms to him.

She couldn't open her arms to him. She wouldn't open herself to anyone's rejection again. She must learn to stand on her own and do the job for which her gifts were given.

"Backward?" he repeated, obviously bewildered.

"We had our wedding night first, and now we must go through the period of courtship where a couple learns to know one another."

He seemed stunned. Her logical, sensible husband had difficulty grasping her intuitive version of their problem.

Just his presence stirred unbidden responses that caused Ninian to regret her decision. She'd never seen Drogo in daylight with his shirt off. She wanted to see *all* of him, in the morning light, in her bed, before and after making love.

"You want courtship?" he asked in astonishment.

"We've done the wedding night, then the wedding. It seems logical." She beamed in approval of her own thinking as she stroked the gray kitten on the bed beside her.

"Courtship." He staggered to one of the fireplace chairs and, collapsing, stared at her with incredulity. "I'm sitting here in my wife's bedchamber, while she wears nothing but a shift — which, by the way, shows your beautiful breasts and the roundness of our child quite delectably — and you want *courtship?*"

Heat bubbled through her at his words. Now that he'd mentioned it, she could feel the taut points of her nipples rubbing against the thin linen, and she very much wanted them touched as he'd touched them last night. But her daughter's future depended on her resisting a moment's pleasure.

"Call it what you will, then, but you must see me as I am before we can go forward." She held up her book and asked brightly, "Shall I read to you?"

He glared daggers. She was gambling he was not a man who took women against their will. That was a very large and dangerous gamble. He could overpower her without even trying, because she'd cave in at the first kiss.

"I think, Wife, that you are as insane as I believed you to be from the first. Do you wish to drive me to the arms of other women?"

She looked at him with interest. "Have you had other women since our wedding night?"

He scowled. "It wasn't a wedding night. It was a moment of madness," he said bluntly. "I took what I wanted, and I wanted you." At her continued look of interest, he shrugged uncomfortably, and apparently thought to soften his bluntness with pretty words. "You're the only woman I've wanted since."

Even though she suspected polite flattery, the news that he'd not had any women but her since they met thrilled her. She radiated confidence now. "Well, in the interest of equality, should you take another woman, I'm free to look at other men."

"*What?*"He almost shot out of his chair as he roared this, but he gripped the arms as if they were her throat and sat down again. "So that's what that equality vow is about?"

"Well, I'm not precisely certain, given I've never married before, but it sounds applicable."

He looked at her shrewdly, finally getting her measure. "You're making this up as you go. You're angry because I won't take you to Wystan, and you want to get even."

"No, I want to teach you a lesson," she said earnestly.

"If I come over there and kiss you now, you wouldn't even put up a fight, would you?" Dark eyes studied her with intellectual curiosity as his temper cooled.

She knew she wasn't much of a teacher, but he was an excellent student. He caught on quickly. Still, she couldn't be any less than honest. "I don't know. I'd like to think I'd try. The future of our child rides on it."

His curled eyebrows almost straightened

as he lifted them. "The future of our child rides on our not making love?"

"On our not having . . . sexual congress." She used the physician's words. "Making love is entirely different. We haven't done that yet."

She thought his eyebrows would fly straight off his head.

"I suppose this is some female nonsense about love and romance. You raise your hopes too high if you expect that to happen. I'm willing to be patient and give you time to fit into my life, but do not expect love songs and sonnets from me."

Disappointment rippled through her, but she knew it had to be so. All she could hope to earn was his respect. "No, I only want you to know I exist," she insisted.

"Oh, I know you exist." He lifted his long frame from the chair and approached the bed. "But we can take some time to know each other. Just do not dally too long," he warned as he stopped beside her.

She didn't have too long. She must learn what she could to help Wystan and return home. But if she wanted to make Drogo understand her needs as well as his own, she would hold out for as long as she could.

"I am not good at sharing," she admitted as he hovered over her. He was so large and intimidating and . . . virile. She didn't giggle at her aunt's word now. She need only glance sideways — like so — to see he was thoroughly aroused and hungry for her. She hastily glanced back to her book. "But I will do what I can to hurry the process."

"I have no experience at courting. I would much rather be inside you right now."

Flames flickered over her skin at the heated roughness of his voice.

"But you are within your rights to ask for what you've been denied," he conceded with a grim twist of his lips. "Give me a report each night on that book you're reading," he suggested, "but not now," he added hastily as she thought to reply. "I do not think I'm capable of keeping my hands off you should I linger tonight."

Then, without warning, he kissed her forehead, straightened, and walked out.

The kitten meowed in protest at thus being disturbed. Ninian scratched its head sympathetically. She'd never sleep now. Her breasts ached for the attention he would have bestowed on them.

The day after her wedding, Ninian gazed dismally at a crudely spelled letter that arrived in the morning post. Mary must have desecrated one of her few precious books to write this; it was obviously written on a torn flyleaf. Just for her to write all the way to London meant the problem was serious. The villagers thought London was another planet.

And they thought Ninian was a witch. Apparently, they must think only a witch could solve their problems now.

She read the letter again. Sheep had died. Mary's sister had miscarried. The castle burn had spilled into the town's water, and the grass and trees along it had turned brown. Mary's letter didn't say so, but the poison must have spread with the flood.

Whether they liked it or not, the village wanted her to come home. But how could she help? She still didn't know what had caused the burn to die.

She must find books, and naturalists willing to help her. She needed Drogo.

Drogo would only say his steward was taking care of it.

Perhaps Lydie and Claudia could act as her eyes and ears since they were already there. In the meantime, she must apply herself to learning everything she could, and convincing Drogo of the importance of her return once she had the knowledge.

"Your solicitor seems concerned about

some odd expenditures you have ordered. Books, and chemicals, and pumps?" Drogo dropped into the man-sized upholstered wing chair beside Ninian's bed, then glanced down to discover what the devil he was sitting on. He didn't remember a chair his size in the delicate boudoir he'd assigned to Ninian. These continual changes in his environment kept him perpetually off balance.

"How I spend my funds is of no concern to my solicitor or to you. If he continues appealing to you, I shall most certainly find another man of business."

Another woman might have sounded angry. Ninian merely stated facts. The idea of a woman controlling her own funds unsettled him, but if whatever Ninian was doing had passed the scrutiny of the Duchess of Mainwaring, he couldn't question it.

"I can recommend another solicitor if you prefer, or your aunts might wish to name one of their own. This one merely seeks to impress me with his conscientiousness. How are you coming with your translation of the diary?"

Drogo hadn't come in here to argue over money. He didn't want to admit he'd entered Ninian's chambers to court her either, but he couldn't put any other face on it. He'd gone four damned months without a woman, then indulged in one of the most sensual experiences of his life, and he damned well didn't like sleeping in a cold bed again. He would simply take a few nights to study the situation.

Knowing that instead of being repelled by his less than extraordinary looks, his wife enjoyed the same passionate attraction for him as he did for her, gave him patience.

"The handwriting in the diary is more difficult to translate than the Latin it is written in," Ninian complained. "My ancestress had a penchant for loops and swirls and strange circles and did not always use the best of pen nibs."

"Rather like Sarah."

She shot him a questioning look, then apparently recognizing his humor, smiled tentatively. It seemed she had as much difficulty knowing what to make of him as he did of her. That reassured him. Stretching out his legs toward the fire and trying not to stare too hard at the tempting thrust of her breasts against the thin nightshift, Drogo folded his arms across his chest and prepared to be entertained.

"I do not know my history well, but I looked up the date on which the diary opens and it begins during Cromwell's reign." She gently turned a brittle page. "The signature in the frontispiece is that of a Ceridwen Malcolm Ives."

"Ceridwen? That's Welsh, isn't it?"

"Yes, but until recently, my family has always drawn on Celtic names. If I had more education, I could possibly understand the connections in our old books and trace them back through history, but I can only make assumptions based on general reading."

"I should think your family would wish their daughters formally educated." It certainly didn't seem as if any man had ever stopped them, Drogo reflected cynically.

"Wystan has no teachers. The cottage has a limited library, and that contains mostly handwritten herbals and miscellaneous scribblings. We're a family who learns best by trial and error. It's not as if anyone can teach us to deal with our talents."

There she went again. Drogo squeezed his fingers together to prevent scoffing at her idea of "talent." "You must have many gardening books then. You have a green thumb when it comes to plants."

Her eyes narrowed and she ignored his observation. "Ceridwen apparently also had a talent with plants. In these first few pages, she seems very young, but she is talking about potting her kitchen herbs for the winter."

Drogo wrinkled his nose in distaste. "If that's all she has to write about, you'll not learn much from there. I thought I'd given you something more interesting."

"Her name is Malcolm *Ives,* and the Ives is in different ink, as if added later. I should think it will be interesting to know how a Malcolm and an Ives came to marry."

Drogo had an uneasy feeling it might be far better if she did not know how they fared, but it was too late to think of that now. He did not know of a single happy marriage on his family tree, including Dunstan's, from the looks of it. He watched her warily. "You will not try comparing what you learn in there to us, will you? I can assure you, I am nothing like my ancestors."

She closed the book, crossed her hands neatly on the cover, then swept his breath away with her direct gaze. She delved straight into his soul with that look. And stirred far lower portions than his soul.

"Your ancestors neglected Wystan. In what way are you different?" she asked.

She may as well have hit him with a brickbat as to accuse him of dereliction of duty. Every time he started to relax in her company, she hit him from a different direction. Scowling, he rose from the chair. "I am doing what I can for them. Sending you back there won't help anyone."

Muttering to himself, Drogo slammed out of her cheery room into the cold damp of his own. Why the devil could women never leave well enough alone?

And why did Ives men always pick impossible women?

Twenty-three

"Joseph? What are you doing here? I thought you'd taken rooms at Temple Bar." Ninian laid down her trowel as Joseph slumped beside Sarah on the garden bench.

"I did. I do." He grimaced. "I'm not meant to be a solicitor."

Sarah carefully tied aster seeds into her handkerchief before scattering the dead petals onto the ground. "Now there's an observation," she said brightly.

Paul, Joseph's youngest brother, jumped from the shed attached to the stables. "We could take those old carriage wheels, run a post through the axle holes, and make a tower you could use as a trellis for the roses."

Drogo's youngest half brothers were supposed to be in school, but they'd been sent down — again — this time for floating a helium balloon off a bell tower and setting fire to a provost's roof in the consequent crash. Their mother was still in Scotland, so they'd ended up with Drogo, as usual.

Concerned about Joseph, Ninian nodded absently at Paul's suggestion. "If you think it will work, but you must finish it and not leave things lying about," she warned. As Paul whooped and carried a discarded wheel toward the shed, she turned back to Joseph. "What happened?"

Joseph shrugged and tried to look unconcerned. "I'm a little better at drawing faces than buildings, I suppose."

"It was you?" Sarah shrieked. "*You* posted that caricature of Claudia's husband at the print shop? The one threatening the suit?"

Ninian could sense the turmoil bouncing back and forth between brother and sister, but she didn't understand the cause of it. She waited for an explanation as the younger boys worked on their projects behind her.

"Well, it was a good cartoon, and I didn't want it wasted. I didn't think anyone would know who did it. It's not as if I signed it or anything. Bastard Twane thought he could sue Drogo over nothing," he said indignantly.

"He really meant to file a crimcon suit?" Sarah cried.

Joseph shoved his fingers through his hair. "Drogo has money and Twane's apparently discovered where Claudia is hiding. Maybe he's hoping Drogo will settle just to avoid a scandal."

That did it. Ninian threw down her gloves. If someone meant to sue Drogo, she needed to know about it. "What's a crimcon suit?" she demanded.

Brother and sister turned to stare at her as if she had just popped out of the ground. Joseph replied first. "Criminal conversation. Polite legal parlance for adultery."

"But Drogo scarcely knows Claudia exists," Sarah hurriedly interrupted. "Claudia's husband beats her, and she came to me . . ."

"But once Twane discovered Drogo was aiding her, he saw an opportunity to sue someone wealthy. He didn't know Drogo had apprenticed me to his solicitor. He must not have seen me, and I heard it all. I got my back up and my pen just flew while they were talking. I've never drawn anything so good in my life."

Sarah chuckled. "I heard it was an exact likeness of Twane. Naughty boy."

Ninian had little patience for the tangled web of London society. She just knew Joseph was upset, and she had yet to discover why. "Lord Twane wants to sue Drogo for adultery? And Joseph drew a picture of him? I still don't understand."

Sarah sobered. "It showed Twane whipping Claudia. That's what he did, you know." She grimaced and turned to her half brother. "I heard you wrote a bubble over his head saying, 'And I'll sue Lord I. for all he's worth for the trouble.' Drogo will be . . ."

"Beyond furious," Joseph finished glumly. "He won't even have to know about the drawing. Twane saw the cartoon, knew he'd only told one person, ran back to the solicitor's, and they threw me out. So much for my apprenticeship."

Ahhh, now she understood. Sort of. Standing, Ninian patted Joseph's shoulder. "You must be very talented for everyone to recognize the caricature. You ought to be taking drawing lessons. I'll talk to Drogo."

"It won't do any good," Joseph replied glumly. "He'll just offer me the military or a vicarage."

"We'll see. Do you think you could climb up there and help Paul with that ladder? I'm afraid he'll fall and break his head."

"You've not had much experience with men, have you?" Sarah shook out her skirts and stood up. "They do what they want and never listen to what we say."

"Unfair, Sarah!" David cried as he appeared around the corner of the shed carrying an armload of debris. "We're at least working while you do naught but sit and look elegant."

Ninian smiled at this familiar bickering. She'd never had a brother or sister to argue with, and she'd worried over their constant skirmishing when she'd first arrived. Now that she'd had time to explore and analyze some of the feelings behind the words, she recognized love and protectiveness and concern combined with the irritation of familiarity. She rather enjoyed the coziness, and she wanted to be a part of it. This didn't require her talent for healing, but perhaps by helping Joseph, she could feel useful.

She tried to dismiss Sarah's complaint that men did what they wanted and never listened, but it hit too close to the heart of her problem. Drogo didn't *need* her. He did what he wanted, regardless of her. Perhaps she should do the same.

The babe within her stirred, and she hurriedly sat, which caused everyone in the yard to turn to her in concern. Cursing her weakness, she covered it with a vague smile and pointed at a Michaelmas daisy struggling to survive in a dark corner. "If I had a shovel, I could dig that up and plant it somewhere sunnier."

"That's your bailiwick, David!" Paul shouted from his perch on the shed roof.

"I mean to dig for Roman ruins, not flowers," David grumbled. But glancing at Ninian, Drogo's militant half brother obediently set off for a shovel.

"You'd better go back inside," Sarah told Ninian worriedly. "All this work can't be good for you."

Neither could the constant confinement of four walls, but Ninian didn't mention that. All Drogo's family looked after her with particular attention and anxiety, but they did it for Drogo's sake, she knew. No matter how much they protested Drogo's controlling behavior, they all adored their older brother and for the sake of the child she carried, they would lay themselves on the ground for her to walk on should she request it.

But it wouldn't be because they loved or wanted or even needed her. It was all for Drogo. Refusing to give in to self-pity, she bottled it up and donned her best smile.

"I'll just sit here awhile and tell everyone what to do."

"Aren't you supposed to attend that lecture with Ewen?" Sarah asked. "The boys don't need supervision. They'll have the garden cleared before you come home."

Superfluous. She was superfluous.

Ignoring a prick of pain at this rejection of her abilities, Ninian opted for the brighter side of her situation. She'd never been the recipient of so much concern in her life. Being considered fragile and helpless was a little annoying, but being the center of attention had occasional merits. Her family had always taken her independence for granted. The villagers considered Malcolms so far above them that they saw no reason to worry over her. Drogo's family treated her as rare and precious porcelain that might shatter should they step too forcefully. Watching all these large males tiptoe around her provided some entertainment.

She rose from the cold stone bench to show David where she wanted the daisy. "Dig the ground up well to soften it. I'll ask Cook for eggshells and scraps to plant with it. We really need a nice bin or hole to dump kitchen and yard scraps in. Come spring, it would make lovely soil."

David looked at her as if she were crazed, but Paul, the youngest, actually nodded approval as he slid back to the ground for another wheel. "I've read that soil can be improved with more than manure. Capability Brown says —"

"Capability Brown is a daft old farmer," Joseph declared. "I've seen what he's designed for Wakefield Lodge. He wants to tear out perfectly good trees just to plant them elsewhere. Stupid, if you ask me."

"No one asked you —"

Ninian left them arguing. According to Ceridwen's diary, all Ives men were prone to quarrelsomeness, inventiveness, and outrageously male arrogance. Nothing had changed over the last hundred years.

Gathering up her skirts, Ninian hastened inside. Drogo had spent these last weeks cautiously courting her — not with balls and soirees, but with lectures and trips to museums, when he had the time from his other pressing business. She liked books well enough, and she was trying very hard to learn about naturalist methods so she could study the burn, but she'd much rather be grubbing in dirt. Still, she'd been the one to suggest this particular lecture. She wished Drogo were taking her so she could talk to him about Joseph, but he'd said he had other appointments.

Ninian slid her hand along the newly polished wood of the banister and admired the new staircase carpet as she hurried to her chamber. Under Sarah's guidance, Drogo's messily male household was slowly gaining a refurbished look. After living in a drafty, dreary cottage the better part of her life, Ninian only knew how to keep the kitchen clean and the beds made. She might notice the disorganization of Drogo's household, but she would never have known what to do about it without Sarah's help.

Hurriedly cleaning her hands and changing her wool dress for a more fashionable silk, Ninian let her newly assigned maid catch her hair up and pin it beneath a cap. Then grabbing the cloak the maid offered, she hurried downstairs again. She wouldn't let her time in London go to waste.

She nearly stumbled and fell on the last steps at the sight of Drogo standing with Ewen in the front hall. She had only to mention a whim, and one of Drogo's brothers would make himself available to her. Perhaps, maybe, she should have mentioned to Drogo that Ewen had volunteered for this one. He'd only just returned from the north, and she was eager to question him about conditions there.

Guiltily, she glanced from one brother to the other. Drogo looked as impassive as ever. Handsome Ewen grinned and bowed at her appearance. Drogo's youngest legitimate brother possessed all the cheerfulness her husband did not.

But it was Drogo's respect she craved.

She dragged her gaze back to his and carefully descended the final steps.

"I have only two tickets to the lecture, my lady," Ewen said cheerily, waving the passes between them. "And as much as I should like to hear the professor on Naturalism in the Study of Our Waterways, I believe Old Ironface here has first claim to your company."

She wished she knew how to react to all this male attention. She was used to hiding behind a witless smile and going her own way. Here, she had no need to dissemble. Ives men didn't fear her as the villagers did. They didn't have a superstitious bone in their bodies. On the contrary, they really did believe her helpless and incapable of causing the least bit of harm. She adored their attentiveness, even if she fretted at their stubborn refusal to recognize her abilities.

Receiving no reaction from Drogo, she dimpled and curtsied for Ewen's benefit. "Heaven forbid that I should stand in the way of the edification of two eminent naturalists such as yourselves."

Drogo snatched the passes from his brother's hand. "Ewen does not know the meaning of honesty. He would rather watch grass grow than attend a lecture. Come along, the carriage is waiting."

Ninian shot Ewen an accusatory glare. "You did this on purpose."

He lifted his hands in a helpless gesture and smiled blindingly. Of all the brothers, Ewen used his charm best. "Drogo would not leave his books and charts otherwise. One cannot claim that he uses his title to win society's acceptance."

"That's because I don't need society's acceptance." Gruffly, Drogo drew Ninian's hand through the crook of his elbow and nearly dragged her toward the door.

"Perhaps you don't," Ninian protested, "but perhaps your family might?"

Ewen looked shocked that she'd understood the truth behind his jest. Drogo merely developed a grim tic at the corner of his mouth. "If society is so bumble-witted as to blame us for the sins of our parents, I have no use for them."

Dozens of things instantly became clear, and Ninian gaped as she tried to comprehend all of them at once. Drogo didn't give her time. He flung open the door and half carried her to the waiting coach.

Naive in the way of society, she hadn't realized how the late earl's misalliances must have irreparably destroyed the reputation of the Ives family. Even Drogo's legitimate brothers must feel the damage. No wonder poor Joseph was struggling. As earl, Drogo could afford to ignore the rejection of his peers. As penniless younger sons, his brothers could not. She understood rejection entirely too well.

"I don't like London," Ninian declared as Drogo clambered in beside her.

"So you have said." Taking the seat across from her, Drogo rapped for the driver to begin, crossed his arms, and proceeded to ignore her as well as he did society — one man against the world.

"I have no use for society." She restated her comment.

"That is agreeable with me."

She would kick his shin but she would bruise her toe. She really needed her country clogs back. "I mean, I never learned the ways of society. My aunts offered to take me in, but I deliberately chose to live in Wystan."

She thought that caught his attention, but he did no more than cock an absurdly curled eyebrow. She drew a deep breath to calm her anger, but winced as the baby kicked.

He instantly transferred to the seat beside

her and wrapped a sheltering arm across her shoulders. She wanted to bury herself in the strength and comfort of his embrace as much as she wanted to elbow him and tell him to let her alone. The big clod didn't have an understanding bone in his body, but she was coming to love the extraordinary combination of tenderness and desire he offered.

"I'll have the driver turn around. You should be in bed, resting."

"I should be in Wystan, potting my herbs for the winter," she said tartly as she recovered her breath. "I am fine. City air does not agree with me." She straightened and edged as far from him as the narrow seat would allow. Her need for his touch had not lessened with time, and she would be tugging at his shirt ties if she did not distance herself.

Propping his feet on the opposite seat, Drogo remained planted where he was. "We will go to Ives for the holidays, and you may smell Dunstan's cows all you like."

Blinking back tears, Ninian gazed out the window. Despite all his concern, he rejected her talents and needs just as her father had done. If she could not make him understand . . .

What would she do? She had gifts meant to benefit the people around her. If the people nearest and dearest didn't want or need her, what was her purpose?

"My aunts can see that your brothers are accepted." Perhaps if she offered help to his family, he would learn to appreciate her, even if it didn't require her gifts.

"I am not a poor man. I'm perfectly capable of providing for my brothers until they can provide for themselves. They don't need society's idle drinking and gambling."

"Or to marry well?" she asked softly.

"They're better off supporting themselves than relying on women."

Ninian bit her tongue. She supposed if Drogo could have fathered a child without her, she would not need to exist at all. She wanted the child. She just hadn't realized it reduced her to the level of the machines that so engaged Drogo's brothers.

"So Joseph must become a solicitor when he would rather learn architecture? And Davy become a soldier when he would rather dig for Roman ruins?" she asked flatly.

He propped his broad shoulders in the corner and glared at her. "Those are indulgences of the idle rich. They need to support themselves. It's bad enough that Ewen thinks he can make a fortune by harnessing steam without the others following in his footsteps. Or would you rather keep him around as your personal pet? He lives off his looks as it is. I'm certain your wealth would keep him entertained for quite some time."

She'd never had a violent moment in her life until she'd met this man. She wanted to smack him hard right now. Instead, she donned the only protective defense she'd ever learned. She smiled like a daft sheep and batted her eyelashes. "How kind of you to think me so pitiful I must buy admiration, that Ewen can be bought, and that you would make a good cuckold. Your opinions are so reassuring."

She couldn't read auras as her cousin Christina could. She couldn't even sense the emotions reeling through the empty hole of her husband's soul. But she thought he turned purple at her words.

"It wouldn't have been the first time I've been made a cuckold," he finally declared, without an ounce of intonation.

"The lady you intended to marry last year?" she asked, searching for under-standing. As he narrowed his eyes in suspi-cion, she said hurriedly, "Sarah told me you decorated the nursery for her."

His expression remained cold and un-readable. "I've never practiced celibacy" —

he dipped his head meaningfully in her direction — "until now."

She wouldn't allow him to lay that guilt on her. He must be hurting. No man could be stoic about asking a woman to marry him, only to discover she carried another man's child. "Why would she tell you the child was yours if it wasn't? Why did she not go to the child's real father?"

He crossed his arms and glared over her head. "Because I'm titled and wealthy and the child's father was not. It's of no importance."

She didn't need her gift to read Drogo's pain. He'd wanted that child. He'd been given perfidy instead. With a sigh, all the anger flowed out of her.

"I'm a healer with a gift for empathy, my lord," she stated as flatly as he. "Some call me witch. But I've never been accused of mind reading. If you would accuse me of being akin to such a terrible person, please state it in words so that I might answer in the same."

"I am not accusing anyone of anything."

"I can read everyone's emotions but my husband's," she muttered in disgust.

"Why not mine?" he asked with curiosity.

All his anger had seemingly fled once expressed. In wonderment, she shook her head. "Because you haven't any?" she suggested.

"Then lust must not be an emotion."

Before either of them could act on the heated look in his eyes, the carriage halted in front of the lecture hall.

Ninian breathed a sigh of relief. Being trapped in a carriage with Drogo was akin to being trapped in a furnace with no escape. She didn't think she would be able to deny him much longer. She mirrored his heat and craved his touch — a most ignoble admission for an independent witch who must leave him behind if he could not be made to understand.

Twenty-four

Unaware that this particular lecture hall was located in busy Covent Garden, Ninian was caught by surprise at the blast of human joys and angers that overwhelmed her as soon as Drogo left the coach. Somehow, her husband's impassivity had shielded her until now.

Concentrating on the good and not the bad as Granny had taught her, she took Drogo's hand to climb down. His touch had a curiously soothing effect, and she clung to it as she looked with interest about the crowded street.

Gentlemen in colorful long coats, cockaded hats, and wearing impressive scabbards topped with silver swords gathered in humming conversation outside a theater door. Several glanced up in interest at their arrival.

Farther down the street, men in drab

coats carrying heavy tomes spoke heatedly in front of the lecture hall. Ninian recognized several from earlier lectures. Educated men of studious natures, they argued everything from philosophy to politics and often wrote and published their opinions — or diatribes against those whose opinions disagreed with theirs.

In between these groups, fashionable ladies in towering wigs and hats hurried along the cobbled street, followed by maids and footmen carrying stacks of purchases. Orange girls swinging baskets of fruit rushed to catch the best rows in the theater, flower girls hawked their posies, and all the myriad street life of urchins and beggars and thieves pushed and shoved around them. Ninian concentrated on balling all their teeming emotions into one solid tangle that she could tuck into a corner of her mind and ignore. She'd strengthened the technique over the years, and could wield it quite well — unless something threatening leapt out at her. As it did now.

Gasping at the impact, Ninian dug her fingers into Drogo's coat and swung around to locate the malevolence aimed in their direction. Half expecting to see the mysterious Ives from the wedding, she shrank back against Drogo's stalwart form as she located a sharp-faced man halting his fashionable imported phaeton amid the stream of traffic. Drivers hurled curses, horses screamed, and pedestrians dashed for cover as the man shook his whip and leapt, shouting, from his seat.

His horse, already unnerved by a stripe of pain, pranced dangerously now that its reins fell lax. Cornered by an ale wagon in front and a stream of sedan chairs behind, the horse could do naught but rear and trumpet its fear. Its owner ignored the rumpus as he shook his whip and hurried through the crowd toward Drogo and Ninian.

"Twane!" Uttering a curse, Drogo shoved Ninian toward their coach. "Inside, hurry."

She couldn't. If she let him go, she would faint with the strength of the hatred and rage foaming around her. He was her only shelter. As she was his.

Drogo could shield her from the emotional weapons Twane flung, and she could shield Drogo physically. Even an insane man wouldn't strike an obviously pregnant lady in front of a street full of witnesses.

Donning her best witless smile, still clinging to Drogo's coat, she stepped in front of her husband and beamed at the angry man coiling his weapon.

Drogo roared, caught her by the waist, and practically flung her toward the carriage. His timing thrown off by Ninian's action, Twane hesitated with whip raised, and slashed it downward a second too late.

The blow glanced off Drogo's shoulder, ripping his coat, then backlashed to strike a curiosity-seeker who had ventured too near. Loosened by the blow and caught by the wind, the man's cockaded hat flew into the street, startling Twane's already anxious horse.

The horse reared, screaming.

"The little boy!" Freed of Drogo's grasp, Ninian acted on sheer force of will alone, shoving into the gathering crowd as the horse reared and battered its dangerous hooves.

With outstretched hand, Ninian reached through the throng and grabbed the coat of a frightened child. She hauled him against her just as the horse's slashing hooves tore off the rear of the cart, sending barrels rolling and crashing into the street where the boy had been standing.

The throng crushed around her as a woman screamed and men shouted. The horse whinnied in fear not inches from their noses, and Ninian pressed the child in a protective embrace. Calmly, Drogo appeared through the mass of humanity to grab the horse's rein.

Sighing in relief, Ninian hugged the crying child as the crowd surged, all talking and gesticulating at once.

The intensity of Twane's anger faltered, but she'd lost her concentration and a barrage of other passions leapt free. Gratitude swamped her as the child's weeping mother flung her silks and perfumes into the milieu. Curiosity and fury emanated from the bystanders who had caught all or part of the scene. Ninian's head spun, and she wanted to weep along with the child. Swaying, she released him into his mother's arms.

Drogo caught her before she fell.

"I'm not through with you yet, Ives!" Twane shouted as Drogo lifted her into his arms and carried her through the path created by bystanders. "I'll make you pay!"

Weakened and vulnerable from the emotional assault, for the first time in her memory, Ninian caught someone else's fury, wrapped it around her, and used it for herself. Shoving against Drogo's shoulder, she forced him to halt. "Put me down, Drogo. Put me down right now."

He looked at her as if she were crazed, then proceeded toward the coach again.

"If you don't put me down, I'll scream

bloody murder," she warned.

"Fine, that's just what I need," he muttered. "Cause another scene, why don't you? The crowd won't need to pay for theater entertainment."

"Put her down, Ives," a familiar, welcome voice intruded warningly. "Ninian did not start this war, you did. She must act as she thinks best under the circumstances."

"Aunt Stella!" Ninian cried with relief as Drogo glared at the large woman bearing down on them like a full-rigged ship in sail.

"She is my wife and I will do as I think best for her," he answered coldly, defying the duchess as no man ever had — except, perhaps, the duke.

Stella drew herself up indignantly, her extra chin quivering with fury. "Ninian is a *Malcolm*, sir. She knows what's best for her better than any Ives could possibly do."

"I must get down. That man is much too mad . . ." Ninian wriggled in Drogo's arms. The fury still emanated from behind her, and she had to shield Drogo, shield herself, and fling it back where it belonged. She had to. She'd never done it before, but she must. Grandmother had said she could do anything.

The woman carrying her little boy broke through the crowd. "My lady, my lady! I must thank you. You cannot know . . ."

With exasperation, Drogo lowered Ninian to her feet but kept his arm firmly around her shoulders, sheltering her more than he knew or understood.

"You saved Tommy's life! I don't know how you did it. He's always escaping me and I don't know how you knew where he was, but you saved his life. Bless you!"

"Bloody miracle, it was," someone muttered. "Never saw the like."

"She couldn't of seen him, him being that small and all."

"Pushed right past me, she did, and I was right there and didn't see it."

"It was a miracle, all right."

Stella did not dignify the crowd's comments with her notice but wrapped Ninian in her embrace. "You did well, child, but you must teach this oaf not to . . ."

"Or witchery," a cruel voice called from the back of the crowd. "Haven't you heard? Ives has married a witch!"

That did it. She would not be called "witch" in that derogatory manner ever again. Unwrapping herself from her aunt's embrace and Drogo's hampering hold, Ninian snatched Drogo's rapier from its scabbard. Raising it in front of her, she stalked through the crowd. Prepared for entertainment, onlookers fell away to let her pass.

She dodged Drogo as he grabbed for her, and helpfully, the crowd fell in behind her, cutting him off as they watched to see what would happen next.

Coming face-to-face with the hatchet-faced man who'd wielded his whip so cruelly, Ninian smiled, startling him.

"For what you've done to your lady wife, Lord Twane, I condemn you to hell," she said calmly. "For what you could have done to that little boy with your carelessness, I merely claim your coat buttons."

Frozen by the look of fury behind her wicked smile, Twane didn't react quickly enough. Carried on the winds of the anger he projected, Ninian denuded Twane's gold-braided coat of its expensive buttons with one decisive slice, uncovering a long vest decorated with a double row of more gold. With a truly evil grin, she sliced again, scattering the buttons across the cobblestones and into the hands of grubby urchins who fought and squabbled and chased the glittering disks across the dirt.

"Witches cast curses, my lord," she said conversationally as Drogo finally caught up with her and grabbed the wrist holding his rapier. "But you're already accursed. I foresee a miserable and lonely death for the likes of you."

Drogo arrived just as the whites of Ninian's eyes rolled up. He caught her by the waist and swept her up before she fell. A woman screamed and men muttered around him, but he concentrated wholly on the problem that was literally falling into his hands. Cuddling his foolish, pregnant wife against his chest, holding his rapier protectively in front of her, he glared at Twane. "I suggest a long sojourn in Paris, Twane. I believe you've already run afoul of one of my brothers. The rest will gladly torment your every waking moment, no matter how I might advise them otherwise."

He thought he said it quite as calmly as Ninian had, but Twane blanched even whiter. The threat of unleashing the nest of hornets that were Drogo's brothers ought to terrify the most courageous, but Drogo didn't think Twane had the imagination to understand his danger. Maybe it was something in his own face that caused Twane to shrink backward, searching for an escape hole. Drogo certainly felt capable of murder.

Although he wasn't entirely certain who he wished to kill most, Twane or Ninian.

Stella strode briskly up beside him and

shook her parasol under Twane's nose. "If you dare show your face in this town again, I'll have it personally removed!"

Whether Twane understood precisely who Stella was didn't matter. Assaulted by demented demons, he took the only sensible path and dashed for the safety of his phaeton.

Urchins ran taunting after him as he attempted to steer his carriage from the tangle of traffic. No longer caring what happened to the bastard, Drogo awkwardly returned his rapier to its place while still holding his unconscious wife.

"She let passion get the better of her again," Stella commented prosaically, not in the least concerned. "She did it often as a child. Take her back to Wystan, Ives. She may be capable of handling London when she is stronger, but the child drains her."

Without explaining that insane statement further, Stella sailed off down the street as if nothing had happened. A footman and a maid ran after her, and the awed crowd let her pass until she disappeared into the throng as if she had never been there at all.

Torn between running after Ninian's aunt with questions and separating Ninian from the prying crowd, Drogo gave up one and attempted the other. He hated being an object of ridicule, speculation, or even interest. Society had ignored him all his life, and he had returned the favor. He certainly didn't wish to court it in this manner, and he couldn't believe Ninian willingly would either. He only wished to see her safe and ascertain that Ninian and her babe hadn't been harmed by her intemperate behavior. His heart pounded fitfully at her lack of response.

"Out of the lady's way!" a pair of urchins grasping golden buttons shouted, clearing a path to the coach. "Make way for the lady!"

"Maybe we could use a few more witches to clear the streets of wretches like Twane," someone murmured from behind Drogo.

"How *did* she see that child?" another queried. "She wasn't even near."

"That's Lady Ives," Drogo heard one of his fellow scholars inform another. "Sweet young thing. Deucedly odd, though. Asked me once if I knew what makes water sour."

Sighing, Drogo lowered Ninian to the coach seat just as she started to stir. He may not like drawing attention to himself, but whether either of them wanted it or not, he'd damned well done it by marrying Ninian. He'd have to learn to live with the consequences.

He could live with consequences. He just

wasn't certain he could repeat the nightmare of Ninian collapsing before his eyes. He didn't think his heart would ever beat properly again.

He drew her into his lap as her lashes fluttered, and ignoring all offers of help, he ordered the doors closed. He didn't think Ninian would appreciate an audience.

"You'll see a physician," Drogo informed her as she came around. "It cannot be right for you to collapse like that." Or behave like that, but he didn't think he'd mention that. Women did not attack men with swords. Had she been in a rage, he might have understood, but she'd seemed perfectly calm.

"I most certainly will not. There is nothing wrong with me." Looking fragile and wan, Ninian rebelliously straightened her shoulders. Her maid's efforts to control her golden ringlets had come undone in the scuffle, and they curled riotously around her shoulders.

She'd wriggled out of his grasp, but Drogo could still reach out and wrap a curl around his finger. "You did not see yourself faint. It was a most daunting sight, and I have no wish to go through it again."

She shrugged and looked out the window as the coach jostled along the crowded street. "I used to do it quite frequently, before I went to Wystan. I've learned to handle it better since then, but I was overwrought. It is nothing. London has far too many people."

He could ascribe her words to a woman's hysteria and forget about it. Pregnant women were prone to fainting spells. Everyone knew that. And she had definitely been overwrought. He'd no idea she possessed such a temper, if temper it had been. Now that he had recovered from the shock, he was rather proud of her ability to wield a rapier. He ought to question her about that, not the matter of London having too many people. But the duchess had said much the same, and it was slowly dawning on him that Ninian often told him things without explaining their importance. Perhaps, to her, they weren't important. They were the same as saying the grass is green and the sky is blue.

But in his fascination with his bewildering wife, everything she said suddenly possessed significance. He really needed to examine her claims more thoroughly. The alternative was to dismiss her as befuddled, and he'd had one too many examples that Ninian knew precisely what she was doing.

"You are saying too many people caused your fainting spell, and not the child?"

Her head snapped around, and she raised her lovely eyebrows at him. "Of course."

"I understand some people are overset by heavy odors, that they cannot tolerate an abundance of perfumes and street stenches and the like. Could that be the cause?"

She rolled her eyes and looked out the window again. "Scent is not a problem. People are."

"There are people in Wystan." Baffled, Drogo searched for her logic.

She sighed and rested her head against the seat back. "I do not have explanations. I am used to the people in Wystan. They aren't strangers, and there are far fewer of them than there are in London, so I suppose I can protect myself against them easier. Here, I am battered from too many un-knowns at once. I am growing accustomed to shielding myself, I think, and for some reason, you act as a buffer also, but I cannot always stop the force of strong emotion. I don't fully understand what just happened any more than you do. I just know I turned Twane's anger against him, but it drained me."

All right, that was going a little too far over the line from natural philosophy into the supernatural. Drogo set his mouth and filed the information for future reference.

He would need more evidence before he could reach any conclusions. "And the little boy?" he inquired, wishing he'd learn to shut up and not ask.

A wistful smile curved the corners of her lips. "That is the first time I can think of that I have actually found a use for my gift. I felt his fear and knew exactly where to find him. Isn't that amazing?"

Amazing wasn't the half of it.

She was sitting here trying to convince him she was a lunatic so he'd send her home, and all he wanted to do was hold her in his arms again, and kiss her until she begged for more.

The question of which one of them was sane remained unanswered.

Twenty-five

October

Court her, Drogo mused, sitting in his empty study, wishing he were anywhere else. Ninian wanted him to court her. He'd tried everything he knew, but he wasn't any closer to her bed than before.

What more could he do? He didn't move about in society much. The kind of families that would accept the Duchess of Mainwaring and her niece wouldn't acknowledge the existence of a ramshackle family like his. His father and his grandfather — and untold Ives ancestors dating back through the annals of time — had stamped "scapegrace, rakehell, and scoundrel" on the family escutcheon. It had never bothered Drogo to any great extent. He was capable of making his own way in the world without the aid of a bored and boring society of fops.

But a wife . . . A wife expected more.

He glanced at the letter Ninian had left on his desk. The barely literate lettering indicated it came from one of her Wystan friends. They needed a healer again. After rejecting and practically throwing her out of town, they begged for her aid now. Typical.

It was too late in the year even to consider it. If the villagers didn't think of Ninian's welfare, he must. Ewen had said winter had arrived early up there, that an ice storm had covered the road when he'd left. Drogo refused to risk Ninian and their child to that sort of danger. The village would have to survive the winter without her.

She would be furious. He'd have to make it up to her somehow. He desperately wanted his marriage to work, to prove the Ives tradition of broken homes and scandal had died with his father.

He desperately wanted Ninian.

Combing his fingers through his hair, Drogo contemplated the problem. His gaze fell on the thriving palm in front of his study window. It had grown a foot or more in the two months since Ninian's arrival.

Out of curiosity, he wandered to a window overlooking his once ragged kitchen courtyard. White and red roses bloomed on an extravagantly designed trellis that concealed the garden shed. Did roses bloom in October?

A riot of Michaelmas daisies bounced on sturdy stems in a sunny corner. The gray-green leaves of unfamiliar herbs decorated newly turned beds of rich dirt. Grass instead of dust surrounded the old stone bench where his brothers once rolled and played games. Next year, he'd have a child of his own gamboling on that welcoming lawn.

Something warm and almost joyous stirred in him at the image of a sturdy child toddling through the grass at his mother's feet. Ninian would be a wonderful mother, a warm and understanding mother who would love their child in a way he and his brothers had never been loved.

Tears stung his eyes, and he turned back to his desk. He would show Ninian how much she meant to him. As a wedding gift, he'd ordered the rebuilding of the Wystan conservatory. He knew little about plants and had intended to leave stocking it to Ninian when they returned in the spring. But he could do better than that.

Pulling out a sheet of vellum, he began scribbling further instructions to his steward and bailiff in Wystan. He couldn't take his wife home yet, but he could see to it that his castle was the home she needed when they arrived.

And then, he'd figure out how to get her back in his bed. He refused to spend the long, cold winter alone just for the sake of a foolish whim.

"The reports I've received from Wystan are alarming," Aunt Stella scolded. "I daresay it is something your foolish Ives husband has done to cause this disaster. It's our duty to correct it."

"But, Aunt Stella, I cannot just walk out on Drogo," Ninian protested.

"You have left this entirely too late, Ninian." Completely ignoring Ninian's protest, Stella paced back and forth across the newly installed sea-green and ivory carpet in Ninian's sitting room. "Winter has set in and you risk much. I'll provide my coach and an army of outriders to escort you."

Ninian's stomach clenched at the thought of leaving Drogo. "He's been hurt too often," she pleaded. "Surely there is something we can do to make him understand."

"He's a man." Stella waved her beringed hand dismissively. "He'll survive. They always do." She pinned her niece with a sharp gaze. "You, on the other hand, might not. And neither will the village. The children are ill and there have already been two miscarriages. With several of the younger girls carrying their first babes, it's no time to leave them without your talents. And you've been oversetting yourself with your foolish jaunts about town. You'll lose your own child if you're not careful."

"But Drogo's family needs me," Ninian whispered, searching desperately for some solution beyond the one her aunt suggested. She *knew* it would hurt Drogo if she left. He wasn't the cold, unfeeling man he pretended to be. He was just so . . . *blind.*

And so was her aunt, but she couldn't politely say that.

"I have done as you asked," Stella replied indignantly. "I have arranged drawing lessons for that illegitimate . . ."

"Joseph. His name is Joseph." Ninian knit her fingers and gazed into the crackling fire. "And you cannot just *give* him the lessons. He must earn them. He's shy, but he's proud. He needs to be out from under Drogo's thumb so he can stand on his own."

"Hmph." Stella sailed back across the carpet and plumped into the chair opposite Ninian's. Her panniers flew upward without disturbing her teacup. "He can design the folly the duke wants for the rose garden. If he's any good at all, half of society will be begging for his talents by this time next year."

Ninian smiled gratefully. "Thank you. He has the talent. He just needs encouragement. But there is still the matter of Ewen. Drogo has refused him any more funds for his foundry. He wants Ewen to go into business with a shipping merchant friend of his, but Ewen gets seasick, and he has no understanding of money at all. He's extremely inventive and can work wonders with mechanical things. I know he can find a way to produce steel cheaply if he only had someone to manage his financial backing."

"Ewen is the legitimate one?" Stella asked sharply. "The one who experimented with electricity and nearly burned down —"

"But it worked," Ninian reminded her. "He showed that we might someday harness the power of lightning."

"So he might burn down bigger and better buildings." Stella sniffed, sipped her tea, and thought about it. "It wouldn't hurt to have him on the other end of the country, far from London and civilization. I don't want him near Wystan," she warned, eyeing Ninian narrowly. "It won't do to have an Ives fouling up Wystan again."

"Drogo has a mining operation north of there. That's where Ewen started his foundry. It was a good idea, having a constant source of coal for his furnaces."

"Yes, well . . ." Stella set down her cup. "Persuade Drogo to provide half the backing, then you can supply the rest. And *you* can handle the funds so the rapscallion doesn't start investing them in helium balloons or electric firestarters or whatever."

Satisfied, she stood up. "That should take care of the worst of it. You should have no reason not to return where you belong now."

"Except Drogo," Ninian murmured, staring down at her hands to prevent her aunt from seeing the tears in her eyes. Solving everyone else's problems was easy. Solving her own never had been.

Stella's voice softened. "He's an Ives, my dear. They have a history of doing things their way and the world be damned. I'm certain he's not a bad man. He will just never know that you exist except as a warm body to heat his bed. Learn to accept him that way, and you can go on as you did before, and all will be perfectly well again."

Calling for her maid and gathering up the bundle of remedies Ninian always prepared for the family at this time of year, Stella swept out, leaving her niece to contemplate her luxurious suite with despair.

Nothing had ever been perfectly well, and now that she had some inkling of what it was like to be part of a family, it might never be well again, because that family needed Drogo more than they needed her. And Drogo didn't know she existed. Loneliness seeped through all the broken cracks of Ninian's soul.

She'd tried regaling her husband with tales from her ancestor's diary in hopes that he would understand the family from which she came. When Ceridwen had married one of Drogo's ancestors, Ninian had pointed out the mistakes they'd made, and Drogo had agreed Ceridwen had been too impulsive and his ancestor too unfeeling. But he couldn't see the application beyond that.

She'd quit reading him passages when Ceridwen bore a baby girl and her Ives husband disavowed it, claiming no Ives had ever fathered a girl. He'd set Ceridwen aside in the cottage Ninian assumed was the one her grandmother called home, and he'd kept the castle that had been his wife's dowry. She couldn't bear to read further.

What could she learn from a book that only spelled out her own fate?

The people of London didn't need her healing talents. They had their so-called physicians to wait on them. They wouldn't believe a woman could be better. Drogo's family needed him here in London. And Drogo loved his duties as much as she loved hers.

She desperately desired her husband's acceptance, but to achieve it, she must give up all that she was. She would become like her mother, and die.

She couldn't let him do that to her. If he couldn't see that she was a person in her own right, with abilities and needs of her own, and not a bed warmer, then she had no choice but to return to Wystan, alone.

The villagers needed her far more than he did.

"A ball! We will have a ball. That's the solution."

Ninian frowned at Sarah's response to her question. "I don't think that's the answer," she said slowly, not wanting to dampen Sarah's enthusiasm. "Drogo doesn't much like social occasions. And how will that persuade him I must return home?"

"Why, if you introduce all of us to your aunts' inner circles, we'll be too busy to annoy Drogo, and he won't have a thing to do. Then he can go with you." In satisfaction, Sarah spun around the downstairs hall. "We'll have to *completely* redecorate. This place is much too unfashionable." She stopped twirling to eye Ninian speculatively. "Unless one of your aunts would offer her home . . . ?"

Ninian shook her head vehemently. "We definitely do not want to involve my aunts." Rather than explain, she made excuses. "They're much too busy for such things. Besides, they spend most of their time in Hertfordshire. Sarah, I really don't think . . ."

"Drogo will be immensely grateful to have us off his hands. Besides, everyone in town is talking about you after the Twane incident. You really must be introduced to society properly. *Everyone* will come. Perhaps I could persuade Claudia and Lydie . . ."

She wandered off, finger to lips, contemplating the aging wallpaper and heavy draperies of the reception area.

In dismay, Ninian remained behind. She didn't think a social occasion the answer at all, but she didn't know what was. Drogo had been unusually attentive lately, bringing her hothouse flowers and even a diamond bracelet. She couldn't hurt him by saying she had little use for cut flowers and stones. She needed to be needed, but not just in the way Drogo had in mind.

As if her thoughts conjured him, her arrogant husband strode through the front door. He started to fling his hat and cloak on the table that was no longer there, then waited impatiently for the new housekeeper to hurry up and claim them. Seeing Ninian, he surrendered the garments, and smiling, came toward her.

"Why the serious frown?" he inquired, caressing her cheek as he did so often.

She loved those touches. Studying the warm depth of his dark eyes, Ninian felt the jolt of need that was always there between them, the tie that bound them more firmly than any other. She craved his touch as a gambler craved cards and dice, no matter whether they ran good or bad.

"Sarah wants to give a ball."

"Sarah has windmills for brains. No one will attend." He threw the suggestion aside without further thought. "How is my son faring this day?" He smoothed the layers of fabric over her growing belly, testing and exploring this new object of his fascination.

The ache within her grew as she studied his rapt attention. Drogo would be fascinated with the growth of any child, she knew, but because this one was his, he felt more comfortable in expressing his interest. It was not her he noticed, just the scientific observation of a miracle at work.

"Sarah thinks everyone will attend," she said tentatively. What if Sarah was right? What if Drogo would relinquish his London duties and accompany her to Wystan if his family was well established in society? Could she afford not to try?

Attention distracted by her insistence, Drogo searched her face. "Would that make you happy? If a ball is what you wish, I'll do all within my power to make it happen."

A ball was the very last thing she wanted. Why could he not see that? If he understood her at all, if he'd listened to anything she'd said, he'd know that.

The way he was looking at her now, the intensity of his gaze as he awaited her answer, gave her a small hope that perhaps, this time, he would listen.

"What I wish is to return to Wystan," she began carefully. "If your steward cannot find the source of the blight, perhaps you could help me —"

He did not even give her time to say more. He brushed her cheek with a kiss. "In the spring, after the babe is born. Payton is doing all he can. You can visit with your friends then and see. Maybe Sarah is right. You need new friends here. Plan a little dinner and dancing, and I'll help you with the invitation list."

He tucked a curl behind her ear and gave her an expectant look. "Make it soon, and we'll call it our wedding reception and start all over," he said suggestively.

Apparently approving his own generosity, he kissed her fingers and took the stairs to his study two at a time, whistling happily.

Below, Ninian gazed after him in broken-hearted dismay. He simply didn't understand the importance of Wystan or her need to help. He didn't understand it was her *responsibility* to help.

She wanted so much for him to see her as she was and not as the convenient receptacle for his seed. But even should he develop blinding insight, how could she conceivably believe that he would love *what* she was? Her father hadn't. If a father couldn't love a daughter, how could a stranger?

Perhaps a clean break was best for all.

Like a gambler, she would risk it all on one throw. She would make him see her, and then he would have to decide once and for all if he wanted the person she was.

The potential for disaster was enormous, but then, the legend had warned of that all along. She'd been the fool who hadn't believed.

Twenty-six

November

The first inkling Drogo experienced that his suggestion for a little dinner might have grown out of proportion arrived with the discovery of workmen ripping out not just his grandfather's beloved walnut paneling, but also the walls bearing it.

The enormous light-filled space that resulted was immediately filled with tile setters laying huge squares of black and white, drapers testing swaths of red velvet, and at one point, Ninian's Aunt Hermione standing on a sofa back, hanging a pomander.

"To drive out the old spirits and welcome the new, dear," she said absently, even though he hadn't asked.

After that, he entered through the rear door and pretended this would all lead to

Ninian's bed — sooner or later.

He knew exceedingly little about the time necessary to redecorate, refurbish, and rearrange an entire household, but it seemed to him that his home was transformed in a miraculously short period of time. Ninian's aunts must have added their considerable wealth and power to expedite the process. He didn't complain. Ninian smiled at him more often now, and she even ventured to kiss his cheek without prompting. It was working. She was happy. She'd finally given up her silliness of wishing to return to Wystan.

Relieved, Drogo signed the invoices for continued improvements to the village's water system, read his steward's reports on the progress of the conservatory, paid the bills for the town-house repairs, and waited eagerly for his "wedding" night.

On the designated evening for the dinner, he arrived home late. An argument on the floor of the Lords had spilled over into a serious debate in the halls, and he hadn't been able to tear himself away. Rushing up the back stairs, ripping off his jabot, Drogo prayed his newly hired valet had his clothes laid out. He'd never seen the point of a valet before, but if his wife wished to hold many entertainments, a valet could be useful.

He stopped short just inside his chamber door at the sight of Ninian waiting for him. Ninian never came to him in his chambers.

She looked beyond lovely against the backdrop of his dark bed hangings. She wore her golden hair swept upward and tangled with pearls in the same manner as ladies of fashion, except her curls were real and not the false ones of society. Candlelight flickered over white shoulders rising from a soft silver-blue bodice adorned with a shimmer of silver gauze. Her panniers and full skirts hid her burgeoning belly, and Drogo thought her thickening waist the most beautiful sight he'd ever seen. She would look even better unclothed and on his bed tonight.

"You are more beautiful than any bride," he whispered, startled by the huskiness of his voice as he approached her.

"And you are late, my lord," she admonished, but a twinkle in her eyes and the dimple at her lips told him he need not worry about a scold. Ninian never scolded. She lit up his life with flowers and smiles and joy, albeit in a confusing array. He would have to shower her with his appreciation, somehow.

"I apologize. Where is my valet? I will be quick."

"Everything has been taken care of. You need only present yourself when you are ready. I have chained Sarah to the wall so she cannot rant at you."

"If you promise to keep her there and feed her thrice a day, I will grovel at your feet forever," he promised.

She laughed, a silvery shimmering laugh that bathed him in happiness. She had been right. They'd needed this time to get to know each other. This was far better than the tense, frantic chaos of their wedding day. Tonight, they would come together in joy, and never be parted again. Cautiously, he opened himself to the airy uplifting of hope.

"You do not value Sarah's talents as you should," she chided gently. "She has far too much time on her hands and not enough to occupy her considerable energy. Perhaps you should turn the raising of your younger brothers over to her."

He rolled his eyes as he pulled off his coat and waistcoat. "She would set them sailing down the River Tick. No, thank you." Was that disappointment he saw flickering in her eyes at his reply? Surely not.

"My aunts will be arriving early. I must see to them. I'll send up a glass of wine and a small tray of cheese and bread to hold you over."

Her soft slippers pattered out, leaving Drogo bereft. He needed a week alone in his tower with his wife. That would cure his ravenous cravings. Until then, he'd have to accept the few crumbs she offered. She carried the weighty burden of his child. For that, he would pay whatever price she exacted.

His valet was still fussing when Drogo heard the arrival of the first carriages. Assuring himself that he didn't have to be there to greet Ninian's eccentric aunts, he bit his tongue and didn't curse as the wretched servant took forever buckling the tiny silver buckles at the knee of his velvet breeches. But when the man started clucking in disapproval over the lack of suitable pins with which to affix the lace of his jabot, Drogo glared his evilest glare, tugged his midnight-blue evening coat into place, and stalked out. The man would be coming at him with hair powder next.

He couldn't get used to the open space at the foot of his stairs. He could almost see himself in the polished tiles. Enormous bouquets — he looked again — enormous *plants* exploded in ivory cascades against the elegant gold silk of what walls remained. In the candlelight, the area was bright as day. Drogo admired a towering branch of trumpet-shaped flowers exuding a powerful perfume, and shrugging, went in search of his wife.

So, Ninian preferred plants in pots to cut flowers. He would remember that.

He raised his eyebrows at a forest of potted trees just inside what had once been his public salon, but he'd already discovered the Malcolm affinity for trees. The greenery looked dignified and elegant beneath the blaze of candles in the crystal chandelier.

Crystal chandelier. Thoughtfully, his gaze swerved upward. He supposed that had always been there, but no one had ever thought to clean or light it in his memory.

He frowned as he realized all the new furniture had been pushed against the walls. Surely a small dance or two did not require the entire room to be emptied? How would he find a quiet corner where he could pick his guests' brains for the information he needed to decide on the upcoming bill?

Hearing feminine laughter, Drogo wandered toward the main dining parlor. Servants had been unpacking and polishing unused silver for weeks. The family had taken to eating in their rooms rather than disturb the feverish activity in here.

His gaze immediately fell on Ninian as he walked through the doorway. All else blended into the perimeter of his vision. She

sparkled more splendidly than the cande-
labra. She waved her hands in animation as
she laughed and spoke, and the bracelet he
had given her flashed rainbow gleams. He
wished all of London could see her as he
did. Then they would know he possessed a
rare and valuable treasure no other could or
would own. To think he'd practically found
her under a stone.

Smiling at that conceit, he widened his
focus to take in Ninian's aunts in their colorful array of silks, and her cousins, flitting
about the room like fair-haired forest
nymphs. Drogo frowned at his brothers —
dark wolves trailing in their wake.

Well, he couldn't very well uninvite
Ninian's cousins or his family. They might
be the only guests who arrived.

"There you are, Ives," Stella boomed.
"We must form a reception line. Take
Ninian into the salon and see that there's a
stout chair behind her. We can't have you
carrying her off every time she grows faint."

Faint? Drogo turned to Ninian, but she
didn't seem to think this odd. She merely
patted her aunt's arm and drifted toward
him with a dancing smile in her eyes.

"Hasn't Sarah done a tremendous job?"

She may as well have asked him how his
visit to the moon had gone. He saw only her.

His ears didn't hear words. They heard beckoning spring breezes and gentle chimes. At her gesture, he glanced blindly about.

The enormous dining table that had once filled the room had disappeared. How would they eat?

"It's too cold for lanterns in the yard or we would have opened up the back so guests could escape the crush. I do hope it won't be fearfully crowded." She took his arm and gently guided him back to the salon. "Our time was too limited to adequately refurbish the library, but perhaps your men guests will like to retire there for brandy. That will ease some of the crush."

Lanterns? Crush? Where was his dining table?

Surely Sarah hadn't set Ninian up for a major disappointment . . .

"Not there, Ives!" Stella called. "I'll stand by the door and guard her as best I can. You must position yourself beside the chair."

Ninian's innocent blue eyes beamed up at him from a face of ivory composure, as always. Drogo couldn't quite untangle the meaning of things.

"Stella frets, but I've been practicing. And Sarah has assured me that Lord Twane has departed for foreign shores, so I needn't worry about him bothering us again."

Drogo took a breath of relief at this glimmer of sanity. They feared she would faint as she had when Twane attacked him. Or she'd attacked Twane. He'd made very certain that wouldn't happen again. His solicitors had acquired all of Twane's outstanding notes and personally escorted him onto a ship to France.

"You could pretend to faint and I will carry you straight upstairs," he suggested.

Her smile dimmed a little, but she patted his arm as she had her aunt's. "Open your eyes, Drogo," she said softly. "My fainting spells really are not a physical weakness caused by the babe. Tonight, listen and learn. You are very good at that, I know."

Learn what? Her words sounded ominously like a warning.

Before Drogo could question, his wife turned at the sound of a carriage driving up. While a footman and driver shouted at each other, Stella sailed in to take the place of honor beside the door. Hermione fluttered into place beside her, tutting and fretting at her scarves. Apparently the duke and marquess had better things to do, but for Ninian's sake, Drogo was glad of her aunts' support.

He glanced dubiously at the gleaming,

nearly empty salon. He had obviously misunderstood the grandeur of the occasion.

Sarah appeared beside him, a triumphant smile beaming on her painted face. He scowled at the glitter of diamonds at her throat. "You've taken this a tad too far, haven't you?" he muttered as Ninian talked with her aunts. "What if no one comes?"

"They will." She fluttered a fan and unholy glee lit her eyes. "I made sure of it. And the stars promise great success for this night."

Drogo rolled his eyes and forced a smile to his lips as their unseen first arrivals shed their outer garments in the reception hall. He wanted Ninian to be happy. That meant he'd best not scowl thunderously and drive her guests screaming from the door.

"That's the Throckwaites," Stella predicted in a whisper that could have passed for a foghorn. "The Burnhams will be right behind."

"I just left Lord Burnham," Drogo murmured to Ninian. "He didn't mention attending."

"Aunt Stella knows these things," she said absently, keeping an eye on Ewen, who had cornered one of her cousins. Her cousin didn't look appreciative of his attentions. "We've invited Dunstan and his wife also."

"That's not a wise idea," Drogo remonstrated. "Dunstan despises London, and his wife is much too fascinated by society to make it comfortable for either of them."

He winced as the Malcolm cousin smacked Ewen's square jaw and flounced off. Well, it served the damned fool right to prowl around the daughter of a rich marquess. He glanced to Ninian's aunts to see how they took the contretemps. Hermione fretted worriedly but smiled a little at her daughter's action. Stella boomed a greeting to the Throckwaites. Drogo discovered a decidedly nervous tic drawing at the corner of his eye.

"How lovely to finally meet you, my lady," their first guest trilled as she reached Ninian. "We've heard so much about you."

"Sarah has done a particularly splendid job in transforming this room, hasn't she?" Ninian replied, seemingly irrelevantly. "I'm sure she'll be happy to tell you where she found the best bargains."

Mrs. Throckwaite blinked in surprise, opened her mouth to say something, apparently noted Drogo's stern expression, and nodding, hastened on to question Sarah about the draperies.

"Envy," Ninian whispered as their next guests greeted Stella. "She was simply brimming with envy."

Before Drogo could digest the full meaning of her comment, Lord and Lady Burnham presented themselves, as predicted.

"Music and good food are always best to ease the sting of petty arguments," Ninian said blithely as Lord Burnham bowed over her hand. "I particularly recommend the pheasant. Drogo is always starved after a heated session."

At no time had Drogo ever doubted his wife's intelligence, but at times like these, he had to question her common sense. Ignoring Burnham's startled expression, he grimly shook the man's hand.

"You must read minds, my dear," Lady Burnham agreed happily. "They are *so* peckish after an argumentative session. I almost couldn't persuade him to come."

It seemed to Drogo that if people could be called ciphers, some of the numbers were missing from this equation. While he tried to figure how Ninian, her aunts, and their guests were bouncing from two and two and reaching five, his wife turned to him expectantly.

"I really don't read minds, you know," she whispered. "Most witches can't. But they were quite angry with each other, and I guessed the rest. I hope you don't mind the gossip, but if I'm to live here, I really must be myself."

She was telling him something important, but Drogo couldn't quite grasp the ramifications. Didn't want to. They didn't fit into the confines of the world as he knew it. Before he could seek an adequate response, a flood of guests poured through the doorway.

Ninian greeted many of them with seemingly irrelevant comments that produced remarkable replies. Lady Driscoll pronounced her a witch for knowing she expected her first child. Drogo stiffened, waiting for a malicious gleam or chuckle, but the woman bubbled with happiness, and Ninian laughed.

On the other hand, when Lord Bolingbroke called Ninian a witch for knowing he'd lost heavily at the tables, Ninian froze, stiffly nodded, and wrapped her hand around Drogo's arm, as if for protection. Except he saw nothing from which to protect her. Everyone knew Bolingbroke was too drunk to mean his comments as insults, but it seemed as if Sarah's idea of filling the ballroom involved telling all of London that Ninian was a witch. The nervous tic in the corner of Drogo's eye accelerated, and he grimaced.

Feeling as if he were swimming in increasingly murky waters, Drogo noted with relief the confrontation between Joseph and still another fair Malcolm cousin. Joseph wasn't much inclined toward arguing with anyone, much less females, but at least the distraction bordered on normal.

"Do you think we have greeted sufficient of our guests, my dear? I do not think the different factions of our family are destined to abide quietly with each other." He nodded in Joseph's direction.

"You may be right," Ninian whispered. "Stella and Dunstan exchanged acrid notes earlier. And if I do not mistake, Christina has taken offense at something in William's aura. She can be quite vindictive when angered. Perhaps we should signal the musicians."

Pretending he hadn't heard the word "aura," Drogo signaled for the first dance, bowed over Ninian's hand, and led her toward the center of the floor. He would have much preferred a quiet dinner and cards, but if the women thought this pomp necessary, he would accept it — especially if it ended with Ninian in his bed.

"I've never danced, Drogo," Ninian whispered. "I know the steps only in theory."

"Then we'll pretend this is the latest variation and our guests shall follow our lead."

The weary downturn of Ninian's lips disappeared, replaced by a blinding smile of anticipation. Drogo's heartbeat accelerated at the promise in her eyes as he led her into the stately steps of the minuet. She was the most beautiful woman here, and she was wholly, unequivocally his. Tonight, then. He had to fight back a fierce surge of arousal. The certainty of the outcome of this evening erased some of his earlier confusion.

Ninian danced as gracefully as she did everything, beaming with every motion, swirling with delight to the music. Drogo thought watching her happiness was almost as stirring as taking her to bed. Almost.

He didn't object as the dance ended and Sarah led Ninian off to introduce her to her cadre of spinsters and widows. He didn't complain when he had to prevent Joseph from building a tower of artichokes, croquettes, and tarts for the amusement of Ninian's cousins. He frowned as women murmured the word "witch" behind fans as he passed, but even this foolish illogic could not dim his elation. Tonight, he'd finally have a wife in his bed.

He glowered at discovering Ninian and Ewen bent in intense conversation near the potted trees, but he stopped politely as Lord

Burnham caught his arm.

"So, Ives, what's it like being married to a witch?" Burnham asked jovially.

"I'd ask that of Mainwaring and Hampton were I you." Irritated by this continuing repetition of the evening's gossip, Drogo brushed him off. Burnham had obviously sampled too much port if he lowered himself to such absurdity. If there were any witches here, Stella and Hermione qualified, but not Ninian. His wife might be a bit scatter-minded and fanciful, but the mother of his child was perfectly normal in every way. That business about reading emotions was the product of an overactive imagination. Witches belonged in fairy tales.

He'd be damned if he'd let Ewen lead Ninian into supper, and ignoring the furtive whispers trailing in his wake, Drogo stalked across the crowded floor. Gossip had as much relevance to him as the heady perfumes wafting through the overheated room. Society gossiped. That was its sole function as far as he could discern. Let them make up fairy tales if it amused them. They had no relevance to him, or the outcome of the evening.

"It is time to go into supper," he said peremptorily as he captured Ninian's arm. He'd never known jealousy before, and he disliked acknowledging such a juvenile reaction now. It just seemed necessary to show the world that Ninian was his in a perfectly normal, sensible manner.

"Will you tell your chuckleheaded wife that a woman cannot finance a foundry?" Ewen complained. "I can't be going to her every time —"

"How is that any different from going to Drogo?" Ninian asked. "Do you wish to spend the rest of your life waiting for handouts?"

"If he wants his damned foundry, then he can work for it," Drogo said dismissively. "The position I've found for him can be quite lucrative. Now, let us go —"

"I'm no drudge meant to sit at a desk, Ives. I'll take orders from your witch of a wife before I'll sit at a desk."

"Ninian is not a witch!" Drogo shouted, all semblance of patience evaporating with this lunacy from the mouth of his logical, scientific brother.

"You have some other explanation of the havoc she's created since your marriage?" Ewen demanded. "She's turned the house into a forest, convinced all London that witchcraft is normal, and even persuaded you out of your ivory tower. If that's not witchcraft, what is?"

"Witches exist only in storybooks!" Drogo roared in exasperation.

Drawing away from him, Ninian visibly bristled and her voice sharpened. "There is no need for you to lose your temper, my lord. Everyone knows Malcolms are witches."

Drogo grabbed the edge of the sofa table and leaned forward to be very certain they heard him. *"I never lose my temper and there are no such damned things as witches!"* His roar echoed through a pause in the music.

"I'm sorry to hear you say that," Ninian said quietly, ignoring their now attentive audience. "Obviously, if we have proved nothing else, we have proved we possess the power to make you lose your temper." Gathering up her skirts, she swept from the room, leaving an expectant hush in her wake.

Twenty-seven

Oh, no, she wasn't going to pull this trick again. He'd courted her and played the fool long enough. He'd intended this as their wedding night, and by damn, they'd settle this foolishness and get on with it.

Tearing after his errant wife, Drogo dodged past Stella in full battle array, eluded an anxious Hermione, only to run straight into Dunstan and his wife, who chose that moment to enter the ballroom, looking as if they'd argued all the way from home.

"We are here at your command," Dunstan stated stiffly, blocking the doorway.

"I commanded no such thing, but you're welcome. Now get out of my way."

Lady Dunstan's pout disappeared beneath an enraptured expression as she gazed upon the crowded chamber. "Oh, you have turned this gloomy old hall into loveliness!

And look at the crowd! It's so perfect . . ." She tilted her head to her husband. "We could have this, too, if you weren't so tight-fisted. Just think of the fun we could have."

"It's not fun; it's hard work," Drogo corrected, "and now, if the two of you will get out of my way —"

"William's drunk and joining the musicians," Joseph announced, appearing at Drogo's side. "He's tired of minuets and wants a fiddle."

"I have to find Ninian." Frantically, Drogo tried to bypass the growing crowd of family.

"Sarah's gone after her." Ewen arrived, looking harried. "But if you don't call off those cousins of hers, we'll have a riot on our hands. And her aunts are on the warpath. I don't think you should have been so vehement about your opinion of the supernatural."

Drogo clenched his hands and glared at them. "Ninian is *not* a witch," he stated coldly and forcefully. "She's a Malcolm. They may be eccentric, but they are *not* witches."

"Well, another of the unwitches sketched a picture of our esteemed representative from Tetbury, and he looks convincingly like himself and a prime sow at the same time," Ewen remarked, glancing nervously over his shoulder. "He's not happy about it."

"Here comes Aunt Stella," Joseph whispered. "I think I'll find the punch bowl."

Grim amusement played on Dunstan's lips as both Ewen and Joseph escaped before the duchess's approach. "I think your married life may go down in the annals of Ives history, big brother." With a wave, he escorted his wife past Drogo, into the ballroom.

A fiddle broke out in the midst of a contredanse, throwing the entire circle of swinging dancers into disarray.

"There you are, Ives. I hope you have an explanation for this behavior!"

Drogo groaned and swung around as the duchess planted herself firmly in front of him, blocking any hope of reaching Ninian soon. Maybe Sarah would bring her around.

Maybe Sarah had set up this disaster in the first place.

Spinning like the emotional weather vane her grandmother had called her, Ninian swung from grief to fury as she flung newly acquired baby linens and pamphlets on water studies and neatly labeled packets of herbs into a trunk. *He didn't believe in* witches! How dare he say such a thing? Didn't he believe a word she said? Did he simply think her insane when she attacked men like Twane or told him how his brothers felt or set up this whole fancy dress ball to show off the talents of her aunts and cousins? Exactly how did the foolish man think her Aunt Stella knew who would arrive and when? And she supposed he thought Aunt Hermione's perfumed pomander was nothing more than an ornament and not an aroma of tranquility to prevent the battling factions of their family from creating chaos while easing the suspicions of society toward the odd and unnatural.

Unnatural. He thought witches were unnatural. Her husband thought *she* was unnatural. That she belonged in fairy tales.

If he'd ripped the heart from her chest, it couldn't hurt more. She had *hoped* . . .

It didn't matter how foolishly she had hoped. She had done what she had come to do. She couldn't do more. It was time she returned to Wystan, where she belonged.

Someday, when witches truly flew on broomsticks, she might recover from this aching hollowness he'd torn open in her center.

A tear dripped on the handwritten diary

411

Drogo had given her for a wedding gift as she carefully packed it with her other treasures. Maybe she should have studied Ceridwen's warnings more carefully.

By the time Drogo reached Ninian's chamber, she was gone.

He searched behind her draperies, hoping to find her on the window seat gazing at the moon, but she wasn't. No fire burned in the grate. No lamp lit the untouched bed. He had a strong remembrance of doing this once before, and a cold chill set up in his innards.

He slipped down the backstairs into the kitchen courtyard. November cold froze his blood and frosted his breath, but no dancing figure transformed his garden. He glanced upward. Just fog and coal smoke clouded the sky, as usual. He stood dangerously on the brink of some precipice, but he didn't know where it was or when it would crumble next. He only knew that without Ninian, he'd slide into an abyss and never be seen again. The black cold of the night foretold the oblivion of a future without her.

Shivering, he hurried into the house. Maybe she'd returned to the ballroom.

Ninian's aunts and cousins had already left in a huff. A number of other guests still circulated, enjoying the gossip and polishing off the food and drink from buffet tables set up across the hall. The musicians halfheartedly attempted to follow William's lead in a spirited round that more properly belonged in a taproom. Absently, Drogo thought his illegitimate brother by a dairy maid had talent, but fiddle players could be had for a ha'pence. He'd hoped a little education would help William find his way in the world, but perhaps he'd been wrong about that, too.

Ninian was nowhere in sight.

Ewen was showing Jarvis a better means of cranking the chandelier down to replace the guttering candles, and Drogo sent up a prayer that he didn't set the newly refurbished hall on fire. Joseph had spread his architectural drawings across the library floor and was trying to convince several inebriated lords that flying buttresses would give their country homes prestige. Ninian wasn't there either.

He might not make a merchant out of Ewen or a solicitor of Joseph or a scholar of William or a happily married man of Dunstan, but he'd be damned if he'd lose his wife.

"Where is she?" he demanded when he discovered Sarah and her biddies clucking in a back parlor.

Pensively, Sarah glanced up at him. "You never should have said that, Drogo."

"I shouldn't state the obvious?" he asked scornfully. "I should tell the world I believe in fairy tales?"

"In just a little bit of magic," she agreed, drifting toward him. "There are things in this world we don't understand. You see the stars, but you don't know their power."

"They're more likely burning gases than prophets." He dismissed her foolishness. "Ninian makes plants grow because she has studied and experimented, not because her thumb is a magical green."

Sarah shook her head in disappointment. "Ninian has more understanding in her thumb than you do in your whole great cumbersome body. I'm sure there's a duke or two left with whom you can discuss politics. Go back to them. They'll enjoy your company."

The cold chill shivered down his back again, and it had nothing to do with the air outside. "Where is she, Sarah?"

She shrugged. "She packed her bags and left."

Stunned, Drogo stood immobile. The mindless chatter around him echoed emptily. She was gone. She'd left him, as all women inevitably left their Ives husbands.

She hadn't even given him a chance . . .

She had. Tonight. She'd asked him to believe in her, and he hadn't listened. He couldn't believe in that which didn't exist.

He might not believe in witchery, but he could read her mind and knew where she'd gone. She'd flown back to the only nest she'd ever known, the damned fool idiot.

She was over six months pregnant. The roads were too dangerous for someone in good health. She would destroy herself and the child returning north in this weather. He would strangle her when he found her.

The despair shattering his insides was worse than anything he'd ever known. He couldn't bear to lose her or the child, to fail as his father had failed. There had to be some solution, some way to keep Ninian by his side, where she belonged.

Icy rain lashed the carriage windows as Ninian huddled deeper inside the warm furs her aunts had provided. She hated to let the driver stay out in this weather, but if they did not go as far as they could before nightfall, the rain was likely to turn to snow. The driver had agreed with her.

They'd made good progress out of London at dawn. The weather had been fine and clear, giving her more confidence than she deserved. She really had no choice. Even her aunts had agreed she must return to Wystan. It was evident she would never convince Drogo to believe in the village's need for her aid or of her responsibility to help them.

She knew Drogo with his practical, logical mind could never understand an instinct he could not see or analyze. He scoffed at her legends, at her gift, at the power of her family. If he could not believe in those, he could not believe in her or her instincts.

She wished it could be otherwise. She had done all she could to make him believe. She had stayed longer than she ought in hopes of convincing him to listen. But he hadn't. She would miss him dreadfully. He'd never forgive her for leaving him. Never. Pain ate at her heart, but she couldn't give in to it.

The carriage lurched in a muddy rut, and she could feel the rear wheel spinning. She held her breath, and the wheel caught on a rock, lurching out of the rut under the pull of the horses. The duke had fine, powerful animals. They would make it. Every jerk and jolt carried her farther away from Drogo and the dream that would never be hers. Being true to herself was incredibly difficult. No wonder her mother had failed at it.

The icy rain turned to sleet pelting the windows as the day darkened. If muddy ruts froze, were they more or less dangerous? She hadn't traveled enough to know.

The driver's curses would have turned her ears blue if the cold already hadn't. She pulled her fur-lined hood tighter over her frozen nose and rubbed her hand over the uneasy tumbling in her belly. Her daughter didn't like this rough ride any more than she did.

The driver's frantic shouts and a horse's terrified squeal coincided with the carriage's perilous sway. Ninian grabbed the strap and tried to peer out the ice-sheeted window. She could see only the ghostly gray of icy rain and fog and the dark shapes of trees beside the road.

They'd have to stop. They couldn't go farther in this weather. She didn't know how the driver could see the road.

She unwrapped the furs to reach for the speaking hole when the carriage bumped again, and she nearly struck her head on the far wall. She must be mad, just as Drogo had once thought her. How could she possibly travel to Wystan like this?

She didn't want to lose her baby because of her own foolishness.

Frantic, she cried out as the carriage shivered to a sudden halt. They were in the middle of nowhere. They would freeze to death out here. What was wrong? Surely highwaymen wouldn't —

Something slammed against the carriage door. Ninian shot back into the far corner of the seat and stared as the frozen door shivered and shook. She heard no protest from her driver. Who was out there in this storm? Low curses emanated from just outside the door as someone attempted to open it through the coating of ice.

A foot slammed into the vehicle's side, shattering the icy glaze from the windows.

Ninian screamed as the door swung open and a drenched, cloaked figure leapt in, spraying sleet and snow over the velvet-padded interior. She swallowed her scream as soon as the intruder hurled his hat on the floor, uncovering familiar dark brows, unpowdered queue, and a scowl that should have petrified her.

Instead, a jolt of fury shook her to the core. *His* fury. She must have truly rattled his walls. That terrified her far more than his scowl. He could easily kill her.

The door slammed, and the carriage lurched into motion, throwing them into separate seats. The fury slid away, disguised behind Drogo's taut control once again.

Hastily Ninian unwrapped one of her robes and threw it over his soaked cloak. "I'm not going back." As he used the fur to dry his face, her heart turned over in foolish joy and terror. He looked so beautiful and fierce . . . He had come after her.

"We'll freeze to death in a snowbank for your whimsy," he informed her coldly.

"I wanted to go home weeks ago," she pointed out, still shaken by the force of his earlier emotion.

"I have had to drop everything to follow you." Ice dripped from every word. "You have taken this notion of equality too far, madam. Forcing me to give up my work to follow *your* foolish whims is neither fair nor equal."

"I didn't think you would follow. I didn't mean to ask you to give up your work." Still stunned, she sought for an explanation in his features, but he hid everything again.

Tossing the fur back, he dropped his sodden cloak, then swung over to sit beside her. Ninian offered him more room on the seat to share her lap robe. Her heart pounded frantically. Would he force the driver to turn around? He would destroy her if he did. How could she make him believe that?

Without so much as a by-your-leave,

Drogo lifted her onto his lap and wrapped both of them up to their noses in furs. "Why?" he demanded. "Why must you go to the back of beyond instead of staying with family?"

"Because I am the Malcolm healer and Wystan needs me. Because my child must be born in Wystan, where she belongs," she said on a pleading note. "Because I have gifts God meant me to use, and Wystan needs them more than you do."

He leaned back against the side of the coach, propped his long legs on the seat, and arranged her on top of him so she shared his heat from head to foot. "In London, I could hire the best physicians," he insisted.

"*I'm* the best physician. You have to believe me in this, Drogo. I know it doesn't make sense to you, but in just this one thing, for the sake of our child, believe in me."

He sat silent, holding her close until they both stopped shivering. Then reluctantly, he conceded. "You are driving me mad, Wife. You ask the impossible, and for you, I'm almost ready to agree to it. Even should we arrive safely in Wystan, which I strongly doubt, we will be trapped there until spring. I must leave my family to their own devices, let my business fare without me, forfeit the rest of the session in Parliament, because of your strange whims."

Ninian buried her head against his shoulder. "I know. That is why I left without you. I'm sorry it has to be this way, Drogo. I'd hoped to make you understand why I must go back, but you do not believe in my gift. You need not accompany me."

Divest of its wet glove, his hand wound deep in her hair and held her head against his shoulder as he stared somewhere into the space beyond them, struggling with their problem. Ninian could feel the power of his heart thumping next to hers, and she wanted it to be like this forever.

"I would not lose you," he finally said, sighing.

She could hear the air leave his lungs and the tension escape him as he admitted this to himself as much as to her. She was the one holding her breath. His air of resignation worried her. If he always expected her to leave, what hope did she have of his ever trusting her?

"If making babies is as easy as you say, then the child does not concern me as much as you do. If it's this important that you risk all to return there, I must believe you in this."

Ninian curled into him as his strong arms held her. She didn't know what to make of his admission, but it moved her, and she would cling to it in the dark hours that would inevitably follow. "Thank you, my lord. You will not regret this, I promise."

"I'm already regretting it," he said grimly. "And if I did not fear for the child's health, I would make you pay by riding you all the way from here to Wystan. I think it's damned well time to call this a marriage and move on with it."

Amused at his gruff surrender, Ninian peered up at the square set of her husband's unshaven jaw and wriggled experimentally in his lap, confirming her understanding of the kind of "ride" he had in mind. "Is that possible?" she inquired cautiously.

He squinted down at her. "You're the witch. You tell me."

Twenty-eight

The violent lurch of the carriage into a wa-ter-logged rut convinced Drogo that witch, physician, or lunatic, his wife would be safer at an inn. Even as she considered his insane proposition, he set Ninian away from him. His entire body screamed in complaint as cold swamped the places she'd snuggled, and he almost said to hell with it and snatched her back, but he'd spent over half his life protecting others. He couldn't kill the habit now.

"There's an inn not too far from here," he said gently as she looked at him in surprise. Had he ever really noticed her eyes before? He'd thought them a clear blue, but they re-flected the mysterious silver light of the moon now. Something in his insides heaved unsteadily and resettled in a different place as he imagined hope behind that light. "I'll send the driver ahead on my horse to secure a room for us. The poor man's half-frozen. I can drive us the last few miles."

"I would not see you made ill in my place," she said gravely.

Drogo kissed her nose and warmed his hands on her rosy cheeks. "Concentrate on healing thyself, physician. I need a wife to warm my bed."

He pounded on the speaking door, halted the driver, and swept into the cold again.

She hadn't really left him, he thought joyously. He might not understand what drove her off, but he'd succeeded in keeping them together, where many an Ives before him had failed. Maybe he would be the one to learn what it took to satisfy a wife.

Their physical attraction gave him a firm start. That was more than most couples had and enough for most. He refused to let the mocking voice in the back of his mind, saying *"Not for Ninian,"* ruin the moment. For now, she was willing and eager.

He suddenly felt freer than the hawk swooping overhead, and his heart did excited acrobatics at the thought of the night to come. The damned ice would melt right off him, the way he felt now. Tonight, his lovely fey wife would warm his bed, and he would teach her the passion that would bind them forever.

Even the icy pelt of sleet couldn't cool his ardor.

Ninian smiled at the frosted feather patterns glowing silver against the dark of their bedchamber window. Tonight would be the wedding night she'd never had.

She glanced wryly at her unwieldy belly beneath the warm flannel of her bed gown. Unlike her more slender cousins, she carried her child low and full. There was no mistaking her condition.

She glanced up as Drogo returned from the taproom with two steaming hot toddies. "You wish me drunk before we retire?" she asked in amusement.

"Warm and willing," he agreed with a leering lift of one curled eyebrow as he set the mugs down.

Her heart pounded a little more erratically. She'd never seen this side of her husband. He seemed almost lighthearted, despite the weather, despite leaving all his responsibilities behind. She'd never expected him to follow her. A tiny sliver of hope pierced her heart as she searched his face, fearful his lightheartedness was forced, that he hid resentment as he had fury, but she saw nothing other than a man eager for sex.

She pressed her gown taut against the bulge of her belly. "Warm and willing perhaps, but a trifle ungainly. Even my aunts were not so large at this stage."

"That's because it's a boy," he whispered wickedly in her ear as he pulled her back against his chest and stroked her roundness. "I tell you, Ives only produce males."

"Just what your family needs, my lord," she taunted, wrapping her arms around his where they rested at her waist, "more virile men to foist upon an unsuspecting world."

"More like what your family needs, my lady." He caught her by the knees and lifted her into the bed. "A rowdy male to disrupt all the family traditions."

"Oh, my, I don't even want to think it." A male Malcolm. The idea spun her head.

She sipped gratefully at the mug he handed her once she settled against the pillows, and watched with interest as Drogo tugged off his clothes and folded them on a chair. They had but the one candle, and she wished for more as his shirt joined his coat and waistcoat and she could admire the full expanse of his muscled back and shoulders. "Oh, my," she repeated, for an entirely different reason as those muscles shifted and swelled.

Drogo swung around and lifted a questioning eyebrow, giving her a full view of the arrow of dark curls sculpting his breastbone and taut abdomen. She gulped and couldn't look away. She'd never really *seen* him without his shirt.

Finally gauging the direction of her thoughts, he reached suggestively for the buttons of his breeches. "If we've had our wedding night and the courtship is over, what do we call this, madam?" he taunted, slowly releasing the first button.

Candlelit shadows played against the hard ridge pushing his breeches flap outward. Ninian licked her suddenly dry lips. "Large," she answered mindlessly. She remembered another time and place she had thought that. Her husband was definitely not a small man.

Or a shy one. He grinned as he took her meaning, and the beauty of his chiseled features almost distracted Ninian from his breeches. Almost. As he shoved the fabric over his lean hips, she forgot about the white flash of his teeth against the sensuous fullness of his lips, or about anything at all beyond the evidence of Ives masculinity. Her aunt was definitely right about that. Ives men were very . . . *virile*.

He removed the mug from her limp fingers before she could spill the contents. "It's good to know there are still a few things I can teach my all-knowing wife." He snuffed the candle.

"I only know about herbs," she murmured as his heat and weight slipped beneath the covers beside her, and the rough hair of his leg captured her thigh.

"Then let me teach you about men, my dear."

A very male hand covered her breast, and a hot, whiskey-flavored mouth parted her lips. She thought surely she'd died and gone to heaven as his tongue stroked and his fingers pleasured.

She was well and truly married then. To an Ives. So far, the only destruction was to her self-control.

She sighed in satisfaction as he guided her hand downward and taught her to touch him. She only needed her woman's power for this, and he held the key to that.

He groaned and buried his bristled chin against her hair as she stroked him.

"I won't last much longer," he murmured, cupping her breast again and creating havoc with any control she'd thought she possessed. "This is safe for the child?"

"For a few weeks more." Ninian moaned as Drogo rewarded her by sweeping aside her bodice and applying his tongue to an aching nipple. Wildly, she thought men need not chase lightning if they wanted electricity. Drogo created it with just his hands and mouth, and she could no more resist his pull than the sea could run from the moon.

The heat of his palms molded her breasts into heavy mounds as he trailed his kisses upward. "Perhaps you *are* a witch," he said as she arched into him, offering herself.

Before she could absorb his admission, he nibbled at the fullness his hands created, then soothed the pinch with his tongue. Ninian wrapped her fingers in his hair, holding his head as he marked her, beyond interpreting anything so simple as words.

"Only a witch could drive me to distraction as you do."

At any other time, his words would have shattered her, but for now, she didn't heed them. "You have magic in your fingertips," she pointed out as he assuaged her need by caressing both her nipples at once.

He chuckled and teased her lips with nipping kisses. "Not just my fingertips." Rolling over and bringing her with him, he eased her nightshift up and over her head.

Ninian held her breath as he uncovered her unwieldy body, but his hands merely stroked and admired the changes their child had wrought. Blossoming under the heat of his stare, she finally followed his meaning as he adjusted their positions. Leaning back against the stack of pillows, he set her astride him, until his male part rubbed temptingly close to where she needed it.

He touched her between her legs, reminding her of their first night, teasing her into aching hollowness, while his gaze caught and held hers. Ninian shivered at the smoldering intensity holding her captive, unable to deny him anything.

"Bewitch me," he commanded huskily.

Without any further instruction, she raised her hips and slowly eased over him until Drogo groaned, caught her waist, and surged upward, filling her to bursting.

No longer herself but a part of him, Ninian surrendered her will to her husband's, molded her body to his command, and cried out in joy as he used her for a soaring pleasure she hadn't known existed. He cupped and suckled her breasts until she was weak with need, then drove into her again until they galloped to a single rhythm.

When they soared off the cliff of oblivion together, he caught and held her while the mindlessness overtook them and they drifted downward, sated and unharmed.

Together, they made magic.

★ ★ ★

"You needn't look so smug, Wife," Drogo complained jokingly the next day as they emerged from the inn into crystal-clear sunshine, "just because we generated enough heat last night to burn off clouds for the rest of the winter."

Ninian demurely hid her smile in her muff as he handed her into the carriage.

Just her smile had the power to jolt his brain into a mindless clatter. That frightened Drogo as much as her smile filled him with pride. He knew better than to trust in women, marriage, or jolting body parts. He knew the best he could hope for was a warm bed and an uneasy truce until their next difference of opinion. But even in the bright light of day, he could remember with clarity the joy and hope his maddening wife had wrung from him last night. She was definitely a witch of some sort.

He would do well to remember that she had twisted him to her will with this non-sensical journey into nowhere. He'd dropped everything he held near and dear to see her safe. He couldn't remember anyone ever diverting him from the path he'd chosen — not since he was fourteen and his father died, leaving him with a mountain of debt. Even the estate solicitors had bowed to his authority.

Not Ninian.

Fortunately for him, she didn't even know what she had wrought. She simply smiled and snuggled close as he joined her, as if they were merely on a holiday excursion. He'd never taken a holiday excursion, and this wasn't one now. They were going back to a blighted land, a frozen nowhere, without friends or family to greet them, and she beamed as if he'd promised her paradise.

He could survive a winter in Wystan in return for the child she would give him. But he damned well didn't appreciate the blackmail that had led him into it. Over these next months, he'd have to teach her who was in charge.

"Have you heard from your steward? Has the burn recovered?" she asked.

On second thought . . . Drogo tucked her firmly under his arm. "The burn will be frozen. Concentrate on hatching that youngling, and not what cannot be changed."

He didn't like the way she narrowed her eyes and crossed her arms in that stubborn manner he was beginning to recognize.

"Who says it cannot be changed?" she demanded.

She said no more and Drogo let himself believe that was the end of it. Expectant mothers did not traipse about the frozen countryside exploring dead streams.

Expectant mothers helped other expectant mothers deliver their babes, Drogo discovered some days later, much to his dismay.

"Thank goodness you're here!" Lydie exclaimed as she rushed into the great hall before the driver could carry in their luggage. "Cook's daughter has been in labor since yesterday, and I can do *nothing!*"

He'd almost forgotten Lady Lydie. He'd rather assumed Sarah had disposed of her somewhere, somehow. His mind instantly sought the legal ramifications of her presence. Surely her father couldn't sue him . . . Well, at least Claudia had returned home now that Twane had departed for France.

"Where is she?" Ninian flung her fur muff to the table without a second look to the husband following her in.

"We brought her here last week since the roads are so bad. Hurry. She's growing weaker." Lydie rushed toward the corridor leading to the servants' wing.

"Ninian!" Drogo halted her before she could follow. When she turned to look at him questioningly, he could see her mind had already followed Lydie down the hall. "You've had a long journey," he said gruffly. "You need to rest."

She beamed that bewildering smile he couldn't fathom. "I love you, Drogo," she murmured, standing on tiptoe to kiss his cheek. "But I can take care of myself."

She was gone before he could even digest that "I love you" or rearrange his thinking to absorb it.

It was undoubtedly some wifely platitude meant to allay his fears, he decided grimly as he directed the servants to carry Ninian's things to his room.

But he was still in charge here. This was his home, and she would learn to live by his rules. After the lovemaking they had shared these last nights, she certainly couldn't object to sharing his bed on a regular basis. He'd be damned if he'd move into the haunted master suite, though.

"You didn't bring that dreadful book with you, did you?" Drogo exclaimed as he came to his bed that night to discover his wife sitting up against the pillows, reading.

She flipped a brittle page and tilted the book to better catch the lamplight. "I keep hoping they will settle their differences and everything will turn out right. The castle was *hers*," she said indignantly, not looking up.

"*Was* hers," he corrected. "Her father gave it to her husband as dowry."

"He had no right. The castle belonged to her mother. It just isn't fair. They were so happy at first. He even improved the conservatory. Her child was born here. But to not believe the child was his just because it was a girl . . ."

Drogo sighed and disposed of his coat and waistcoat. He obviously didn't have his wife's full attention tonight. "She married an Ives, my dear. We are not known for our trust in women or wisdom in marriage. I suppose he's sired a bastard or two by now?"

"Two," she said crossly, glaring at the pages. "Stupid man. Both boys, thus proving his masculinity, I suppose, while his wife pines with loneliness and lets her love wither. At this point, he's returned to London, and the village is suffering from flood, and no one is doing anything about it." She finally looked up at him. "I've not noticed stupidity as an Ives trait. Why would he do that?"

Drogo lowered himself to the mattress and removed the book from her hand. "It was a logical assumption," he explained patiently. "It's a matter of common knowledge that we always sire boys. He'd been away on business and came home to find his wife with child. That would have stirred the suspicion of almost any man. The girl was all the proof he needed."

"Ives men don't stay with their women long enough to know if they could sire girls." She punched her pillow into shape and slipped down between the covers. "And it only takes one night to create a child of any sex. You know perfectly well that he would have taken her to bed the night before he left on an extended journey."

Drogo pried off his boots and flung them toward the wall. "If she was anything like you, love, he was mad not to have taken her with him."

"What's that supposed to mean?" she demanded as he blew out the light.

He slid between the covers and wrapped her securely in his arms before answering. "It means the only time a man can be certain of a woman is when she's under him."

He caught her cry of outrage with his mouth and did his best to teach her that being under an Ives was no bad thing.

And perhaps, having a Malcolm woman under him wasn't half-bad either.

Twenty-nine

"How does your daughter fare this morning, Mrs. White?" Ninian asked of the portly woman removing oatcakes from the oven.

The cook carefully shuffled the hot pan onto a cooling rack, then turned with a wide smile. "She and the bairn are well, thank you, my lady. It's grateful we be to you and the good Lord above that you arrived in time."

"They say He works in mysterious ways." Ninian poked at the steaming cakes and decided to wait before burning her mouth on one. "Where is everyone? I thought Lady Lydie said she'd sent for the other servants. I want to start cleaning out the master suite."

Cook blanched. "You no want to be doing that, my lady. It's a gloomy old place, it is. The chimney howls something fierce, and the panes rattle, and damp has set in. I'll air one of the newer chambers, shall I?"

Ninian dipped her finger in a bowl of cake batter, then sucked it clean. This was Drogo's house. Sarah had been the lady here and in London. Ninian had never dealt with servants or been much use at ordering people about. But she sensed this simple woman's fear and sought to ease it.

"Feeding Lord Ives is a full-time chore," Ninian assured her. "You needn't air anything. Does this mean the others won't be returning?"

Mrs. White clasped her doughy hands in her apron. "They're afraid of their shadows, if you don't mind my saying so, my lady. They'll come when they're hungry."

Ninian sighed. She hadn't expected better. After all, even she'd believed the superstitions of Ives's devils and feared the legends when the village flooded. Living with Drogo had certainly widened her mind to look for new explanations.

She was beginning to understand why her grandmother had spent so much time telling people what they wanted to hear and giving them foolish amulets to conquer their fears. It wasn't easy being a witch.

"All right, Mrs. White. You just take care of that daughter and new grandbaby of yours and see that we have meals, and Lady

438

Lydie and I will take care of the household."

Selecting one of the cooler oatcakes, Ninian drifted out of the kitchen, her mind racing furiously despite her body's ungainly pace.

Her grandmother had said she was the Malcolm healer. To be a healer, she must be accepted by those she must heal. Otherwise, she was nothing but a breeding machine for an earl. Some women might aspire to that, but she wasn't one of them.

She had to be true to herself whether Drogo liked it or not.

"Hello, Mary. Am I welcome here?" Ninian asked as the cottage door opened.

Mary's eyes widened. "Ninian!" Then remembering herself, she executed a clumsy curtsy. "I mean, Lady Ives. I . . ."

"I'm still Ninian, but Lord Ives really only has one wife, and I'm it." She couldn't resist the jest, but bit back the ridiculous urge to smile. She didn't know where she stood in her own home, and she prayed frantically as her childhood friend looked uncertain.

Mary cast a nervous glance to Ninian's plain woolen skirt and the bulge only slightly concealed beneath it. "Aye, and he made short work of his duties, too. What is he thinking to let you wander about like this?"

She opened the door, and with a huge sigh of relief, Ninian followed her in. "Oh, we'll hear his shouts soon enough, I wager, but I could not wait for him to find time to bring me here. Walking is good for me."

"Walking in this damp is not," Mary scolded. "Sit down and let me fix some tea."

The children crowded shyly into a corner as Ninian took a seat at the trestle table. Smiling, she reached in her pocket and produced a sack of sweetmeats. She needed to go back to wearing the aprons she'd abandoned in London. She never had enough pockets.

At a nod from their mother, the eldest boldly crept up to inspect the offering.

"You have grown, Matt. I bet you're strong enough to carry water from the well." Ninian didn't need the child's shy smile to tell her of his pride at her recognition, but she liked it just the same. Learning to read Drogo through his expressions and actions had taught her to read the way others expressed feelings physically so that now she could better interpret the vague empathic vibrations she received. That knowledge could be a useful tool when her patients were hurting and too confused for her to understand.

The children giggled happily over the treat and before long, the youngest had crawled into Ninian's lap. She felt good there, and Ninian happily smoothed silken locks. "I have missed the little ones."

Mary still watched her with wariness as she prepared the tea. "You left them readily enough for the ballrooms of London. I'm surprised you returned."

"I did not leave them willingly," Ninian protested. "You didn't want me around. What was I supposed to do? Grow old and keep cats for company?"

"You never kept cats before *he* came along." Mary smacked the mug on the table. "The burn never flooded until Ives and Malcolm came together, just like the legend."

"The burn *has* flooded before," Ninian corrected, without mentioning the Malcolm and Ives connection. "And I never kept cats because Grandmother wouldn't let me. I feared Lord Ives as much as you did, but he's only a man, like any other."

Mary smiled wickedly. "And he's proved his manliness. You'll not have time for the likes of us once the babe arrives."

"Don't be foolish. Of course I will." Ninian relaxed as they fell into the easy bantering of their childhood. "Tell me how everyone fares. Did Harry marry Gertrude?"

"After she got fat with child, he did. Beltane produced a fine crop this year." Worry flitted across her face, but she didn't mention the reason she'd written. "It looks as if you'll have your own to deliver, and we'd best look to ourselves."

That was a problem Ninian had already considered. "I am teaching Lady Lydie what I know. She was quite adept at helping with Mrs. White's daughter. Perhaps she can act as my hands as I did for my grandmother."

"A fancy London lady delivering children? That'll be the day the sun doesn't rise."

"Well, let's not borrow trouble just yet. We have over two months." Two months in which she hoped to teach Lydie the things she was eager to learn. Lydie had been remarkably underestimated by everyone, but she'd survived out here on her own, raising her daughter without complaint, stalwartly resisting her family's plans to marry her to wealth. Ninian had learned a few things in London and understood now how much courage that had taken.

With Mary to lead the way and the news that she had saved Cook's daughter in childbirth to smooth the path, Ninian visited Gertrude to reassure her that she would help in her delivery. She stayed with the safe topics of local gossip and childbirth and didn't mention the burn. That was next on her list, but regaining the confidence of the village was of first importance.

Worried about her ailing mother, Gertrude set aside her wariness to take Ninian to her parents' house. Several of the older women were there, and Ninian's arrival stimulated a discussion of ailments and remedies that took much longer than she'd anticipated. By the time she stepped outside the modest cottage, the sun had traveled well past noon, and weariness had set in, but triumphantly, she knew she had her foothold in the village again.

"Going somewhere?" a welcome voice asked dryly as she reached the square.

"Drogo!" She spun around to find him leaning against the stone wall of the tavern, apparently waiting for her. Her husband looked gloriously rugged in his country boots and old wool coat without the fripperies of London lace. He also appeared on the edge of fury. "You never lose your temper," she reminded him evenly.

"A man must start sometime." He unfolded himself from the tavern wall so he towered over her. "Are you out of your mind, madam?"

"Not at all." She pulled her cloak more comfortably closed and met his glare without fear. "I am ready to return home, however."

"Whose home?" he demanded. "Perhaps you would prefer returning to your old one and pretending I was just a passing fancy."

She cocked her head and tried to interpret what went on beyond his inscrutable expression, but she could only see the anger. In Drogo's case, it seemed safest to be herself and watch what happened.

She tucked her hand around his arm and started down the street. "People don't seem to be afraid of me. The flood and superstition scared them, and maybe they're still wary, but at least they're listening. How did you get here? Surely you did not walk."

Silence. She was comfortable with that. It took Drogo a while to work out hidden meanings, interpret, and decide on a reply. He was a very cautious man, and she smiled at him to show she didn't mind.

He appeared totally disconcerted by her smile. She smiled wider, and he scowled. Ninian's heart soared. He might not understand why she was smiling, but he was actually *seeing* her and wondering what she thought instead of ignoring her thoughts in favor of his own. That might not be as good a thing as she had hoped, but it was a more solid place to be than before, when she was just another cipher on his book of responsibilities.

"I can't turn you over my knee or cut your allowance or send you back to school or any of those things I do with my brothers. How the devil am I supposed to command your obedience?"

"You don't, no more than I command yours," she replied cheerfully. "Equality, remember? Is it so difficult to understand?"

"Equality," he repeated glumly. "You're carrying an impossible burden and can barely stand for weariness, and you expect me to treat you like a man?"

He halted before a gray palfrey with a small, nearly flat saddle. Without further discussion, he swung her sideways onto the saddle, then climbed on behind her. His legs dragged the ground as he gathered the reins in one hand and held her with the other.

"Not like a man." Ninian skeptically eyed the distance to the ground and granted his wisdom in choice of mounts. "I will freely admit that I cannot ride a horse as you do, although I should not mind learning on one this size. It is not *quite* so far to fall."

"And this one walks like a swaying bed." Drogo kicked the mare into a slow saunter. "Which is better for you than the farm cart, at least."

She watched the ground until certain she would not immediately slide off, then relaxed enough to appreciate the strength of her husband's arms around her. He pulled her closer as she leaned into him.

"Will you teach me to ride? It could be a very useful thing to know."

"You are seven months gone with child!" he exclaimed in exasperation. "People fall off horses when they're learning. Accept it, Ninian. You cannot do anything but grow that child right now. The village is too far."

"I am not a melon ripe enough to burst." She concentrated on swaying with the horse. "Walking is good for me. Remember, I'm the midwife, not you."

"And you will tell me the cold and damp are good for you, too? And that growing so weary you can scarcely stand is healthy? I have six younger brothers who have tried every excuse known to mankind, Ninian. I know when I'm being gulled."

"I am a healer, Drogo. I cannot heal if I cannot visit the sick. These people are my responsibility as much as your brothers are yours. Can you not accept that?"

Silence. Ninian thought she'd tear off his shirt and drive her fingernails into that thick skin to see if he was human, but she knew he was as human as she, and that was the problem.

"I've accepted that you carry my child, that you are a Malcolm, and that you know something of herbs. I accept that you're my responsibility now, and that I must protect you as well as the child from harm. Why can you not accept that protection?"

She patted his chest instead of shredding it. He really did not understand. "I'm not your responsibility, Drogo. I don't need your protection. I can very well take care of myself. Accept that, and we've found a starting place."

"If you don't need me for anything, then what the hell do you want me for?" he shouted, losing the temper he claimed never to lose. "Am I to be your breeding stud and nothing more?"

Ninian laughed with a carefree joy that bounced off the icicles coating the trees. "Now we are getting somewhere, my lord," she said approvingly, snuggling into his warmth. "For in your eyes, I am no more than a brood mare. Just because I have the appropriate plumbing for the task does not mean that is who or what I am."

447

"You are an extremely annoying bit of baggage with far too much intelligence and freedom," he grumbled. "Your family was mad to let you grow up wild."

"My family accepted from my birth that I would grow up as I am. Their only choice was in whether to teach me to use my skills or abandon me to learn on my own. My mother preferred abandonment. I was miserable not knowing who or what I was, only knowing I was different. My grandmother showed me how to make the most of my differences."

He rubbed his hand thoughtfully over the place where their child grew. "And since I can teach you nothing, I have no purpose? What is it you want of me?"

"Acceptance, my lord." She closed her eyes and rested against him, hearing his heart beat. "I wish people to accept what I am and not ostracize me for my differences. That's all I've ever asked. Perhaps, someday, I could learn to help you with your responsibilities, and then we could work together."

"Right. I'll give you the books from the mining operation when we reach home, and you can find where we need to cut costs."

He still didn't understand, but he was listening and not rejecting her. That's all she could ask, for now. "Introduce me to your foreman, and I will tell you if he's cheating you," she answered dreamily, half asleep with the sway of the horse and the warmth of his arms. "I'll bring you children and teach you to laugh."

"And if I don't want to laugh?"

"Then I'll cure you of that, too."

She nodded off in his arms, reawakening Drogo's terrified feeling that he walked a precipice beyond which he had no idea if air, water, or rocky boulders waited.

Marriage had been a mad idea. He should have stayed in London, where he knew where he stood and what was expected of him.

But sitting here with his wife and child in his arms brought him a joy he'd never known, even as his head spun with uncertainty.

One way or another, he would solve the problem that was his wife.

Thirty

Drogo carried his sleeping wife into the castle. She woke enough to hug him but her sweet breath soon warmed his neck again as she returned to slumber.

He didn't know what he was doing with a woman like this. He'd once thought he might marry some graceful doe-eyed beauty who would drift through his life like a butterfly, going about whatever odd business women tended during the day, warming his bed occasionally at night. If he'd given it any thought at all, he'd imagined she would be content with flattery, a little jewelry, and whatever attention he could spare. He was quite certain that if his father had given his wife that much, his parents would have stayed together.

But no, he had to bed a moon-eyed country bride who thought London a bore and delivering children her task in life. Instead of inspecting his estate in Ives, gathering his brothers for the holidays, and exploring the profitability of a new shipping venture, he was stranded in the back of nowhere, dancing to his wife's merry tune — all because she carried the child he'd thought never to have. This wasn't how he'd planned his life.

He supposed he could humor her for a few months. He could explore expanding his mining ventures and look into the canal some of the other owners wanted to build — if only he could be certain Ninian would stay where she belonged, the obstinate wench.

Today hadn't been a reassuring experience, but he thought he might have the answer to that.

Gently, he carried her through the winding corridors to the conservatory in the back wing of the castle. He hadn't comprehended Sarah's suggestion to rebuild the glass room until Ninian had fully entered his life. After these last months of watching plants spring to life everywhere he turned, he had a better grasp of Ninian's talent.

With satisfaction, he lay his sleeping burden on the settee he'd carried down for her use. Not that she would ever use it, he acknowledged ruefully. Maybe he could tie her down so he wouldn't have to chase after her.

She woke again as he stepped away. Drogo watched with secret pleasure as her sleepy blue eyes widened with astonishment. He didn't think he had ever seen anything so innocently beautiful since his brothers were babes in the cradle.

"My word!" she whispered, pushing herself onto her elbows and staring.

He'd ordered all her potted plants carried in here, and after consulting with a few of London's noted botanists, he'd had quite a few more delivered. He didn't understand their purpose or appeal, but Ninian's fascinated wonderment was satisfaction enough.

"I wasn't certain if the servants were keeping it warm enough," he admitted as she continued her wordless examination from the settee.

"Oh, my." Ninian struggled to sit, accepting Drogo's hand as she drank in the sights and smells of moist earth and green leaves. She clung to that strong hand as she stood and touched a fern. It was sending out new fronds — in the midst of winter.

Tightening her grip on his hand, uncertain if she was dreaming or not, she brushed her fingers against the fragrant leaves of a bay bush. Its aroma filled the air.

"I never imagined . . ." She didn't even have the words as her gaze fell upon a rose-bush with a single perfect pink bud. "My roses!"

"I told them to carry in the things you had at your grandmother's. I wasn't certain how they'd fare without you."

Ninian thought she would cry. All this time, she'd thought he hadn't *noticed* . . . If he could see her love for plants, surely, *surely,* he could be made to see her love for Wystan. And then . . . She shouldn't hope for too much all at once.

Blinking back tears, she gazed up through a watery film at this remarkable man who was her husband. His dark eyes held a hint of uncertainty, but otherwise, he main-tained his usual stoic composure. She touched wondering fingers to his square jaw and caught a small smile curling the corner of his mouth.

"I didn't think you meant to return me to Wystan." She didn't understand anything about him. She searched his face for under-standing now. "Why would you do this?"

"I thought we would come here in summer, and these seemed important to you."

She didn't know what to say. No one had given her such an astonishing gift before.

He'd rebuilt the conservatory! She gazed up at the panes of glass overhead. She could see blue sky and puffs of clouds. It was like being outdoors, except warmer. Her gaze fell downward and swept the tiled floor, finding the secret figures of moon and sun and stars. Those tiles were older than Ceridwen. They traced back through generations of Malcolm women. This is where her roots were.

"I can't thank you enough," she whispered. "I don't even know how to begin."

Drogo drew her back against his chest and rested his hands above the child she carried. "You have given me a greater gift. The plants are small in comparison."

The bonds they had forged together tightened around her, frightening her more than a little. She was his as surely as this castle belonged to him. He'd bought her a pretty cage. Did he also expect her to sing sweetly and remain loyally where he placed her? She had never asked for that.

"Perhaps I can grow some of the plants that no longer grow along the burn."

"Tell me what you need and I will send for them," he agreed. "Perhaps you will be content to stay here and not wander the woods alone."

He'd said the words she dreaded. She

tried not to imagine the silken bonds knot-ting tighter. She could not argue with him in the face of his generous gift.

"I like wandering the woods," she said gently so as not to upset him. "But I shall like working here just as much."

"Good. Then I need not wonder where you are while I visit the mines." He heard only what he wanted to hear, kissed her cheek, and released her. "I thought I would leave while the weather holds. The roads are nigh impossible, but I'll take the fields."

She didn't want him to leave. The bonds with which he held her were strange indeed.

Ninian forced a smile and turned to pat his cheek. "Do not be gone too long. It will be lonely here without you." And that, too, was the truth. Cupid's arrow had truly pierced her heart. She didn't want to be without him again. She had been alone far too long, and this man offered her under-standing far beyond that of most others.

"It will be very strange without Joseph popping out of closets and watchmen drag-ging David home. I fancy we won't know what to do with ourselves." He kissed her again and then wandered off on his own pursuits.

Ninian didn't dare tell him that she had five expectant mothers, three feverish children, and an ailing old woman to tend in the village. He'd surely chain her to the walls.

Drogo's first suspicion that his plans had gone awry occurred upon his return to the castle after living for a week at the mines. He'd only recently learned the pleasures of a shared marital bed and had certainly never intended to stay away so long, but the weather had turned bad again, and even the hills were treacherous, so he'd sensibly availed himself of the opportunity to learn more of the canal the other owners wished to build. Perhaps he should have worried more about leaving his new wife alone, but Ninian had wreaked havoc with all his theories about marriage. He actually trusted her.

Now he wondered if he had been a little hasty in placing that trust.

The new maid taking his hat and gloves at the door didn't disturb him. He had no objection to Ninian's hiring servants without his help.

The tapestries hanging over the stair rail didn't bother him greatly either. He understood that women had nesting instincts he didn't possess, and he rather appreciated the results.

He didn't understand why there was a hustle and bustle in the moldering master suite, however. He should have bolted the damned thing shut.

Taking the stairs two at a time, he discovered Lydie at the first landing, carrying her infant and an armful of linens. "What the devil are you doing?" he demanded crossly. "And where is Ninian?"

Lydie looked startled. "I don't know. Should I? She could be in the conservatory, I suppose."

"What's going on up there?" he repeated as a loud crash echoed from the suite.

"Oh." Lydie appeared vaguely guilty as she glanced over her shoulder. "They're cleaning. The chimney was a disgrace. I'm taking these down for washing. Here, would you hold Henrietta? I'll be right back."

Dazed, Drogo stared at the wide-eyed infant she thrust suddenly into his arms. The infant blew a bubble and gurgled as he held it at arm's length.

He'd been only fourteen the last time he'd held an infant. At the time, his stepmother had been wailing with grief, Joseph and David had frightened the nursemaid into hiding, and Paul had been howling as if his little heart would break. He'd tried rocking him and patting him on the back as he'd seen the maids do, but nothing worked. The experience had terrified him. He'd disliked being helpless ever since.

Well, at least this baby wasn't howling. Holding the squirming bundle upright with both hands, Drogo stalked up the stairs to see what the hell was happening in the haunted suite. He certainly hadn't authorized any repairs in there.

The first thing he noticed upon entering was the room's warmth. He raised his eyebrows in surprise at the roaring fire in the hearth, then gazed at the wood panels stripped of their musty tapestries. Someone had replaced the cracked panes in the solar window and sunshine streamed through the undraped expanse. It looked almost cheerful.

The child squirmed more forcefully, and terrified of dropping her, Drogo heaved her over his shoulder as he wandered into the next chamber where the bed had been. The men working on the walls tugged their forelocks in respect and returned to pounding. Apparently Ninian had worked some magic and the servants were slowly returning. Women did have an uncanny knack of managing things like that.

If Ninian didn't mind this accursed chamber, he supposed he could endure it. The women were the ones who had complained of it before. He'd thought the constant repairs a nuisance, and he suspected the paneling ought to be ripped out and not just painted.

Thinking to locate Ninian in the conservatory, he started down the stairs, and met Lydie as she hurried up again.

"Oh, there you are!" she exclaimed breathlessly, not taking the infant he shoved in her direction. "Your bailiff is in the study and I can't find Nanny. I promised to take some of Ninian's arthritis remedy into town. Would you mind watching Henrietta until Nanny returns? And there's a letter from Ewen in the hall. Will he be here for the holiday?"

She didn't wait for an answer but grabbing up her skirt, flew back down the stairs.

Drogo noticed she wasn't wearing panniers or powder. Ninian probably kept her too busy for such frivolity. Realizing he still held the brat, he tucked it under his arm and stalked toward the conservatory. To hell with his bailiff. He wanted his wife.

"Oh, my lord, you're back!" Cook exclaimed as she hurried from the kitchen. "I've none to stir the pudding, and my kettle is boiling. Come along, or it'll spoil."

No longer amazed by the chaos his wife had apparently created in his absence, Drogo preceded Cook's shooing gesture into the kitchen. He didn't think he'd ever been in a kitchen before. He glanced around in curiosity but couldn't discern the purpose of the iron and wooden utensils upon the walls.

Cook shoved a wooden spoon at him, and he shifted the babe to one shoulder and caught the handle. He stirred the contents of the bowl cautiously. It smelled like pudding all right. Why were they making pudding? There was enough here to feed a village.

The kitchen maid returned bearing firewood, which crashed to the floor upon sight of a devil earl in the kitchen, stirring pudding and dandling a babe on his shoulder.

When the girl looked as if she would faint, Drogo decided he'd had quite enough. Shoving the bundle of flailing arms and legs into the girl's now empty hands, adding the spoon for good measure, he nodded curtly and all but ran out.

He didn't know how women managed it all. Where the hell was Ninian?

Not in the conservatory. He saw evidence of her presence in the apron draped over the settee and the partially planted seedlings on the potting bench. Already, a row of neatly labeled herbs had sprouted on the shelves. She'd been busy.

Feeling somewhat relieved at that, he headed for the tower. Perhaps she was actually napping through all this racket. Expectant mothers were supposed to sleep a lot, weren't they?

His bailiff caught him in the great hall before he had a chance to reach the stairs.

"My lord, a word with ye, if I might."

What was he doing hunting his wife in the middle of the day when there was work to do? The fresh air must be affecting his brain.

"Of course, Huntley. What is it?" Abandoning his chase, Drogo crossed the wide expanse of towering hall.

"It's the burn, my lord. Mr. Payton said as to tell you as soon as you arrived. Her ladyship insisted that he take her to the source of the blight. They've gone off over the hills and it's been since early this morn."

Drogo's heart slid into his throat. He thought he would kill her, if she did not kill herself before he got there.

Thirty-one

"This is the end of the earl's property, my lady. You can see there is no sign of the source of the problem." Mr. Payton stood stiffly beside his placid mare as Ninian stared at the barren wasteland leading back to distant hills.

"The stream must come from somewhere," she insisted. "You have had all summer to explore. It's impossible to tell much of anything at this time of year."

"It could come from Crown land, for all I know. Or Scotland. There is naught we can do beyond this property."

"We could find the source of the blight and stop it," she said crossly, kicking at a dead limb lying in the brown leaves at her feet. She knew she couldn't walk farther this day, and the sight of the barren hills discouraged her. She would need a horse; only it would be months before the child was born and she could learn to ride.

Mr. Payton had a horse. And Mr. Payton was lying. She twisted the dying tip of an evergreen and the needles fell off in her hand. "I can find my own way back. I want to look around some more. You may go about whatever it is you do." Furious, she found it took no effort to summon the imperious tones of her grandmother. It came as naturally as breathing, more naturally than the pleasant face she'd worn for so many years. If she was to be herself, she may as well begin practicing with this annoying insect.

"I cannot leave you here alone, my lady," the steward responded stiffly.

"Of course you can. I've walked these woods alone all my life. I'm a witch, remember? Go away and leave me be." Muttering under her breath, she set out along the stream bank, taking more time to examine what she had missed in her hurry to reach the source of the blight. Perhaps her grandmother had been wrong when she'd insisted Ninian always be pleasant and not frighten the village with her gifts. Wasn't that denying who she was?

She certainly should have frightened the stupid man into letting her go beyond Drogo's boundaries. Perhaps she could persuade Drogo to invent more filters. They could experiment by passing the water through different types and determining which was most effective. Drogo would know how to go about that.

Drogo would no doubt chain her to the wall for venturing out.

She heard Payton riding away as she scrambled down a hillside he hadn't allowed her to traverse earlier. Men! They must think her some breakable china ornament. How did they think the human race had survived all these years? Certainly not by women putting their feet up and doing nothing for nine months out of every year.

At the bottom of the embankment, she crouched quietly, listening to the burn's burble and the wind blowing through barren tree branches. Sometimes, she could hear things in the wind, if she opened up her senses to her surroundings.

The crunch of dead leaves, the slipping of a hidden log, and a loud curse weren't exactly the sounds she'd had in mind. The resulting crash brought her to her feet.

"Who's there?" she called. She already knew whoever it was had hurt himself.

"The bogeyman," a deep, irritated male voice called. "Are you all right?"

"Of course I am." Brushing dead leaves from her woolen skirt, she grasped a nearby sapling, tested it for sturdiness, and pulled herself upward.

"Of course you are," the rough male voice mocked. "You're a Malcolm. Whyever would I think elsewise?"

"Malcolms can be harmed, just the same as anyone else." Puffing a little at the exertion of climbing the steep embankment, Ninian steadied herself on an oak and glanced around. "You!"

The uninvited guest from their wedding lay sprawled in the dead leaves and debris in a washed-out gully beneath some rowan roots. Massive arms crossed over his wide chest, he managed a magnificent, insouciant pose with one boot turned at an uncomfortable angle, his breeches torn by the bare rocks, while glaring at her from beneath brows more thunderous than Drogo's.

"My nose recovered," he said dryly. "My pride is still bruised."

"It looks as if more than your pride is bruised." She found a perch on the rocks where she could kneel beside him and tug at his boot.

"Leave it alone," he grumbled. "Just find a sturdy stick and I can reach my horse."

"Ives men are occasionally stubborn, but usually not stupid." Ninian tugged at the boot as gently as she could, but he still grimaced as it loosened. She noticed he didn't deny his family connection. "The foot will swell and you will have to cut a perfectly good boot if you leave it too long."

"I'll steal another." He pulled his leg from her grasp and with a painful wince hauled the stiff leather off his foot. "There, are you happy now? Find a stick, and go back where you belong."

"Since this is my husband's land, I am where I belong," Ninian said placidly, testing the bones of his sturdy ankle. "They're not broken, but the tendons are strained. I'll wrap it for now. You can soak it when we reach the castle."

"I am not going to the castle." Curtly, he jerked his leg away. "I merely wanted to see that you were unharmed. Now go about your business and I'll go about mine."

Ignoring his orders, Ninian worked at her shift hem with a rock until she'd torn a gash in it. Without any particular sense of delicacy, she lifted her heavy skirt and ripped the hole wider until she had a strip the proper length. The blamed man couldn't even stand without help, so she didn't see much point in arguing with him.

"This is my business," she reminded him as she laid her hands on his swelling ankle and concentrated. He radiated pain, and she worked to ease it. "I can give you willow bark once we are home, and it will feel better. There's not much I can do out here."

"I'll not go to the castle," he repeated, leaning on his elbows as she massaged away the pain. "You really are quite good. A Malcolm with a useful talent is rare."

Ninian understood that more than the pain of his injury was talking. "People do not often appreciate our perceptiveness. Ives men in particular seem to have difficulty grasping things which they cannot see. Do you have a name?"

"Just call me Adonis and wrap the blasted ankle."

"Adonis?" She grinned at him and he scowled in return. The resemblance to Drogo was quite remarkable. She'd judge him to be several years older and a stone heavier — all muscle and probably all between his ears. She sensed no evil in him.

"Greek gods are a rare breed in these woods. Why were you following me?"

"For lack of anything better to do." He grunted as she pulled the cloth tight.

"Do you live around here?"

"I don't live anywhere. Cease and desist, madam!" he howled as she pulled the cloth with all her strength.

"It will feel better when I'm done. If you

don't live anywhere, then there is no reason you cannot come back to the castle. The ankle needs to be soaked."

"There is every reason in the world why I cannot go to yon blasted castle. Now find me a stick, madam, and be off with you. And if I were you, I'd not mention this encounter to your husband. In case you have not noticed, Ives tend to be jealous men."

"Now that really would be stupid." Knotting the bandage, Ninian stood and looked about. "Malcolm women cannot tolerate stupid men. No wonder the legend warns us against you."

"If you know that, why the hell did you marry the earl?" Cursing as he pushed to a sitting position on one of the rocks, he pointed toward a dead tree on his right. "One of those limbs should support me. Can you pull it loose?"

"Drogo is not a stupid man." She tested the limb but it did not crack. She scuffled about in the leaves, looking for a better one. "He is an extremely considerate but very busy man who just has different goals than I do. That does not mean one or the other of us is right or wrong."

"Fool. You're in love with him. You don't have a chance. What in hell are you doing out here risking his precious heir anyway?"

Ninian spotted a stout limb on an out-cropping and pulled herself toward it, ignoring the abrupt curses of the man behind her. "Looking for the source of the burn's blight. You wouldn't happen to know where it begins, would you?"

She slid back down, stick in hand, and handed it to the angry man who had pulled himself upright in his apparent haste to rescue her from the rocks. She offered him a dimpled smile but he merely scowled more blackly.

"Don't give me that innocent look, my lady. I'm not so blind to Malcolm charms as my fool . . ." He didn't finish that statement but grabbed the stick and tested his weight against it. Satisfied it would hold, he met her gaze more calmly. "The blight begins at the mines to the north of here. Your husband's family does not teach their sons of the malignancies they perpetrate on the face of the earth in the name of progress. Perhaps Malcolms can point it out to them before it is too late and they destroy us all."

He heaved himself up the hill by brute force, using the stick as a brace. Fascinated despite herself, Ninian followed him up, carrying his boot. His shirt looked as if it had seen better days, and he wore no waist-coat. His long coat appeared tailored for a younger, smaller man.

"Drogo's mines?" she inquired as they reached level ground. "Does he know this?"

"Probably not." The man — Adonis? — whistled loudly and waited. "He is only interested in productivity and profit and things that he can see and measure. His steward suspects though, and says nothing. It would cost too many people their jobs, were the mines closed."

Ninian heard the sound of a horse galloping toward them. Shortly, he would ride away, and she would never know more. Curiosity wouldn't let her give up. "Please, you must come home with me. Drogo is away on business, if that's your fear. I think he would like to meet you, though."

"No, he wouldn't." The horse appeared around a copse of trees, and he whistled again. It slowed and obediently trotted in their direction. "I'll follow you part of the way to be certain you're safe, but I'll stay out of sight. If you know what's healthy, you'll not mention any of this to his noble lordship. I'm no hand at swords." He caught his mount's bridle and swung up.

Ninian handed him his boot. "Drogo isn't violent," she chastised him. "And I see no reason for violence. I'm quite certain he would listen to your theory about the mines."

"And I'm quite certain he would run a stake through my heart, should we be introduced. It's late. You'll have to hurry to return to the castle before dark."

She wanted to tell him she would arrive much faster if she rode, but his horse was a large, restless stallion she had no desire to sit upon. Before she could formulate another argument, he trotted off into the woods, leaving her alone on the empty road.

"Dratted man," she muttered, searching the place where he'd disappeared but seeing nothing of him.

Who was he and why was he following her? Was it a coincidence that no one had known of his existence until her wedding day?

Very strange. Pondering his words about the mines, she abandoned her search of the burn and followed the more direct road home. She occasionally sensed his presence, but he didn't represent danger, and she could shut him out easily. She should have bound and gagged him while he was helpless and then gone to fetch aid.

Kicking at frozen dirt clods and simmering with resentment as well as curiosity, Ninian didn't notice the pounding of hooves in the distance until she felt the stranger's alarm. Coming alert, she searched for some signal to identify the approaching rider. When she found none, she grinned. Drogo. Well, that was one way of identifying him.

Moses could have carved commandments in the granite monument of her husband's face as he caught sight of her and slowed his mount to a walk. He hadn't brought the palfrey this time, she noted. He apparently hadn't thought he would find her.

"If you'll ride back into the woods, you'll find the missing Ives from our wedding," she informed him. "But he'll probably escape before you can catch up with him."

Apparently believing that her comment was as lamebrained as everything else she did, Drogo swung down from his horse. "What the devil do you think you are doing?"

He sounded so much like the surly stranger that Ninian couldn't help smiling. He always looked so startled when she did that. "You sound just like Adonis. The two of you must have been separated at birth." She looked up at his massive gelding with a frown. "I'll not ride that monster. I'm much safer down here."

Without reaching for her, Drogo pulled his horse around and walked beside her. He said nothing, and she figured he was grappling with his temper. Her husband was very good at concealing anything resembling emotion. She thought he'd done it for so long that he'd forgotten how to express his feelings.

"I can make you lose your temper, you know," she said, kicking the mud clods again. "But I'm rather afraid the result would be so explosive after all this time that you might blow us both up."

"You are not making sense, madam," he said stiffly. "I do not lose my temper. I do, however, worry when I cannot find my seven-months pregnant *wife*."

The last words were strained through clenched teeth. Ninian cast him a sidelong look of amusement. "You cannot keep a leash upon me. Perhaps you would be more comfortable back in London where you do not know what I'm doing."

"I don't think I'll ever be comfortable again." His voice sounded hollow and vaguely perplexed.

"I'm sorry," she said honestly. "I truly did not mean to disturb you. You weren't home and the opportunity opened and I simply took advantage of it. Your steward wasn't very helpful, but Adonis — that's what he said to call him, although I'm certain it's not his name — Adonis says the blight begins far past the hills and into the mines, so there is naught I can do about it."

With a resigned expression, Drogo finally looked down at her. "You really aren't making this up, are you?" He sounded as if he needed reassurance.

She laughed at his bewildered expression. "I think he was following me today, but he fell and twisted his ankle. He said not to tell you, and he refused to return with me to the castle. Do you think he might be another of your father's by-blows?"

Drogo thought about it. Ninian waited expectantly.

"I know little of my father's life before he married my mother. I don't like the idea of him following you, though. Will you stay in the castle from now on?"

He didn't sound very hopeful of receiving the reply he wanted.

Ninian took his arm and patted it consolingly. "I won't go farther than the village until after the babe is born, all right?"

His expression was bleak as he turned to her. "You, madam, will almost certainly drive me mad."

Ninian just smiled.

Thirty-two

"There's something wrong, Drogo."

Reluctantly pulling himself back from his study of the stars, Drogo set aside his telescope and watched with concern as his very pregnant wife swayed into his tower study.

Into her eighth month of pregnancy and with the onset of severe December weather, Ninian had finally given up her forays into the village, much to his relief. That hadn't stopped a steady trickle of villagers from traveling to his back door for Ninian's healing remedies. She thought he didn't know about the small infirmary in the servants' quarters, but he didn't object as long as she took care of herself and the child.

Climbing to the tower was not taking care of herself. "Couldn't you have sent someone up here to me? You're not supposed to be on the stairs."

She collapsed on a cushioned window seat

and caught her breath, protectively holding her belly. Her immense size worried him. He wanted to carry the burden for her. He should never have forced a child on her. He really didn't need a child. He needed Ninian. Life without Ninian lacked color. Life with Ninian meant flowers in unexpected corners, brothers who occasionally behaved with good sense, and nights filled with rapture.

Life with Ninian meant a constant stream of terror as she escaped his protective nets. He ought to follow her advice and go back to London so he didn't have to know about her escapades.

He didn't want to need her, any more than he wanted to need the child. Need did frightening things to his insides that had him waking up in a sweat in the middle of the night.

But then Ninian would curl her warmth against his, and he'd fall asleep again.

Heaven and hell, all wrapped together in one bountiful bundle of golden curls.

The bundle of curls scowled at him. "You're supposed to ask me what's wrong, not scold me. I was in a hurry and didn't want to look for someone."

He'd given up any hope of logic from her months ago. She had a brain. She just didn't use it as he used his. Moving to the window seat, Drogo curled his arms around her and felt her relax against him. It was the only way he could share her burden.

"What is wrong?" he asked, hoping to pacify her.

"I don't know."

He smiled above her head. He'd almost expected that. "If something was wrong with the baby, you would know that, wouldn't you?"

"Yes, of course. It's not that. Maybe the ghost is telling me something."

Drogo sighed. "I told you not to refurbish that dratted suite. It only upsets you. We'll use my old chamber tonight."

She dug her fingers into his arms. "The ghost has been quiet since I've carried your child. No one has complained of screaming or noises since then, have they?"

"That's because I had the roof and chimney fixed. If you hear whining again, it's just the north wind in the old paneling. We should have ripped it out."

"No, it's not that." She swung her head vehemently, batting him with soft curls. "For some reason, I sense it's Dunstan. Has he written to you lately?"

"No, but I hear from Ewen regularly. He would have told me if anything was wrong at the estate."

"Dunstan never should have married that foolish twit. They have nothing in common." Irritably, Ninian rose from the cushioned seat and paced. "I'd hoped she'd be content with a holiday visit with my aunts."

Patiently, Drogo tried to follow the path of her thoughts. "I encouraged the marriage. As a younger son, Dunstan needed the portion she brought. She's young and a little flighty. They'll settle down."

"No wonder Ives do not make good marriages," she scoffed. "They think with their heads and not with their hearts. Celia will not settle down. She will drive Dunstan mad with her demands. She will cost him far more than her dowry. You must learn to let your brothers live their own lives." She nervously twisted his telescope, then fidgeted with the notes on his desk. "How can I empathize with someone who isn't even *here?*"

Drogo smiled. "You can't. You're just worrying for naught, as usual. Now let us go downstairs and I'll tuck you into bed. You need your sleep." He'd given up questioning her "empathy," deciding she just noticed people more than most.

"Dunstan must be close," she asserted firmly as he led her to the door.

That worried him more than he wanted to

admit. He didn't believe in empathy, but Dunstan usually sent him monthly reports. He hadn't heard from him since London.

"There is nothing we can do." He was trying to reassure her, as well as himself.

"He's in pain, I know it," she insisted. "Send one of the grooms to the nearest inn. There is no other explanation. He must be nearby."

"The roads are pits of ice. No sane man would travel them." He lifted her in his arms and carried her down the stairs. "Dunstan is eminently sane, probably more so than the rest of us."

"Not tonight," she whispered. "Send a groom, Drogo, please."

And because it was almost Christmas, and she was far gone with his child, he did.

"They're here." Sleepily, Ninian nudged her snoring husband. Drogo didn't snore loudly, but he breathed deeply. Most mornings, she loved lying there listening to him, basking in the warmth of his muscled male body. Even though she had told him it was best to limit their relations until after the child's birth, he insisted they continue sharing a bed. She didn't object.

But this morning she didn't have time to be idle. "Hurry, Drogo. They're here and they're angry and they'll tear the walls down if we do not do something."

Awkwardly, she eased her legs over the edge of the high bed. She would be quite happy when this child was in her arms instead of her belly. If she didn't know better, she'd think it a contrary Ives male who sat on her bladder. She didn't know if she could endure over a month more of this discomfort.

The cold of her departure apparently aroused Drogo from his torpor. He'd lit a candle and donned his breeches by the time she emerged from behind the dressing screen.

"What the devil are we doing up at this hour?" he demanded as he grabbed a shirt.

She dearly loved admiring the masculine contours of his chest and shoulders outlined in the shadows of the candle as he dressed, but she would have to forgo the pleasure now. She hastily donned the linen chemise she'd worn last night.

"Don't ask me why they would travel at night in weather like this. They're your brothers, after all. I suppose we could assume they wished to arrive before the snow."

"What the devil do my brothers have to do with anything?"

A sudden pounding and shouts at the front portals answered that silly question. Ninian struggled into a loose wool dress and began hooking the bodice over her heavy breasts. She carried the child low, but the bodice was still a struggle.

Drogo tugged the top hook in place for her. "I don't think you've ever looked more radiant," he murmured, taking his time.

"And you must be quite blind, my lord." But she blushed at the compliment anyway. She was learning to deal with the fact that he was an earl and an Ives and didn't reveal his emotions. She was still having difficulty absorbing the physical intimacy of him as a man. She felt self-conscious and awkward next to his masculine grace.

"I daresay the noise is just one of your villagers with a wife about to give birth. We'll have to order the Beltane festivities spread throughout the year rather than on just one night."

She slapped his hand as it encroached upon her breast. "The villagers go to the kitchen, where they know they can rouse someone. It has to be your brothers."

She started for the door as soon as he released her, but Drogo caught her arm and held her back.

"No stairs, remember? I either carry

you, or you wait here."

She hated this. She hated being helpless, coddled, and left out. She was used to her independence. She pouted as Drogo drew on stockings and shoes. He didn't have to be so damned *calm* about someone breaking in the door. If their visitors had an ax, she was quite certain they would have used it by now.

"Wait here," he ordered as he grabbed his coat and started out.

So, maybe he was more anxious than he showed, or he would have taken the time to carry her. She was learning to read him, if she didn't go off on an emotional tangent of her own, like wanting to fling a knife between his shoulders for leaving her behind.

Barefoot, she wandered to the hall and stood at the top of the stairs, listening as Drogo hauled the bar from the doors.

Ninian heard an argument as the door burst open. Dunstan. And Ewen. Perhaps she was better off here, out of sight, until Drogo calmed them. She didn't think her child needed this kind of upset. Perhaps becoming too close to people was detrimental to the child's health. Maybe the ups and downs of loving a large family was why her grandmother had advised her to stay in Wystan and live a solitary life. Ninian had never experienced anything quite so sharply as this Ives fury.

As angry male voices escalated, accompanied by the calmer tones of the groom Drogo had sent to the inn, and finally joined by the sleepy voice of the housekeeper, Ninian sighed in exasperation and settled her bulk on the top step. "If you do not all behave like civilized people and come up here to greet me, I shall roll down these steps to join you!"

She didn't think they would hear, but the angry exclamations ceased abruptly, as if Drogo had collared his brothers and cut off their windpipes.

She suspected Drogo loved his family so fiercely, he didn't dare express it for dread of being made too vulnerable to deal with them.

As she'd anticipated, Drogo appeared on the landing, Dunstan's and Ewen's neckcloths in a firm grip as he shoved them upward.

"They're drunk, and they've left Sarah at the inn," he announced with disgust from below. "Go on to bed. Mrs. White and I will see them to their rooms. I'll have someone take a carriage to fetch Sarah in the morning."

Ninian tilted her head and concentrated.

Usually, she did not seek out the pain of others unless called upon to heal them, but Dunstan would never ask for help. Beneath the drunken belligerency that any fool could see, he registered an emotional pain so deep, it physically hurt. She closed her eyes against the anguish of it.

"I think not," she said quietly, trying to arrange her scattered thoughts while Dunstan's agony bounced off the walls of her mind. "Send Mrs. White for some coffee. Cook will have oatcakes shortly." She dared open her eyes to squint at Ewen. "Thank you for bringing Dunstan safely here, but you'd best follow Mrs. White to the kitchen."

All three men stared at her as if she were insane. Nothing new. But she was learning that brawny Ives men bent easily beneath feminine breezes. With a sigh, she made an exaggerated attempt to pull herself upright by grabbing a newel post.

Drogo instantly dropped his brothers and took the steps two at a time to rescue her. Dunstan staggered at thus being left to his own power. Ewen caught the stair rail and stared at her with a slowly awakening grin.

"By all means, Countess," he agreed with only a slight slur and sway as he attempted a bow. "Coffee and a roaring fire for me." He toddled back down the stairs.

Drogo helped her to her feet. "I'll handle Dunstan. You go back to bed."

Sometimes even the brightest of men could be so obtuse. She stood on tiptoe and kissed his scratchy cheek. "Help Dunstan to our sitting room. I'll stir the coals."

Dunstan was already heading back down the stairs after Ewen. Torn, Drogo looked from one of them to the other, and giving up, chased after Dunstan.

The tinder Ninian added to the coals was burning merrily by the time Drogo steered his brother to a chair and flung him into it. Dunstan collapsed like a broken doll and buried his face in his hands.

"He's drunk," Drogo said unnecessarily. "He never used to drink."

Behind Dunstan's back, she patted Drogo's arm. "Hurry Mrs. White and the coffee. He's frozen clear through." Drogo would understand physical peril much better than if she told him his brother was dying of shame.

Nodding reluctantly, acknowledging there was little he could do, Drogo strode off in search of hot refreshment.

As soon as he left, Ninian pulled a second chair close to Dunstan's. He didn't look up or respond to her presence. She'd seldom dealt with grown men in pain. They came to her for cuts and scrapes, not with wounds so deep they weren't visible. She wasn't entirely certain how to proceed, except that she knew she must. This was Drogo's heir.

"Dunstan." Quietly, she reached for his hands, sliding her own between his callused palms and his face. The potential for violence she felt in him was almost unbearable, but this was something she knew how to control. She channeled it to a part of her mind that could deal with it while concentrating on her patient.

"Dunstan. It's just me. Tell me what is wrong."

His fists gripped hers so hard it hurt. His huge frame shook with the force of his torment. Anger burned as deep as the pain, however, and anger won out.

He tore his hands away, sat up, and glared at her. All the mighty Ives rage wrote itself across his thunderous brow and stubbled jaw.

"I'm going to murder my wife."

Thirty-three

"And an early Merry Christmas to you," Ewen said wearily, sipping black coffee and stretching his legs before the roaring kitchen fire. "Don't say I never gave you anything. Dunstan is a damned rough gift to deliver."

"I don't suppose you're capable of telling me *why* you delivered him?" Drogo poured a cup of bitter brew while listening for any unexpected noises from above.

Ewen glared blearily in his direction, grimaced, and took another sip of coffee. "Not a pretty tale at this hour. Go back to your omniscient wife and ask her."

Stubbornly, Drogo dug in his heels, although the crack about his wife's "omniscience" rang alarms. How had Ninian known Dunstan was near? And in trouble? She'd never claimed to be a mind reader. But empathy? He shook his head. Perhaps Sarah had written, and Ninian hadn't

487

wanted to tell him of it.

"Ninian will be prying Dunstan's version of the tale from him. You'd better state your case here."

Ewen grunted something incomprehensible and managed another swallow of coffee. Emptying the cup, he held it out for another. "He thinks I slept with his wife."

Pouring more, Drogo sank onto a bench and stared at his besotted brother. The usually dapper Ewen looked as if he'd been dragged through every mud puddle between here and London. A bruise scored one side of his jaw, dangerously near his eye. Ewen disliked marring his pretty face with fisticuffs, and he wasn't as strong or as quick as hot-tempered Dunstan.

"Why?" was the only word that came to Drogo's bewildered mind. Why Dunstan, his heir, the brother he relied on most? Why was the sky blue? Nothing made sense.

Ewen shrugged out of his damp coat. "Because Celia left him to sleep with everyone in town, and I told her I'd strip her naked and drag her through the streets of London if she continued." Morosely, he retrieved his cup from the table and sipped again. "She must have given Dunstan a slightly different version of our talk." He looked at his coffee with distaste.

"Couldn't we add whiskey to this?"

Excellent idea. Grabbing the cooking brandy, Drogo added a large dollop to both their cups. He could deal with brawls and exploding carriages and the juvenile mischief his brothers dumped at his door — but not emotional turmoil. Every specter of his father's failed marriage rose before him. And Ninian thought *she* had ghosts. "Where does Sarah come into this?"

"She hit Dunstan over the head with a vase before he could murder me, then demanded she accompany us as her reward. Apparently her mother has returned from Scotland, so she wanted to run the other way. I've had a damned hard time trying to keep Dunstan from murdering the both of us all the way up here."

Drogo rubbed his brow and wondered how soon he could go to Ninian with this tale. Then he wondered why he should bother her with it. He was the one responsible for his brothers, not her. Since when had she become such an indispensable part of him?

"Where is Celia?" he demanded, wishing he could get his hands around the silly twit's neck right now.

"With her current lover," Ewen answered grimly.

Oh, damn. Oh, thrice-bedamned curse of the Ives. He should have emphasized the dangers of ever linking themselves to any woman.

Then why the hell did he think he was any different?

"Who?" Drogo asked with deadly calm.

Seeing the murder in his eyes, Ewen shook his head. "It doesn't matter. She's left Dunstan, and it's killing him. In his own way, he loved the little bitch."

Very carefully, Drogo set his cup down. Holding his shoulders back, trying not to breathe too deeply, he dragged himself up. He'd thought he could rely on the older two of his brothers to look after themselves, but it seemed his duties never ended. It would take all the power of his position in the Lords to obtain the divorce Dunstan would need. "The housekeeper will have prepared a room for you. Get some rest."

Every fiber of Drogo's body protested as he strode stiffly from the kitchen. He relied on Dunstan's stability and sense. Dunstan should have thrown the lying slut out of the house — just as their father had their mother. He groaned as the circle came 'round without fail.

How could Dunstan love Celia? How could a man as sane as his brother love a twit of a female like that? Or any female, for all that mattered. Women were for warming beds and for bearing children. Men simply couldn't let them rule the household. They were all emotion and no logic.

Like Ninian.

Oh, God, none of this made sense. He needed distance. That worked best. He would take care of Dunstan's problem, then return to work as he should have done instead of giving in to his wife's whimsy. Let her coddle plants and occupy herself as she would. He had business and a family to take care of. With the appropriate distance, his life would suffer no more irrational disruptions.

With the right amount of distance, he could deal with Ninian and her foibles logically, as Dunstan had failed to deal with Celia. Emotional involvement was akin to witchcraft, warping the thought processes, blinding sound men to the correct paths, causing them to do things they would never have considered had they been in their right minds. Had Dunstan not fallen in love, he would never have indulged his twit of a wife by taking her to London and leading her into temptation.

Had Drogo not succumbed to the desperate need for a child, he would never have bedded Ninian, never deserted his family, and Dunstan would not be in this predicament. He could not let his needs and desires blind him to his duties again.

Ninian looked up as her husband strode in like some iron automaton that Ewen might have invented. With only a nod to her, Drogo grasped Dunstan's elbow and hauled him from the chair.

When she tried to halt him, her husband shook her off. Looking as if he stood beneath a hangman's noose, Dunstan straightened his shoulders and with only a cool nod in her direction, walked out of his own accord. Wordlessly, Drogo followed him, firmly shutting the door between them.

Ninian didn't need to read his emotions to analyze that action. Her husband had just formally shut her out of his life and out of his family. Again.

Staring at the gloomy paneling the workmen had yet to remove, she prayed to the spirits inhabiting this place for guidance.

After ascertaining that Drogo had closed himself in his tower, Ninian defiantly climbed the narrow stairs to corner him in his lair. She couldn't remember ever demanding anything of anyone at any time, but she had gathered her strength, and she refused to let Drogo return to the distant monster she'd first met without a fight.

"I will have a door and a lock installed at the bottom of those stairs if you don't cease climbing them," he said coldly as she entered, not looking up from the mathematical calculations on his desk.

"Dunstan is *dying* inside," she raged at him, at herself, at the obtuseness of the entire Ives family. "I can't help that kind of pain. He needs you, Drogo." How could she prove to him that she knew how Dunstan felt, knew what he was suffering, even though he would never admit it to his cold and practical brother?

"There's nothing a divorce proceeding won't handle. You, madam, may go back to your plants and patients and leave me to deal with my family's problems."

"Divorce! Is that your family's solution to everything?" Outraged at this denial of Dunstan's pain, she wanted to heave something at him, wake him up, jerk his heart out of his chest and show him he had one.

But she didn't have that power. He'd reduced her to the role of Wife again. He'd listened to her and brought her here and they'd grown closer than ever in these past months. And now he was denying that intimacy had ever existed.

"You, sir, are playing the obnoxious fool, and I won't stand for it!" With a sweep of her lace-bedecked sleeve, Ninian sent all the papers on his desk flying into the air. The cold contempt in his expression as he turned to her incited her anger further. "I am *not* a helpless nitwit to be patronized and treated as your brood mare! We are *equal* partners in this marriage. Dunstan is now my brother as much as he is yours, and if you will not help him, I will!"

Drogo stood, and catching her flailing arms, lifted her from the floor and carried her out the door and down the stairs. "You, madam, are more trouble than all my brothers put together. If you do not stay off these stairs, I will lock you in your room."

Her feeble attempts at kicking and swinging produced no effect other than a wince as she grabbed his queue and pulled as hard as she could. Seizing this one advantage, she wrapped his thick locks around her palm and held on as he deposited her in the master suite. She wouldn't let him walk out that easily.

Without a word, he caught her wrist, twisted it until her fingers loosened, then stalked out, his granite face as immobile and inflexible as his mind.

Damn! If she were a real witch, she'd put a hex on him, turn him into a frog, and turn his damned tower into a lily pad where he could croak to himself all he liked. Stupid, stupid, *stupid* blind Ives men.

She hurled Ceridwen's diary at the door and burst into tears.

"It's Christmas Eve." Ewen sidled into the study and flung himself into the window seat. Trapped by snow and ice, he and Dunstan had avoided each other this past week. "Shouldn't you be downstairs celebrating with the others?"

Drogo adjusted the lens of his telescope and peered deeper into the night sky. "I don't see you or Dunstan down there."

"Ninian has live hollies decorating the hall, and the whole town is bobbing for apples. She promised a flaming pudding and spiced cider. Sarah is playing the piano and there will be dancing. Shouldn't you dance with your wife?" Ewen balanced a compass between his fingers.

Drogo didn't turn around. At the moment, he wasn't even sleeping with Ninian. He'd left her to the suite and her haunts and returned to his old room. It was much saner this way, her with her pursuits, he with his.

His theory on togetherness in marriage needed a few kinks worked out of it. It was impossible to be near Ninian and not desire her. It was impossible to desire her and not want more. "More" seemed to include an emotional involvement he couldn't afford, so togetherness just didn't appear to be an alternative.

"I shouldn't think dancing possible for her at this stage," he said without inflection.

"With Ninian, I expect anything is possible. Her family is . . . unusual."

Grunting noncommittally, Drogo set aside his telescope to return to his desk and jot down a few notes. According to his calculations, he should be able to see his planet again in a few weeks. "The whole Malcolm family is cork-brained. Peculiarities develop in families that are bred too closely, and Malcolms were isolated here for eons. The royal family ought to look into that close breeding business." He checked another item off his list.

"Sarah made Ninian give Dunstan an amulet."

Drogo dropped his quill and glared at his brother. "An amulet?"

Ewen shrugged. "And a small pouch of herbs to wear around his neck. Ninian told him the amulet would help him gather his grief and anger so he could deposit them in the pouch, that he can't be rational until he rids himself of ill humors."

Drogo rolled his eyes and picked up the quill again. "Maggoty-brained females. Do yourself a favor and stay away from them. What did Dunstan do with the claptrap?"

"He's wearing it. He's helping roll rocks into the stream. Ninian said you didn't have time to help but had told her how to do it. Some kind of filter system?"

Drogo kneaded his forehead. He felt as if he'd explode out of his skin with all the constant demands pounding at his door. He just wanted peace and time to think, to distance himself, to put his world into some sensible, logical form as it had been — before Ninian. "I'll have Payton hire someone to move the rocks. Dunstan will be fine once he realizes he's wasting his grief on a tart like Celia."

"Drogo, I don't think you understand," Ewen said a little more adamantly as his brother returned to his work.

Impatient, Drogo looked up again.

"Dunstan believes Ninian's a witch," Ewen said, setting the compass down gently on the desk, "and that Ninian is helping him. He hasn't had a drink in days."

Drogo's thick brows formed into a thunderous cloud.

Ewen hurried on. "She's told him it is our duty to provide an heir. So Dunstan is staying sober and politely refraining from killing me while waiting to see if you have a boy, which of course we all know you will. I suppose he thinks that will free him to murder me, or Celia."

Drogo wondered if the spiced cider his wife was serving contained a strong dose of brandy. He couldn't believe his sane, sensible brother believed that faradiddle.

He *could* believe that Ninian was thoroughly convinced the child was a girl and that she was saving both Dunstan and Ewen from their stupidities.

Standing, he reached for his discarded coat while Ewen watched him.

Drogo shrugged and adjusted his neckcloth. "The woman's a witch, but not the way you think. Come along, let's make Dunstan grovel some more. Take it from me, earls in this family need to learn humility."

Thirty-four

Ninian watched with more anger than trepidation as her husband descended the staircase with his thick brows curled into thunderclouds. She'd thought Ewen's early departure from the festivities ominous, and Drogo's stony face verified her instincts.

She would have been happy to discuss all this with him if Drogo hadn't ignored her all week. She could have returned to her grandmother's house and raised cats for all the good it did being married to a man like him.

Yes, she should have moved to her grandmother's house. At least there she wouldn't have footmen stationed at all the stairs, preventing her use of them.

But rebelliously, she'd decided she didn't want to live alone. Admittedly, for the past week living with Drogo had left her more lonely than she had ever felt in her life. She missed his dry humor, his thoughtful conversation, his physical presence in her bed. Living without the Drogo she'd come to know would no doubt kill her if she didn't find an alternative. Perhaps, if he could not give her the love and acceptance she craved, she might obtain some satisfaction from his more open family.

As she watched Drogo descend with that granite expression of his, it occurred to her that she'd never demanded what she wanted before. She'd always accepted what her grandmother told her, what the villagers thought of her, what her family wanted. Well, it was time that changed. She certainly couldn't continue living this way indefinitely.

Tickling her cat's belly, she watched as Drogo inspected the chair Ewen had attached to the banister with pulleys. If Drogo meant to waste servants on guarding the stairs, at least now they were usefully employed pulling her up and down in Ewen's contraption.

Laughter exploded around the mistletoe as the baker caught Lydie with her hands filled with pastry and planted a kiss on her cheek. Pies and scones flew everywhere and a mad scramble ensued as the village children chased after them.

The village was bleakest at this time of

year, with summer's bounty far behind and the worst months of winter still ahead. Ninian wouldn't let Drogo spoil their holiday fun. Rather than watching him, she eyed Sarah conversing with Mary. At least Sarah wasn't a true Ives. She couldn't cause too much trouble, although giving all the children whistles would certainly cause a few headaches.

"Am I invited to this gathering?"

Drogo's presence struck Ninian with such force that she could feel him deep inside her, where her heart lay. She no longer needed to seek his emotions to know where he was. She could sense him in ways she could sense no one else. She didn't bother turning to look at him. She continued petting the cat.

"It's your house," she said. "I can scarcely forbid your appearance."

"Immensely practical." He pulled up a chair and watched as two children scrambled to hide behind their mother's skirts. "Do the children see me as an ogre?"

"They've not met you and anything new can be terrifying." She adjusted her skirts so the cat could depart now that she'd had her required share of attention.

"Where is Dunstan?"

"In the kitchen, turning the spit."

"In the kitchen? Why the devil isn't he part of the party?"

"I doubt that you'd understand or believe me if I told you, so don't worry yourself. He's keeping busy, and I've hidden all the alcohol."

"I am capable of understanding his pain," he replied stiffly.

"Perhaps, but you're not inclined to share it. The rest of us poor mortals will simply wallow in our emotional weaknesses while you pursue your more toplofty intellectual interests."

"I do my best to provide for my family. That's all anyone can ask."

"Certainly." She dipped her head in polite agreement, then beckoned to a small boy clutching his new whistle. "Come here, Matthew, show me what you have won."

Warily skirting Drogo, Matthew clambered into Ninian's lap from her other side, and proudly displayed his latest acquisition. She felt Drogo stiffen beside her, and instinctively, without any thought, she dropped the boy into her husband's lap. "Show Lord Ives how you can play, Matthew."

To Ninian's amazement, Drogo froze. He showed no evidence of knowing how to hold the child, how to show interest in the boy, how even to speak with him. Wide-eyed, child and man stared at each other in uncertainty.

Drogo had spent half his life providing for his brothers, but he'd never learned how to show them his love. To ease his nervousness, Ninian leaned against her husband's arm and placed the whistle at Matthew's lips. He tooted on it briefly, then scrambled from Drogo's lap and ran for his mother.

"You have six brothers!" she exclaimed impatiently. "Did you never once hold or play with them?"

"They had mothers and nursemaids to hold them," he answered, not looking at her. "It wasn't as if I were their father. I was no more than a boy myself."

The picture was too painfully clear. Denied his own mother at an early age, denied the company of the brothers closest to him, then denied the company of his youngest brothers by their grief-stricken mother and a battalion of nursemaids during their early years, Drogo had never been taught the affection and understanding of a close, loving family. He'd never been held by warm, grubby hands or cuddled a tot in his arms. What a horrible, horrible way to grow up. At least she'd had the village children to hold, and her smaller cousins, when they'd visited.

Tears rimmed her eyes as she pulled away from him and felt him relax. Even *she* made him nervous. He didn't know how to deal with an emotional female who wailed and railed and expected understanding. He could bed her and protect her, but he didn't know how to love her. She was beginning to doubt that he ever would.

"I'm sorry," she whispered.

He looked at her with curiosity. "For what?"

"For asking for far more than you can give." Sadly, she pressed a kiss to his cheek and rose to pull Lydie's daughter from under the banquet table.

It scarcely mattered that he didn't ask her to dance when the fiddlers struck up their next tune.

January 1751

"You'd best hurry and have that babe so you can climb between your husband's sheets again," said Lydie. "He's near snapped the heads off all the servants. Even Ewen blew up at him and left for the mine-fields rather than tarry here longer."

Lydie efficiently snapped a fresh sheet across an empty cot in the infirmary. Ninian had just returned from seeing off their last patient.

"I asked Ewen to check on the water in the mines to see if he could locate the source of the damage," she said. "I'm afraid many of these babies are being born too early because of that water. It's never happened like this before."

Ninian wearily settled into a chair and let Lydie do the physical labor. They really needed to hire more help. Sarah wasn't much inclined toward midwifery.

"Ewen kissed all the maids good-bye, but he did not even try to kiss me," Lydie complained. "I must have lost all my looks. I have become old and decrepit."

Ninian smiled at this vanity. "You are all of seventeen. You have a few more years before decrepitude sets in. And I warned Ewen I would have him shot if he played light and loose with you. Have some respect for yourself, and men will respect you."

"And what good does respect do me?" Lydie grumbled as she tucked in the sheet. "They nod politely and keep their distance and go off to play with their flirts and marry the chits their mothers choose. And their mothers never choose the likes of me."

Ninian finished jotting down her notes on the treatment she'd used for the last infant's cough and pulled herself up again. "If you are tired of living here, we'll think of something else you can do once the roads are open. But I need you for a little while longer, if you do not mind."

Lydie dropped the sheet and rushed to hug her. "I do not mean to sound so spiteful! I love it here. I love the babies, and I want to help with yours. I'm just mad at Ewen, and I'm tired of Drogo looking through me."

Ninian hugged her back. "You must hit an Ives over the head with a large stick to gain his notice. Find someone who will love and adore you and worship at your feet instead. Large sticks are burdensome."

"And Ives men are lousy at choosing women to worship," a sarcastic drawl intruded from the doorway.

Covered in dirt from his toils at the burn, Dunstan leaned against the door frame, looking as surly and disheveled as a cross bear. Ninian had known he was there, but he was so lifeless these days, she'd hoped to arouse some animation. He couldn't really be looking forward to killing Ewen or Celia. He was much too sane a man for that. But the Ives pride had to be assuaged somehow. Perhaps she could persuade him she had an amulet for erasing transgressions. Sarah had been remarkably closemouthed about the astrological chart she'd tried drawing of Dunstan's future.

"Is there aught we can do for you?" she asked pleasantly.

"Besides strangle your husband? Probably not. But there's someone in the woods who requests your presence."

"Who?" she demanded. "I can't go into the woods, or Drogo will clap me in irons."

"Rightly so, I daresay. I think I must insist that I escort you." Suspicion wrote itself easily across his expression.

Ninian threw up her hands. "You're all madmen! Every last black one of you. Why does this visitor not come here like any decent . . ." Her eyes widened as she realized what she'd just said. "Adonis?"

"Is that what he calls himself?" Dunstan straightened and frowned even more darkly. "Bastard is more like it. If it's a measure of the man's desperation that he talked to me, you'd best see what he wants."

Ninian halted Lydie's protest with a pat on the arm. "I am fine. He won't be far. Ives men may all have heads of stone, but they take care of their own."

"I didn't," Dunstan muttered as he took her arm and helped her out the door.

"Even Ives men have limits," Ninian answered callously. "Next time, choose a woman who loves you."

"There will be no next time."

"There is always a next time, if not in this life, then in the next. God may forgive your mistakes, but He expects you to learn from them." She leaned heavily on his arm, forcing him to adapt his stride to hers. She understood his pain and bitterness, but she didn't have to suffer for Celia's mistakes. Dunstan needed a woman who could wield a stout stick to tear down his walls of anger.

"Then God must have sent you to make Drogo pay for his failings," Dunstan grumbled. "How in hell have you hidden yon Adonis from him?"

"I haven't. Like any Ives, he does as he pleases. Shall I turn him into a toad?"

"I'd say he's already an encroaching mushroom if he claims he's an Ives."

Ninian looked at him in disbelief. "How can you doubt it?"

Drawing his lips grimly shut, Dunstan said no more.

Ninian had to smile as they reached a clearing not far from the clump of birch trees she'd been eyeing with wistful plans for a garden. Adonis sprawled his lengthy masculine frame upon some rocks and moss, much as a fairy king might oversee his kingdom while awaiting his attendants to present themselves.

"I see your boot shows no sign of disrepair," she said with amusement as this mysterious Ives rose casually to his full height — not out of respect for her, she suspected, but to intimidate Dunstan, who glared at him ferociously. As much as these men frustrated her, she didn't know how she had lived without the constant entertainment they provided.

"My gratitude to you for that, my lady." Adonis bowed perfectly while still keeping a wary eye on her escort.

"If you had the proper respect for the countess at all, you would not force her outside in this weather but would come to the door like any civilized person," Dunstan admonished him.

She shot Adonis a warning look as she held Dunstan's arm tighter. "I'll turn both of you into toads if you do not behave. Now, what is it that you wish to tell me?"

"Beside the fact that you've married into a family of self-destructive bedlamites?" Legs akimbo, arms crossed over his massive chest, Adonis appeared to guard the forest as he studied Dunstan's distrustful demeanor with amusement.

"I assume the insult applies to yourself as

well?" Dunstan countered.

"It does, else I would not be here."

"Stop it, both of you! I am weary of this posturing. You may insult your heritage after I leave. For now, tell me what it is I need to know so I may go back to my fire."

Reminded of her delicate condition, they instantly retreated from their battle positions, although neither looked particularly abashed about their neglect.

"I apologize, but I thought you might like to know I've discovered that your husband's mine is directly responsible for poisoning the burn. To locate new seams, they are pumping water filled with coal sludge from the ground and dumping it down a hill that drains directly into the burn. Ives have never given thought to the land they mutilate, nor to the effects of that mutilation."

"That's a damned lot of —" Dunstan raised clenched fists but halted immediately as Ninian grabbed his arm and moaned. A frown of pain creased her forehead as she tried to stand upright.

"Ninian?" Panicking, he grabbed her waist to support her.

With a frown of concern, Adonis stepped forward but Ninian waved him off. Panting, she let the pain roll away and straightened.

"I thank you for the warning. I have asked

Ewen and Drogo to look into it. I would appreciate it if you could guide them, since they do not take me seriously." Seeing Adonis stiffen and back away at this command, she waved it away. "I understand if you cannot. I might be a trifle . . . indisposed . . . for a while, but I shall do what I can."

"My apologies, my lady, I should not have disturbed you." Glancing to Dunstan with deep concern, he asked, "Shall I help carry the countess to the house?"

Hesitating, studying the stranger, Dunstan shook his head. "Drogo is in the village. Send someone for him. I think the child is early."

Ninian would have smiled as the brawny stranger looked petrified, then recovered sufficiently to nod and run off, but the next contraction was swift and fierce and she barely managed to hold back a cry of pain.

The child was not only too soon, but too quick.

Thirty-five

"You'd best have someone prepare a few guest rooms," Ninian said absently as Drogo dashed into the suite, nearly breaking his neck on a cat winding around his ankles. He scooped it up and deposited it on a chair, where it curled contentedly.

"Sarah told me —" he started to say, but his otherwise-occupied wife waved away his interruption.

"My family has a tendency to descend without warning. I'm sorry, I should have informed you of that."

What the devil did her family have to do with this? Why the *hell* wasn't she in bed? Damned woman . . .

He may have been mistaken thinking he could overcome the Ives curse, but that didn't mean he couldn't protect his son. If his addled wife didn't lie down, their son would drop out on his head. He stalked her cautiously, hoping to capture her without a fight.

She paced in front of a roaring fire in the master suite, wearing naught but a ruffled shift. Expecting his son to fall out at any moment, Drogo couldn't help staring at her belly.

"You need to be in bed," he said firmly, uncertain where it was safe to grab her.

She stopped at a table to slap a portable writing desk in his hands. "Better make a list. I don't want to forget anything. Adonis says the mine is causing problems —"

"Adonis?" Drogo roared. Or thought he roared. He'd never roared before. Flinging the desk down, he grabbed his obviously hysterical wife above her nonexistent waist, intent on placing her in bed where she belonged.

She slipped from his grasp, caught the back of a chair, and began breathing deeply.

Terror nearly blew the top off his head as Drogo recognized the pain tightening Ninian's suddenly pale cheeks. His curses riddled the room, but he didn't dare touch her until she released the chair.

Finally, she breathed easily and straightened. "Five minutes apart. We have time. Do take note, Drogo. I can't do everything."

She couldn't do everything? "You damned

well can't do *anything!*" he exploded. "You're supposed to be having a child!"

"There's that temper you don't have," she reminded him, pulling a worn, leather-bound book from the shelves she'd filled from her grandmother's library. "I've never done this for myself. I'm sorry this is happening so soon. I'd counted on my aunts . . ."

She flipped the book open to a marked page. "You'll have to recite the welcoming ceremony. Perhaps I can say it with you, if you speak slowly enough."

"Welcoming ceremony?" he shouted. Instead of grabbing his manic wife, Drogo sank both hands in his hair and pulled to make certain he wasn't dreaming. Or having hallucinations. Was she or was she not having the child? And if she was, why in hell wasn't she lying in bed, surrounded by women?

"We always welcome new Malcolms," she answered with a diffident shrug. "It seems to ease labor. I don't seem to be dealing very well with the pain. I had no idea —" She gasped and bent double.

This time, his roar brought the rest of the household running.

By the time they arrived, Drogo had Ninian on the damned bed. She clung to her book as she gasped and prayed and curled

514

up in agony. He thought her pain would rip the heart and lungs out of his chest if it did not cease soon. Sweat poured down her brow by the time she straightened and handed him the book again.

"I've marked the place. You may start anytime. Your daughter is in a hurry."

"My *son*, madam, doesn't need any superstitious nonsense chanted over his head." Drogo turned and glared at Lydie, who stood in the doorway bearing a bowl of steaming water. "Help her!" he commanded.

"There is nothing I can do yet," Lydie said simply, setting the bowl down.

Ninian's face looked small and exceedingly fragile against the pillows. The enormous lump of her stomach seemed to fill the bed as Lydie covered her with a sheet. Drogo swallowed hard. Ninian was too small. Even he could see that. He had thought her healthy peasant material, but she was like a transparent wraith who would shatter at the merest loud noise. Just the wind howling through this accursed suite could fracture her.

"Ninian," he whispered as she closed blue-veined lids over the lovely pools of her eyes. Her skin was like the finest glass as he brushed it with his fingers — and just as cool.

Her lids snapped open and she smiled vaguely. "I'm afraid I won't be of much use for a while. Dunstan must tend the filter, if you would be so kind as to see it's done properly. Perhaps, if you send for Ewen —" She bit her lip and breathed deeply, her hand instinctively covering her lower abdomen.

"Damn the burn and Dunstan and all else! Just tell these confounded women what to do to deliver the child safely." Drogo was aware of Sarah and several of the village women in the shadows behind him. Dunstan was back there somewhere, too. He couldn't concentrate on any of them.

She smiled faintly. "They can do nothing but wait, my lord, just like you. You would fare much better if you listened to me just this once."

"Fine, I'll listen." He drew up a chair and gestured for someone to bring him the abandoned writing desk. This was something physical he could handle.

He obediently jotted notes as Ninian rambled. He had no idea what he was writing or what she was saying, but the exercise of applying quill to paper was sufficient to calm them both, until she whimpered and arched and clenched the bedsheets. Then quill, desk, and ink flew into the air.

While a maid hastened to clean the spill, Drogo transferred to the bed and held his wife awkwardly, not knowing how to offer comfort but giving what he could as Ninian bit back screams and clutched his coat sleeves. Her agony seared him, and he could not imagine how much worse it was for her. His son was tearing her apart. He was killing her.

He would surely die if she did. That would leave Dunstan.

Frantically latching on to this thought, Drogo sought his brother as the contraction subsided and Sarah hurried forward to wipe Ninian's brow. He wasn't any good at this comforting business. He needed something solid to sink his teeth in. Where was Dunstan?

Without a word, he rose from the bed and elbowed his way through the crowd of women until he located his heir pacing in front of the fire in the sitting room.

"If the child dies, and Ninian with it, I'll have none other," he announced as Dunstan swirled to look at him. Marrying Ninian had been the first selfish thing he had done in his life, and he'd created disaster. He should have known better.

Eyes empty, Dunstan said nothing.

Drogo wanted to shake him. "Someone

has to look after our mothers, the estates, the younger ones. I'm counting on you. Don't let me down!" he ordered.

"You'll live to be a hundred," Dunstan replied bitterly. "Don't look at me."

"I'm killing her more surely than you ever wished to kill Celia!" He didn't shout. He was certain he hadn't shouted. He paced, not daring to face his brother with his fear, not daring to meet the matching pain in Dunstan's eyes. All his life he'd managed to keep fear and pain at bay by concentrating on what could be done logically. He didn't know how to handle fear and pain when there were no logical parameters to grasp. If he could pull his son out right now, he would do so.

The wind howled down the chimney, shooting embers across the hearth. Drogo grabbed the poker and shoved the coals deeper into the grate. Here was something he could do. "Dammit, I thought I had this thing fixed."

"Women have children all the time. Ninian will live," Dunstan said crudely. "You'll have your heir. You won't need me."

Drogo ignored him, lost in his own discovery. "We don't give a damn what we do to the women as long as we plant our seed. That's the curse of Ives. We plow and plant and walk away, content we've done our duty, when they're the ones who toil and strain and dutifully produce our offspring until the soil grows barren and wasted from the effort. We *kill* them," he announced vehemently, "in one way or another."

"We should rotate crops?" Dunstan asked. "Or fields? That's what our father did."

A scream echoed through the darkening chambers, bouncing off the walls. Terror escalating, Drogo swung on his heel and stormed back to the bedchamber.

Ninian lay serenely, eyes closed.

Wildly, Drogo glanced around. The scream had shattered his brain. Where had it come from? Perhaps the wind whistled through the chinks in the stone behind the paneling. The still form on the bed drew his frantic gaze — she still breathed.

He relaxed warily as Ninian opened her eyes. To his horror, she suddenly gasped, drew up her legs, and grabbed her belly in agony. Her scream joined the one still echoing in his head.

The scene in front of him dwindled to a distance. He watched the women surround the bed, saw the golden waterfall of curls across the stack of pillows, knew it was his wife bearing down in agony to produce his child, but he was no longer with them. He stood apart, watching from afar — separate, as he had been the night he'd met her, as he had always been.

The wind howled, the draperies blew inward in the draft, and the fire in the grate sputtered. Ninian writhed in pain, and he could only stand here at a helpless distance.

Fury at his uselessness stirred him into action. Why had nothing made this room comfortable? Drogo strode past the bed and pulled the heavy draperies across their rod to seek the source of the wind's howls. Nothing but the black glass of nightfall and the reflection of candle flame flickered back at him.

The chimney. Determinedly, he lifted a poker. A solid wallop to the stone shook loose centuries of dried mortar. He slammed it again, hoping to shake loose the blockage that must be causing the wind's lament. He beat the stones until the poker bent and broke and the wind howled through every particle of his body, just as Ninian's moans filled the room.

A cloud of soot smashed into the burning grate, wafting outward, coating everything in a film of black. Women shrieked and scolded and chattered like magpies. The scream still wailed, if only in his head. He spun on his heel, but Ninian had collapsed against the sheets. Sarah looked at him as if he were crazed and continued wiping Ninian's brow with a cool cloth.

"Read her the book, Drogo." She nodded at the volume on the chair.

Books and prayers and silly ceremonies would not stop the howling.

Grabbing a kindling ax, he stalked the room, searching for the source of the shrieks. Sarah must have planted whistles in the walls just to drive him mad. She was probably laughing up her sleeve right now.

Dunstan grabbed his arm and tried to lead him away, but Drogo shook him off.

Locating a knot in the rotten paneling, he swung his ax and splintered the wood. Why hadn't they fixed these walls by now? He would not have Ninian suffer the discomfort of the wind. He was master here. He'd have them plaster the walls.

"He's gone mad," one of the maids whispered as Drogo swung the ax into the paneling until it popped and peeled from the wall.

"I've never seen him lose his composure like this," Sarah murmured to Dunstan in delighted horror. "What on earth is wrong with him?"

A corner of Dunstan's mouth curled

grimly. "A woman. Big brother has finally found one that's got under his skin, and he doesn't know how to handle it."

"Shouldn't you do something? Take him downstairs," Sarah ordered.

Crossing his arms, Dunstan shook his head. "No, ma'am. I'm enjoying this."

The frail figure in the bed seemed oblivious of the destruction. Overcoming another contraction, she reached for the book her husband had abandoned. "Drogo," Ninian called softly. "Hurry, please. I need the words."

Words. Drogo blinked. He glanced blankly at the ax in his hands, then up at the havoc he had wreaked in the room. He absorbed Sarah's expression of horror and confusion. Puzzled, he set aside the ax and turned in the direction of the voice calling him.

"The words, please," she whispered between pants, handing him the book as he returned to the bedside.

Words had no power. They were just . . . words. Drogo gazed blankly at the ancient page. From memory, Ninian began to recite the first line.

Seeing the agony creasing her forehead once more, Drogo hurriedly offered her the next line, reading slowly so she could follow between breaths. *"Wind and rain, sorrow and woe, begone from this moment of birth. Bring in the joy."*

Ninian smiled and seemed to relax, even as she writhed with the pressure contracting and bearing down on her insides. The howl of the wind disappeared as Drogo concentrated on Ninian.

Together, they read the whole silly ritual of flowers and trees and birth and life. Drogo ignored it when she removed a pouch of fragrant herbs from her bodice and sprinkled them across the covers. He said the words for as long as they eased her.

Sitting on the bed facing his wife, his back to the women, Drogo read in the flickering lamplight, blocking out the wailing wind and howling chimney. Ninian reached out her hand, and squeezing her soft fingers, he read louder.

"Thank you," she murmured, blue eyes focusing steadily on his face — just before she raised her knees and groaned so deep, he swore the sound tore from the bowels of the earth.

"Here it comes," Lydie shouted excitedly. "Bear harder, Ninian."

Hair matted and wet with perspiration, straining into the pain, Ninian didn't tear her gaze from Drogo's.

Heart in his mouth, he clasped her hand with both of his and willed her his strength, pouring everything in his power into her slender fingers. He could swear she smiled broader through her tears.

"I love you, Drogo."

The words whispered through him even as Ninian's face crumpled with pain and her scream split the air.

She'd said them once before, but he'd not listened. He'd not believed. He couldn't believe she'd said them again, not after all he'd done to push her away.

He was supposed to maintain his distance. He should be downstairs, getting drunk, waiting for the women to bring him the announcement of his child's birth. What the hell was he doing here, hearing words he'd never wanted? He clung to her hand as her scream died, but its echoes haunted the air.

An infant's weak cry filled the silence following Ninian's collapse.

She lay so still. Worriedly, Drogo watched for the blink of an eyelash, the restless rise of her breast.

Ninian, please, he pleaded inside his head, where none could hear but himself. He couldn't show his fear, but it was there, growing wider and deeper and clawing with terror at his rib cage as her hand lay limp in his. *Ninian, don't leave me alone.*

Her eyelids moved, and great heaving sobs of relief shook his whole body.

He laid his head down on her breasts and wept like the babe she'd just borne as her hand squeezed his.

"Alana," she breathed in satisfaction next to his ear.

Light poured through him. Drogo no longer heard the howls as serenity filled him with a strength he'd never known, not physical strength, but something far different as he lifted his head and looked into Ninian's shining blue eyes. "Alan," he declared firmly, grasping the invisible connection between them and holding on for all he was worth. "No mere slip of a girl could make that roar."

She studied him for a moment, then turned her gaze wonderingly to the babe Lydie held out. The roars emanating from the bundle certainly had a masculine edge to them.

"Your son, my lady," Lydie announced proudly, laying the squalling, kicking infant in Ninian's arms.

Obviously stunned, Ninian pulled back the infant's swaddling to verify what couldn't possibly be. Blinking in astonishment as her son proved his masculinity, she smiled with motherly pride, tucked the now wet toweling around him, and offered up the black-haired babe for Drogo's admiration.

As he daringly reached to push back a blanket edge for a better look at his screaming offspring, she murmured tauntingly, "He doesn't have a temper either, my lord."

Drogo's grin nearly split his face.

Thirty-six

"You have your heir, Drogo," Dunstan pronounced glumly, inspecting the babe in Ninian's arms the next day. "With that hair, there's no doubt he's an Ives."

"Had he been a girl, there would have been no doubt," Drogo replied stoutly, experimentally brushing a black curl on the babe's head.

"You should be glad he's not a Malcolm for all Malcolms are" — Ninian blinked, bit back the word "witch," and stared at her son in curiosity — "are fair," she amended.

Surely . . . ? She had no way of knowing. No Malcolm within living memory had carried a son. Of course, no Malcolm had married an Ives in ages. Was this the true foundation of the legend? If a Malcolm bore an Ives male, was there some danger he had Malcolm gifts? An Ives witch? Or did one call them warlocks?

Oh, my. Ninian studied rosebud lips sucking hungrily at a chubby fist. Could he read emotions as she did? Was he sensitive to auras, like her cousin Christina? How would she tell — especially if he turned out to be as closemouthed as his father?

She'd felt gratitude and relief filling the suite the night of Alan's birth, but what did that tell her? She glanced around at the walls Drogo had uncovered. In daylight, a wonderful mural had emerged depicting trees and Druids. Perhaps this was what the ghost had hoped to show them, but it wasn't the ghost's feelings she needed.

Her attention reverted to her enigmatic husband. He'd wept last night. He'd utterly lost his self-possession and fallen to pieces. Except that was just one moment out of the many stretching before them. She couldn't give birth to a child every time she wanted his attention.

And what of his child? Would Drogo ignore his son the way he did Lydie's baby? Would he ignore his child's real needs as he did his brothers? Would he teach Alan to be as cold and distant as he was? If he couldn't love her, could he love his son?

She glanced up at Drogo, who had not stopped smiling since the child's birth. *He* had no doubts, that was certain. He had what he thought he wanted. Let him deal with it.

She held the babe out for him to take. "I'm tired," she said with her best dimpled smile. "You hold him."

She saw the panic in his eyes, the reluctance as he looked down at the helpless infant squirming in the blankets. Other women might assume that men had only one part to play in the creating and raising of a child, but she had no such misconception. He wanted a child, he could care for it as well as she. And learn to love him, in the process.

"Just put your arms out," she ordered. "Put a hand under his head."

With Dunstan as an amused audience, Drogo could do no less. Awkwardly, he tried to wrap his arms around the bundle and manage his son's floppy head at the same time. Startled by the change in position, Alan whimpered in protest.

Frantically, Drogo tried to press the babe back in Ninian's arms. "He wants you."

"He doesn't know what he wants." Impatiently, she adjusted the blankets but refused to take him back. "We must teach him to want you as well. He's an *Ives*, remember?" she asked maliciously.

The infant kicked the blanket from his

feet and Drogo hastily attempted to adjust it. Instead, tiny pink toes emerged from a long linen gown, thrashing in freedom.

"I can't do this," Drogo muttered, balancing a head of dark curls and tugging at gown and blanket while juggling the whole awkward bundle without dropping it. "I have to take care of . . ."

"Your son," Dunstan said, watching over his brother's shoulder with a hint of amusement. "He's big. He'll be climbing the castle ramparts in no time. You can't ask Ninian to follow him."

Dunstan turned to Ninian. "You have done a fine job, Countess. I congratulate you. Now, I must be on my way."

"No!" she said sharply, catching him by surprise. "Not until the village's water is safe. Once the snow starts melting and the spring rains arrive, the burn will rise again, and Drogo can't do everything. It's time all of you accepted your responsibilities and stopped acting like children. You owe Drogo that much."

Startled, both brothers stared at her. She glared right back. She might be half their size and nowhere as formidable, but by the goddess, she would have her way in this at least.

Drogo succeeded in balancing his son's

head in the crook of his elbow while tugging the blanket to cover the tiny feet. He raised questioning eyebrows at brother and wife but opted to leave the argument to them. He had his hands full already.

"And once we save the water — providing such a thing is possible — I suppose there is still another task I must perform to fill this never-ending debt?" Dunstan asked dryly.

"Drogo has taken care of this family all his life," Ninian replied. "He has provided you with all your worldly goods. What have you done in return? Your debt is so enormous you cannot begin to fill it anytime soon. An *honorable* man would attempt to pay his debts."

Fury blazed in Dunstan's dark eyes. She could sense the shame still swamping him, but plain black Ives fury inundated the air. He might be as burly as a bear and lack Ewen's pretty face, but he wore passion handsomely. "I thought you meant to *help* me, my lady," he cried, dragging the charm bag from his neck and flinging it at her. "That's the last time I'll believe any woman." He stormed out, slamming the door.

Drogo hurriedly attempted to return Alan to Ninian so he could follow.

Stubbornly, she crossed her arms over her

breasts. "Dunstan is a grown man and will do as he wishes, no matter how much you interfere. He is beyond your help. Your *son*, however, needs you. It's your choice."

Dumbfounded, Drogo looked from her, to the door, to the helpless infant whimpering in his arms. Defeat rose in his eyes as he hugged his son closer to his chest.

"We may both regret this," he warned.

"I doubt any of us lead lives without regret." Wearily, Ninian rested her head against the pillow and prayed that she was doing the right thing by driving Drogo's family away. Instead of just tolerating her, Drogo might end up hating her.

Drogo sat before the fire, rocking his son and watching his wife sleep. *His* son. *His* wife.

He wanted to find that distance again, that undisturbed plane where he could look down on his possessions and responsibilities and manipulate them like men on a chessboard. The child in his arms prevented it.

He studied Alan's sleeping features. The babe had already found his thumb and sucked on it dreamily. Round baby cheeks gave no evidence of the square man's jaw he would someday possess, but the pugnacious chin hinted of a strong streak of Ives temperament.

Somehow, he had to lead this child into adulthood, teach him responsibility and duty, steer him clear of life's perils and pitfalls, as he had failed to do for his brothers.

Ninian stirred against the pillows, drawing his gaze to her and away from his morose thoughts. With the draperies pulled back, moonlight streamed across the bed, catching in her golden curls and illuminating her translucent features. He no longer knew what to make of her — not that he ever really had.

He'd tried to analyze her as he'd tried to analyze the problem with the burn, with equally dismal results. He'd tried to think of her as a mathematical calculation where two plus two gave him four every time, but that hadn't worked either. Ninian's moods guided her behavior as erratically as the winds blew.

How could he remain distant from a son who needed his constant guidance and from a wife who demanded attention with her mere presence?

He couldn't.

Ninian had accused him of controlling his family, and she was right. He felt much less helpless when he could predict their behavior with the scratch of quill on bank note.

He couldn't manipulate Ninian or his son that way. They would do as they willed, with no thought to him. She could leave him anytime she wished. From the wariness with which she had taken to watching him, he had to wonder if she was already considering it. The thought terrorized him down to the marrow of his bones. If their son didn't tie her to him, how could he keep her and still hold that distance he needed to survive?

As if she heard the panic of his thoughts, Ninian opened her eyes and smiled sleepily, striking a blow to his heart from which he would never recover.

He could never leave her, but she could walk away anytime. He was doomed. Ives wives always left.

Frantically, he grasped for some way of binding her. Glancing down at his sleeping son, he thought the answer lay there, somehow. Ninian would not wish to be parted from her child.

February

"You look as if you've swallowed a lemon, my lord," Ninian teased as Drogo appeared beside the bed, carrying their whimpering son.

"The brat has loaded his napkin and none of your nursemaids has appeared to take care of it," he grumbled, handing her the soggy bundle.

"I could teach you," she offered.

He handed her a dry cloth and poured warm water into a bowl, but stepped back in disgust at her offer. "Not a chance, madam. I'll drag someone up here by the hair of their head first."

She didn't know what had come over him, but he'd been the kindest, most considerate man in the world this past month. Still, he categorically refused to change dirty nappies.

She'd forgive him this one weakness. Alan kicked and squalled and doused everyone in sight when he was displeased, and hunger and dirty linen displeased him. Skillfully, she caught his flailing legs and rearranged his clothing to her satisfaction.

"Master Alan needs to learn patience," she observed once the infant was clean and dry and sucking greedily at her breast. She still found it hard to believe she'd borne a boy, but his strength and hunger proved he was his father's son, without a doubt.

"Lord Alan," Drogo corrected. At her questioning look, he explained. "The eldest son of an earl bears the courtesy title of 'lord.' If my title included a viscountcy, then he would be Lord Wystan, but I have two earldoms instead."

Ninian sniffed. "He has as much chance of lordliness as your brothers. Crack-brained rogues, the lot of you." She glanced anxiously at the window. "Is it still snowing?"

Tearing his gaze from the sight of her bared breast, Drogo strolled restlessly to the window. "No, it's stopped, but no one will come in or out for a while, I wager."

She recognized his male restlessness. He'd managed to submerge it in his work, but she'd caught him looking at her with hunger more than once these past weeks. She was grateful he had not taken another woman to his bed as many men did, but they still had problems she must sort out before she gave in to that look again. She would not end up like Drogo's mother — perpetually burdened with children and no husband to show for it.

"Dunstan?" she inquired softly.

"He can't leave any more than your family can arrive. He's sleeping it off with the horses right now. It seems he's found a drinking partner somewhere." He shrugged and returned to hover over her as she nursed Alan.

Drogo's unabashed stare heated her flesh, and Ninian suspected he knew it. The makings of a smile curled his mouth as she tried to adjust her bodice more modestly.

"You cannot hide what nature gave you," he noted with satisfaction as he sprawled in the chair beside the bed.

"It need not give me quite so much," Ninian muttered.

He was in shirtsleeves and waistcoat, with his shirt unfastened to reveal the strong column of his throat. Ninian let her gaze drift to the flap of his breeches and swallowed at the sight of the bulge there. His gaze mocked hers as she hastily returned it to his face.

"Should I say the same?" he asked with a straight face. "I can scarce hide that I miss sharing your bed."

"You are the one who moved out of it," she said tartly, switching Alan to her other breast despite his sleepy protest. "Perhaps it's best left that way. I would not burden you with any further *responsibility*."

The mocking light left his eyes. "And I would not use you for my convenience and kill you with the agonies of childbirth. I can keep my breeches fastened."

Oh, dear. When he said things like that, it reminded her of how much she loved him, no matter how exasperating, calculating, or plain old mule-headed he could be. She loved the man behind the cold demeanor, the vulnerable man who must be taught to hold the child he adored. But that man was as inaccessible as the Himalayas.

If she could not teach Drogo to love, what kind of future could they have?

"Fastened for another month, at least," she agreed. Perhaps he didn't love her in the same body-and-soul manner as she loved him, but she thought he cared for her in his own way. Perhaps it was a Malcolm gift to love this deeply and thoroughly, and she shouldn't expect others to return it. She just didn't think he would ever — all evidence to the contrary — believe she had abilities beyond the natural, and if he couldn't accept her as she was, she could never expect him to accept her as more than a bed warmer either.

It simply wasn't within the limits of his philosophy. He would never have love enough to believe what he couldn't see. In turn, she didn't know how she could survive without the love she needed as much as she needed the air she breathed.

Drogo took a deep breath and tore his gaze away from her to studiously watch the fire. "A month. By then, you'll be well enough to travel?"

She should have seen that coming. "It will be March. With the melting snow and spring rain, the roads will be swamps." She was more concerned about the burn and floods, but she knew better than to broach one difficult topic on top of another.

He lifted one curled eyebrow in her direction. "If we can travel to Wystan in sleet, we can travel it the other way in mud."

Grandmother had said she belonged in Wystan, that the people needed her here. She needed to be needed. To *feel* needed. Of course, if Drogo needed her . . .

His tears at Alan's birth had raised her hopes, but Drogo was an immensely self-sufficient man who prided himself more on conquest and accomplishment than anything so ephemeral as love. She had only love to offer. Could he accept that?

It would seem not. He never responded to her words of affection.

As she eased Alan from her breast and buttoned her bodice, Ninian eyed her husband's broad shoulders casually slouched against the chair back, the long, muscled limbs sprawled across the carpet, and doubted the likelihood of Drogo ever needing anything. His noble lordship already had it all — including her.

Thirty-seven

March

"Water's out of its banks," Dunstan declared blearily, staggering into the breakfast room where Ninian and Drogo dined.

"Oh, dear, I was afraid of that." Ninian dropped her spoon and stood up. "And it's raining. With all the melting snow, we'll soon be sitting on a great bog. Do you think you can hitch the wagon? We must evacuate the village."

Drogo had jumped up when she did. "*You* will do no such thing."

Dunstan shook his head. "Can't. There's sickness. The babe will catch it."

"Sickness? Why didn't someone tell me? What are the symptoms?" Anxiously, Ninian balled her napkin between her fingers.

"How else do people know they're sick?

They make great messes all over and lie about and groan," Dunstan answered carelessly.

"Fever? Is there a fever?" Ninian demanded anxiously.

"It doesn't matter," Drogo intruded. "You cannot endanger yourself or Alan by going into the village."

"If there's no fever, I can help." Ninian threw down her napkin and headed for the door.

Drogo caught her by the waist and hauled her back. "If everyone has it, it must be contagious. You are Alan's only source of nourishment. We cannot risk it."

She hesitated, looking from one towering man to the other. It was her job to protect the village. She couldn't desert her friends, yet she couldn't harm Alan.

The choice she'd made when she'd first left Wystan rose up before her now. She had chosen a larger world, and that world contained a child and husband. She couldn't do everything any longer, but if her husband truly saw her as an equal, as a partner, she wouldn't have to do everything. Could she trust him?

"If I cannot go, you must," she whispered. What if they wouldn't? What if these Ives men laughed off her fears? Or ignored the

541

village as generations of Ives had?

"I will take care of it," Drogo said, watching her as if he did not believe she would do as he commanded. "You will remain here."

"If you will be my eyes and ears," she agreed hesitantly. "You must tell me their symptoms, observe them closely, *listen*."

Dunstan scowled. "What can I do?"

"Carry the sick ones to my grandmother's house. It's on high ground."

She turned and looked into Drogo's stern-jawed face. She was asking the impossible of him. Whether he realized it or not, he commanded from an ivory tower while she was the one who walked among his family and tenants, listening. He didn't know how to hear the pain and sorrow behind brave words.

"You realize that if it is contagious, we cannot come back," he said.

She nodded, biting her lip, knowing what she was asking of him, fearing it. She might not see him until the crisis passed. Drogo could become ill himself. She wouldn't be able to go to him. "Someone must tell me what you've found so I know what cures to use."

"I will write down all that I find and pass it to you through a window."

"But if the water continues rising, the village will not be safe," she reminded them, trying not to think of anything but the immediate danger. If she considered what might happen, she would be of no use to anyone.

"One thing at a time, moonchild. Gather up your linens and bedding and whichever of the servants you trust to follow orders. We will do what we can."

Torn, she watched them go with a prayer in her heart.

What they could do wasn't enough. Dunstan reported that her grandmother's house was overflowing with the sick. Ninian's potions, plasters, and prayers weren't working.

When Drogo appeared to tell her that all of Mary's children were ill, Ninian resolutely reached for her herb pouch and began picking among her jars, choosing from the contents.

Standing outside the conservatory windows, Drogo narrowed his eyes. "What do you think you are doing?"

"I thought the herbs healed," she yelled back. She didn't have time for the nicety of pen and paper. "But maybe it's not the herbs. Maybe they really need *me*."

"That's ridiculous." He flung open the door and barred her way. "All of London's physicians could not cure this."

"All of London's physicians are quacks." She reached for a pot on a high shelf. She wished she had the agrimony from the burn. Drogo had reported no fever, but he wasn't a physician.

"I've ordered up the carriage to take you and Alan back to London. You'll be safe there." Like a mountain, he would not be moved.

"Lydie is still nursing. She can nurse Alan. Or we can wean him to cow's milk." She swung and glared at him. "Would you leave your brothers if they were ill?"

"You're my wife, mother of my son, dammit!" Drogo roared. "I will not let you risk your life for people who turned their backs on you!"

They had at that. They'd pushed her to the outside, never accepted her, and turned their backs when she'd needed them. But it no longer mattered if people accepted her. All she really needed was to accept herself and use her gifts and talents to their full extent. Drogo had given her the confidence to do so. She hated to test him this way, but she must.

She stood on tiptoe and pressed a kiss to

her husband's stubbly cheek. He was such a handsome man, even when he was scowling ferociously. She wanted to make love with him again. She was healed. She didn't dare tell him that now, though. "They did not have the power to help me as I have the power to help them. You cannot stop me, Drogo. This is who I am. If you cannot accept that, then you are no better than they are."

Irrational panic bubbled through Drogo's blood as he watched Ninian packing her bags, sorting through bits of dead leaves and grass as if they were of as vast importance as the infant sleeping in his cradle. As if they were as important as their marriage.

She might die out there. He couldn't let her. Alan needed her. She had no idea what it did to a child to lose his mother. He couldn't let her go. *He* needed her.

Clamping an iron bar on his fear, Drogo did the only thing he knew to do. Knowing he would hurt her but preferring hurt to the inevitability of death, he heaved her over his shoulder.

Ninian screamed. She kicked and grabbed his hair and called curses down on his head that grew more malevolent as his direction became evident.

"Drogo, you cannot!" As she realized he

would not be diverted, her curses calmed to more coherent pleas. "I cannot let them down, Drogo! Please! I can help."

"So can I, but you are the one who is not listening this time." Her curses and threats tore at him, wounding newly exposed vulnerabilities, but he would not be deterred. She and Alan could survive without him, but Alan could not survive without her. And there was a distinct possibility he could not survive without his insane wife. He was protecting himself as well as her.

"Drogo!" she screeched as he slammed her into his tower room and reached for the key. "If there's no fever, there's no contagion! It's the water! Please, you don't . . ."

He shut the door and turned the key on her furious screams.

He ignored the astonished looks of Sarah and Lydie as he returned down the stairs. Ninian might never forgive him, but for the moment, she was safe.

"Don't you dare let her out," he ordered. "There is nothing else to be done about the sickness, and she can't stop rain. I'll look for some way to divert the water."

"No wonder Ives men cannot stay married," Sarah said in amazement, shaking her head. "The lot of you have steel where your hearts should be and clockworks for brains."

"I'd rather have her alive and hating me than dead and beyond caring."

The very real terror of what Ninian would do when he returned shot arrows through Drogo's supposedly steel heart, but he could not give in to feminine hysteria.

"This is the only place narrow enough to dam." Dunstan gestured to a rocky ledge under which the burn ran.

"The water will build up behind any boulders we roll off," Ewen observed. Drenched from the wild ride back from the mines he'd taken after receiving Drogo's message, he hadn't had time to change his clothes or even reach the castle before Drogo had intercepted him.

"Wouldn't it spill down the hill, away from the village?" Drogo studied the distance from hill to stream. If he concentrated on this problem and not the woman who was no doubt attempting to climb down his tower wall, he might cling to his sanity.

Only, his particular talent was for math and finance, not mechanical operations. He might waste a few spare hours on the impractical study of the stars, but he knew nothing of building dams or diverting water. He needed his brothers for that.

From this hillside he could see the stone

tower rising above the trees, and follow the path of the flooding burn as it spilled toward the distant village. Smoke rose only from the chimneys of Ninian's cottage on the highest rise. Even that wouldn't be safe if the warming air melted the remaining snow, and the rain continued. He glanced back toward the barren hills where his mines pumped water by the gallons from deep within the land. Could Ninian be right? Could he have caused this flood?

A dark figure striding down the distant stream could easily be seen from where Drogo stood. He watched the confident gait with growing suspicion. Abruptly leaving his brothers to argue the mechanics of the problem, he took off downhill.

The other man had to have seen him coming but stuck to his intended path. With cold gray rain obscuring the landscape and a fog rising off the flooding water, Drogo continued on a course that would intersect with the stranger's.

The newcomer evinced no surprise as Drogo appeared in front of him. Shoving his rough, ungloved hands into his coat pockets, he tipped his tricorne hat so the water ran away from his face.

"Adonis, I presume?" Drogo asked dryly when the stranger remained silent.

The other man bent his head in what could have been agreement. "The so-called Earl of Ives and Wystan?" he countered.

"The same. My wife claims you can tell us the origin of the burn's problem."

"Ives's machinations," he replied without hesitation. "Your mine is poisoning the water. You're pumping acid from the bottom of the mine, and it's flooding into the river."

Wondering if there was any possibility of truth in this, Drogo held his questions for the moment. "Shall we go somewhere drier to discuss it?" He wanted to know more about this man who looked like himself, but mostly, he needed to know more about the burn so he could prevent the flood, maybe even the illness, and go home to Ninian.

The larger man regarded him warily. "You haven't much time for discussion." He nodded toward the rising water. "The flood will reach the castle walls soon."

The castle. Had he left Ninian and Alan in worse jeopardy than if they'd gone to the village? Panic licked along Drogo's veins. "Who are you?" he demanded. "Or should I ask, *what* are you?"

The other man looked as if he would refuse to answer, then shrugged. "Half Malcolm, half Ives, and crazier than both for lingering. Are you in this with me, or not?"

An offspring of Malcolm and Ives? Why didn't the Malcolm women know of this anomaly? Why hadn't he? Ives had spread bastards across the land for generations, but none other looked quite so like him.

Drogo studied the stranger's guarded expression, then nodded, accepting what he didn't have time to thoroughly investigate. He needed help, and this man was offering it. "Come meet my brothers. We're in this together."

And so they were. For the first time in memory, he wasn't the one in charge.

"Where's Ninian?" a young voice cried from the front entrance of the castle.

"Where's Alan?" an older one called no less eagerly as its owner swept into the great hall trailing an assortment of silks and scarves.

An entourage of fair and chattering Malcolms streamed across the threshold, followed by a collection of servants bearing trunks, carpetbags, and assorted oddments.

"Where's Drogo and those fascinating brothers of his?" another feminine voice purred as an enchantingly beautiful Malcolm in full powdered wig drifted into the room to admire a tapestry.

"You have come at just the wrong time. Th-there is illness . . ." Sarah stuttered as she raced to the head of the stairway to circumvent this invasion.

The small, gray-haired lady trailing scarves hurried forward. "Yes, yes, we know. We have come at just the *right* time. But first, show us darling Alan. A Malcolm-Ives! We've never had a male. Do you think he could be a witch? Be a dear . . ."

From above, Ninian's howls of outrage carried more effectively than any tantrum the resident ghost might have thrown.

Glancing at one another in wonderment, the women swept past Sarah in a sea of foaming petticoats and silk.

Thirty-eight

Ninian didn't have time to regale her family with tales of Drogo's perfidy. He'd done what he'd thought he had to do. Now she must do as she must. Racing down the tower stairs once the chamber was unlocked, she threw orders over her shoulder as she aimed for her aunt's carriage. Her amazing cousins were useless in a sickroom, but they would take care of Alan and her household for her.

By the time she reached the rose-covered gate of her granny's garden, one of the tenants was rolling kegs of ale from a farm cart. Two milk cows mooed loudly from their tethers at the back of the cart. To her utter amazement, Drogo had actually thought to test if the water caused the illness by providing other forms of liquid. Now, if he could only stop a flood.

She was furious with him. She wanted to scream and rail and beat him with her fists, but he would only look at her in bewilderment if she did. She knew her husband well now and understood he had taken the only solution he could see to protect his family. He hadn't really rejected her, or her gift. He had *cared* for her, in his own obtuse, bullheaded manner, though she would have some difficulty persuading her family of that.

"They'll all be drunk," Mary whispered in puzzlement as Ninian entered the makeshift hospital behind the ale.

"Better drunk than dead," Ninian answered, stopping at the first pallet she reached. "No one is to drink the water until Drogo has found the solution." She bent to examine the weakened child at her feet. Vomiting could be caused by many things. She probed gently at the boy's abdomen, and he groaned.

"But it's been a year and no one has found a solution," Mary protested as Ninian stood up. "We haven't even figured out the *problem* yet."

"But that's what Ives are good for." Still furious at Drogo's thickheadedness but cheered by this proof that he understood that he had a responsibility to the world around him as well as to his family, Ninian hastened toward the service room to mix the elixir that worked best on vomiting. "Ives men are not devils. They're geniuses. One cannot expect geniuses to think the way others do."

"No, I suppose not," Mary said doubtfully, following her. "But why haven't these geniuses done something sooner?"

"Because they're idiots." At Mary's puzzled expression, she explained, "Men cannot be smart about everything. Ives are idiots about people and geniuses about things. Adonis will explain it. Tell me when he arrives."

She swept off, not hearing Mary's weak "Adonis?"

Stuck in a cramped cottage worrying frantically about his wife and son, Drogo could scarcely contain his impatience with the men who were engineering the impossible. "What do you mean, we can stop the flow with gunpowder!"

"Well, he's right." Ewen scribbled a quick calculation and sketch on the battered page he'd torn from a book in his coat pocket. "A keg or two, at just the right angle, and we can bring a good part of that hillside down, creating a dam that would divert the mine water as well as the flood. That much, we can do immediately. I'll need time to study the chemicals you must be pumping out of the mine. If there's an acid causing illness —"

"A keg or two? Where the devil would we get a keg of gunpowder, providing we're insane enough to attempt it?" From the door of the cramped cottage, Drogo glared at the misty gray rain covering the countryside while worry gnawed at his guts.

"I can find it," Adonis declared without inflection.

"He's Scots," Dunstan commented, with seeming irrelevancy.

Ewen and Drogo swung to stare at Dunstan. The stranger merely tipped his chair back and waited.

Ever curious, Ewen asked the less obvious question. "How do you know?"

Dunstan shrugged and took a gulp of ale. "Accent. English tutor, apparently, but definitely Scots underneath the polish. One of my tenants has a Scots wife."

"What the devil has that got to do with the way the world turns?" Drogo asked acidly. He didn't even know the damned stranger's real name. His national origins were of small concern.

"If you want to trust a Scot with gunpowder, you're more a bedlamite than your wife. What do we know of him, anyway?"

Dunstan asked impassively.

The stranger crossed his arms over his chest and raised a questioning eyebrow, as if he, too, were interested in the answer.

"Ninian trusts him. She said he has the answers." Even as he said it, Drogo knew how insane that sounded.

Dunstan was quick to point out the flaw in his thinking. "When was the last time an Ives could trust his wife?"

There the question stood in all its stark, cold logic, asked by the latest victim of an entire string of failed Ives marriages dating back generations.

With a history like that to draw on, why would any sane Ives trust a wife?

Drogo scowled at Adonis's look of expectation. One more question to be solved — who the devil was this damned Adonis? As far as he was aware, his father was the only son who had survived adolescence. He supposed there could be uncles and cousins elsewhere. The Ives weren't precisely a close-knit family, given their tendency to lose wives and children on a regular basis. And the earls had only been gone from these parts for fifty years or so. The features could have carried through several generations.

His mind had wandered from the crux of the matter. Why would an Ives trust his wife?

The crushing weight of that question nearly floored him. Could he believe Ninian's dimpled look of innocent abstraction? Or should he believe that everything she'd done since she'd first come to his tower had been a ploy in a Malcolm plot to force him to suffer the torment of the damned in some obscure revenge he couldn't discern? She'd told him often enough that Malcolm and Ives don't mix, and she had the diary to prove it.

But Ninian had given him a son.

He thought of Ninian casually scooping up a village child and kissing his cheek, of Ninian scolding his younger brothers back to school, of her surprised and pleased expression when he brought her a musty old book for a wedding gift.

If he had been fooled by those performances, then he deserved to play the part of fool now. Trusting Ninian and her instincts — her "empathy" — meant risking the village, his brothers, and everyone around them, but he had no choice. Not to trust Ninian would mean the death of everything he had come to believe since meeting her.

He fixed his gaze on the stranger Ninian trusted, the stranger who looked like a slightly older version of himself. Adonis met his gaze squarely, defiantly. Could he trust this man with dynamite? Ninian would. He would trust his wife, but keep the man under surveillance. He had little choice. Ninian would never leave Wystan while the flood threatened, and saving her and his family held priority.

"Ewen, have the men start digging holes to plant the charges. Adonis, take Dunstan with you to fetch the gunpowder."

Adonis dropped his chair to the ground and nodded. Dunstan and Ewen looked at Drogo as if he'd lost his mind.

Drogo ignored their concern. It was damned well time they shouldered a few responsibilities. "If the charge goes off wrong, it could blow up the whole hillside and send the river down the valley with it. I have to warn Ninian."

Adonis gulped his ale as Drogo walked into the rain. "Well, hell," he muttered when no one else said a word. "That's some welcome to the family."

"We've driven the sheep to the highest shelters we can find, but the wind is picking up. They hate wind. And if it starts to thunder . . ."

Nate's father didn't have to finish the sentence. This was a farming community. Everyone knew the erratic temperament of sheep. They'd dive off the nearest cliff if they were frightened enough.

Ninian peeked out the window. Water ran down the road in front of the rose gate. Wind tossed and turned the leafless limbs of the trees. This was even worse than the night she and Drogo had first made love. Well, she couldn't blame herself or the legend this time. They hadn't made love in months.

"I see your family has arrived, my lady," a soaked Adonis commented as he emerged from the kitchen to navigate the crowded parlor full of occupied pallets. Located on the highest ground, the house had gradually filled with villagers, whether ill or not.

Every head in the room turned. Adonis ignored the attention as he doffed his dripping hat. Silence suddenly reigned, and Ninian knew all eyes had swung to her.

The wind was howling, the rain was increasing, flood waters were rising, and her family had arrived. The villagers needed no more than that to believe witchcraft was at work.

Impatiently, she dismissed their suspicion, concentrating instead on the wariness and curiosity emanating from the man who was watching her like a hawk. "Have you come to lock me in the tower, too?"

Adonis grunted as he reached the place where she stood. "That's probably the first smart thing your husband has done. I've come to warn the village that I've just delivered gunpowder to your husband and his brothers and they're about to blow up the burn. You might want to be with your fair cousins when they do. The water is as likely to run toward the castle as the town."

"Does Drogo know that?" she asked in horror.

"Like all Ives, he and his brothers are completely confident they know what they're doing. They do not take into consideration all the things that can go wrong."

He was right. He was so terribly right. Drogo and his brothers thought themselves invincible. They would experiment first and consider the results later.

Frantic, Ninian grabbed her cloak. "Mary, you know what to do here. All we can do is stop the vomiting for now. I must return to my family." She turned to Adonis, who watched her without expression — just like Drogo. "How did you get here?"

"Horse, how else?"

"It can go through the flood?"

He shrugged. "I'll get you there."

She could sense he was torn about it, but

she didn't hesitate. The water had been too high for the carriage when she'd arrived. It would never make it through the mud now. Pulling her hood over her hair, she headed for the door, Adonis trailing behind, hastily donning his hat. She would never persuade her family into the discomforts of the flood and storm. Perhaps if she herded them all into the tower, they would be safe.

The rain had become a cold mist as she stepped into the ruin of her cottage garden. In the lane below her, water roiled, carrying with it chicken coops and smashed farm carts. If the water carried illness, it would be in every well and stream for miles. She prayed Drogo could divert the poisoned tributary. She prayed for his safety.

She looked up sharply as Adonis brought his horse around. "Is Drogo safe?"

"Depends on whether he stays where he is or tries to reach the village." He caught her by the waist and heaved her onto the horse's bare back.

Drogo had barely escaped the castle and the fury of Ninian's aunt and cousins in one piece. Like a nest of hornets, they'd circled and buzzed and stung, and he could do nothing more than shout at them for their stupidity in freeing Ninian from the tower.

They'd ignored his admonitions about the sickness, his fear of leaving her in the unprotected village, his desperate need to see her safe. They'd scorned his fears and chastised him for his audacity, and he'd finally run out, frantic to reach Ninian before the powder blew.

How the devil could she endanger herself like this, deliberately defy his orders?

As he neared the cottage and saw her clearly outlined on a massive horse with the stranger, his heart quit beating. No matter what fears had charged through his head, not once had he expected to find her in the arms of another man — like the wife of every other Ives over the ages.

Not Ninian. She wouldn't do that to him. She was his, in every way imaginable. She'd given him everything.

In return, he'd refused to let her go to Wystan, denied her his bed and the affection she craved, then locked her in a tower. What the hell had he expected?

The impossible, obviously. A piercing arrow of pain shot through his heart, and he knew it wasn't made of steel, as Sarah claimed.

Belatedly, Drogo recognized that Ninian lived inside his skin. She was the soul he didn't possess. Without her, he couldn't exist. The realization terrified him, and he panicked — irrationally, unreasonably, illogically.

By the time Drogo whipped his horse to a gallop to reach the top of the hill, the other man had slid off his stallion to the ground. Without preamble, Drogo dismounted, and shoving Adonis backward into the mud to reach his errant wife, he caught her by the waist, retrieving her from her precarious perch on the prancing horse.

She beat him soundly about the head and shoulders as he did so, pounding him with soft fists, calling him more names than he'd thought she knew. Impervious to the blows, Drogo dropped her to the ground. "What the *hell* do you think you are doing, madam?"

"Knocking sense into your bloody head, you idiot! You lunatic! You could blow up the entire countryside and everyone I love with it. What the *devil* do you think you are doing?"

She was back to pounding him with her fists, kicking at him with her muddy clogs. Unable to totally comprehend her words through her fury, Drogo merely caught her wrists and held her safely away. "I went to warn you," he informed her coldly, "but you weren't where I left you. I had to fight my way through your cousins before I could get here. It's too late to leave now. Go back inside. I have to return to Dunstan and Ewen."

"I have to go to Alan!" she screamed. "What if the castle floods? Don't you care what happens to my family?"

Fighting weariness, confusion, and anger, Drogo watched over her shoulder as Adonis picked himself out of the mud and stood idly brushing himself off, not offering further interference. Not a particularly loverly way to act. Drogo glanced back to Ninian whose face was still suffused with fury. She didn't even look at the man she was about to ride off with.

"A flood won't harm the castle. I told your family to stay on the upper floors. Alan is fine." Drogo's heart still rode in his throat as he clasped Ninian's arms and wished he had the power to pull her against him and kiss her senseless. Would she fight him in that, too? "Who is he?" he demanded, not daring to ask for more while her potential lover stood waiting. "Why would you leave me for him?"

She stopped struggling and looked blank. "Who?"

"He thinks we were running off together." Behind her, Adonis looked disgusted at

Drogo's implication. "You've got maggots for brains if you think I'd take a fancy to a Malcolm. They're the most malicious, meddlesome, quarrelsome, useless lot of lunatics a man could hope to avoid."

Ninian threw one of her deceitfully sweet smiles over her shoulder. "And Ives are such pleasant, loving, helpful creatures, too."

Those weren't the words of a lover. Those were the words of the bewildering woman he was coming to know too well. Drogo didn't know whether to shake her or hug her. "Ninian . . ."

As if to mirror his confusion, a muffled explosion shook the distant hills.

A scream rang from inside the cottage. "Matthew! Where's Matthew?"

Thirty-nine

Lightning struck the oak in the corner of the garden, cracking its sturdy trunk, sending it crashing across the garden gate, ripping the rose canes to shreds. Thunder rolled again, and behind them children joined Mary's screams with cries of fright.

"Let go of me, Drogo," Ninian ordered hastily. "I can't find Matthew if you're holding me. You block the fear."

Impatient to check the results of the gunpowder explosion, Drogo almost didn't listen, but some warning in her voice halted him, advising him that if he did not listen this time, there would never be another chance to do so.

Reluctantly, he released her and watched doubtfully as she held her hands to her temples. The storm winds increased, and wails of terror escalated as another explosion echoed from the hills. The sound of rushing water changed.

"Oh, by the goddess, he's down by the burn!" Before Drogo could react, Ninian picked up her skirts and ran for the only opening left in the demolished tangle of roses and fence, straight toward the raging river.

Running after her, Drogo dragged her from the ground and slammed her backward into the solid figure of Adonis. "Take her back inside. We don't know which way the water will flow once the valley is dammed."

"You can't find him without me!" she screamed as Drogo ran for his horse.

"There's only one path not covered by water!" he shouted back, spurring his horse into a jump over the fence and flying down the hill faster than she could have run. He was on a mission of madness, but not once did he doubt that she was right. He had no way of understanding how Ninian knew where the child was, but he trusted her enough to act impulsively on her beliefs. She would not send him into those waters without reason.

Fear gripped Ninian's heart as she watched Drogo disappear over the hill. He'd listened. He'd accepted that she knew what others didn't. Stunned, she didn't even recognize she wasn't touching the ground until her captor lowered her to the mud.

"You staying put?" Adonis asked warily.

"Go after him," she whispered. "He doesn't know the meaning of fear."

"I do, and it's scaring the hell out of me." He released her and strode off in the direction of his own mount.

Clamping down on her own trepidation, Ninian returned inside to comfort Mary. Murmuring reassuring words as several of the men donned slickers to follow Drogo and help as they might, she glanced around as other mothers attempted to quiet their small ones over the sound of the rising storm. Whether it was her herbs or her touch or the ale and milk Drogo had sent, the illness seemed to be diminishing. There were no new cases. Perhaps it wasn't contagious, but in the water, as she'd suspected.

Another explosion rocked the floor, and she dropped to her knees and prayed with growing hysteria.

Drogo had rescued his brothers from enough trouble to know the path of a childish mind. Following a branch-littered lane toward a once dry streambed strewn with large rocks, he recognized the temptation of a large boulder at the edge — except the boulder was no longer on the edge of anything but surrounded by rapidly rising water. A small boy huddled terrified on top, clutching a makeshift boat, a boy who had scrambled away from him at the Christmas party. He didn't know how or why Ninian knew where to find the child, but she had been right.

Removing the child to safety before another explosion diverted more flood waters was his first priority. If he was lucky, there wouldn't be another explosion.

If he wasn't . . . He hadn't time to consider that.

Riding into water that rose rapidly around his horse's legs, Drogo leaned over and held out his arms to the weeping child. He could remember yelling at his brothers, hauling them out of trouble, sending them off in the arms of tutors and nursemaids. He could not remember once holding out his arms to them as he did to this small boy now. With trepidation, he prayed the child would accept him.

Sniffing, Matthew wiped his nose on his sleeve, watched Drogo warily, and then without a word, accepted his rescuer's help.

The explosion shook the valley just as Drogo leaned over to hand the child to the men following him to the water's edge. Already frightened by the rising water, his horse reared. His hands on the boy instead of the reins, his balance off as he leaned from his seat, Drogo couldn't control his mount and couldn't remain in the saddle.

Just as he plunged into the rampaging river, another wave of water crashed down the valley. To the horror of the onlookers, the horse scrambled out of the streambed without the earl.

"Drogo!" Ninian screamed as the front door flew open, letting in a squall of rain. Two men carried the inert figure of her husband while Adonis carried a sobbing Matthew.

She thought her heart would tear from her throat as a silent path cleared through the room and she raced toward her husband. He was so pale . . .

Behind her, Mary reached to cuddle her frightened child, but Ninian had no thought for anyone but the man they lay upon the hearth, where the fire's warmth could dry him.

Except that he looked as if no fire would ever warm him again.

"We're sorry, my lady," Harry whispered, removing his hat as Ninian fell to her knees beside Drogo's still form. "He saved the boy, but fell in and the water poured down and carried him away, it did. We pulled him out down by the road."

"Drogo," Ninian whispered, testing for a heartbeat, breathing, anything . . .

He was nearly blue with cold, and she couldn't find any sign of life. Panic welled but she refused to give into it. The physical presence that flowed between them beat through her blood where her fingers touched his icy throat and temple. Blocking out the grief and consternation of the people hovering around her, blocking out all but the man who held her heart in his, she pressed her hands against his chest and sought deep within her where instinct dwelled and let the healing power guide her.

Her fist slammed into his chest. Solid bone and muscle hurt her hand, but she pounded again, and again, forcing his heart to acknowledge her presence. If she could find Drogo anywhere, it was through his heart. He hid it from others, but she knew it was a large one, that he loved and loved deeply but simply didn't know how to express it. She would wake up his heart if it killed her.

Faintly, the beat thrummed beneath her fingers, and she instantly fell on his mouth. She would breathe life into his lungs now, breathe in the air his heart needed to expand.

Someone tried to pull her away, thinking her gone mad with grief, but she shook them off. She was strong. They couldn't take her where she didn't wish to go.

A woman started a prayer, and Ninian breathed with relief, pouring the air she gulped between the lips of the man in her arms, pushing on his chest, forcing his heart to pump and his lungs to take what she offered. Tears streamed down her cheeks as she breathed and pumped and her arms trembled. She could do this. God had given her more gifts than she'd ever accepted. She could feel Drogo's heart, his lungs, his soul. He was here with her. She knew it. She just needed to reach him.

A surge of warmth and love flowed up her fingers, seeping from the flesh she touched, swamping her with a giddy ecstasy as she realized the heat and emotion emanated from the man beneath her. She could *feel* him.

He gasped and choked on a breath, and cheers resounded at this sign of life. The women continued praying, adding their spirit to Ninian's, warming her, returning her strength, holding her in the moment so she didn't disappear entirely into that place inside her where she'd found the knowledge and healing she needed. She wept, and collapsed against Drogo's chest as it heaved up and down.

Drogo coughed, and Ninian debated whether she should push on his chest some more. When she tried to stir from his embrace, he wrapped his arms around her, crushing her against him with surprising strength.

"Don't move," he croaked. "Don't you dare move."

Laughing, crying, she buried her face against his chest and let him dig his fingers into her hair. He was alive, and he was the same odiously demanding man he'd always been, and she loved him dearly. And he loved her. She could feel it, at last. She thought she would drown in the flood of love pouring from him as strongly as water rushed from the burn.

"You're soaked, my lord. You will catch your death if we do not dry you out." She was soaked, too, from lying upon him, but the heat flooding through his body was so welcome, she didn't mind the damp.

"I have a distinct feeling I have already caught my death and you called me back." His eyes popped open and he lifted her chin to study her face. "You *are* a witch."

She watched him silently, to see how he

accepted that knowledge. She was just beginning to understand the enormity of it herself. She had called upon some deep, underlying knowledge in a time of need. A gift.

Drogo stared into the innocent blue that mirrored his own amazement, and knew the wall about his heart had cracked as wide as the valley they'd dammed, and love spilled as free as the burn's water. She was the part of him that was missing, the soul he'd never known, the love he'd never expressed. Her breath breathed inside of him now.

"Consider me bewitched," he murmured. "I'll love you until the stars stop shining and beyond. Now tell all those women that it's merely magic and to go away so you can get me out of these damned clothes."

Ninian grinned and swallowed the tears she'd been holding back. He could see the tracks of them down her shiny cheeks. His little witch was here with him completely, not in some world of her own making. It shook him to know how much she cared.

"Perhaps we should go home and take those clothes off, my lord," she suggested with a wicked smile.

That was the best idea he'd heard in a long time.

Unfortunately, to ensure the safety of the castle and village, there were other things they must do first. Her magic must wait.

The rain stopped not long after. Payton carried news of the burn's slow receding as the diverted waters spilled into the new lake. Adonis rode out in search of Dunstan and Ewen, and garbed now in borrowed dry clothes, Drogo took Ninian onto his horse and progressed slowly through the last light toward home.

News of the rescue had preceded them, and Ninian's fair cousins rushed to welcome their return.

"Christina tried to tell us your aura was benign, but we didn't believe her," Hermione apologized, patting Drogo's arm. "She always likes to see the best in everyone."

Given Ninian's astonishing abilities, he really needed to learn more about this aura business, but not tonight. Drogo watched with joy and pain as Ninian cuddled their cooing son in her arms. She was a living miracle. How could he deserve a woman like that?

"We knew as soon as you were safe," one of the cousins said shyly.

Drogo thought he actually read admiration in her gaze. He needed to start differentiating one blond head from the other. As

Hermione fluttered off to hug Ninian, Drogo tore his attention from his wife and focused on the brown-eyed cousin. "How?" he asked innocently, before realizing he probably didn't want to hear the answer.

"Alan cried all evening until you were safe. He's been cooing ever since."

He'd been right. He really hadn't wanted to hear that. Turning to watch as Ninian carried their son up the stairs, Drogo shut out all the terrifying possibilities that leapt to mind and concentrated on Ninian as she lifted her head and smiled beckoningly in his direction. Perhaps he could learn not to question anything in return for the peace of his wife's arms. If nothing else, she had taught him that anything was possible.

Standing naked in the privacy of their chamber, Drogo and Ninian warmed themselves before the fire, clasped in each other's arms, flesh heating flesh.

"I haven't changed," Drogo warned. "I'm still the man you've berated and accused of stubbornness and lack of understanding."

"I love that man," she murmured contentedly from within his embrace. "And I'll still yell at you for your denseness. And prick your arrogance until you're forced to see the world around you. Just tell me you love me again, and I'll accept your obtuseness."

He smiled against her hair and drew his hand down over a well-rounded posterior, snuggling her closer to where he needed her. "I'll tell you every morning when we wake, and every night before we go to sleep. But I'll never admit such foolishness in public."

She chuckled, and he could feel the vibrations deep in his chest.

"I will. I'll yell it at the top of my lungs and embarrass you daily. Every time you do something stupid, I will yell my love at you."

"That should cure me," he admitted dryly. "My brothers will laugh me into an early grave."

"Your brothers," Ninian whispered, sliding upward so their bodies brushed against each other as she kissed his jaw, "need to stay in school where they belong. Then we would not need to visit London so often."

Thoughtfully, he played a devastating tune upon her breast. "Perhaps there is merit in your suggestion that Sarah have the London house so they may run to her. You and I will visit my and your family's country estates when we must travel. Will that be far enough from the city for you?"

"You shield me from the city," she murmured, exploring his chest as he explored hers. "If you can accept I have responsibilities here, I can train Lydie —"

He covered her mouth with his, and she nearly drowned again in the heat and love he offered. For this, she would do anything.

He released her mouth and their gazes met. She stumbled down the deep tunnel he opened into his soul.

"Our responsibilities are one and the same — equal. We will work it out, moonchild."

And she believed him.

He kissed her forehead, then seared a trail along her throat, drawing closer to the tempting pout of her full nipples. "Tell me the time is right, that the moon is in its proper phase, and that you want what I want."

She caught the tail of his hair and tugged until he lifted his head and looked down at her.

As she met his gaze and struck him with the full brunt of her adoration, Drogo nearly staggered beneath the enormity of it. The woman breathed love, bathed him in it, and eased all the nagging doubts always simmering beneath his surface. If he just let himself *feel* instead of inquiring into the logic of it, he would never question their marriage again. The bane of Ives marriages was too much logic and not enough trust.

"For you, the moon is always in its proper phase. I want your children, Drogo. I want you. Take me to your stars."

He didn't require further reassurance. Carrying her to the downy warmth of the bed, he covered her with his body and pulled the feather-stuffed covers over them.

"It stopped raining," she whispered as he nibbled her ear and tried to absorb all the nuances of her giving curves beneath him.

With a moan of delight, he cupped her breasts and felt her swift intake of breath as he caressed the tips. Just the brush of her breath aroused him to the point of driving need. But he wanted to savor this moment. His wife, his love, the mate of his soul . . . He'd never thought such a thing possible. "The stars are out," he agreed, stroking lower, bringing her hips closer to his. "We're safe, and I want to lose myself in you and not discuss the weather."

She quivered as he touched her where she was wet. "In that case," she murmured with a groan as she arched into him, "we didn't cause the flood this time."

With that utterly inexplicable, illogical statement, she stroked him, and incapable of anything else, Drogo drove deep inside her, where they understood one another on levels beyond the ken of mankind.

Epilogue

Blazing sparks leapt high into the night sky as the Beltane fire roared heavenward and the fiddle struck up a dance. Laughing figures rushed to throw their branches on the flames, then danced off in one another's arms.

On the outskirts of the clearing, in the twilight between fire and forest, Ninian perched on an upright stone and smiled at the merriment.

"I heard Nate married a miner's daughter." Gertrude lifted her fussy babe to her shoulder and watched as a new crop of maids and bachelors wove a spell of seduction in the firelight. "Seems the miners don't take well to men who won't accept responsibility, and they were a little harsh with him."

"He has twins." Ninian tried to muffle her laughter at Nate's fate. "Imagine how many wee ones he'll have at his feet in a few years time."

Gertrude glanced at the teething babe on her shoulder. "One is enough for a while."

Tapping her toe to the music, Ninian merely shrugged, then slowly smiled as a tall, dark figure emerged from the forest's edge. Even after all these months, her heart pattered faster at his approach.

He'd been inspecting the new pump at the mines, ensuring that the dangerous runoff never harmed the burn again. She'd missed him.

He didn't ask, didn't speak at all as he reached for her and drew her toward the music and the dancing. He merely watched her face with the studious expression she loved so well, and finding what he sought, smiled and guided her into the steps.

They twirled and laughed and let the rhythms of the night sweep through them, knowing with the confidence of lovers how the night would end, with no need to hasten the thrill of excitement coursing through them.

Normally, an earl was too lofty a personage for his tenants and the villagers to approach, but on a night like this, with a keg of good ale to share and the music to blend them, even an earl wasn't a stranger. Ninian laughed as she danced off with Harry, leaving Drogo to discuss sheep breeding with Nate's father. Her husband's long queue of midnight hair fell over his shoulder as he tilted his head in concentration. Drogo knew nothing about sheep breeding, but he would learn, she had no doubt.

As the moon slipped down the far side of the sky, he returned to claim her, swinging her into the shadows outside the fire's light. Murmurs of other couples blended with the cries of night birds and the rustle of other nocturnal creatures, as the pounding thrill of their blood matched the thrum of the earth.

"Now," Drogo commanded, flinging his cloak over a bed of pine needles behind a wall of shrubs and drawing her into his embrace. "I'll not wait another minute."

"It's Beltane," she teased, slipping the buttons of his waistcoat from their holes and seeking the heat of his chest. "A night of power. Can you not feel it?" The vibration thrummed through her fingertips as she rubbed against him. "A child conceived tonight —"

"Don't tell me," he groaned, attempting to unfasten her fingers from his clothing. "The moon is in its proper phase and unless I wish to spend next winter in Wystan, I'd better keep my breeches buttoned."

"Well, I did agree to spend winters in the

south with you," she murmured demurely, deftly avoiding his hands and reaching for the breeches buttons he'd just defamed. "And the moon is definitely in its proper phase. We would make a lovely baby tonight."

"No." Firmly, he caught her wandering hands and held them back. "If you insist on having our babes here, I insist they come in the summer so I can summon physicians and midwives and your whole damned family. You are more important to me and Alan than this moment's pleasure."

"I do so adore you, Drogo." She stood on tiptoe and kissed his jaw, then moved to cover his mouth with her own as she drew her wrists from his grip and reached for his buttons again.

"Ninian," he moaned in protest against her mouth, trying to hold her and catch her hands while not releasing her lips, fighting the impetuous irresponsibility she always led him into.

"It's all right," she murmured, finally parting the ties of his shirt and neckcloth and running her hands through the crinkle of curls on his chest. "This is sheep country. I have a present for you. I even wove a ribbon around it. If you're very, very good, we will not have to worry about the phases of the moon tonight."

"You *are* a witch," he muttered as he parted her bodice and slipped his hands beneath it. "And you'd best be talking about what I think you are talking about."

"I've shown *all* the women how to make them," she replied after gasping for breath from his thorough kiss. She blinked in amazement at the night sky overhead. How had she come to be lying down already?

"Excellent. I'll have Ewen establish a factory just to supply all my brothers," Drogo replied with a hint of grimness as he kneeled between her legs and his hand slid up her thigh. "Why didn't you think of this sooner? Joseph has just written me for an increase in his allowance to pay for his new dolly bird."

She sighed as he caressed her where she needed to be touched. "I made certain they all have samples." She cried out as he suddenly withdrew and glared down at her. She smiled back. "Dunstan delivered them. Surely you did not think I —"

He caught her mouth with his and drowned any further protest.

When he finally surged into her, ribbons and sheath and all, Ninian was already halfway to the moon and ready to fly to the stars. He took her there and back, showed her the heavens from his perspective, then held her gently as they tumbled back to earth again, where she reigned. Magic, indeed.

"Has the Society verified your finding of a new planet yet?" she whispered, still spinning among the stars, although Drogo's heavy weight pressed her into the earth.

"Our equipment needs refining. I would ask Ewen, but it is a full-time task to keep his attention on the foundry. We can wait." With care, Drogo rolled on his back, carrying her with him. Now he could see the stars while holding heaven in his arms. "He has some notion that the chemicals in the runoff from the mine might be useful, and I have had to persuade him that he must spend his days on something that can provide him with a living and use his spare hours on his less profitable ideas."

"He'll learn. You have taught your brothers well. Have you heard from Dunstan?"

Reluctantly, Drogo adjusted her wool skirt to cover her more warmly. "The lack of all that frippery women wear is a definite advantage of this place," he murmured.

Ninian propped her elbows on his chest and practiced lifting her eyebrows in the same manner as he did.

He grinned at the result. "I could keep

you in nothing but shifts in London. It's warmer there."

"Not that warm. Now what have you heard from Dunstan?" she demanded sternly.

Drogo sighed and rested his gaze on the bounteous beauty revealed by her open bodice. "He is working as steward on one of your uncle's estates so as to earn money to pay what a divorce will cost. You didn't have to send him away from my estate," he grumbled.

"He won't murder Celia, trust me," Ninian murmured. "And I didn't send him anywhere. He chose not to be in your debt any longer. I will never understand the workings of the male mind." Tauntingly, she leaned forward so her breasts brushed against his chest.

"You understand this part too damned well." He lifted her so he could taste the ripe fruit she offered and almost forgot where they were until he heard her cries echoed elsewhere. Deciding this was not a respectable thing for an earl to do twice, he reluctantly pulled back.

She punished him by rolling off and buttoning her bodice. "This part has nothing to do with minds," she said firmly, although Drogo noticed with interest that her hands shook and her nipples appeared ready for plucking.

He stopped her progress by sliding his hand beneath the cloth and stroking her. "It's all of one piece. This" — he pressed a kiss to the place his hand fondled — "eases the mind so it can function properly. We'll need to test that theory."

She laughed and slapped his hand away. "If your mind functioned any better than it does now, we would never get anything done. I found agrimony near the burn today."

"Did you?" Some other time, he might have cared, but she was escaping him, and proper or not, he wasn't done. Hastily, he fastened a few buttons so he could leap after her.

With her back toward him, she shook her skirt out. "Life is returning all along the bank. Adonis was right. The runoff from the mines was poisoning the burn. But just in case, I shall gather seeds as they appear and try to start them in the conservatory."

"We're going to London, remember?" He pulled her back against him and rested his chin on her hair. "Have you seen Adonis and squeezed some answers out of him?"

"He'll tell us of his heritage in his own time. I think he went off with Dunstan. I believe he's lonely and is looking for a family."

To Drogo, Adonis seemed capable of looking after himself. He didn't need shepherding. Drogo couldn't help worrying about Dunstan, but Ninian had taught him to let go. He was learning. Besides, he had Ninian and Alan to occupy his thoughts now. His thumb unerringly found the pointed tip of her breast beneath the wool of her bodice.

"And I'm teaching Lydie about herbs," she said with a hitch in her voice at his caress. "She learns quickly, and she's teaching Mary's sister. I don't see why it must be just Malcolm women who learn these things. All women can be educated."

Uh-oh, they were moving swiftly into one of her latest crackbrained notions. Knowing better than to argue, Drogo cupped and kneaded her breast. "Sarah is still searching the library in hopes of lost treasure."

Ninian laughed, a crystal-clear chime that rang through the night as she snuggled closer into his arms.

"We have found a treasure," she informed him as Drogo wrapped his arms about her waist and she dropped her head against his shoulder to smile up at him. "It is just not the gold and jewels that Sarah expects. And she'll not find it reading the stars any more than you'll find it by calculating them."

He lifted his brows and waited.

Her lips bowed into that enigmatic smile he loved so dearly as she replied, "The only curse on Malcolm and Ives is our inability to share our strengths or learn from our differences."

"I'm learning," he declared, staring down at her innocent expression in bewilderment. "What has that to do with treasures?"

"Everything." Her laughter lit the sky as she turned and wrapped her arms around his neck and obliterated all thought with her kiss.